Dillon knew it was rude to stare.

But he couldn't help himself. He was so amazed to be seeing *her* again after so many years. She'd literally knocked the wind out of him, and now, in typical Isabel style, she wanted to run away.

"Stay a while," he said, his gaze lingering a little too long on her face. "Stay and tell me why you were taking my picture."

"No." She tried to move away. She didn't want to be with Dillon Murdock.

But he refused to let her go. "Then stay long enough to tell me why you came back to Wildwood."

Wanting to show him he couldn't get to her the way he used to, Isabel retorted, "I think a better question would be—what are *you* doing here?"

"Well, that's real simple, Isabel," he said sarcastically. "I came back at my mother's request." Backing away, he called, "Yes, the prodigal son has returned."

Books by Lenora Worth

LENORA WORTH

grew up in a small Georgia town and decided in the fourth grade that she wanted to be a writer. But first, she married her high school sweetheart, then moved to Atlanta, Georgia. Taking care of their baby daughter at home while her husband worked at night, Lenora discovered the world of romance novels and knew that's what she wanted to write. And so she began.

A few years later, the family settled in Shreveport, Louisiana, where Lenora continued to write while working as a marketing assistant. After the birth of her second child, a boy, she decided to pursue her dream full-time. In 1993, Lenora's hard work and determination finally paid off with that first sale.

"I never gave up, and I believe my faith in God helped get me through the rough times when I doubted myself," Lenora says. "Each time I start a new book, I say a prayer, asking God to give me the strength and direction to put the words to paper. That's why I'm so thrilled to be a part of Steeple Hill's Love Inspired line, where I can combine my faith in God with my love of romance. It's the best combination."

LENORA WORTH

Wedding at Wildwood

Steeple
Hill®

Published by Steeple Hill Books™

STEEPLE HILL BOOKS

Steeple
Hill®

ISBN 0-373-80971-9

WEDDING AT WILDWOOD

www.SteepleHill.com

Printed in U.S.A.

It was right that we should make merry and be glad,
for your brother was dead and is alive again,
and was lost and is found.

—*Luke* 15:32

To my brothers, Windell, Waymon
and especially Jerry

And in memory of
my father,
Delma Humphries

Chapter One

She hadn't planned on coming back to Wildwood. But now that she was here, Isabel Landry realized she also hadn't planned on the surge of emotions pouring over her like a warm summer rain as she stood looking up at the stark white mansion.

Wildwood.

The house, built sometime before the Civil War, was old and run-down now. Abandoned and gloomy. And so very sad.

But then, most of her memories of growing up on this land made Isabel feel sad and forlorn, too. Staring across the brilliant field of colorful wildflowers in shades of pink, yellow and fuchsia, she clicked her camera, focusing on the old house, deliberately blurring the pink phlox, purple heather, and yellow black-eyed Susans that posed a sharp contrast to the wilted condition of the once grand mansion. Now shuttered and closed, its paint peeling and its porches overgrown with ivy and wisteria, the house with the fat

Doric columns and the wide, cool verandas on each floor didn't seem as formidable as it had so long ago.

Isabel had never lived in Wildwood, but oh, how she'd dreamed of living in just such a house one day. Now, she saw that fantasy as silly, fueled by the imagination of an only child of older parents, raised on land that did not belong to her family. Born on the Murdock land, in a quiet corner of southwest Georgia, known as Wildwood Plantation.

Glancing away from the imposing plantation house, she saw where she had lived off in the distance, around the curve of the oak trees and dogwoods lining the dirt lane. The small white-framed farmhouse hadn't changed much in the ten years since she'd been away, and neither had Isabel's determined promise to herself to rise above her poor upbringing.

"I don't belong here," she said to the summer wind. "I never did."

Yet she lifted her camera, using it as a shield as she took a quick picture of the rickety little house she remembered so well. Just therapy, she told herself. That's why she'd taken the picture; she certainly didn't need or want a reminder of her years growing up there.

Looking up to the heavens, she whispered, "Oh, Mama, why did God bring me back here? I don't want this." Silently, she wondered if her deceased parents were as at peace up there in Heaven as they'd always seemed to be when they were alive and working here on Wildwood Plantation.

Mentally chiding herself, she smiled. "I know, Mama. Grammy Martha would scold me for doubting

God's intent. You are at peace. This I know. So, why can't I find that same peace here on earth?''

Lifting up yet another prayer, Isabel knew she wouldn't find any answers here on this red Georgia clay. Ever since her grandmother, Martha Landry, had called asking her to come home to take pictures of Eli Murdock's upcoming wedding, she'd been at odds. But between assignments and with nothing pressing on her agenda, she'd had no choice but to come. Isabel knew her duties, and she was good at her job as a professional photographer. Besides, she could never turn down a request from Grammy Martha, even if it did mean having to face the Murdocks and bow to their commands once again.

She hadn't been home in a long time, and she missed her grandmother. Often in the years since her parents had died—first her mother, then two years later, her father—Isabel had hurried home for quick visits with her grandmother. But on those occasions, she'd distanced herself from the Murdocks, always staying only a couple of days, sleeping in her old room at the farmhouse and keeping a low profile. During those rare trips, she'd never once ventured up the lane to visit the people who'd allowed her grandmother to stay on their land and still employed her grandmother's services on occasion.

Now, she'd be forced to socialize with them, to snap happy pictures of Eli's wedding to a girl Isabel had graduated high school with, a woman almost ten years younger than Eli. Well, at least Susan Webster was a wonderful woman. She'd make Eli a good wife, though for the life of her, Isabel couldn't understand what had attracted petite, perky Susan to such a bully bear of a man.

"Oh, well, that's none of my concern," she reminded herself as she turned back to the mansion. She'd do her job, get her pay, then be on her way again to parts unknown. But right now, she wanted to get a shot of the house with the brilliant sunset behind it, and the wavering wildflowers out in the meadow in front of it. Then she'd head back to have supper with Grammy.

Finding a good angle, Isabel focused on the house, finding a side view so the massive columns lining the front of the two-storied house would be silhouetted in the sun's glowing rays. With a flip of her wrist, she pushed her long blond hair back over her shoulders, then lifted her camera to click.

Then her heart stopped.

Through the lens, she saw a man standing at the edge of the wildflower patch on the other side of the house. Gasping, she dropped her arms down, almost dropping her expensive camera in the process. But surprise aside, Isabel knew a good shot when she saw one. She wanted to capture the man, whoever he might be, in the picture because the expression on his dark, rugged face clearly mirrored the mood of the mansion he stood staring up at.

Watching him as if he were a wild animal, Isabel barely moved for fear he'd spot her and bolt away. He looked that untamed, that intense. So intense in fact, that he wasn't even aware she was just around the corner, hiding underneath a clump of tall camellia bushes.

For a minute, Isabel analyzed him, preparing herself for her subject. Tall, at least six feet, fit enough to fill out his faded jeans nicely, and…brooding. Definitely brooding. From the five o'clock shadow on his face and the stiff tufts of spiky hair on his forehead, he looked as if he had a chip on his broad shoulders that couldn't be knocked off. His clipped dark hair mocked the wind playing through it, and every now and then, he'd lift a hand to scissor his fingers through the clump of hair that refused to stay off his face, the action speaking much louder than any gruff words he might want to shout out. This man was angry at someone or something. And…his actions seemed so familiar, so stirring.

Isabel wanted to capture that mood on film. Her artistic instincts had never failed her before. And the way her heart was beating now was a sure sign that she was on to something big here. She might not ever sell this photo, but she had to have this picture. Right now, while the light was playing off the planes and angles of his shadowed face.

Lifting her camera, she once again focused and then, holding her breath at the sheer poignant beauty of the shot, clicked the camera—once, twice, three times.

The third time, she moved closer.

And that's when the man looked up and spotted her.

"Hey!" he shouted, a dark scowl covering his face as he began a mad stalk through the wildflowers like a raging bull about to attack. "What do you think you're doing there, lady?"

Not one to take any unnecessary chances—she'd been in far more dangerous situations, but for some strange reason this man scared her—Isabel smiled and waved. ''Just taking a picture. Thanks.''

Then she turned and as fast as her sandaled feet and flowing skirt could carry her, headed toward the lane, the echo of that deep, commanding voice wafting through her head on that vague mist of familiarity she'd felt on first seeing the man.

''Hey, wait a minute!''

She could *feel* him stomping after her. Picking up her pace, she trudged over delicate wildflowers, forgetting to follow the worn path that had been molded through the field over the years. Whoever he was, she'd apparently made him angry by interrupting his solitude. Maybe she should at least apologize and explain, but too many warning bells were clashing loudly in her head, telling her to get away.

''You're on private property,'' the man called, nearer now.

Isabel didn't dare turn around, but from all the thrashing sounds, she knew he was gaining on her. Then, telling herself this was silly and that she really should speak to the man at least, she whirled just as he reached her. And came crashing into his firm chest.

The action sent the unprepared man sprawling backward even as he reached out a hand to grab Isabel. Which meant she went sprawling down with him, her camera still in one shaky hand.

Her breath coming hard, Isabel looked down at the man holding her, the scent of sweet flowers and rich loam wafting out around them as he stared up at her, a look of surprise coloring his features as his gaze moved over her face.

When she looked down into his gray eyes, Isabel

gasped again as recognition hit her hard and fast, and a very real fear coursed through her. "Dillon?"

He squinted up at her, then as realization dawned in his deep blue-gray eyes, he dropped his hands away from her shoulders so she could get up. In a voice as hard-edged and grainy as the soil beneath them, he looked her over, his surprised gaze sweeping her face. "Isabel."

It was a statement, said on a breath of disbelief.

Fussing with her blouse and skirt, Isabel used the brief time to gather her skittish thoughts. Had she also heard a bit of longing in his voice? Refusing to acknowledge her own longing, she turned to look him square in the face. "I'm sorry, Dillon. I didn't realize who you were until you got close."

Something in her drawling, soft-spoken words made Dillon Murdock's squint deepen back into a scowl. He'd remembered that sweet voice in his dreams, in his memories, and he'd often wished he could hear it again in reality.

Maybe he was just wishing again now. The dusk was obviously playing tricks on his mind. After all, it wasn't every day a man found a beautiful woman with long waves of blond hair and eyes as green as a pine forest, standing in the middle of a field of wildflowers as if she'd been waiting just for him. The same way Isabel used to wait right here for him.

To waylay the uneven beat of his heart, he said, "Well, since *you're* the one who knocked *me* flat on my back, maybe you'd better tell me what you're doing taking pictures of Wildwood."

He didn't know why she was here, Isabel thought wistfully. But then, he had no reason to know anything about her. They hadn't exactly kept in touch over the years. And they'd both changed, obviously.

Last time she'd seen Dillon, he'd only been out of high school a few months, and in a rebellious resistance he'd sported long, scraggly hair and a thick beard. Now, the hair was different, cut short and spiky, and only the remnants of a day's worth of beard covered his brooding face. Yet, she'd sensed something so familiar in him. Too familiar.

Determination and bitterness clouding her dreams away, she rose to her feet to stare down at him. "Relax, I'm just here to take pictures of your brother's wedding."

Dillon sat still, then let out a hissing breath before he stood to follow her retreating floral cotton skirts. Isabel. The minute he'd said her name, all the memories had come rushing back. Boy, she'd certainly changed from the scrawny, dirty-faced kid with cropped blond hair and bony knees. The last time he'd seen Isabel... He wasn't ready to remember the last time he'd seen her. Not yet.

"Isabel?" he called now, refusing to go back to the dark days of his youth. "Hey, wait a minute, will you?"

"You told me I was on private property," she reminded him with a haughty toss of her long locks. "I'm late, anyway."

Stubborn as ever, Dillon thought as he hurried his booted feet after her. And more beautiful than he'd ever imagined. Little Isabel, the poor kid whose father had worked the land so hard it had eventually killed him. Little Isabel, whom Eli and he had teased unrelentingly all through grammar school and high school. Isabel, afraid and ashamed, defiant and lost, a young girl who'd worn her feelings on her sleeves and carried her heart in her hand.

He'd known the girl all his life. Now he wanted to know the woman. "Isabel," he said as he reached out to grab her arm. "I'm sorry."

She whirled to face him in the muted dusk, thinking his apologies always had come too easily. "Sorry for what? I was the one who got caught where I wasn't supposed to be. Some things never change."

He jammed a hand through his hair in frustration. "Well, you're certainly right about that." Her words only reminded him of all the things he'd done to bring his life to this point. Glancing back at the house looming in the distance, he said, "I don't know why I came back here."

"Me, either," Isabel said, some of her anger disappearing. Why should she be angry with Dillon for questioning her about being on Murdock property? She'd always been a hindrance to the powerful Murdocks, anyway. And she'd do best to remember that now, when her heart was pounding and her mind was reeling at seeing Dillon again. "I'd better get back to Grammy," she said at last, to break the intensity of his dusk gray eyes.

Dillon knew it was rude to stare, but he couldn't help himself, and besides, he'd never been one to fall back on manners. He was so amazed to be standing here, seeing her again after so many years. She'd literally knocked the wind out of him, and now in typical Isabel style, she wanted to run away. "Stay a while," he said, his hand still on her bare arm, his gaze lingering a bit too long on her face. "Stay and tell me why you were taking my picture."

"No." She tried to pull away. She did not want to be with Dillon Murdock.

But he refused to let her go. "Then stay long enough to tell me why you came back to Wildwood— and don't tell me it was just to take a few pictures."

Wanting to show him he couldn't get to her the way he used to when they were younger, Isabel retorted, "I think a better question would be—what are *you* doing back here, Dillon?"

He dropped her arm then to step back, away from the accusation and condemnation he saw in her eyes. "Well now, that's real simple, Isabel," he said in a voice silky with sarcasm. "I came back at my mother's request, to witness my brother's happy nuptials." He shrugged, then lifted a hand in farewell, or maybe dismissal. Backing away, he called, "Yes, the prodigal son has returned."

With that, he turned into the gathering twilight, his dark silhouette highlighted by the rising moon and the silvery shadow of Wildwood—the house that once had been his home.

"Dillon, wait," Isabel called a few seconds later. When he just kept walking, she hurried after him. "I'm sorry. I shouldn't question your being here. You have every right to be here."

"Do I?" he asked as he whirled around to face her, his hands thrust into the pockets of his jeans, his eyes flashing like quicksilver. "Do I really, Isabel?"

"It's still your home," she reminded him as they faced each other in front of the house. "And it's still beautiful."

Dillon snorted and inclined his head toward the other side of the country road, away from the mansion. "*That's* not my home, and that house is not beautiful. Not to me."

Isabel shifted her gaze to the big house sitting across the way. Eli's modern new luxury home. Grammy had told her he'd built it a couple of years ago. Now, their mother, Cynthia Murdock, lived there with her son.

"I guess Susan will be moving in soon," she said, very much aware of Dillon's obvious scorn for the elegant brick house with the lavish landscaping.

"I guess so," Dillon replied, his gaze reflecting the timid moonlight covering them like a fine mist. "Hope she can stand the squeaky clean linoleum and all the gadgets and gizmos my brother had installed."

"It's probably more convenient for your mother, at least," Isabel said, trying to be tactful.

Dillon scoffed again. "Yeah, well, Eli always did have Mother's best interest at heart."

He turned then, his eyes moving over the old plantation house. He stood stoic and still, then said in a voice soft with regret, "I miss this house. I wanted to come home to *this* house."

Isabel's heart went out to him. Dillon, always the wild child, always the scrapper, getting into trouble, getting into jams that his father and older brother had had to pull him out of. Dillon, the son who'd left in a huff, mad at the world in general, and hadn't looked back. Now, he was home, for whatever reason.

Isabel could feel sympathy for whatever Dillon Murdock was experiencing. He'd had it all handed to him. His life had been so easy, so perfect. And what had he done? Thrown it all back in his parents' faces. What she would have given to have been able to live with that kind of security, with that kind of protection. But instead, she'd had to live in a house so full of holes, the winter wind had chilled her to the bone each night as she'd lain underneath piles of homemade quilts. She'd had to live in a house with rundown plumbing and a leaky roof, simply because the Murdocks didn't deem her family good enough for repairs. They lived in the house for free; what more did they want anyway? That had been the consensus, as far as the Murdocks were concerned. No, she couldn't feel sorry for Dillon Murdock. Yet she did, somehow. And that made her put up her guard.

"I always loved this house," she said now as she strolled over to the raised porch of the mansion. Swinging her slight frame up onto the splintered planks, she sat staring out into the night, into Dillon Murdock's eyes. "It's a shame it has to stand empty. Some people don't realize what they have, obviously."

She hadn't meant the statement to sound so bitter, but she could see Dillon hadn't missed the edge in her words. He came to stand in front of her, his eyes lifting to meet hers. "You're right there. It took me a long time to learn that lesson."

Isabel studied him, searching for clues of the life he must have led. But Dillon's face was as hard as granite, blank and unflinching, unreadable. Until she looked into his eyes. There, she saw his soul, raw and battered, his eyes as aged and gray as the wood underneath the peeling paint of this old house.

"So, you've come home," she said, accepting that

he didn't owe her any explanations. Accepting that she didn't need, or want, to get involved with the Murdocks' personal differences.

Dillon stepped so close, she could see the glint of danger in his eyes, could feel the warmth of his breath fanning her hair away from her face. His nearness caused a fine row of goose bumps to go racing down her bare arms, in spite of the warm spring night. Yet, she didn't dare move. She just sat there, holding her breath, hoping he'd back away. But he didn't.

"We've both come home, Isabel," he observed as he leaned against the aging porch. "But the question is, what have we come home to?"

With that, he turned and stalked away into the night, leaving her to wonder if she'd made the right decision after all. Taking a deep breath, she pushed her hair away from her face and wondered if maybe she should have stayed away from Wildwood a little longer. Well, she was here now. But while she was here, she'd be sure to stay clear of Dillon Murdock.

She didn't like feeling sorry for him. She didn't like feeling anything for him.

Yet, she did. Even after all these years, she still did.

Chapter Two

The smell of homemade cinnamon rolls greeted Isabel as she entered the screened back door of the old farmhouse. Grammy had already set the table, complete with fresh flowers from her garden. Touching her hand to a bright orange Gerber daisy, Isabel closed her eyes for just a minute. It was good to be home, in spite of her feelings regarding Wildwood. The meeting with Dillon had left her shaken and unsure, but being here with Grammy gave her strength and security. Grammy always made things seem better.

"There you are," an aged voice called from the arched doorway leading to the long narrow kitchen off to the right. "I was getting worried."

Isabel set her camera down on a nearby rickety side table, then stepped forward to take the two glasses of iced tea from her grandmother's plump, veined hands. "Sorry, Grammy. I got carried away taking pictures of the wildflowers."

She didn't mention that she'd also gotten carried away with seeing Dillon Murdock again. She wasn't ready to discuss him with her grandmother.

"You and that picture taking," Martha said, waving a hand, her smile gentle and indulging. "The flowers are sure pretty right now, though." Settling down onto the puffy cushion of her cane-backed chair, she added, "Miss Cynthia always did love her wildflowers. I remember one time a few years back, that Eli got it in his head to mow them down. Said they were an eyesore, what with the old house closed up and everything."

"He didn't do it, did he?" Isabel asked, her eyes going wide. "That would have ruined them."

Martha chuckled as she automatically reached for Isabel's hand, prepared to say grace. "Oh, no. He tried, though. Had one of the hired hands out on a mower early one morning. Miss Cynthia heard the tractor and went tramping through the flowers, all dressed in a pink suit and cream pumps, her big white hat flapping in the wind. She told that tractor driver to get his hide out of her flowers. She watched until that poor kid drove that mower clear back to the equipment barn. Then she headed off, prim as ever, to her Saturday morning brunch at the country club."

Isabel shook her head, sat silently as Grammy said grace, then took a long swallow of the heavily sweetened tea. "I was right. Some things never change."

Martha passed her the boiled new potatoes and fresh string beans. "Do you regret taking the Murdocks up on their offer?"

Isabel bit into a mouthful of the fresh vegetables,

then swallowed hastily. "You mean being the official photographer for Eli's extravagant wedding?"

"I wouldn't use the same wording, exactly," Martha said, a wry smile curving her wrinkled lips, "but I reckon that's what I was asking."

Smiling, herself, at her grandmother's roundabout way of getting to the heart of any matter, Isabel stabbed her knife into her chicken-fried steak, taking out her frustrations on the tender meat. "Well, I'm having second thoughts, yes," she admitted, her mind on Dillon. "But I couldn't very well turn them down. They're paying me a bundle and I can always use the cash. But, I mainly did it because you asked me to, Grammy."

"Don't let me talk you into anything," Martha said, her blue eyes twinkling.

"As if you've ever had to talk anyone into anything," Isabel responded, laughing at last. "You could sweet-talk a mule into tap dancing."

"Humph , never tried that one." Her grandmother grinned impishly. "But I did bake your favorite cinnamon rolls, just in case—Miss Mule."

"For dessert?" Isabel asked, sniffing the air, the favorite nickname her grandmother always used to imply that she was stubborn slipping over her head. "Or do I have to hold out till breakfast?"

Martha reached across the lacy white tablecloth to pat her granddaughter's hand. "Not a soul here, but you and me. Guess we can eat 'em any time we get hungry for 'em."

"Dessert, then, definitely," Isabel affirmed, munching down on her steak. "Ah, Grammy, you are the best cook in the world."

"Well, you could have my cooking a lot more if you came to visit more often."

Isabel set her fork down, her gaze centered on her sweet grandmother. She loved her Grammy; loved her plump, sweet-scented welcoming arms, loved her smiling, jovial face, loved her gray tightly curled hair. Yet, she couldn't bring herself to move back here permanently, a subject they'd tossed back and forth over the years.

Her tone gentle, she said, "Grammy, don't start with that. You know I have to travel a lot in my line of work and I don't always have an opportunity to come home."

Martha snorted. "Well, you told me yourself you didn't have any assignments lined up over the next few weeks, so you can stay here and have a nice vacation. Living in a suitcase—that is no kind of life for a young lady."

"I have an apartment in Savannah."

"That you let other people live in—what kind of privacy does that give you?"

"Very little, when I manage to get back there," Isabel had to admit. "Subletting is the only way to hold on to it, though."

"And you always going on and on when you were little about having a home of your own."

Her appetite suddenly gone, Isabel stared down at the pink-and-blue-flowered pattern on her grandmother's aged china. "Yeah, I did do that. But I never got that home. And I've learned to be content with what I do have." Only lately, she had to admit, her nomadic life was starting to wear a little thin.

Wanting to lighten the tone of the conversation, she

jumped up to hug her grandmother. "And I have everything I need—like home-baked cinnamon rolls and a grandmother who doesn't nag too much."

Martha sighed and patted Isabel's back, returning the hug generously. "Okay, Miss Mule, I can take a hint. I won't badger you anymore—tonight at least."

"Thank you," Isabel said, settling back down in her own chair. "Now, how 'bout one of those rolls you promised me?"

"Glad to be home?" Martha challenged, her brows lifting, a teasing glow on her pink-cheeked face.

"Oh, all right, yes," Isabel admitted, taking the small defeat as part of the fun of having a remarkable woman for a grandmother. "I'm glad to be home."

"That's good, dear."

Isabel smiled as Martha headed into the kitchen to retrieve two fat, piping hot cinnamon rolls. Martha Landry was a pillar of the church, a Sunday school teacher who prided herself on teaching the ways of Jesus Christ as an example of character and high moral standing, but with a love and practicality that reached the children much more effectively than preaching down to them ever could.

Isabel knew her grandmother wouldn't preach to her, either; not in the way her own parents always had. It was a special part of her relationship with her grandmother that had grown over the years since her parents' deaths. She could talk to Grammy about anything and know that Martha Landry wouldn't sit in judgment. One of Grammy's favorite Bible quotes was from First Corinthians: "For if we would judge ourselves, we should not be judged."

Isabel knew her grandmother believed in accepting

people as humans, complete with flaws. And that included their mighty neighbors. Yet Isabel couldn't help but judge the Murdocks, since they'd passed judgment on her a long time ago.

"I saw Dillon tonight," she said now, her gaze locking with her grandmother's, begging for understanding. "He's home for the wedding."

Isabel watched for her grandmother's reaction, and seeing no condemnation, waited for Martha to speak.

"Well, well," the older woman said at last, her carefully blank gaze searching Isabel's face. "And how was Mr. Dillon Murdock?"

"Confused, I believe," Isabel replied. "He seemed so sad, Grammy. So very sad."

"That man's had a rough reckoning over the past few years. From what I've heard, he hasn't had it so easy since he left Wildwood."

Hating herself for being curious, Isabel asked, "And just what did you hear?"

Grammy feigned surprise. "Child, you want me to pass on gossip?"

Isabel grinned. "Of course not. I just want you to share what you know."

Martha licked sweet, white icing off her fingers. "Yep, you want me to spill the beans on Dillon Murdock. Do you still have a crush on him, after all these years?"

Isabel cringed at her grandmother's sharp memory, then sat back to try to answer that question truthfully. "You know, Grammy, I had a crush on him, true. But that was long ago, and even though I saw Dillon each and every day, I never really knew him. And I don't know him now. It was a dream, and not a very realistic one.''

''Amen to that. And now?''

Isabel couldn't hide the truth from her grand-mother. ''And now, I'm curious about the man he's become. Seeing him again tonight, well, it really threw me. He seemed the same, but he also seemed different. I'm hoping he's changed some.''

Martha gave her a long, scrutinizing stare. ''That's all well and good, honey. But remember, the boy you knew had problems, lots of problems. And as far as we know, the man might still be carrying those same problems. I'd hate to see you open yourself up to a world of hurt.''

Isabel got up to clear away their dishes, her eyes downcast. ''Oh, you don't have to worry on that account, Grammy. When I left Wildwood, I promised myself I'd never be hurt by the Murdocks again.''

''Including Dillon?''

''Especially Dillon,'' Isabel readily retorted. Then she turned at the kitchen door. ''Although Dillon never really did anything that terrible to me.''

''Oh, really?''

''Really. Oh, he teased me a lot, but mostly his only fault was that he was a Murdock. Eli, on the other hand, made no bones about my being the poor hired help. I just can't tolerate their superior attitudes and snobbery. Not now. I did when I was living here, but not now. Not anymore.''

Martha followed Isabel into the kitchen. ''And did Mr. Dillon Murdock act superior tonight, when you talked to him?''

Isabel surprised herself by defending him. "No, he didn't. Not at all. In fact, he was…almost humble."

"I just hope that boy's learned from his mistakes."

"Me, too," Isabel said. "Me, too."

Dillon's soul-weary eyes came back to her mind, so brilliantly clear, she had to shake her head to rid herself of the image. "You don't have to worry about me and Dillon Murdock, Grammy. I don't plan on falling for any of his sob stories."

"Should be an interesting wedding," Martha commented, her hands busy washing out plates.

Isabel didn't miss the implications of that statement. She never could fool her grandmother.

Dillon stood at the back door of his brother's house, every fiber of his being telling him not to enter the modern, gleaming kitchen. But his mother was standing at the sink, dressed in white linen slacks and a blue silk blouse, her curled hair turned now from blond to silver-white, her small frame more frail-looking than Dillon remembered. He smiled as he heard her loudly giving orders to the maid who'd been with their family for years.

"Now, Gladys, we want everything to be just right, remember? So finish up there, dear, then you can go on back to tidying the guest room for Dillon. He'll be here any minute."

Cynthia had written to him, begging him to come home for his brother's wedding.

And so here he stood.

The minute he opened the glass door to the room, he was assaulted with the scent of dinner rolls baking, along with the scent of fragrant potpourri and a trace of his mother's overly sweet perfume. At least some parts of Eli's new home were familiar.

"Hello, Mama," he said from his spot by the door.

Cynthia whirled from directing the maid to see who'd just entered her kitchen, her gray eyes wide, her mouth opening as she recognized her younger son. "Oh, my…Dillon. You came home."

Dillon took his tiny mother into his arms, his hands splaying across her back in a tight hug, his eyes closing as memories warmed his heart even while it broke all over again. Then he set his mother away, so he could look down into her face. "This isn't my home, Mother. Not this house. It belongs to Eli."

"Well, you're welcome here. You should know that," Cynthia insisted as she reached up to push a stubborn spike of hair away from his forehead. "You look tired, baby."

He was tired. Tired of worrying, wondering, hoping, wishing. He didn't want to be here, but he wanted to be with his mother. She was getting older. They'd kept in touch, but he should have come home long ago. "I could use a glass of tea," he said by way of hiding what he really needed. "Where's Eli?"

"Right here," his brother said from a doorway leading into the airy, spacious den. "Just got in from the cotton patch." Stomping into the kitchen, his work boots making a distinctive clicking sound, Eli Murdock looked his brother over with disdain and contempt. "Of course, you wouldn't know a thing about growing cotton, now would you, little brother?"

"Not much," Dillon admitted, a steely determination making him bring his guard up.

His brother had aged visibly in the years that Dillon had been away. Eli's hair was still thick and black, but tinges of gray now peppered his temples. He was still tall and commanding, but his belly had a definite paunch. He looked worn-out, dusty, his brown eyes shot with red.

"So, it's cotton now?" Dillon asked by way of conversation. "When did we switch cash crops? I thought corn and peanuts were our mainstay."

"*We* didn't do anything," Eli said as he poured himself a tall glass of water then pointed at his own chest. "I, little brother, I did all the work on this farm, while you were gallivanting around Atlanta, living off Daddy's money. Why'd you come back, anyway—to beg Mama for your inheritance?"

"Eli!" Cynthia moved between her sons with practiced efficiency. "I invited Dillon home, for your wedding. And I want you to try to be civil to each other while he's here. Do you both understand?"

Dillon looked at his mother's hopeful, firm expression, then glanced at the brooding hostility on his brother's ruddy face. "Why don't you ask the groom, Mother?"

"I'm asking both of you," Cynthia said, her eyes moving from one son to the other. "For my sake, and for Susan's sake."

Eli hung his head, then lifted his gaze to Dillon. "As long as he stays out of my way. I won't have him ruining Susan's big day."

"Thoughtful of you," Dillon countered. "But, hey, I won't if you won't, brother."

"I'll be too preoccupied with my bride to pay you

any attention,'' Eli retorted, a distinct smugness in his words.

Wanting to counter his lack of tact, Dillon said, ''Well, it certainly took you long enough to find a woman willing to put up with you.''

That hit home. Eli set his glass down, then placed both hands on his hips. ''I don't see you bringing any young ladies home to meet Mama.''

Cynthia clapped her hands for quiet. ''Enough of this. Can we please sit down to have a pleasant dinner together? Gladys and I made baked catfish and squash casserole.''

''Why did you have to invite him back here?'' Eli asked. ''And for my wedding, of all things?''

''I wanted your brother here,'' Cynthia said, tears glistening her eyes. ''I wanted my sons to make peace with each other.''

Eli stomped to the sink to wash his hands and face. Then turning to dry himself with a dish towel, he said, ''I don't have to make peace with Dillon, Mama. He's the one who should be doing the apologizing. He ran off.''

''No, you drove me off,'' Dillon said, then he turned to his mother. ''I'm sorry, I can't stay in this house. I'll be at the wedding, Mama, and I'll show up at all the required functions, but if you need me, I'll be at Wildwood.''

''You can't stay in that run-down house,'' Cynthia said, grabbing his arm as he headed for the door.

''I'll be fine.''

''Let him go,'' Eli called. ''Let him try to survive in this heat, with no water or electricity. He'll be back across the road soon enough.''

Dillon gently extracted himself from his mother's fierce grip. "I'll see you later, Mama."

"That's just like you," Eli said. "Turn and run again. You never could stick around long enough to do any good around here."

"Eli, hush," Cynthia said. Then she called to Dillon, "I'll bring you a warm plate over later."

Dillon just kept walking, and he didn't stop until he reached the wildflower field. Then he fell down on his knees and stared up into the starry sky. He wanted to get on his motorcycle and ride away. But, this time, something held him back. This time, Isabel's green eyes and sweet-smelling hair haunted him and held him while her words came back to taunt him.

What are you doing back here?

Maybe it was time he found the answer to that question.

Maybe this time, he *would* stay and fight.

The next morning, Isabel remembered just how interesting things could become in a small town. The wedding of one of the most eligible, elusive bachelors in the county was the talk of the small hamlet, so everyone who was anyone would be invited to the event. And those who weren't invited would bust a gut trying to hear the details.

Isabel was scheduled to meet Susan Webster at the bridal shop on Front Street at ten o'clock. Susan's mother wanted Isabel to see Susan in the dress, then they'd decide where to start taking the preliminary pictures of the bride in all her splendor.

Pulling her rented Jeep up to the curve of the Brides and Beaus formal wear shop, Isabel got the strange sense that the curious townspeople were watching *her* return closely, too.

"Guess I'm a strange creature," she told Susan after hugging the other woman. "The radical free spirit comes home to Wildwood."

"We gave that particular honor to Dillon," Susan said, her bright blue eyes lighting up in spite of the wisecrack. "Did you know he's moved back in the old house? Opened up a couple of rooms. He refuses to stay in Eli's house."

Hoping she didn't sound too interested, Isabel tossed her long braid aside and shrugged. "Dillon always was a loner."

"Understatement," Susan replied, dragging Isabel into the back of the long, cluttered shop. Past the pastel formals and tuxedos that went flying off the racks at prom time, they entered the bride room where Susan's plump mother, Beatrice, sat going over the final details of the bridesmaid dresses with a clerk.

"Hello, Isabel," Beatrice said, smiling up at her. "Isn't this exciting? My baby's finally getting married, and to Eli Murdock. I'm so proud."

"It is exciting, Mrs. Webster," Isabel replied, bending down to hug the older woman. She'd have to be careful about keeping her real feelings regarding this match to herself. "And I'm touched that you both wanted me to be a part of it."

"Wait until you see the dress," Beatrice enthused, her attention already back on her job as mother of the bride.

"Wow, look at all this lace and satin," Isabel quipped, holding a hand to her eyes as she looked around at all the dresses and veils hanging in the prim room. "So bright and so white."

"Still wedding shy, I see," Susan said, sweeping around with her arms wrapped to her chest. "Not me, Isabel. I'm very happy."

Isabel eyed her high school friend, wanting desperately to ask her how she'd fallen for a cold fish like Eli Murdock. But she wouldn't dream of saying anything to hurt kind, gentle Susan. "You look sickeningly happy," she told Susan, her smile genuine. "You were meant to be married."

"Took me long enough to notice Eli, though," Susan said as they settled down on a cushioned sofa. "Imagine, all those years in the same town, then one day we ran into each other at the Feed and Seed...."

"Very romantic," Isabel said, grinning. "Tell me, did it happen over the corn seeds or maybe the... er...manure pile."

"Oh, you!" Susan laughed, then patted Isabel's hand. "I'm so glad you'll be taking the pictures. I insisted, you know. I told them you were nationally famous and we might not be able to get you for such a frivolous assignment, so I convinced Eli to pay you big bucks."

Isabel didn't hide her surprise. "Well, that explains a few things. I couldn't understand why the Murdocks wanted me so badly."

"Oh, they do," Susan assured her, her face flushing. "I mean, Mrs. Murdock agreed wholeheartedly—"

Seeing the other woman's embarrassment, Isabel shrugged again. "I understand, Susan. Eli wasn't too keen on the idea of hiring me to take your wedding pictures, huh?''

"I can explain that," Susan began, clearly appalled that she'd let that little tidbit out.

"No need," Isabel replied. "Eli and I never did see eye to eye. But that's all in the past. And if the request came from you, then I accept completely, and...I don't mind taking some of Eli's money off his hands. Now, show me this dress everyone keeps raving about.''

Ever the excited bride, Susan hopped up. "It's so beautiful!" Then she turned to stare down at Isabel, a troubled look on her pretty features. "Eli's changed, Isabel. Really, he has.''

"I know you wouldn't marry him if you didn't believe that, Susan," Isabel replied softly. "And I do hope you'll always be as happy as you look right now.''

Just to prove her point, she snapped a picture of Susan. And captured the tad of sadness she saw flickering quickly through the girl's eyes. Had Eli already started causing worry to his young bride?

"Susan," she asked as she watched her friend chatting with one of the clerks, "you'd tell me if anything was wrong, right?''

Susan whirled around, her features puzzled. "Wrong? What could be wrong?" Then lowering her head, she sighed, "It's just...I'm so excited I haven't been able to eat or sleep. I'm so in love, Isabel." With that, Susan was off to the dressing room to put on her elaborate bride dress.

Not good at waiting, Isabel got up to saunter around the shop. She'd brought her own gown to wear to the wedding, but some of the dresses offered here were quite lovely. Remembering her first prom, she balked as a vision of a young Dillon in his prom tuxedo, with a popular cheerleader encased in satiny pink by his side, came to mind. Isabel's dress that night had been homemade, an inexpensive knockoff made from a pattern with some gaudy material her mother had found on sale.

It had been Dillon's senior year, but Isabel had still been a junior in high school. Dillon had teased Isabel about her date, a football player who had a reputation for taking advantage of young girls' hearts, then later that night Dillon had asked Isabel to dance with him. She'd promptly refused, too afraid of her own mixed feelings to get near him. And too obsessed with Dillon to let the football player make any moves on her.

"Get over it, Isabel," she told herself now as she watched a bright-eyed teenager drooling over the many formal dresses crushed together all around them like delicate flower buds. She refused to think about Dillon Murdock.

But when the front door of the shop opened and the man himself stepped into the room, she had no choice but to acknowledge him. His masculine presence filled the dainty store with a bold, daring danger. And his eyes on her only added to the rising temperature of the humid summer day.

"Dillon," she said, too breathlessly.

"Isabel." He strode toward her, his eyes twinkling with amusement. "I see they've put you straight to work."

"Yes. I'm here to get a few shots of Susan in her

dress and to set up a more formal location for her portrait shots.''

He nodded, then ran his fingers through his hair. ''Mama wanted me to get fitted for a tux. I tried to get out of it, but—'' His shrug was indifferent.

The image of him in a tuxedo made Isabel want to drool just like a teenager. But she quickly reprimanded herself, and putting on a blank expression, said, ''But your mother persuaded you to come in anyway.''

He nodded, a wry grin slicing his angular face. ''You know the woman well.''

Isabel wanted to remind him that she knew all the Murdocks very well. Well enough to be wary of any association with them. Instead she asked, ''How is your mother?''

Dillon hesitated, then decided to keep his family problems to himself, not that it mattered. The whole town would probably soon be talking about his renewed feud with his brother, and the fact that he'd moved into the run-down plantation house.

He shrugged. ''You know Mama. She's tough. And she's okay, I reckon. Stressed about this wedding.''

And probably about having him back home, no doubt, Isabel decided.

Just then a nervous female clerk came forward. ''Mr. Murdock, I'm Stacey Whitfield. If you'll just follow me, we can have you fitted in no time.''

''Thanks, Stacey,'' Dillon said with a winning smile. ''Give me a minute, all right?''

The fascinated woman bobbed her head, then hurried to stand behind the counter, her eyes glued to Dillon and Isabel.

Dillon fingered a bit of lace on a nearby sleeve while the teenaged shopper Isabel had noticed earlier now had her wide eyes centered on *him* rather than a new frock. Isabel watched in detached amusement as the young girl's mother shooed her out the door, the woman's look of disapproval apparent for all to see.

"My reputation precedes me," Dillon observed on a flat note. "Mothers, lock up your daughters. He's back in town."

"Should they be worried?" Isabel asked, all amusement gone now.

"No," he replied as he came closer, his hand moving from the trailing lace to a strand of curling hair at her temple. "But maybe *you* should be."

Her breath caught in her throat, but she stared him down anyway, challenging him with a lift of her chin. "Why me?"

He leaned closer. "Because if I chase after anybody while I'm here, it'll be you, Isabel. We've got a lot of catching up to do."

Snatching his hand away, Isabel busied herself with checking her camera. "I don't have time for catching up, Dillon. I'm only here as a favor to Susan and my grandmother."

"Right."

"I'm serious."

"So am I."

Angry at herself more than him, she snapped, "You can stop playing games with me, Dillon. I'm not the naive young girl I used to be. And I won't be taunted and teased by a Murdock, ever again."

Clearly shocked at the venom in her words, Dillon backed away. "I guess I didn't realize you could hold such a grudge. But you're right. And wise to stay away from the likes of me.'' Turning to stalk toward the door, he called to the confused clerk waiting to take his measurements, ''I'll be back later, Stacey. It's a little too confining in here right now.''

With that, he slammed the front door, leaving a stunned silence to follow him, and all eyes clearly on Isabel.

Chapter Three

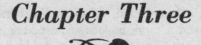

She refused to feel guilty about what she'd said to Dillon. The man needed to know right off the bat that she wasn't interested.

But, she reluctantly told herself, Dillon had looked so dejected, so hurt when she'd accused him of taunting her. She'd seen it in his stormy eyes just before he'd shut down on her. Then, he'd warned her away, as surely as he'd tried to draw her near. Now the whole town would probably be talking about the little scene in the bridal shop.

When Isabel went into the back with Stacey to tell Susan that Dillon had left, the bride-to-be was clearly flustered.

"What do you mean, he left?" a frazzled Susan asked poor embarrassed Stacey. "We have to fit him for that tuxedo!"

Stacey shuffled her loafered feet and looked over to Isabel for support. "He...he was talking to Isabel and he—"

"Dillon couldn't wait," Isabel explained, shooing Stacey away with the wave of her hand. Turning Susan back around to view herself in the three-way mirror, she commented on the exquisite bridal dress. "This is incredible, Susi."

Looking over her silk-and-lace reflection, Susan soon forgot all about Dillon's leaving. "Do you like it?"

"I do," Isabel said, although she herself would have chosen a more understated wedding gown. All that pearl beading and lace seemed a bit overwhelming. But then, she reminded herself, she wasn't the one getting married. "I knew you'd make a lovely bride. Now, let me just get a few candid shots of you here, and then we can talk about the formal portrait for the newspaper. You know, I thought about the wildflowers. How would you feel about setting up a shoot there?"

Susan's excitement changed to worry in the blink of her blue eyes. Looking over at her mother for support, she said, "Oh, I don't know—Eli hates those flowers. He calls them weeds."

Mrs. Webster fussed with Susan's veil, then nodded. "It's true, Isabel. Eli doesn't like the wildflower patch. It's been a bone of contention between him and his mother for some time now."

Susan lowered her voice to a whisper. "Something about it being Dillon's favorite spot—"

"What?" Isabel raked a hand through her long hair to keep from saying something she'd regret.

"Couldn't we do it somewhere else?" Susan questioned, her blue eyes big and round. "How about in the garden behind Eli's house? He had it especially landscaped—that big nursery from Albany did it. They did such a good job, too.''

The image Isabel had of Susan in her wedding gown amid the wildflowers died on the vine. Eli certainly wouldn't want his bride centered in a field that only reminded him of his unwelcome brother. Remembering how lonely Dillon had looked the night before, she couldn't help the little tug of regret in her heart. Maybe she shouldn't have been so nasty to Dillon earlier.

Reminding herself she was being paid to please the bride *and* the groom, and that she had to stand firm regarding Dillon Murdock, she nodded. ''If that's what you want, of course, we can do the shoot there. But Eli can't see you in your dress, remember?''

''Oh, no.'' Susan's big eyes widened. ''That'd be bad luck and we don't need any more of that.''

Curious, Isabel asked, ''Have you had some problems?''

Beatrice Webster pursed her lips, then started to speak.

Susan hastily shook her head to stop her mother, then gazed at her reflection in the mirror, her eyes glistening. ''No, everything's fine. It's just that Eli has this cotton crop to worry about, and well, he works so hard. And now, Dillon's already started showing himself. I won't have him ruining my wedding, Isabel, I just won't. We only invited him back because his poor mama wanted him here for his brother's wedding, and he doesn't even have the common decency to try on his tuxedo.''

Isabel stopped snapping pictures to stare up at her friend. ''Susan, Dillon left the shop because of me.

We…we kind of got into a little argument and I'm afraid I was rude to him. I'll try to smooth things over with him, I promise.''

Clearly relieved, Susan clapped her hands together, her number one concern right now her wedding. ''Would you please try to get him back in here, tomorrow morning if possible? We've only got a few days left before the rehearsal supper, then the wedding.''

''I promise,'' Isabel said, dreading the whole affair all over again. She must have been crazy to even accept this assignment.

An hour later, she found herself in the wildflower field, amid the honeybees and the butterflies, dreading having to see Dillon again. But she had to apologize and persuade him to do his duty. A promise was a promise, and she *had* caused him to leave the shop.

Only she didn't run into Dillon in the field. Instead, she saw his petite mother hurrying across the path, a huge plate covered with a white linen napkin balanced on her wrinkled hands.

''Miss Cynthia,'' Isabel called, rushing to help the woman with the heavily laden plate. ''My goodness, you've got enough food here to feed an army!''

''Isabel! I heard you made it in. Susan's mother—that woman calls me at least three times a day.'' Cynthia stopped to take a long, much needed breath. ''How are you, dear?''

Isabel dutifully leaned down to kiss the woman's rosy powdered cheek, noting that Miss Cynthia was dressed impeccably just to cross the road and tramp through a field. She wore a pink cotton shell, pearls, and dressy gray slacks with matching pumps.

"I'm all right, Miss Cynthia. Do you want me to carry that for you?"

Cynthia shifted the platter, then laughed nervously. "Heavens, no. I'm just in a hurry. Eli will be home soon, and I'll have to answer to him. He doesn't want me carting food over here to his brother."

Isabel hurried along with Miss Cynthia. "Just like you used to do—sneaking Dillon food after he got sent to bed with no supper."

"I'm just an old softy, aren't I?" Cynthia said, her sharp eyes moving over Isabel. "My, you've changed. You've turned out to be quite a lovely young lady, Isabel."

"Still a little tomboy left, though," Isabel said, remembering how Cynthia Murdock used to encourage her to wash her face and put on some makeup. Isabel had resented the woman's heavy-handed suggestions at the time, but now she only smiled. Apparently, Beatrice Webster hadn't wasted any time updating the whole town on Isabel's improved grooming habits. Straightening the flowing skirt of her soft linen dress, she told Miss Cynthia, "I did remember some of your fashion tips."

"I can tell," Cynthia agreed as they reached the back porch of the old mansion. "That red sundress is mighty fetching with your blond hair."

Fetching. Only Cynthia Murdock could use an old-fashioned word like that and make it sound classy and completely perfect. But the woman could also cut people into ribbons with a few well-chosen words, Isabel remembered.

"Let me get the door," Isabel said now without thinking.

The two women were busy laughing and talking as they entered the long central hallway of the cool, shuttered house. Which is why they didn't see the man standing at the end of the long kitchen, splashing water from an aluminum bucket sitting on the wash drain all over his face and bare chest, until it was too late to back out of the room.

Dillon heard the commotion, then looked up to find his mother and Isabel standing there in the doorway, looking at him as if he were doing something scandalous.

"I didn't hear a knock," he said, his lazy gaze moving from his shocked mother's face to the stunning woman standing beside her. "And I don't recall inviting two pretty ladies to dinner."

Cynthia quickly got over her shock and set the heavy platter on the cracked counter. "I found Isabel walking through the wildflowers. And…there's plenty enough here for two."

Dillon didn't bother to hide his bare chest, or the surprise his mother's bold suggestion brought to his face. "Mama, are you trying to fix me up with our Isabel?"

Cynthia snorted. "I was trying to cover up for your lack of manners, son. Where is your shirt, anyway?"

"Over there." He pointed to a suitcase tossed carelessly up on one of the many long counters. "Throw me one, will you, Isabel?"

Gritting her teeth, and pulling her eyes back inside her head, Isabel chose a plain white T-shirt to hurl at him, her small grunt of pleasure indicating that she wished it had been something that could do a little more damage.

Dillon caught the shirt, his eyes still on Isabel. With lazy disregard, he pulled it over his damp hair, then tucked it into the equally damp waistband of his jeans. "Sorry, Mama, but I didn't know I'd have an audience for my bath. Guess it's a good thing I kept my breeches on."

Cynthia threw up her hands. "He's still a charmer, isn't he, Isabel?"

"Oh, he is indeed." Isabel turned to leave. "And I really can't stay. I just wanted to say hello, Miss Cynthia."

Dillon leaned across the old, planked table standing in the middle of the kitchen. "What's your hurry?"

Isabel turned to see him reclining there, bathed in a golden shaft of afternoon sunlight, his gray eyes almost black with a teasing, challenging light.

She wanted to take his picture again. But she wouldn't, because she wasn't going to stay in this hot room any longer. She'd just have to figure out some other way of getting him to cooperate with Susan about that tuxedo. If she stayed here right now, she couldn't be sure she'd be in control of her wayward feelings.

Tossing back a long strand of hair, she said, "Actually, I was taking pictures and I ran into your mother. I didn't mean to disturb you."

Cynthia cleared her throat and shooed Isabel back into the room. "Stay and talk to my son, please. Maybe you can convince him to come over to Eli's house, where there's plenty of fresh water and air-conditioning."

Isabel hesitated, her gaze locking with Dillon's. "I

don't think it's my place to argue with your son, Miss Cynthia.''

"And why?" Cynthia questioned with a diamond bejeweled hand on her hip. "You two used to argue all the time. That boy used to send you running, nearly in tears. But only after you'd given him a good piece of your mind."

Isabel lowered her head to stare at a crack in the pine flooring. "Well, that was then—"

"And this is now," Dillon finished. "Mama's right. I'm not minding my manners. Stay and talk to me a while, Isabel. I'll be on my best behavior, I promise."

"That's more like it," Miss Cynthia said, nodding her approval. "You two can keep each other company until we all get through this wedding."

Dillon lifted up off the table then to come around and kiss his mother. "Thanks, Mama. Now, you'd better get back. I suspect Eli doesn't know you've been feeding me."

"I'll take care of Eli, son."

"Yep, you always have, haven't you?"

Cynthia stopped at the wide doorway. "I'd be more than happy to take care of you, if you'd stay here long enough to let me."

Dillon's smile was bittersweet. "I'm fine, Mama. Really. Now, scoot."

Cynthia gave an eloquent shrug, then waved to Isabel. "Bye, now. Tell your grandmama hello for me, honey. Oh, and I might have some alterations to bring down to her next week. A couple of dresses that need taking in. I don't trust anybody else to do the job."

"I'll tell her," Isabel promised, thinking that as

always, Miss Cynthia had reminded her of her place. Her grandmother was still the hired help, no matter how fond Miss Cynthia was of Martha Landry. She waited until she heard the click of Miss Cynthia's heels on the back steps, then looked up at Dillon. "I'm not staying for supper, and I can see myself out."

He reached out a long tanned arm, catching her by the hand to hold her in her spot. "Was it something I said?"

She glanced back up to find his eyes centered on her with that questioning, brooding intensity. "No, Dillon. Actually, it was something *I* said. Susan is upset that you didn't get your fitting this morning. Will you just go back in tomorrow and get it over with?"

He dropped her arm to move to the red ice chest he had propped in one corner of the room. "Want a soda?"

"Okay," she said without giving it much thought. Just like she'd come bursting in here without much thought, to find him half-clothed. How she wished she'd knocked, but then, he probably would have come to the door bare-chested anyway. When he came back to hand her the icy cold can, she told herself she'd take a couple of sips then leave gracefully.

Then he pulled the white linen cover off the fried chicken. "Mmm, Mama does know how to fry up a chicken. Doesn't that smell so good?"

Her stomach growled like the traitor it was. Taking a bit of meat that Dillon tore from a crispy breast, she nibbled it, then tried to put the fat and calorie content out of her mind.

Unrolling the silverware his mother had thoughtfully provided, Dillon dipped a spoon into the white mound beside the chicken, then held it out to Isabel. "Want some mashed potatoes?"

"Stop it!" Isabel said, taking out her frustrations on the pop top on her drink. The sound hissed and sizzled almost as loudly as the tension between them. "Just tell me you'll go back in and get your tux."

"I might," he said after shoveling the potatoes into his own mouth. Then he picked up a drumstick and bit into it. Chewing thoughtfully before he dropped it back on the plate, his eyes on her, he said, "Then again, I might just show up like this." He shrugged and waved the white napkin over his jeans. "Or, I might not show up at all."

That comment caused her to set her drink can down with a thud. "Oh, that would be just perfect. Show everyone around here that they're right about you after all. Make Susan feel even worse and cause your mother even more heartache. Yeah, Dillon, I'd say just blow the whole thing off. Why should you try to do something for someone else, anyway?"

In a blur of motion, he dropped his napkin and stood before her, one hand on her shoulder and one braced on the panelled wall behind her. "Don't, Isabel. Don't make me feel any worse than I already do."

She took a shuddering breath, her face inches from his. "Why do you fight so hard against everything?"

His gaze traveled over her face, then back to her eyes. "Why are you standing in my kitchen telling me what I should or shouldn't be doing?"

She stared him down, though she knew she'd be a

nervous wreck later because of it. "Good question. So, let me go."

"No."

Glaring up at him, she said on a breath hot with rage, "You haven't changed a bit. Still the macho tough guy, still trying to make me feel small and insignificant."

He moved an inch closer. "Is that what I'm doing? Is that how you feel right now?"

She backed farther into the wall. "Yes, to both questions. I'm right up there on your list along with Eli and all the other people in this town you're still holding a grudge against, aren't I?"

"I thought you were the one with the grudge," he said, his hand lifting off her shoulder to come up and cup her chin. "You told me I'd never get to you again. Did I get to you before?"

"No," she said, hoping she'd be forgiven for lying. "No."

"Yes," he said. "Yes."

Then he lowered his mouth to hers and kissed her with a tenderness that contradicted everything she believed about him. No man this tough could kiss with such a whispered gentleness that it left a woman's soul dancing.

No man except Dillon, of course.

When he lifted his head, the kitchen was still and warm, the house silent and waiting. And his eyes were alive with a fire of surprise, of awe, of longing. "I wasn't teasing just now, Isabel."

Isabel swallowed hard, then tried to find what little sense of reason she had left. She shouldn't be here with him. She should run away as fast as she could.

Instead, she reached up a hand to stroke away that irresistible spike of hair centered on his forehead. "Are you sure, Dillon? Are you sure that kiss wasn't just a way to inflict pain on me?"

He ran a hand down the length of her hair, then gave her a wry smile. "Right now, darling, I'm not sure about anything, except that maybe I have a champion in you."

Surprised, she asked, "Why do you think that?"

He backed away then, letting her hair trail through his fingers to fall in cascading waves back around her shoulders. "Because, you *didn't* run away. You came here to fight me, and maybe, to fight for me. And you stayed even after I insulted you." Tipping his head to one side, his hands on his hips, he added, "And you stayed even after I kissed you."

Isabel moved away from the wall, and on shaking knees, tried to walk to the counter where she'd put her drink. Taking a long, cool swallow of the amber liquid, she turned to face him again. "I didn't have much choice. You had me against the wall."

A smug indifference replaced the gentleness she'd seen in his face. "That's how I court all of my women."

Tired and frightened of her own soaring feelings, she snapped at him. "We're not courting each other."

He came back strong. "Then what are we doing?"

Sighing, she threw her wavy hair back off her face, holding it tightly against her head with her hand. "I came here to ask you to behave, to show Susan some respect. But since it was my fault you left the shop this morning, I just wanted to make amends."

"Well, you did," he said, his voice going soft again. "You did that and a whole lot more."

Isabel dropped her hair over her shoulder, then crossed her arms over her chest in a defensive manner, still holding her soda with a loose hand. "Will you go back and get yourself a tux for the wedding?"

"Will you sit by me during the ceremony and dance with me at the reception?"

"I asked first."

"I'm asking now."

She smiled, then set her nearly empty can down. "You haven't changed a bit, Dillon."

He tipped a hand to his head in an acknowledging salute, then leaned back against the creaky table. "Ah, but you have. And for that, dear Isabel, I might be willing to behave—for my brother's wedding, that is."

"And wear the tux?" she said, tossing him the challenge.

"And wear the infernal tux," he added. Then he grabbed her to pull her back into his arms. "Just remember, save the last dance for me, okay?"

"Okay," she said as she allowed him to hold her close. Battling with Dillon Murdock had always left her drained.

Dillon didn't try to kiss her again. Instead, he just closed his eyes and held her. Isabel couldn't help feeling as if she'd come home. But she knew in her heart, that Dillon couldn't give her a home. Neither of them would linger here at Wildwood for very long. They were both still searching for something, some elusive something to ease the ache in their souls.

And all around them, the waning sun cascaded

through the tall kitchen windows in rays of gold, white and muted yellow, revealing dancing fragments of dust that had long lain as dormant and still as the pain buried deep in both their hearts.

Chapter Four

"**D**on't open the door!"

Isabel stood in the dark bathroom at the back of the house, watching through the red glow of the safelight as the picture she'd taken of Dillon developed in a chemical bath. If her grandmother opened the door now, the picture would be ruined. "I'll be out in a minute, Grammy."

"It's not your grandma," a deep masculine voice said through the closed door.

Dillon.

Isabel almost knocked over her whole tray of developer. "Just a minute!" Taking a deep breath, she checked the timer, then stood back to see the emerging picture of the man who'd kissed her not two days ago, and who'd kept her awake thinking about him since then. With quick efficiency in spite of the flutter in her heart, she lifted the picture out of the developer, then dropped it in the stop bath for thirty seconds.

Another minute in the fixer, then a good wash for a couple of minutes, and the picture was done.

But the knocking at the door wasn't.

"Hey, you getting all dolled up or something?"

"Or something," Isabel retorted as she clipped the finished picture up on the clothesline she had extended across the cracked tub. "I'm working."

"Sorry, but that excuse won't wash. It's a pretty summer day and I have a hankering to take a walk down to the branch—with a pretty woman by my side."

Isabel stared at the picture of Dillon, her smile bittersweet. She'd captured his spirit as he stood there looking up at Wildwood. And somehow, since then, he was coming very close to capturing her heart. She'd have to be very careful about that. She wasn't ready to admit that Dillon had always held her heart.

Blinking, she called out, "Couldn't talk anyone else into it, huh?"

"Right. You seem to be the only woman around these parts willing to put up with me."

Opening the door just a fraction—she surely didn't want him to see that picture of himself—Isabel pasted an indulgent smile on her face. "You have such a unique way of asking a woman for a date, Dillon."

Dillon stood back in the small hallway, his eyes sweeping over her face, his half grin teasing and tempting. "And you, dear Isabel, sure have a way of looking as refreshing as a tall glass of lemonade. How do you do that?"

Ruffled, she lowered her head and crossed her arms around her chest, sure that she looked raggedy and drained from working in her makeshift darkroom all afternoon. Conscious of her faded cotton T-shirt and old shorts, she asked, "Do what?"

"You look different now, you know," he said instead of explaining himself. "I think it's the hair. You never wore it long before."

She left the bathroom and moved up the hall to the front of the rickety old house, running her hands through the swirls of loose curls falling away from her haphazard ponytail. "No, I didn't. Mama made me keep it cut. Said it was too much of a handful, what with all these waves and curls. I hated wearing it short."

He caught up with her in the kitchen. "So you let it grow."

"And grow," she said as she turned to hand him a glass of iced tea. "I guess it's silly, wearing it so long—"

"No, it suits you."

"Thank you," she said, acutely aware of his eyes on her. "I think it's probably more of a personal statement than a fashion decision."

"The rebellious daughter doing what her parents didn't approve of?"

She nodded, then lifted a brow. "Takes one to know one, I guess."

"I am one," he agreed. He set his now empty glass in the wide single sink and held out his hand. "C'mon, Issy, let's go for a long walk."

Stopping, Isabel stared across at him. "You called me Issy."

"Yeah, well, don't tell me you don't allow people to do that anymore."

"No, it's just that…no one besides you and my

immediate family even knows about that horrid nickname.''

"Issy, Issy, Issy," he teased, his grin widening.

Isabel's breath lifted right out of her body. She had forgotten what a lethal smile Dillon had. Maybe because she remembered his smiles being so rare. Coming up for air, she said, "Dilly, Dilly, Dilly," as a retort.

"Oh, boy. I should have never reminded you."

She took his hand in spite of all the name calling, very conscious of the rough calluses on his fingers. "I really need to finish developing that roll of film."

He gripped her fingers against his. "It'll keep."

He led her out the back door. The late afternoon air was ripe with the scents of early summer. Peaches growing fat on nearby trees, lilies blooming in her grandmother's carefully tended flower beds, roses drifting like rich cotton candy in the warm summer breeze. How could a woman resist such a day? Isabel believed God saved such days for special times, when people needed them the most.

She sure needed one. But with Dillon? How was she supposed to resist him and the sweet summer air, too?

"Who let you in, anyway?" she asked, looking around the yard for her grandmother.

He let go of her hand to turn and walk backward in front of her, much in the same way he used to do when they'd walk home after getting off the school bus. "I saw Martha on the road. She was headed to the Wedding War Room to help Mama with her dress. Told me to come and keep you company."

"How very thoughtful of my dear old grand-mother."

He gave her a sideways glance. "I thought so. Took her right up on her suggestion."

"Don't you have anything better to do?"

"I've made a few calls, done my work for the day."

Catching up to him, she asked, "And just what is your line of work these days?"

He turned serious then. "I run my own company, so I can set my own hours."

"Really?" Surprised at this revelation, she asked, "What sort of company?"

As smooth as the flattened red clay underneath their feet, he changed the subject. "I don't want to talk about work. I want to enjoy what's left of the day."

Isabel sensed his withdrawal, remembered it all too well from their years of growing up together. "Okay. You want to be irresponsible and play, right?"

He gave her that classic Dillon salute. "Right. It's what I do best, or so they tell me."

She didn't miss the sarcasm or the tinge of pain in his words. But she wouldn't press him to talk. That had been one of the things between them way back when, that is, when he hadn't been ribbing her or pestering her. Sometimes, they'd just sit quietly, staring off into nowhere together.

"Race you to the branch," she said, her long legs already taking off, her baggy walking shorts flying out around her knees.

Dillon was right on her heels. Just like always.

The branch was a shallow stream of clear, cool water that ran through a pine-shaded forest toward the back of the estate. The path to get there took them through the rows and rows of cotton just beginning to bud white on ruffly green vines.

"Eli and his cotton," Dillon said, the note of resentment in his voice echoing through the trees. "Our ancestors raised cotton on this land, but we quit growing it years ago. They say cotton's making a comeback, though. A good moneymaker, I reckon. And Eli sure likes his money."

"Is that so wrong?" Isabel questioned as she settled down on the same moss-covered bank she'd sat on as a child. "I mean, do you resent your family's wealth?"

Dillon snorted, then picked up a rock. With a gentle thud, he skipped it across the water, then plopped down beside her. "No, I don't resent my family's wealth. Thanks to my mother, I certainly spent my share of it before I settled down. It's just that Eli puts money and prominence before anything else."

"And you don't?"

"Not anymore."

Isabel glanced down at him, her heart skipping like the rock he'd thrown earlier. He looked so at home, lying there on a soft bed of pine straw in his faded jeans and Atlanta Braves T-shirt. She hadn't realized until this very moment how much she'd missed Dillon.

And he chose that very moment to look over at her, his eyes meeting hers in a knowing gaze that only reminded her of his kiss, his touch, his gentleness.

"You're pretty, Issy," he said, his voice as low and gravelly as the streambed.

To hide her discomfort, she said, "Don't sound so surprised."

"I am surprised," he admitted, his gaze moving over her face. "I don't remember you being so attractive."

No, he didn't remember much about her, Isabel thought. Even though he'd seen her every day of their growing up years, Dillon had taken her existence for granted. To him, she'd always be the poor kid next door. A fixture in his mind, just like his precious wildflower patch. Well, the wildflowers were the same. But she wasn't.

She looked away, out over the flowing water. "I don't remember me being so attractive, either. I was all legs and teeth."

"Not anymore," he said as he lifted up on his elbows. "I mean, you've still got legs, that's for sure, and when you smile—well, you have a pretty smile."

"Thank you, I think," she replied, her words lifting out over the breeze. "I guess the braces paid off after all." She took a long breath to retain some of her dignity. If she looked at him again—

"I like your lips, too."

That did it. "Dillon," she said, jumping up to move away, "are you deliberately flirting with me?"

He rolled over on his stomach, a lazy grin stretching across his swarthy face. "Well, of course. And if you come back over here, I intend to kiss you again."

She moved farther away. "No. We can't do this, Dillon."

"Why not?"

"You know why not."

He sat up then, brushing his hands together to scatter the pine needles he'd collected. "No, I honestly don't know why not. We're adults now, Issy. And no one can tell us what we can and can't do."

Isabel walked to the water's edge, then looked down at the sparkling stream where a school of tiny minnows danced in perfect symmetry. "But...we're still us, Dillon. I'm still the poor farm girl, and you're still the rich second son."

He came up in one fluid movement, then pulled her around to face him. "That's ridiculous. You can't still feel that way."

She looked up at him, wanting to touch him. But she didn't. "I do. Because it will never change. I wasn't ever good enough for you. And I never will be good enough for you."

Dillon's expression changed from perplexed to resolved. "I'm sorry, Issy. I never realized you wanted to be good enough for me. You see, I always thought it was the other way around."

"What do you mean?"

He came closer then, his eyes boring into her. "I always figured you didn't think I was worth your trouble. I never thought I was worthy of anybody's consideration around here."

Touched by his admission, Isabel reached a hand up to his face. "You never bothered to find out about me, Dillon. You never took the time to consider *me*."

Dillon stared down at her, seeing the hurt mixed with pride in her misty green eyes. If she only knew....

He placed his hand over hers, then brought their joined hands down between them. "Is that why you're fighting me now? You think I'm just playing with you, the same way I played with you when we were kids?''

''Well, aren't you?''

Dillon dropped her hand, then turned to stalk a few feet away, the honesty of touching her too much to bear just yet. Playing it cool, he chuckled. ''Yeah, maybe I am, at that. Maybe I'm just bored and restless and, maybe I don't really want to be here.'' Shrugging, he said over his shoulder, ''Yep, you sure got me all figured out.''

Hearing the resentment, the anger, in his words only made her more determined to keep things clear between them. ''I'm just being honest, Dillon. I didn't want to come back here, either. But I promised Grammy and Susan.''

''That was noble of you.''

Stomping over to him, her hands jammed into the deep pockets of her shorts, she said, ''Look, I'm here for the same reasons you are. We're both here out of a sense of duty and obligation.''

''Speak for yourself. As for me, I just wanted to come home—just for a little while.''

Something, maybe that slight inflection in his voice that made him seem so vulnerable and lonely, brought her head up and made her want to understand him. ''Because your mother asked you to, right?''

''Right. But, hey, everybody knows Dillon Murdock doesn't have a sense of obligation or honor. And I certainly don't know what duty means, now do I? I'm just bad ol' Dillon, enticing a pretty girl to the woods like the big bad wolf.''

She'd wounded him. Somehow, she'd cracked that uncaring, cynical veneer. And what she saw there in the shimmering depths of his eyes tore her heart apart. "Dillon?"

He looked up just in time to see the sorrow in her eyes. "Don't, Isabel. Don't feel sorry for me. I don't want your pity."

"Dillon."

He lifted a hand to stop her from coming to him. "No, you're right, Isabel. This is a bad idea—you and me. You're right to have doubts about me." With that, he shrugged again, then gave her a bitter smile. "I guess I was just lonesome. I guess I just thought we could talk."

Completely confused, she said, "Then why did you tell me you wanted to kiss me again?"

"Just flirting," he said, his face blank, his tone indifferent. "Won't happen again."

"Okay," she said as she hurried to catch up with him. Behind them, the sun was snuggling up against the tree line. Another beautiful summer sunset. Isabel wished she had her camera. She also wished Dillon didn't walk so fast. "Listen, if you want to talk, that's fine—"

"I'm over it now," he said, his words curt and clipped. "I'll go on home and talk to myself."

Feeling smaller by the minute, she grabbed his arm. "Dillon, I mean it. I don't mind talking. And I'm a good listener."

He gave her a harsh laugh. "I've heard that line before, sweetheart."

"It's not a line. I...oh, I don't know what kind of games you're playing."

They were in the cotton patch now, moving down the dirt lane toward the main road. Off in the distance, the putter of a tractor's grinding motor vibrated through the field. But Dillon kept on walking.

Finally running to match his stride, Isabel yanked him by the arm. "Slow down, for goodness' sake."

He turned then to stumble into her arms, his eyes raking her face with longing and regret, while his hands gripped her elbows. "I gotta keep moving, Issy."

"Why?"

He lowered his head to hers. "Because if I stop, if I keep standing here with you in my arms, I'm gonna do something we'll both regret."

She understood what he meant, but she didn't try to pull away. "Let's talk about this, Dillon."

He shook his head. "You see, there's the rub. I don't want to talk."

"But you said you needed someone to talk to."

"I'll find someone else."

"I'm here."

His eyes, so misty gray, so clear, held hers. "This is a bad idea."

Not understanding, but wanting to desperately, she protested. "No, Dillon. We can be friends. We can help each other through this wedding."

"Can we?"

"Yes. I promise. I know it's hard for you, being here again. I'll help you."

"Will you?"

Isabel looked up at him, at his face, so open now, so willing to trust her. She saw hope in the clouds banking in his eyes. "I'll try."

"And what if I try to kiss you again?"

"You wouldn't, would you?"

He touched a finger to her lips. "I want to, right here, right now."

"Dillon—"

"I want to, Issy."

Isabel felt a sigh move through her. A strange humming sound lifted out over the wind, maybe it was her heart beating much too fast. Somehow, she knew, knew that they'd never be able to just talk. There was a sweet, special something here that she'd never felt before with any other man.

"Issy?"

She had her eyes closed. "Hmmm?"

"I'm going to kiss you."

She sighed right along with the pine trees. "Okay."

"Okay, I just wanted to warn you."

"Okay."

Dillon leaned down to pull her close. With one hand pulling through the tangles of her long hair and the other one gentling on the small of her back, he lowered his head to hers. Knowing that he shouldn't be doing it. Knowing that she deserved so much more than he had to offer her. Knowing that they'd both be moving on soon.

Knowing that it felt so right, so pure, so wonderful that he'd never be able to let her go. And while he kissed her, he thanked the God he'd so often fought against for giving him the strength to come home again, to find her here. Even though Dillon hadn't relied on prayer in a long time, he prayed about his feelings for Isabel, and he asked God to release him from all the bad memories. But maybe The Good

Lord didn't want him to forget. Maybe he'd been asking for the wrong things.

It didn't matter right now. Right now, he felt a burst of sheer joy, felt his heart settling down for the first time in a very long time, felt as if he had indeed come home again. Lifting his head, he stared down at her, unable to voice his feelings. Except to say her name. "Isabel."

Isabel watched his face, saw the peaceful expression falling like soft sun rays across his weathered features. "It's going to be all right, Dillon. I promise." Then she lifted up to kiss him again.

For a few minutes, they were lost in each other, there on the edge of the cotton field. Until the roar of an approaching tractor brought them out of their embrace.

And brought Eli Murdock face-to-face with his brother and Isabel Landry.

Eli glared down on them, then cut the engine, leaving a quaking silence to shatter through the trees.

"I told you this was a bad idea," Dillon whispered, all traces of serenity gone from his face now. But he held her hand tightly in his as he turned to face his brother. "I'll handle this."

"No," Isabel said, lifting her head to stare up at Eli. "We'll handle your brother—together."

She didn't miss the pride shining through Dillon's eyes, or the tightening of his fingers around her own.

Eli sat back in his seat, then hopped down from the cab, his harsh features red from heat and disapproval. "I see you two are up to your old tricks."

"Hello, Eli," Isabel said in a level voice, even though her whole body tensed at seeing him again.

She'd avoided him as long as she could. Might as well show him right here and now that she wasn't a scared little girl anymore.

"Isabel," he said by way of greeting. "I mighta known you'd take up with my no-good brother again. Y'all are like two peas in a pod."

Dillon glared at his brother, a steely look cresting in his eyes. "Well, these two peas don't want to be bothered, Eli. What Isabel and I do together is none of your business."

"It is when you're standing on my land," Eli reminded them, his eyes purposely centering on Isabel. "What would Mama think, if she saw you two kissing right here in the middle of the cotton patch."

Dillon let out a long sigh. "First of all, this is my land, too. And I don't think Mama would make a big deal out of this. Isabel and I are adults, after all."

Eli's look of disdain made Isabel feel sick inside. He'd never regard her as anything but poor farm trash. His next words only confirmed that notion.

"Yeah, I can see things have certainly taken a new turn with you two. Used to chase each other around, playing tag and baseball, innocent enough. I reckon you've both grown up, but that doesn't mean you should become careless and irresponsible—with no thought for the consequences."

"Shut up, Eli," Dillon said, the echo of his frustration rising out over the trees. "I won't listen to your insults and I won't let you talk that way about my relationship with Isabel."

Isabel lifted her chin, her gaze meeting Eli's. "It's okay, Dillon." Then to Eli, "You're right, of course. Dillon and I are adults now, and we're also a whole lot older and wiser than we were when we used to run around this place teasing each other and playing games. Don't worry, though, Eli. I wouldn't dream of doing anything to ruin Susan's wedding. And I hope you won't, either.''

Turning defensive, Eli said, ''And what's that supposed to mean?''

''Take it any way you want,'' Isabel said, shrugging. ''Now, gentlemen, I have to get back to work. Susan wants to see the first shots of her wedding dress. And, in case you've both forgotten, she's having a pantry shower tomorrow night. I'll be taking pictures of that happy occasion, too. So, I'd better get back and finish up today's negatives.''

Dillon stood silent, his hand on Isabel's arm. Then he said, ''Don't rush off.''

''Not on my account anyway,'' Eli said with a mock smile. Then he added, ''Oh, by the way, Isabel, I hear you're making a nice living with that fancy camera of yours. Don't go gouging me for too much money on these wedding pictures. I'd hate to think you'd take advantage of my good graces just 'cause you've gone and got a big head.''

Seething, Isabel smiled sweetly at him. ''I'm doing this as a favor for Susan and my grandmother,'' she explained. ''And unlike some people, I don't take advantage of others. You can rest assured I'll quote you a fair price for my services, Eli.''

Eli nodded, his gaze sweeping her face. ''I'll just bet.''

A shiver of revulsion slipping down her back, Isabel turned to hurry toward her house, memories of Eli's past innuendoes coming back with all the clarity of the chirping crickets singing to the approaching darkness.

While Dillon had always teased her relentlessly, his youthful flirtations had only fueled her own longings. Eli, on the other hand, had been much older and much more direct with his barbs. He'd always cornered her, making suggestive remarks about her station in life and about her lack of a social position, making her feel small and worthless even while he implied he could give her whatever she wanted—if she'd be willing to pay the price. Isabel had never taken him up on any of his offers. And apparently, he'd never forgiven her for it. Or for her closeness to Dillon.

Isabel tried to block the ugly past and Eli's condescending cruelness out of her mind. But it wouldn't work. Dillon's sweet touch, followed so closely by Eli's implied threats, only reinforced what she'd been telling herself all along.

She should have never returned to Wildwood.

Nothing good could come of this. Especially if she and Dillon didn't halt things between them right now.

Reaching the back porch of the little farmhouse, Isabel turned to stare out into the golden dusk. And then she saw Dillon, moving like a desperado through the wildflowers. Heading toward home.

"Only we don't have a home, do we, Dillon?" she whispered to the night wind. "You and me, we're like that field of flowers, wild and uncultivated, scattered."

And if Eli Murdock had his way, they'd both be mowed down and cleared out.

Chapter Five

~❧

"More rice and flour," Cynthia Murdock said, laughing out into the crowd of about twenty women scattered around the opulent formal living room of Eli's home. "Susan, sugar, you'll have to cook rice every night for a year if this keeps up."

Susan laughed, then passed the basket laden with staple provisions around the group, her eyes shining with pleasure. "But isn't this basket so lovely. I can use it in the kitchen maybe, or out on the sun porch." Then, her gaze flying to Cynthia, she hastily added, "That is, if you don't mind me adding my own decorating touches here and there, Mrs. Murdock."

Cynthia took the floral-etched wicker basket filled with not only rice and flour bags, but spices and seasonings, too, then turned to her future daughter-in-law. "Of course not, honey. As far as I'm concerned, when you move in here with my son, my work is done. I plan to fade to the background. I think I'll travel a lot and you know, I might even invest in one of those fancy condominiums down at Panama City Beach. I do so love the Gulf of Mexico.''

''Wish I had an accommodating mother-in-law,'' one of the shower attendees chirped. ''I'd gladly buy mine a condo far away from here, if I could afford it.''

Isabel, standing near the high arched doorway to the kitchen, laughed at the offhand joke, then snapped the moment with her camera, her stance aloof and observant as always. She was comfortable being on the outside, looking in. Maybe because she'd been born into that position here at Wildwood, it just came naturally for her now. Perhaps that was why she'd taken up photography at an early age, with an inexpensive camera Grammy Martha had given her one Christmas. Now, she could watch the world from her vantage point and capture the parts of it she wanted to preserve.

Like tonight. Being here in Eli's excessively furnished home only reminded her of being with Dillon in the sparse, ragged remains of Wildwood. Like Dillon, Isabel didn't feel any tuggings toward the new house. No, her heart would always belong to the old mansion across the way.

And her heart was strongly leaning toward the man who'd taken up residence inside that old house. She'd much rather be there, trying to decipher Dillon, than here watching her friend tear open the silver-and-white patterned paper of yet another shower gift. Here amid the belles and matrons of the local society, Isabel felt out of sorts and at odds. She'd never been a part of the inner circle. No, she'd been more of a curiosity for Miss Cynthia's rich friends—someone to patronize and tease. And because of that, she now felt as if she'd been on display all evening.

With comments ranging from, "My, my, it's Isabel Landry, the world traveler. Whatcha doing back in the boonies, sugar?" to "Isabel's gone and got herself citified. I do believe I've never seen shoes like those. And that hair—your poor mama, rest her soul, would take a pair of scissors to that tangle right away, darlin'," she only wanted to finish her pictures and escape the sugary-sweet facade of southern blue-blood wedding shower mania.

"Want a cup of punch, Isabel?" Martha Landry, who'd been hired to help serve, asked from behind her granddaughter. "You look drained."

"Thanks, Grammy." Isabel took the rich red juice concoction laced with a dollop of vanilla ice cream. The creamy mixture felt cool and smooth on her throat. "I am tired. I didn't sleep very well last night."

"I know, honey," Martha said above the din of feminine chatter. "I heard you roaming the house. You used to do that when you were little, remember?"

Isabel smiled, then dipped her head. "Yes, and I'd usually wind up sneaking into your room."

Martha winked. "Grammy's quilts are guaranteed to calm any nighttime fears away. You could still stop in for a visit—you'll never be too old for some comfort."

Tears misted Isabel's eyes. "I might take you up on that offer, Grammy. I'm having a hard time being back here."

Concerned, Martha said, "But your pictures...

Isabel, they're all so pretty. Susan is real pleased so far."

"Then that's worth the trip," Isabel replied, meaning it. "I wouldn't want her to be disappointed, in me or this wedding."

"Don't sound so cynical, dear," Martha whispered. "Just look at the girl. Even if you can't find it in your heart to soften toward Eli, at least be happy for Susan's sake. She's glowing."

"Yes, she is," Isabel said, deciding she wouldn't share the rest of her doubts with her grandmother just yet. "And don't worry, I wouldn't dream of bursting Susan's bubble."

"It's more than a bubble, Isabel," Martha replied, patting her granddaughter's slender arm. "It's a lifelong commitment between two human beings."

"It's downright scary," Isabel admitted, her thoughts automatically slipping to Dillon. "What makes a good marriage, Grammy?"

Martha sighed, then took a sip of her own punch. "Well, that's a loaded question. I guess it's both simple and complicated—it takes love, faith, hope, commitment and compromise. A really good marriage always includes that very important element—the firm belief in God as a guiding force. You know, your parents had all of those things."

"They did adore each other, and they did rely on God's help."

"But?"

Isabel shifted on her chunky sandals. "They just seemed so…resigned. They didn't try to make a better life for themselves. They worked so hard, and for somebody else. I'll never be able to understand that."

Martha's keen eyes scrutinized Isabel's face. "Child, have you ever stopped to consider that your parents had everything they wanted right here?"

Isabel shook her head. "But they could have had so much more. Remember the time Daddy wanted to buy Mama that house in town? They were so excited, so happy. I know they wanted to get away from this place. But nothing ever came of it. It's as if they just gave up on all their dreams."

"Maybe that was more your dream than theirs, sugar," Martha said gently. "You can't misjudge Leonard and Miriam. They had the life they wanted—you see, they had each other."

Seeing the pain and disappointment in her grandmother's eyes, Isabel quickly set her empty punch cup down. "Oh, Grammy, I meant no disrespect. I loved them dearly—you know that. I just didn't always understand them."

Martha put a hand on Isabel's shoulder. "My son was a kind, proud man. A hard worker, like his father. Maybe he was too softhearted, true. He let others dictate to him." Her gaze shifted ever so slightly to Cynthia Murdock. "But he was content with life. He had a strong faith that everything would work out, with The Lord's help."

"You want me to find that kind of faith, don't you?" Isabel said.

"Yes, I surely do," Martha replied in a soft whisper. "And...I want you to find the kind of love your parents had, the kind of relationship I had with your dear grandfather. That, Isabel, is where you'll find your treasures."

Isabel nodded, then looked out the wide window,

over toward the dark shape of Wildwood. "Somewhere out there, I guess I'll find some sort of peace one day."

"Might be closer than you think," Martha said.

Isabel shot her grandmother a look, but Martha was already clapping and admiring the next gift Susan had opened.

Wondering what her grandmother had meant by that pointed observation, Isabel automatically busied herself with taking another picture of Susan. The gift wasn't a kitchen item, however. It was a bath basket, complete with colorful pastel gels and soaps that smelled like a tropical paradise.

"I know it's not officially kitchenware," Beatrice Webster said to her surprised daughter. "But I did get you a food processor. I just couldn't resist throwing this in, too, honey. I got it for your honeymoon—you can take some of the lotions and soaps."

"Oh," Susan said before placing the gift off to the side, her usually bright eyes going flat. "That's so nice of you, Mama." Then to everyone's surprise, at just the moment Isabel snapped another shot of her, Susan blurted out, "There's only one problem. We might not have a honeymoon. Actually, there might not even be a wedding!"

With that, the woman burst into tears and ran to the kitchen, leaving the entire room in a shocked, awkward silence.

"Oh, my," Cynthia said, clearly embarrassed. After all, Murdocks didn't show vulgar displays of emotion in public. Turning to Beatrice, she said, "Maybe I should go and talk to her."

"It's my fault," Beatrice wailed, her face as red as

the ribbon curled around her pudgy fingers. "I shouldn't have sneaked that gift in. I'll go and see what's wrong."

"Let me, Mrs. Webster," Isabel said, stunning not only herself but everyone else in the room. "I mean, it might be better if Susan talks to someone who's not so...involved in all of this."

"Good point," Martha agreed, urging Isabel into the kitchen. "Now, ladies, let's finish these cheese straws. I made them myself and I'll be highly offended if we have any left. And let me see that beautiful tablecloth Irene Stratton sent over—Battenburg lace, isn't it?"

With the even flow of her grandmother's calming voice echoing in her head, Isabel searched the long kitchen for her friend. She found Susan out on the patio, staring into the glistening waters of the kidney-shaped swimming pool.

"Are you all right?" Isabel asked, hesitation making her whisper.

Susan waved a hand, then wiped a couple of fingers under her tear-smudged eyes. "Just prewedding nerves, I guess. I sure made a fool of myself in there, though, didn't I?"

Coming to stand by her friend, Isabel put a hand across Susan's back. The woman was trembling. "Susan, tell me what's going on?"

Near bursting, Susan turned to hug Isabel close, a new batch of sobs racking her body. "It's just...Eli can be so stubborn at times. We had a terrible fight today—he was so moody and mean to me. Something about boll rot or boll weevils—I can't remember which. And now I feel horrible, fighting over some silly bugs!''

Hiding her smile, Isabel hugged her friend tight. ''Oh, Susi, I'll bet he was just worried. I'm sure he didn't mean to take it out on you. But boll weevils can be bad for a cotton crop. And so can boll rot— the crop won't yield as much if the plants can't mature properly.''

Susan let go to stand back and stare at Isabel. ''You think I'm being spoiled and selfish, don't you?''

''No, I think you're a bride—maybe a bit emotional and overstressed, but that's to be expected, I imagine.''

Susan let out a sigh, then plopped down on a wrought-iron bench. ''I never knew such a happy event could cause so many hurt feelings. Eli means well, I know. But...he gets so mad when I suggest even the smallest of changes.''

Wanting to understand, Isabel sat down, too. ''You mean with the wedding?''

''With everything,'' Susan blurted out. ''He doesn't want me to change a thing about this house— not that it needs changing. It's perfect. But that's the problem. I want to add my own touches. You know, make it homey. It seems so lofty and grand, I'm afraid to walk through it for fear of knocking something over and breaking it.''

''I understand,'' Isabel said, looking around at the immaculate yard. ''It needs children running through it and a swing set over there. Little things that make a house a home.''

''Exactly,'' Susan said, bobbing her head. ''And Eli refuses to even discuss children. Plus, he's watched over the plans for the wedding like a general watching over a battle plan. He wants everything to go off without a hitch. 'What would people think if a Murdock had a tacky wedding?' That's exactly what he said to me when I showed him the teal material I'd picked for the bridesmaid dresses. Said it was too loud and bright.''

"I'm sure it was lovely."

Susan hung her head. "No, I have bad taste. I know I do, but Miss Cynthia's helping me there. We settled on a pale pink instead. Oh, Isabel, what if I can never measure up?"

Angry that Eli had inflicted the same kind of pain on Susan as he had her, Isabel jumped up to pace in front of the rippling pool. "That's ridiculous. You more than measure up to Eli Murdock. That man had better tread lightly, or he'll lose the best thing that's ever happened to him."

"I won't leave him at the altar, Isabel," Susan said, her eyes widening. "I truly love him with all my heart, and besides it would devastate him. Not to mention the embarrassment. I'd never be able to hold my head up in Wildwood again."

"Hogwash," Isabel said. "Is that all anybody around here worries about, appearances? If you're having doubts about this wedding, Susan, you'd better halt it now. Before it's too late."

Appalled, Susan jumped up to stop Isabel. "No, I didn't mean to imply that. I fully intend to marry Eli. I love him. I…I just get so confused and worried. And I know he loves me, and he can be incredibly sweet about things. But on days when he's in one of his tempers... Well, I just start doubting if I can ever make him happy.''

Isabel didn't want to tell her friend that she seriously doubted anyone could ever make Eli Murdock happy. The man just didn't seem to have any compassion or understanding for his fellow human beings. But she'd already pressed Susan enough, and she knew her interference would only cloud matters.

''Of course you'll make him happy,'' she told Susan, patting her friend's trembling hand. ''You've just got to relax and enjoy being a blushing bride.''

Susan still looked dejected. ''If he'd only quit being so stubborn—he could hire someone to help oversee things around here. He's trying to run this place with so little help, and it's making him very hard to live with. Not to mention, he never gets to rest. I worry about his health.''

''Farming is very demanding work,'' Isabel said, remembering how hard her father had worked. Rain, drought, wind, fire, pests, a hundred things could go wrong at any given time when you farmed the land. Your livelihood depended on nature and good luck. ''Does he have someone reliable who could take over some of the responsibilities?''

''He's got good workers, but...'' Susan stopped, her expression guarded and unsure. ''Eli says he can't trust anyone else to be in charge. And his mama runs him ragged, demanding his attention.''

''Miss Cynthia is a very capable woman herself,'' Isabel said. ''Maybe she could at least take over some of the paperwork.''

''But Eli doesn't trust her with any of it,'' Susan said. ''Besides, he doesn't want his mother working.''

Giving Isabel another measured look, she said in a shaky voice, "If Dillon would offer a hand—"

"Dillon?" Isabel couldn't help but laugh. "You expect Eli to let Dillon help out on this place, after the way they feel about each other?"

Recovering remarkably, Susan nodded, then sniffed. "Well, I could talk to Eli and you could work on Dillon. I'm sure between the two of us, we could make them see eye to eye on this."

"No," Isabel said, shaking her head as she whirled away. "Dillon doesn't want to get involved in his brother's problems."

"This land isn't a problem," Susan retorted. "This land has been in this family for generations, and the money from this place has helped Dillon through the years. He owes it to his mother and to Eli. He deserted this family. He should be thankful he's even welcome back here at all."

Angry now that Susan had just blurted out all her own problems regarding Wildwood and had just as quickly turned the blame toward Dillon, Isabel said, "I don't know what Eli's told you, Susan. But from what my grandmother's told me, whatever happened between Dillon and Eli all those years ago wasn't all Dillon's fault. Eli, as you're beginning to discover, can be as hardheaded as anyone. And he was always the hardest on Dillon. I just don't think this is a good idea."

"Then I guess I'll just have to handle this the best I can, and hope my groom doesn't call off the wedding." Giving Isabel another pleading look, she said, "At least think about it. If Dillon could stay on a while, that would give Miss Cynthia some time with him, distract her from pestering Eli so much, maybe. And you and Dillon could have some time alone— it's obvious you two are growing close again.''

Hating the logic in Susan's words, and ignoring that last remark, Isabel decided she hadn't given her friend nearly enough credit. Beneath that ditzy persona grew a regular steel magnolia.

''Why, Susan Webster, if I didn't know better I'd think you were deliberately trying to manipulate me.''

Grabbing her arm, Susan said, ''Of course not. I just know that Dillon needs some time here, to reconcile with his mother. And he'd listen to you—you did get him to agree to the tuxedo.'' Lowering her voice, she added, ''And the talk around town is that you two are getting reacquainted in a very big way, if you know what I mean.''

Isabel knew exactly what her friend meant. ''We're friends, good friends. That's all.''

''But Dillon confides in you,'' Susan said on a low whine. ''He's never been civil to anyone around here. He must have some feelings for you.''

''Not really, and that's why I don't want to go another round with him,'' Isabel said, remembering how hard fought the tuxedo victory had been, and how much it had cost her. Many more of Dillon's kisses, and she'd be forever lost here at Wildwood. ''I can't do it, Susan. I won't act as a go-between with Dillon and Eli. Eli's already suspicious enough of my relationship with his brother.''

''Well, you care about Dillon, don't you?''

''Yes, but it's not what you think.''

Her expression hopeful, Susan plowed on.

"Wouldn't you like to give Dillon an opportunity to prove himself? This is the perfect chance for him to get back in Eli's good graces."

"I'm not so sure he needs to prove himself where Eli is concerned. And I won't trick him into doing something he might regret."

"But if you don't at least suggest this to Dillon, you might wind up regretting it yourself," Susan argued. "I just want some time with my new husband, Isabel. I really want to start this marriage off on the right path. Eli needs help, and Dillon's the perfect replacement."

"Dillon hasn't worked this farm in years."

"He's smart. He can figure it all out. Him and his books—he'll get with the program real soon."

"Books? What on earth are you talking about?"

Smiling now, Susan playfully slapped Isabel's arm. "You really are in another world. Dillon owns a chain of bookstores up in Atlanta. That's how he made his money. So he might not be a cotton farmer, but he can sure figure out how to become one. Dillon will just read up on it until he gets it right. That's how he always does things." Clearly recovered now, Susan turned. "I'm going back in. I feel better already. I'll explain to everyone that Eli and I had a little spat and I was feeling sorry for myself."

Pivoting, she said, "Think about this, Isabel. And talk to Dillon, please. He'll listen to you."

"Okay, I'll think about it." Right now, however, she was more surprised about Dillon's new life, than Eli's bad attitude.

Watching in amazement as Susan pranced back inside, Isabel let out a low sigh. So Dillon's business venture happened to be a bookstore or two?

Books. The man had never once mentioned anything about being bookish. He'd said he owned his own business, but she'd never dreamed it was a bookstore. Oh, it was just like Dillon to let her jump to conclusions and assume that he was still as wild and unsettled as he'd been as a youth. He never was any good at defending himself or talking about himself.

Maybe because he knew everyone would automatically think the worst, just as she had. What if Susan had a point? What if Dillon could use this opportunity to end this bitterness with his brother. Eli could certainly use the help and support, and his mother would be thrilled to have her family back together.

"No, I won't talk to him." But even as she denied it, Isabel looked toward the dark mansion. "No, I can't get involved in this." She was about to turn away, when a light flickered on in the back of the house, in the kitchen.

A single candle burning in the darkness like a beacon. A beckoning glow, reaching out to her in the night.

Telling herself she was crazy, she followed that light.

Maybe it wouldn't hurt just to see how he felt about helping out around here—just for a couple of weeks.

After all, all he could say was no.

Chapter Six

"**No.**"

Dillon said the one word into the cellular phone nestled at his ear, his eyes scanning the screen of the laptop computer blinking in front of him. "I don't care if we will lose money or momentum. I don't intend to compromise on quality, Sanford. If the quality isn't there, then we don't expand right now. All five stores are holding steady, especially the original on Peachtree. We'll survive until next year without expanding into the Carolinas just yet."

Clicking the small phone shut, Dillon sat staring out into the summer night. The lullaby of singing crickets mingled with the strands of a warm, soft wind flowing through the open windows in front of him. His business manager and lawyer, Sanford Reynolds, wasn't too happy with him right now. Sanford had advised more expansion, but Dillon wasn't quite ready to tackle everything that went into building and opening another store.

Not now. Not when he was back here at Wildwood and he had a million scattered emotions blinking through his mind like fireflies. Rhyme and Reason, as his chain of eclectic bookstore-coffeehouses, was aptly called, would just have to wait.

He needed a little rhyme and reason of his own right now. He needed to stop thinking about Isabel Landry.

Remembering yesterday, remembering kissing her there in that field, Dillon let the darkness shroud his doubts while he remembered the feel of her in his arms.

But the ugly vision of his brother staring down on them with condemning wrath quickly broke through the sweetness of that particular daydream. Eli would cause trouble for them, just as he always had. Dillon could handle it; he'd learned to let his brother's taunts and disapproval roll right off his back—or at least he'd learned to avoid Eli by staying away. But he wouldn't allow Eli to inflict any more pain on Isabel. Yesterday's encounter in the cotton patch had only reinforced the uneasy feeling Dillon always had around his older brother. Things had gone from bad to worse after Isabel had left them.

"I can't believe you're taking up with her again," Eli had said, contempt clear in each word.

"That's none of your concern, brother," Dillon had retorted. "Anyway, why do you care? You're engaged, remember? You're about to be married. I don't think your lovely bride would appreciate the way you stare at Isabel Landry."

And Dillon certainly didn't appreciate it. It made him sick—just as it always had. Eli might be attracted to Isabel, but she would never, ever be good enough in Eli's eyes to take the attraction any further.

But Eli was obviously still in denial where Isabel was concerned. "I don't know what you're talking about."

Dillon inched closer to his brother. "Oh, yes, you do. We both know what I'm talking about. I walked away from you once, Eli, to protect Isabel and her family. And I've regretted it ever since. You might not get so lucky this time."

"Are you threatening me, little brother?"

"No, I'm telling you that I want you to stay away from Isabel. She's done nothing to you. She never did. You just can't seem to tolerate anyone who doesn't have blood as blue as yours. So stop playing your cruel games and concentrate on your marriage."

"While you concentrate on that low-class woman who's sponged off us all her life?"

Dillon's whole body had tensed; he came close to hitting his brother. And the dare in Eli's eyes only fueled that need. But, sanity and practiced self-control kicked in as Dillon remembered all the other times his brother had set him off, then had blamed him for the whole thing. This time, it would be different. This time, he'd stay in control. Instead of doing what Eli expected him to do, he'd pushed past Eli, determined to keep a civil tongue for his mother's sake.

Then he'd turned, pointing a finger at his brother. "Isabel Landry has more class in her pinkie than you'll ever have your whole life, brother. And you know as well as I do that Isabel never took advantage of living here. Good grief, Eli, they lived in a shack. They barely made ends meet."

"That so-called shack was rent-free," Eli had reminded him with self-righteous disdain. "And they lived off this land, had plenty of fresh meat and vegetables. And still Isabel walked around like she ought to be a queen or something. Now, she's even worse. I didn't want her here for the wedding, but Mama and Susan insisted. That girl thinks she can flaunt it over us now that she's been away from here for a while if you ask me."

"I didn't ask you," Dillon replied, disgusted that his own brother could have such an attitude about someone who'd never done a thing to him. But that didn't matter to Eli. His narrow-minded snobbery was very intact, and buried so deep Dillon doubted his brother would ever change.

Because Isabel was a distraction, because Eli was as attracted to her as Dillon had always been, his older brother had taken out his frustrations on her. He didn't want to like Isabel, didn't want to feel anything for her, so he turned his feelings into intolerance, lashing out at the very source of his woes.

And he'd lash out again, if Dillon didn't stop him. Torn between wanting to get reacquainted with Isabel, and the need to protect her from Eli's rash behavior, Dillon wondered if he'd be able to control his own yearnings. It wasn't fair to Isabel, when he knew he couldn't stay here much longer.

His thoughts coming back to the blinking cursor of his latest sales report, Dillon reminded himself he only had a few more days here. He took a long, heaving breath, focusing on something serene—the green of Isabel's eyes maybe, but the thought of looking into her wild, forest-rich eyes only agitated him more.

Then he stretched back in the rickety old desk chair he'd dragged to the table by the window. He could do this. He could attend his brother's wedding, be civil, then get away from here all in one piece.

That is, if he could just stop thinking about Isabel.

Thinking about her conversation with Susan, Isabel walked the worn clay path through the iridescent wildflowers, moonlight guiding her to the back steps of the old plantation house. She shouldn't be here. She should stick to her plan of doing her job and nothing else. Despite Susan's pleas, Isabel had not wanted to get involved with the Murdock brothers again.

But here she stood—yet again.

When she heard the sad, beautiful sound of Spanish guitar music coming from a radio, she closed her eyes and listened to the soothing melody. Maybe now would be a good time to lift up a prayer for guidance. She could sure use some. So she stood there for a moment, silent and waiting, while the music and the night soothed her worries to a slow simmering.

Through the long kitchen windows she saw Dillon sitting at a desk, a lamp burning brightly at his side, the window nearest him thrown open to the night. Well, he must have ordered the electricity to be turned on, at least. Curious, she inched up on the porch to get a better look. And was surprised to find him hard at work with a laptop in front of him there on the table.

Dillon, working at a computer! Another myth shattered. She wouldn't have believed he even knew how to turn one on. No, cars and motorcycles were more his mode of operation. Fast cars. Fast motorcycles. Like the one parked out in the tractor shed, sleek and black and loaded with chrome. And classical guitar? She had Dillon pegged for loud rock and roll.

Bookish? Did a man who drove such a machine really read books and listen to classical music?

Apparently, in the ten years that he'd been away, Dillon had made some sort of peace with himself. He'd obviously gained a certain strength from what he knew to be true in his heart. She wondered, though, if being back here might shatter that peace and test that strength. Shaking her head, she supposed it was possible she had misjudged Dillon. After all, there had always been a side to him that he'd kept hidden from the world. Even her.

High time she found out about that side.

She stepped up on a creaky plank, then stopped. This could be dangerous. She was already infatuated with Dillon, always had been. Maybe it would be best if she just left things the way they were. She didn't want him to endear himself to her anymore, and seeing this side of him—this gentle side of the boy she'd always remembered—might make her long for things she could never have.

She turned to leave.

The back door swung open. "Spying on me, Issy?"

Too late to run away now.

She did a hesitant twirl, smiled up at him, then sucked in the breath that rushed out of her body at the sight of him in jeans and a loose, half-buttoned shirt, his dark hair spiked across his forehead. "Yeah, you caught me. But I guess that's the only way I'm ever gonna find out about what makes you tick, Dillon.''

His dark eyes reflected the pale gray of the moon's light. ''That curious, huh?''

''I...I heard your music,'' she hedged. ''I was intrigued.''

''Intrigued?'' He chuckled, then reached a hand out to her. ''There's nothing intriguing about me, honey. Just trying to get through another day.''

Easing up onto the porch, she stared at him, the touch of his fingers on her hand a reminder of how he made her feel inside. ''Why didn't you tell me?''

His chin lifted a notch. ''Tell you what?''

''That you like to read? That you're...how did Susan put it...bookish?''

He dropped her hand. ''Susan chatters too much.''

''What do you do for a living, Dillon?''

''Didn't Susan tell you all about that, too?''

''She said you own a chain of bookstores. I thought I'd heard her wrong.''

Her doubt, so honest, so straightforward, stung Dillon like a wasp. He was so very tired of trying to prove himself. ''I get by.''

''Then it's true?''

''Don't sound so shocked,'' he said, mimicking her very words when he'd told her she was pretty.

Realizing he was on the defensive, Isabel changed her tactic. ''I'm not shocked. I'm impressed. Very. If I recall correctly, you had a certain disdain for any and all books in high school. Never studied, never even opened a textbook.''

''I passed, didn't I?''

''Yes, you did.'' She'd forgotten that his grades

were always just about as good as her own. And she'd had to study for hours on end. But Dillon—he'd never seemed too worried.

Then, she'd chalked it up to irresponsibility.

Now, she wasn't so sure. About anything. Except the dark light in his eyes and the way his fingers stroked her skin as he stood there daring her to doubt him.

"I'm sorry," she said finally. "I guess I didn't really know you after all." Pulling away, she added, "And I guess you don't really *want* me to know you, after all."

He tugged her back. "Yes, I do. More than you can possibly imagine."

She was imagining lots of things right now. "Then talk to me, Dillon."

"I told you—I don't want to talk."

With that, he pulled her into his arms and kissed her without self-defense or self-doubt. Then he let her go, his breath like a warm wind moving over her hair. "I could hurt you, Isabel. And I won't risk that."

"I'm a big girl," she managed to whisper. "And...I've survived being hurt before."

"I won't hurt you again," he said, each word a declaration.

Something in his tone told her that he knew her deepest, darkest secret. Dillon knew that she'd always cared about him. And now, he was deliberately trying to warn her away, because he couldn't return her feelings.

"I'd better go," she said, needing to distance herself from his touch, and from the truth.

Susan would just have to find some other way to

help Eli. Isabel wasn't about to ask Dillon for anything. Not when she felt so raw and in pain that even the humid summer wind on her back felt like bramble moving across her skin.

"Yes," Dillon said, the one word heavy with regret. "You'd better go. And you'd better stay away. I'm no good for you, Isabel. No good."

Dazed, she said, "Maybe it's still the other way around. Maybe I'm no good for you."

She'd walked down the steps, when she heard him call out to her. "Isabel, do you think...do you think God listens to Spanish guitar music when He's feeling lonely?"

Isabel stopped, her back to him, her gaze lifting up to the stars. Oh, how she wanted to be immune to that sweet pain she heard in his words. "I'm sure He does, Dillon." Then she turned to face him. "And, He listens to lonely people, too. If you won't talk to me, then I know in my heart you can talk to God."

She turned, and though she couldn't see his face, Isabel knew Dillon's eyes were on her.

"I don't think God will want to listen to a loser like me," he said.

"God doesn't see us as losers, Dillon. You know that. God sees us as His children. And He's always willing to listen."

"I've tried to talk to Him, really I have. I've tried to pray about things—about coming home. We just never know when it's really right, do we?"

"We have to trust in Him, or so Grammy tells me."

"So you have doubts, too?"

"I do, sometimes." She glanced around at the

beautiful night, then back at the silhouette of the man in front of her. "But when I look up at the stars or see these beautiful flowers that keep coming back here year after year, I know that God is watching over us. It's up to us to let Him take control, Dillon."

Dillon was silent for a minute, then he said, "Do you think God's watching over Wildwood?"

"Always," she said without hesitation. "Can't you see Him here, Dillon? Can't you feel Him in the wild-flowers, in the oak trees, out in the wind in the fields? He's here."

"I wonder why He brought me back here," Dillon said."

"Because it's home," Isabel answered, more to herself than to Dillon. "We're both home for a reason."

"And it has nothing to do with Eli's fancy wedding, does it?"

"I can't answer that," she replied softly, her hands wrapped against her chest, her head down as she stared at the dirt and the soft, ethereal glow of flowers all around her.

"I know," he said into the night. "Now, go home and get some rest. The rehearsal supper is in a few days."

"Will you be there?"

Dillon hesitated, thought about his need to be near her, thought about his brother's need to be cruel. Maybe he should be there, just to watch over Isabel. Telling himself he shouldn't do this, he asked her, "Will you sit by me when you're not snapping pictures?"

"Should I, after you just warned me away not five minutes ago?"

"Probably not, but you don't seem the type to heed warnings, anyway."

"I'm not afraid of you, Dillon. I'd like to get to know you—the real you. So will you come to the rehearsal dinner?"

"Will you sit by me and make sure I behave?"

Smiling, she remembered they'd had this conversation before. "All right, I'll sit by you, if you *promise* to behave."

"Then I'll be there. I'm not the best man, of course. But I get to be an usher, at least."

"I'm proud of you—for doing this for your mother."

"Are you, really?"

Repeating his earlier words, she said, "More than you can ever imagine, Dillon."

Silence, then a shifting of feet. "Good night, Issy."

"Good night, Dilly."

Then, "I do own a chain of bookstores. And I do love to read. Come on back some night and I'll pull out a volume of Keats or Shelley and I'll read poems to you by the light of a single candle."

Touched by that gentle image, she said, "A romantic, too? Dillon, you are full of surprises."

"Yeah, that's me."

With that, he was gone. She heard the soft thud of the screen door, then watched as the lamp went out.

Turning, Isabel was left with only the moon to guide her home. The way looked long and empty and lonely.

*   *   *

The rehearsal dinner was being held at the Camellia Country Club, an exclusive golf and tennis retreat for the few in the area who could afford the monthly membership fees.

Isabel had never been invited to any of the social events at the club, but she'd often heard stories about the tradition and beauty of the place from Susan and her other school friends who had been part of the more popular crowd.

Tonight, Isabel stood on the stone steps leading up to the glass doors of the banquet room, wondering how she would be received now. It was funny, really, that the very people who'd shunned her when she was growing up poor on Wildwood, now welcomed her back with open arms and glowing praise. Funny how a little fame and fortune could turn people's opinions around.

Once, Isabel would have relished being a part of Wildwood society. Now, she only wanted to run away from the glare of its too harsh light. Because, she knew in her heart, they were curious simply because she had seemed so hopeless to them before. It was a morbid curiosity, not a friendly one. They wondered how she'd done it. How had the poor, odd farm girl succeeded against so many obstacles? And, she believed, they somehow envied her even while they regarded her with a quiet disdain.

Well, I survived all of you, she told herself now as she stared up into the chandelier-adorned entrance, her hands sweaty and her breath coming too fast. *I went out and made it, in spite of your low opinions of me.* Her victory, however, was hollow. She would never really triumph over this small-town mentality until she could learn to accept and forgive it. But she would go in there and do her job.

"You were the prettiest girl at the church," a deep male voice said from behind her.

Whirling, she saw Dillon standing by a potted cedar tree, his eyes bright with amusement and questions. "I mean it, Isabel. You far outshone the nervous bride and her stand-in, and any of the fifty or so bridesmaids. I like your dress."

Nervous herself, Isabel smoothed the floral cotton of her sleeveless fitted sheath, then patted the upswept coil of hair centered on top of her head. "Thank you, but there's only about seven bridesmaids in all."

"Looked like at least fifty to me," Dillon commented as he sauntered up the steps. His tie was crooked, and so was his smile. "Of course, I stopped counting once you started flashing that camera. It was more fun to watch you. You really enjoy your work, don't you?"

"Yes, I do," she admitted as he came to stand on the same step with her. "I got a few shots of you, you know."

"Give me the negatives," he said briskly, while his eyes teased her. "Can't have any evidence lying around."

"Evidence that you did indeed show up?"

"Yeah, something like that." Then he leaned close. "How'd I do, anyway?"

"You were the best usher I've ever seen." And the best-looking one. Dillon filled out his casual sports coat and khaki pants rather nicely.

"No, I mean, how did I act?" he asked, his eyes on her.

"You were a perfect gentleman, but do you really care?"

"I care about your opinion of me. And I did see my mother beaming a time or two."

"She was proud of both her sons tonight."

Dillon nodded, looked around, then took her arm under his. "Now, on to the celebration. I think I can manage this if you stick with me. I'll be the envy of every other usher in the place."

"So, you're using me for your own purposes?"

"Haven't I always?" The teasing light went out of his eyes then. He stopped her as they entered the carpeted lobby. "Isabel, I hope you know that I'd never use you. You...you mean a lot to me. Seeing you again has meant a lot to me."

There was a *but* in there somewhere. You mean a lot to me, but...we can't be together. We have to remain just as we always were, secret cohorts. We can't take it any further than that.

It would be so hard, but she'd have to honor his silent conviction. Because it was the only thing she could do.

Touched, she said, "Me, too, Dillon. I'm glad you're my usher tonight."

He leaned close again. "Let's get this show on the road, then we'll sneak out and go back to Wildwood."

"Sounds good."

They both looked up to find Eli staring at them across the expanse of the lobby, his brown eyes flashing disgust and disapproval.

"Get a shot of that," Dillon said, then winked at her as if to ease her concerns.

Isabel didn't miss the uneasiness in his words, though. Nor did she miss the unbridled hostility between the two brothers as they passed each other.

Eli gave them a plastic smile. "Mother wanted you both here tonight," he reminded them, his features set in a serene line for any passersby. "But I expect you both to be on your best behavior. I won't have either of you making a scene at this dinner."

"You mean like this?" Dillon said just before he pulled Isabel close and gave her a quick kiss on the cheek.

Pulling away, Isabel shot a warning look at Dillon, then turned to Eli. "Relax, Eli. Dillon and I are just friends. Nothing more."

"Yeah, she's right," Dillon said, regret evident in his words. "Nothing more, brother. And certainly, nothing less."

Chapter Seven

"**N**othing less than the best for my bride," Eli announced to the people gathered in the private dining room at the Camellia Country Club. Amid the clatter of crystal and the sighs of those surrounding him at the elaborately decorated table, he raised Susan's hand and kissed it. "Here's to you, Susan."

Everyone applauded the happy couple then settled in to enjoy the dinner of prime rib and all the trimmings. Susan beamed, her eyes bright and shining, her sighs filled with dreams and hopes, her hand touching on her future husband's sleeve now and again.

"Kinda sickening, don't you think?" Dillon whispered close to Isabel's ear. "My brother can really lay it on thick when he needs to. Does the word *hypocrite* come to mind?"

"Don't sound so cynical," Isabel whispered back. "Even if you and I aren't the marrying kind, you have to admit Eli seems to genuinely love Susan."

Dillon shrugged, wondering where she'd gotten the impression that he wasn't the marrying kind, then speared a cut of the juicy meat centered on his gold-rimmed dinner plate. "Yeah, he loves her all right. Like he loves his hunting trophies and his Peanut Farmer of the Year award. Susan's another conquest to add to his many accomplishments."

Surprised at the venom in his words, Isabel dropped her fork to stare over at him. "Why do you and your brother hate each other so much?"

Dillon leaned back on the mauve brocade chair. "Just your basic sibling rivalry, darlin'."

"It's more than that, and you know it. I remember you fighting when we were growing up, but this goes deeper. What happened between you two, Dillon?"

He glanced over at her, his eyes going into that deep gray zone that she knew meant he didn't intend to answer her question. Except with a question. "What happened to celebrating this blessed occasion?"

Determination clouding her better judgment, Isabel leaned close. "Oh, no, that trick won't work tonight. I want some answers."

"And I want you to smile for me," he countered, his expression guarded and cautious. "If I wanted to talk about my troubles with big brother, I certainly wouldn't do it here, tonight."

He had a point there. She sat back in her own chair and glared down at the remains of her baked potato and marinated asparagus spears. She was just about to tell him they'd discuss this later when Susan motioned to her from the doorway of the room.

"Want to come with me to powder my nose, Isabel?"

"Sure." Seeing the desperation and determination in the other woman's eyes, Isabel couldn't refuse. Turning to Dillon, she said, "I'm going to the ladies' room. Hold my spot."

"Of course." Dillon glanced up in time to see Susan's worried expression. "Don't tell me the bride's getting cold feet?"

"Just a case of the jitters," Isabel assured him. "She probably wants me to get some more shots of the dinner crowd."

"Well, tell her you're off duty now."

"I'll be right back," she assured him, wishing she could feel confident about Susan's intentions. She had a sneaking feeling Susan was going to press her about getting Dillon to stay and help with the crops.

And she was right.

"Have you talked to him?" Susan asked the minute they entered the vanity area of the elegant powder room.

"No," Isabel replied firmly, glaring at her friend in the gilted mirror's reflection. "Susan, I can't do this. I can't ask Dillon to stay here—he's only here tonight because of his mother."

"Well, isn't that just great. Doesn't he even care that Eli's working his fingers to the bone to try to save Wildwood?"

Alarmed at Susan's exaggerations, Isabel turned to face the other woman. "Don't be so dramatic, Susan. Wildwood seems to be thriving. You just need more attention from Eli."

Gripping Isabel's arm, Susan shook her head, causing her golden curls to spill around her face. "No, I'm not being selfish, Isabel. Eli needs to find some help before this place kills him."

"What's going on?" Isabel asked, real concern filtering through her resistance. Susan looked so panicked, so afraid, that Isabel knew this was about more than wedding jitters.

Falling across the mint green velvet divan centered in the small lounge, Susan glanced around to make sure they were alone. "It's Wildwood. Eli's trying so hard to hang on, Isabel. But…things aren't so good."

Shocked, Isabel bent down in front of Susan. "Tell me."

Susan lowered her head, then whispered, "Well, Eli hasn't come out and told me anything, but I've figured it out for myself. I think he's heavily in debt…what with the house and this huge investment in getting this cotton crop going. He's overextended himself a bit and now he's worried sick about it. That's why he's been so moody lately." Grabbing Isabel's hands, she looked up, her eyes wide with fear. "I don't care about the wedding. I just want Eli to be happy. I want to make him happy, but if he loses Wildwood—"

"This can't be happening," Isabel said. "Wildwood has always been so secure, so formidable. What about all the money Mr. Murdock left to the family?"

Susan wiped a hand under her eyes. "Apparently, there wasn't a whole lot of that after Mr. Murdock died. And with Dillon taking every penny his mother could give him and leaving Eli to take care of things—well, maybe now you can understand why I think he needs to help his brother out."

Isabel sank down on the divan beside her trembling friend. "You're right. This is much worse than I imagined. I'm surprised Eli's even coherent enough to go through with the wedding. I'm sure he's worried sick."

"He is," Susan said, tears springing to her eyes. "I've told him over and over I'll call the whole thing off. We could have something simple and less expensive, but he insists that we're going to keep up appearances. And besides, my folks are paying for most of it, anyway."

"Appearances!" Isabel sprang up to pace the length of the narrow sitting area. "Now, that's a Wildwood tradition, if I ever heard one. Appearances mean everything. Mustn't let people know the truth, no matter the cost. How antiquated and futile, Susan. That old southern pride kicks in every time, though."

Susan stood, too, worry causing tiny wrinkles to appear between her carefully plucked eyebrows. "You can't say anything to Eli, Isabel. But you've got to explain this situation to Dillon. Let him offer to stay and help, that's all. Make it look like a peace offering."

"Just to keep Eli's pride and ego intact! Susan, that would be like sending Dillon to the slaughter. He'd have to bow down to his brother all over again. I can't do it."

"Do what?" Cynthia Murdock said from the doorway. "My goodness, girls, this is a celebration, remember. Why do you two look as if someone just died or something?"

"She doesn't have a clue," Susan whispered

through stiffly clenched teeth, then turned with a bubbling smile toward her mother-in-law.

"We were just discussing last minute details, Mrs. Murdock," Isabel said, hating all of this deception. "I was trying to convince your stubborn future daughter-in-law that I don't think I can pull off the shot she's requesting."

"Oh, we'll work on such stuff later," Cynthia admonished, waving jeweled fingers in the air. "Right now, I want you both back in the dining room. I have a special surprise." Smiling like a conspirator, she said, "I'm going to officially welcome Dillon back into the fold—publicly—so there will be no mistake that I'm glad to have my son home."

Isabel's eyes widened as she watched Susan's strained features. Tonight wouldn't be a good time to try to bring her sons together, but Cynthia looked very determined.

"Do something," Susan mouthed while Cynthia checked her hair and makeup in the mirror.

Isabel didn't have time to wonder what she was supposed to do. Cynthia, pleased with her bright red lipstick, ushered them out into the lobby.

"Come along, children," she said, her cream pumps clicking on the marble floorway. "Everyone is waiting."

"What took so long?" Dillon asked when Isabel sank back down into her chair. "You missed dessert—I ate your lemon pie."

"I couldn't eat another bite," Isabel said in what she hoped was a controlled tone, wondering how in the world she could possibly stop Cynthia Murdock from inadvertently causing further hostility between Dillon and Eli.

"You don't look too hot," Dillon said, his eyes flashing between concern and cynicism. "Are you all right? Did Susan say something to upset you?"

Isabel's chuckle was shaky. She supposed she could bring a halt to the proceedings in the old-fashioned way—she could faint. But that wasn't her style. No, best to just let the evening take its course, then get Dillon out of here as soon as possible.

"I'm okay. I just got a little warm—it's so stuffy with the humidity outside. Maybe we could leave early—it looks like rain."

"That wouldn't do for Eli's cotton crop at this stage," Dillon said dryly, missing her request to leave. "Boll rot." Then, "Here, drink some water."

Isabel took a big gulp of the sparkling water with lemon. It felt good going down, and calmed her nerves to a more rational state. Dillon's attention had certainly perked up at the mention of rain. Maybe he was more worried about his brother's doings than he was letting on. "Do you know a whole lot about growing cotton?"

"I know a whole lot about farming," he countered. "Remember, I grew up on a farm."

"I remember," she replied, thinking this could be a good time to suggest that he might want to stick around and help his brother. "It's just that you never seemed as dedicated as Eli."

Dillon's features sharpened into the scowl she remembered so well. "I loved Wildwood," he said simply. "Loved the smell of the wet peanuts after a spring rain, loved the feel of corn silk rushing through my hands. Sorry, I'm getting a bit too poetic on you, Isabel, but I always loved farming. It's just that with Eli hovering over me, I didn't get to put any of my theories into practice."

"Theories?" She stared at him as realization hit her. Dillon was a thinker. He stood quietly and listened, really listened, to the world around him. Yes, he probably did know everything there was to know about farming. And, he was probably chomping at the bit to be included in his brother's new venture. Maybe Susan had a point after all. Maybe. But if she didn't try to get Dillon out of here soon, it wouldn't matter.

"Dillon—"

"I'd like to thank everyone for coming tonight," Cynthia said just then, standing at the head of the table, her smile wide. "I'm so proud of my sons— both my sons—and since this is a celebration, I have a special announcement tonight."

Eli glanced over at Susan, his dark eyes immediately questioning. Isabel figured he didn't like surprises; Eli liked to be in control at all times, nothing was supposed to escape his attention or his approval. Susan's smile was a strained line against her pale face, but she gave a valiant effort at comforting her fiancé by patting his hand and kissing him chastely on the cheek.

Dillon shrugged and quirked a brow toward Isabel. "Mother's always up to something, isn't she?"

"She loves her family," Isabel said by way of a warning.

Cynthia's soft gaze moved from Eli's frowning face to Dillon's puzzled one. "Tonight, I'd like to officially welcome my younger son, Dillon, back to

Wildwood. We've missed you, son, and we just want you to know that you will always have a home with us." With that, Cynthia came around the table and stopped at Dillon's chair, then leaned down to hug her son close.

Surprised and clearly uncomfortable at being thrust into the spotlight, Dillon stood to return his mother's affection. "I love you, Mother," he said, his voice low. "Thank you."

Cynthia let go of her son, but held a hand on his arm. Then she looked down the table at Eli. "Son, won't you join me in welcoming your brother home?"

Isabel held her breath as she watched the play of expressions moving over Eli's harsh features. He stood, shock and anger evident in his every move. Throwing down his white linen napkin, Eli stalked around the table to confront his stunned mother.

"So, we kill the fatted calf for my brother? Is that it, Mother? We welcome him back with open arms and no questions asked, after the way he abandoned us, after the way he squandered Daddy's hard-earned money?" Glaring at Dillon, Eli extended a hand, but the gesture was anything but brotherly or forgiving. "Welcome home, brother. Did you run out of money? Did your fancy bookstore go under? Is that why you came back to Wildwood?"

A hiss of embarrassed shock rushed through the hot, crowded room, followed by a rush of sandpaper sharp whispers. Dillon didn't reach for his brother's hand. He just stood there, his features etched in granite, the pulse at his jaw vibrating a pounding beat as blood rushed to his face.

Clearly appalled, Cynthia grabbed Eli's arm. "Son, please. You have to let go of all of this bitterness. It's time you forgive your brother and remember that he is family."

Eli jerked his arm away. "I can't do that, Mother. Not now, not tonight. You can forgive Dillon if you want, but I can't."

With that, he turned and motioned for Susan. She rushed to his side, her eyes bright with unshed tears, her head down. But before Eli could take his intended and leave, Dillon sent his chair crashing across the soft carpet as he pushed away from the table.

"Stay, brother, and celebrate your wedding. I'll go and you can pretend I was never here. That's what you've been doing for years now." Then he turned to his mother. "I'm sorry."

With that, he pivoted and stalked out of the room, his back straight and his head high. Only Isabel had seen the gleam of tears forming in his stormy eyes.

And only Isabel knew the hurt he was feeling right now.

Which is why she got up and ran after him.

"Dillon, wait," Isabel called as she followed him out into the parking lot. Off in the distance, thunder warned of an impending storm.

"I don't think so," he said over his shoulder. Then he reached his motorcycle and slung one leg over the padded leather seat. "I've had enough celebrating for one night, Issy."

"Then I'm coming with you," she said, throwing her leg over the seat behind him. Quickly pulling her skirt down, she slung her camera bag across her shoulder and held on to his waist. "Let's go."

"Go home," he said. "You don't need to baby me, Isabel. And you certainly don't need to be seen with me."

"I'm not babying you," she snapped at his neck. "And since when does it matter who I'm seen with around here? I don't want to stay in there—they're wrong about you, Dillon."

That statement brought his head around. "What makes you think that, sugar?"

Looking up at him, then down at the dark concrete, she shook her head. "I don't know. Or maybe I do know. I know you, Dillon. And until you tell me everything, I'm just going to have to go on my instincts and faith."

"Faith?" His laugh sounded more like a snarl. "You know, I was beginning to have some faith, until tonight. Now I'm not so sure."

"Just drive," Isabel replied, her hands clutching his waist. "Just drive, Dillon."

He did, fast and as far away from the bright gleam of the country club's deceptively welcoming haze as he could get. Past the city limit sign out on the county line road, past the rolling farmland and the creekbeds and the rows of pecan trees, past the fields of Wildwood Plantation. Dillon didn't stop the Harley until there was nothing but night and stars left in the world.

Night and stars and Isabel.

She'd come with him. She'd believed in him. Maybe God had heard some of his prayers after all.

Finally, he pulled the snarling machine off the side of the road and down a dirt lane that led past cotton and cornfields to a big pond on the far back side of Wildwood property. His father used to bring Eli and him fishing here. But he refused to think about that tonight.

Instead, he turned to Isabel and lifted her off the long seat, then stood her there in front of him, his hands never leaving the small of her back.

Isabel heaved a deep, calming breath. "That was some ride."

His wild eyes roamed her face. "Did I scare you?"

"No, not really. I was more scared for your emotional state than any physical danger."

"I'm fine, sweetheart. After all, I'm used to being the black sheep of the Murdock family."

"You're not a black sheep, Dillon."

"And how can you be so sure?"

She tossed her heavy camera bag on the bike's seat, then put a hand to his face. "Because, I know you. I've always known you. But, I have to be honest— you had me going there for a while. You played your part so well."

"And what part is that? The bad son, the one who brought ruination to the entire clan?"

"Something like that. You've just let people believe what they wanted to believe, haven't you? Why haven't you ever defended yourself, Dillon?"

He stared down at her, wondering how she could see into his very soul. Wondering why her words hurt even while they brought a tremendous relief. Finally, he said, "I got tired of defending myself."

"So, you just gave up?"

He wasn't ready to tell her everything; to tell her that he'd witnessed such hatred and such venom in his brother's heated words all those years ago, that he didn't think he'd ever be able to forget it. And he wasn't ready to tell her all the reasons he'd left like the coward he was. So instead, he told her, "Yes. I gave up. My brother will never...love me, Issy."

The catch in his words tore through her. Wasn't that what everyone wanted, deep down inside, to be loved, to be accepted?

She certainly knew how he felt. "Why can't he love you, Dillon?"

Dillon shifted, brought her closer. "I don't know for certain. But I think it has something to do with Eli's paranoia about my father." He hesitated a moment, then continued. "Eli always thought I was my father's favorite."

Isabel remembered Roy Murdock very well. Remembered his stern, no-nonsense countenance, his my-way or no-way attitude, the unrelenting grip he had held over his sons and the whole town. And she also remembered his soft spot—Dillon. In spite of his gruff exterior, Roy had always helped Dillon through the worst of escapades.

"Well, you were his favorite. Everybody thought that because of the way he protected you and spoiled you."

Dillon laughed harshly. "That's because my father played his part well, too. He got me out of jams and stood up for me to keep the family name intact. But he always let me know my shortcomings when we were alone. And my poor mother never went against his word, except to send me money here and there."

Surprised, Isabel asked him, "You mean, your father wasn't just spoiling you, the way everyone thought?''

"No, he was inflicting his authority, flexing his power. Eli tried to be the golden boy, the one who could do no wrong. Always there, working hard, trying to make our parents proud.''

"And you, you did everything you could to be a rebel?''

"Yeah, that was me. That's the Dillon they all remember so well.''

Isabel was beginning to understand and see the pattern. Eli, so proud, so conscientious, so willing to please. And Dillon, not really caring, not really trying. And yet, the Murdocks kept forgiving him, kept giving him one more chance. Just as the Bible told them to do, or just to save face? Maybe Eli hated his brother because of that.

"He can't forgive you, because your parents always did, or so it seemed,'' she said, the words coming out in a whisper. "So much bitterness, such a long time to hold a grudge.''

Dillon moved away from her then, turning in the moonlight to stare out into the black waters of the rippling pond. "And I deserve every bit of it. I deserve everything Eli throws at me and more.''

She touched a hand to his arm, forced him around. "What makes you say that?''

Dillon held her by her shoulders. He had to make her understand why he kept fighting against her. "He's right, Issy. I deserted him. I left them—all of them. I wasn't even here when my father died. Didn't even come home for the funeral.''

She believed there was good in him. She'd seen

that good in the dark corners of his beautiful, sad eyes. "I'm sure you wanted to be here, Dillon."

"You're so sure about me, huh? So sure. My beautiful Isabel. You could almost make me believe in myself again, the way you cling to your honorable defense."

"But you don't believe in yourself, do you?" she asked. "Is that why you keep pushing me away?"

Dillon looked down at her trusting face and knew he could never let her go again. "I didn't want to taint you—with my past, with my problems, and I didn't want Eli to do the same."

Frustrated, Isabel refused to back down. "Forget that. I won't let you push me away anymore, not when I can clearly see you need a friend, not a flirtation. I believe you wanted to come home a long time ago. I believe you wanted to be at your father's funeral, but you were too afraid—"

"I'm not afraid."

"Yes, you are. You're so afraid, you'd rather run away than face up to the people you love the most. So you let Eli hurl insults at you and think the worst of you, because that's what you believe about yourself. Am I right?"

He closed his eyes, lifted his face to the wind. "No."

"Yes." She brought her hands back to his face. "Yes."

Dillon could only stand there, staring at her pretty face in the moonlight. The hum of mosquitoes, the sound of distant thunder, the moon's light poking through the scattered clouds above him, everything intensified in her evergreen eyes. And it all reflected the truth she had discovered. Suddenly, he was so tired. So tired of fighting against himself, and against his need to be with her.

"Yes," he said at last, pulling her tightly against him so she couldn't see the shame in his eyes. "Yes, I'm afraid. I did things, Isabel. Horrible things. And now, I've changed, but I don't know how to go about showing everyone I've changed."

Isabel looked him in the eye. "You've already made the first step, Dillon. You came back to Wildwood."

"Yes, I came back—to a brother who hates me, to a mother I've hurt so badly, to a dead father. And to an empty house."

"It's not too late."

He wanted to believe that. He wanted to hold her here forever in his arms and tell her that she'd helped him find a little peace. But, he'd lived on speculation for so long, nothing seemed real anymore. Yet, because she was willing to fight for him, he had found some hope. "Maybe it's *not* too late, after all."

"You've got to believe that," Isabel said. Moving her hands over his face and shoulders, she nodded her head. "Because *I* believe in *you*." She kissed the moisture away from his eyes. "I trust you." She kissed the warm skin on his cheekbone. "I want to help you." She kissed his forehead.

Dillon held back, stiff and unyielding, his eyes drawn tightly shut. He wanted to block her out, wanted to keep this distance between them, even though she could feel the coiled tension rolling inside him like the roaring thunder headed their way.

Her own heart pounding, Isabel drew in a deep

breath. She hadn't wanted to come back here. But then, she'd never expected to find him here, almost as if he'd been waiting for her. Closing her eyes in a silent prayer, she wished she had the strength to walk away. But she'd done that once before. Now, she used her last hope and her faith in God—the faith Grammy had always assured her she did indeed possess, to help this man she cared about so much. "Let me show you, Dillon."

She kissed his lips, closing her eyes to the pain of his indifference. But she felt the quickening of his pulse when her lips met his. Then she lifted her head and said, "We'll find a way, together, with God's help."

Dillon didn't stop to think about the implication of her honesty. Instead, he kissed her, pouring his soul into being able to touch her at last. He wouldn't tell her how he felt, not now. Not yet. He couldn't take that chance. Because he still had some secrets to guard.

Finally, he pulled back, then moved a few feet away, his words lifting out over the night like a soft wind. "You don't know how much that means to me, Issy."

"You can do this," she said, tears choking her words. "That's what faith is all about, Dillon."

He glanced over at her then. "I've been wrestling with my faith and my feelings for you. It just didn't seem possible with all these problems with Eli. I didn't want to drag you into it again."

"I'll be all right," she said, rushing to him, wishing she could hold him close until he learned to trust again. "Let me help you, Dillon."

Dillon lifted her arms away, then walked to the water's edge. Looking down, he asked, "Do you think God has enough love for someone like me? Do you think He's willing to forgive just one more time?"

"I know He is. I believe that with all my heart."

Dillon's chuckle was low and grating. "Then He's sure got his work cut out for Him."

"Grammy always says God can handle anything."

He turned back to her then, reaching out to tug at a wayward blond curl. "And how about you, Isabel? Can you handle anything?"

She swallowed hard, prayed harder. "I can handle you, if that's what you're asking."

"So, you think you can save me, huh?"

The awe in his words fueled her ridiculous hopes. "No, I think you can save yourself."

He lifted his head, then tilted it sideways, eyeing her. "Oh, really. How?"

"You can start by learning to trust again," she suggested. "I'm willing to stay here at Wildwood with you, until you can talk to Eli."

She braced herself, thinking now would be the time to suggest that Eli was in trouble, without actually revealing what she knew. She honestly believed it would be better to let Dillon and his brother work things through without her interference.

"From what Susan tells me, Eli could really use a brother right about now. Maybe if you settle things with him, you can both face your past and get on with your future."

Dillon buried his hands in the pockets of his khakis,

then rocked back on his heels. "You'd do that for me—stay here with me?"

"I will. You and your brother need to get to know each other again. And if that's too hard for you, I'll be here to help you."

"Simply because you care about me?"

"Simply because I told you I wanted to help you."

"We'd be risking everything—Eli won't take too kindly to being waylaid or ambushed. You realize that, don't you?"

"Yes, I realize that. And I think you're wrong. I think Eli needs your help, just as you need mine."

"And yet, you'd still be willing to risk his wrath?"

"Yes." She couldn't tell him that she hoped Dillon and his brother could work this land together. That would be the best solution for everyone right now. But she didn't think Dillon was ready for that step just yet. Maybe with a little nudge, she could ease him into it. Only because tonight, she'd seen how much he needed this land in his life.

And she needed him in her life—she'd realized that tonight, too.

"I can't make you any promises, Isabel," he told her as he pulled her back into his arms.

"You don't have to. I believe in you, remember?"

"It's nice to have someone saying that for a change."

He kissed her, and Isabel savored the gentleness of that kiss. And realized she had fallen back in love with Dillon.

Only this time, it was much more than a schoolgirl crush.

Chapter Eight

"**W**hy don't you come home with me?" Isabel said later as Dillon wheeled the Harley into the dilapidated shed behind the mansion.

It was well past midnight, and while the rain had held off, the sky was now dark with roaming clouds. The night air felt heavy with moisture, humid and waiting—the quiet before the storm.

"On our first date?" he quipped as he helped her off the bike. "Do you think that's wise?"

Isabel smiled at his humor. At least he was in a better mood now. "Silly, that's not what I meant. I want you to talk to my grandmother."

"What?"

"Grammy Martha has a way of making you feel so…good about things," she said, hope in her words. "She'll listen, then she'll hug you so tight, you'll never feel alone again."

He scowled. "Meaning no disrespect to your grandmother, I'd rather be hugging you."

Isabel knew the feeling. But before they could even begin a relationship they needed some guidance and some advice. And her grandmother was an expert on both.

"I'm serious, Dillon," she said, taking his hand to tug him toward the dirt lane. "Grammy can help us through this."

"So, we're just gonna go in and wake your poor old grandmother in the middle of the night, then pour all our troubles at her feet?"

Isabel smiled and bobbed her head. "Something like that, but she won't mind. She's good about things like this. And I, for one, really need to talk to her."

He held back, his words coming low and lifting softly out on the thick air. "About me and how you're willing to stay here and help me? Are you already having doubts about that?"

He still didn't trust her enough to believe her, Isabel realized. He couldn't say the words. He couldn't say "I need you" and he couldn't even say "I trust you." As close as she felt to him right now, Isabel also felt hurt that Dillon could still hold a part of himself back from her. Especially after she'd just realized she was in love with him.

All the more reason to talk to Grammy. She'd bring some perspective to this turmoil. Grammy would know what to do.

"Please, Dillon," Isabel said as they strolled through the sleeping wildflowers. "You need this. You've been out there alone for so long, you don't even know what it's like to have someone to lean on."

"I'm beginning to see what it can be like, though,"

he said, his fingers squeezing hers tightly. "And I'm starting to appreciate it."

"Then come inside with me. We'll raid the cookie jar and talk to Grammy."

"You lead an exciting life, Isabel."

She saw his grin and laughed. "Yeah, always on the edge. That's me."

He tugged her around as they reached the back door, his expression changing from cynical to serious. "We were both on the edge, weren't we? Until we came back here and found each other again."

"I think you're right," Isabel said, loving him all the more for being just a little honest at least. "I don't know…lately I've been so restless. My work is still important and fulfilling, but I seem to be drifting…not quite sure which way I need to go next." She shrugged, then looked out over the distant cotton fields. "I think that's why I agreed to come here and be a part of this wedding. I didn't realize it, but I needed to see Wildwood again, just to make peace with myself. And as much as I always wanted to get away from here, I have to admit it feels good to know I have a place to call home."

Dillon looked out into the night, out toward the looming shadow of the house he'd lived in as a child. "But I don't."

"Yes, you do," she said, careful that he didn't bolt on her. "You can rebuild Wildwood, Dillon. Have you ever thought about that?"

"Every waking minute of my life," he said on a rush of breath. "I've been thinking of doing a little touch-up work while I'm here. But—"

"You won't fail," she replied, guessing his doubts. "I know you won't."

"What makes you so sure? You don't know where I've been all these years, the things I've done—"

"I know everything I need to know. And I don't believe you've done anything terrible. Sure, you've made mistakes, but you've obviously accomplished a lot. You're a self-made man, Dillon. Whatever brought you to this point, I believe you're a better man for it."

"You amaze me," he said, tugging her close for a quick kiss. "And I do believe I'd like to wake up your grandmother and have some milk and cookies, just so I can tell her what her granddaughter has done for me."

"What have I done?" she had to ask.

"You've made me face my greatest hopes and my worst fears. Not bad for a night's work."

Isabel turned to open the door, afraid he'd see the truth in her eyes. What would he do if he knew she was deliberately setting him up to help his brother? What would he do if he found out that Eli was close to losing everything Dillon had ever held dear? She should just tell him, but then he'd lash out at Eli and they'd be right back where they'd started. No, better to let him ease into things. Better to let him make the decisions, call the shots. Yet she couldn't help but feel small and deceitful.

I'm doing it for him, Lord, she said silently. *He needs his home again.* Selfishly, she reminded herself that she needed Dillon. Was that why she was willing to pull him—and herself—back into Wildwood's uncertain arms? Just so she could keep him near?

No, it was more than that. Dillon wanted to be back here at his home. And she was determined to make his dream come true. Only, she had to wonder if the end justified the means.

They didn't have to wake Martha Landry. She was sitting in the small den, reading her Bible.

"Hi, Grammy," Isabel said as she poked her head around the door frame. "Feel like some company?"

Not missing a beat, Martha finished the verse she'd been studying, then placed her hand-crocheted bookmark across the page to keep her place. "Of course. Who'd you bring home?"

Isabel yanked a reluctant Dillon into the room, beaming with pride. "It's Dillon, Grammy."

"Well, well." Getting up out of her padded recliner, Martha automatically opened her arms. "Dillon Murdock, come here and give me a hug. It's so good to see you again."

Shocked and clearly uncomfortable, Dillon strolled across the rickety wooden floor to place tentative hands around Martha's rounded shoulders. "Hello, Mrs. Landry."

Martha gave him a good hug, her eyes smiling over at her granddaughter while she held Dillon's hand tightly in hers. "And what have you two been up to this late at night?"

Dillon stood back, unsure how to begin. He had a lump in his throat the size of a watermelon just from hugging the woman. If he actually unburdened himself on her, he'd probably cry like a baby and make a complete idiot of himself. Glancing over at Isabel for help, he could only stand there and wonder what had come over him. He didn't understand why being hugged should have such an effect on him but he wasn't so sure he wanted to open himself up to it completely. So he just stood there, his head down, his lips pressed together, his eyes centered on Isabel.

"Uh, we went to the rehearsal dinner, of course," Isabel began, motioning for Dillon to take a seat next to her on the couch.

"How did that go?" Martha asked, her expression pricelessly bland, her hands folded primly in front of her.

"Not too good," Dillon blurted out. Then, frustrated with himself, he sliced fingers through the spikes of his dark hair. "I…I made a scene."

"Did you now?"

"Yes, ma'am. I guess I really messed things up—again."

"Eli messed things up," Isabel retorted. "He could have been more civil and forgiving."

"Well," Martha said, her eyes widening, "we can't mess up things so bad that The Lord can't help fix them. How 'bout I get us some lemonade—it's too humid and hot for coffee, isn't it?" Already padding toward the kitchen, she called, "And Isabel, you can bring out those ladyfingers we had left from the shower."

"Okay," Isabel said, glancing over at Dillon to make sure he wasn't about to head out the door. Sitting there on her grandmother's couch, his stormy eyes wide and searching, he looked so much like the young boy she remembered. "Are you all right?"

"I think so," he said, gratitude in the words. "I'll come help with the cookies."

She smiled at him, then reached over to pat his hand. "It's going to be okay, Dillon."

"Is it, really?"

"Yes."

"Tomorrow night's my brother's wedding."

"Yes, and you'll be the best usher there."

"If I show up. It seems pretty clear that Eli doesn't want me there," he said, following Isabel into the kitchen.

"Dillon, come and eat some cookies," she told him.

"You're not going to let me get out of this, are you?"

"No," Isabel said after settling him at the small dining table. "If I have to be there, so do you."

"Hey, Mrs. Landry," he said, his smile wry, "did you know your granddaughter has decided to be my champion, my defender, my lady of the realm?"

Martha poured him a tall glass of fresh squeezed lemonade. Looking down at him with wise eyes and her own wry smile, she nodded. "Hey, Dillon, did you know that my granddaughter has always been on your side?"

He looked across the table at Isabel, his heart skipping a beat at her beauty. "No, I didn't know that. But I sure wish I had."

And he had to wonder—could Isabel possibly feel something beyond friendship for him? Could she possibly love him in the same way he loved her? Was that why she was so willing to fight for him, to help him mend his torn family? And did she know that he had always loved her? How could he tell her that he'd fallen for her way back in their high school days, or maybe even beyond. If he told her that, then he'd have to tell her the ugly truth about his leaving Wildwood.

Martha patted his hand, surprising him so much he almost spilled his lemonade. Then she settled down in her favorite chair and reached for a crescent shaped, sugar-dusted cookie. "Now, children, tell me why you're keeping an old lady up so late."

Isabel told her grandmother what had happened at the rehearsal dinner. "Eli was downright rude, Grammy. I felt really bad for Miss Cynthia."

"She is trying to bring her family back together," Martha said, dusting the powdered sugar off her fingers. Turning to gaze at Dillon, she asked, "How do you feel about all of this?"

With a shrug, he said, "I think I should have stayed in Atlanta."

Martha nodded. "You think that would make things easier for everyone?"

"I do believe so, yes."

"And what about your mother? You know, she's talked about this wedding—and you being a part of it—for months now."

Dillon lifted his head then, his eyes slamming both Martha and Isabel with pain and denial. "They don't want me here, not really."

Martha leaned forward a bit, adjusting herself on her chair. "Your mother certainly does. And, your brother could use your help right now."

Surprised, Dillon snorted. "That's exactly what Isabel has been telling me. But I don't believe it. Eli has always been able to land on his feet. I used to think he really needed me, but I finally figured out he's never needed anyone's help, especially mine. And after all this time, I'm the last person he'd want around.''

''Now how do you know that?''

Dillon looked around the worn old kitchen. This was where Isabel had spent her childhood. Right here, on Wildwood, just like him. Yet he only had to glance around at the faded curtains and the cracked kitchen sink to know that they'd lived completely different lives. The guilt of that realization ate away at him, causing him to remember things he'd tried so hard to forget.

Instead of answering Martha's question, he looked over at Isabel. ''You had it all, Issy. Did you know that?''

Isabel's head shot up. ''What do you mean?''

Dillon lifted his hands, then let them fall across the table. ''Look at us, sitting here in the kitchen in the middle of the night. This could never have happened in my house, in my family. No, there everything was so formal, so stilted, everything in its place—Murdock's don't show great displays of emotion. Murdocks *don't* sit around the kitchen, munching on cookies.''

''Are you uncomfortable?'' she asked defensively, wondering if he found it distasteful to be here in this shack of a house.

''Yes. No. What I'm trying to tell you is that while I grew up in the mansion, you had the real home. Do you know how lucky you are?''

Isabel felt as if she'd just been pinned to the wall. ''I've never thought about it. I've certainly never considered myself lucky.''

"No, because all you could think about was how poor you were, how you wanted to get away from here, to have a better life? Is your life better now, Isabel?"

Confused by his questions, and more than a little angry that he was giving her the third degree, she asked, "Why are you turning the tables, Dillon? Grammy asked *you* a question."

"And I'm trying to answer her."

"By telling me how lucky I am?"

"Yes!" He shoved a hand through his hair, then sat back to look at her. "Do you know how many times I wished my father would just hug me, or tell me he was proud of me? Oh, he bragged to his friends, of course. But he never really showed either of us much real affection. Not like this, not the way your grandmother shows you affection."

Bitterness coloring his words, he said, "And he passed his misguided traits on to Eli, too. Do you know what it's like when your only brother won't even speak to you, that if you try to call just to hear a voice from home, he'll only hang up on you?"

Isabel saw the torment in his eyes, but couldn't believe a brother could treat another brother that way. "Eli did that?"

"The few times I called and he answered, yes."

Bringing a hand to her mouth, Isabel sank back on her chair. "I never knew it was *that* bad between you two."

"Well, it was, and it still is," he said on a low, calm breath. "Your parents loved you, Isabel. Sure, they were old-fashioned and strict, but they loved you. And they showed you that every day. Me, I had

to search for any traces of real love in my dad's eyes.
His love always came with certain conditions. I don't
think he was ever really proud of me—he just toler-
ated me because of my mother, and he presented a
solid front for everyone else, for the Murdock name.
We couldn't have anyone thinking things weren't perfect in the Murdock household.'' Dropping his shoulders, he added, ''So, I guess you both know how I
feel about things now, huh?''

Martha sat silent, her gaze moving from her granddaughter's surprised face to Dillon's resigned one.

Isabel shook her head, her eyes widening as she
tried to reason with Dillon. ''But he had to have loved
you. Why, he gave you and Eli everything, without
question.''

''No, he *bought* us things, Issy. There's a big dif-
ference. It was almost like he was paying us off, for
being what he expected us to be. And when I failed,
well—''

Martha said the same thing Isabel had said earlier.
''Everyone thought you were his favorite, the way he
defended you.''

''In public, yeah. He had an image to maintain. He
and mother always put such high store in appearances. But I made one slip too many, though, and
suddenly, I was no longer the image of a perfect son.
I guess he realized all the glossing over in the world
couldn't change how I felt the day we had that terrible
argument. And I fell out of his favor pretty quick after
that.''

''One slip too many?'' Shaking her head again, Isabel got up to pace the room. ''Dillon, you made
some mistakes, but your father always forgave you.

Maybe if you'd stayed here, it would have all worked out.''

"I don't think so. Not this time. I used to get into trouble, yeah," Dillon said, nodding. "But that was different. That didn't involve turning against my family. My father demanded loyalty, and…in the end, I couldn't give it to him."

Placing her hands on the table, Isabel asked, "What did he want you to do? What on earth happened?"

Dillon looked up then, his expression going blank. Raising up with a push, he headed for the door. "I've got to go. I've said too much as it is."

"Dillon?"

He turned at the door, pushing her away. "I appreciate the talk, ladies. Let's just get through this wedding. I'll see you both tomorrow." Before Isabel could speak, he nodded to Martha. "Thanks for the refreshments, and thanks for listening."

With that, he was gone, gently closing the screen door behind him. Isabel watched as he made his way down the wildflower path, back toward the old mansion.

"What's the matter with him?" she said, throwing her hands up in the air. "Why can't he tell me what's bothering him?"

Martha came to stand by her granddaughter. "I think I understand what's wrong with Dillon."

"Then please explain it to me. I thought we'd made some progress."

"Isabel, he doesn't want to reveal the Murdock family secrets. Whatever happened that day, Dillon is still trying to honor his father by keeping quiet about it. He has to make his own peace with his brother, and especially, with himself.''

Whirling around, Isabel said, ''Am I just supposed to sit back and wait for that to happen? I've got a bad feeling about all of this—this wedding, Eli's attitude, Dillon's indifference. I'm telling you, something has got to give.''

''Since when do you care so much about the Murdocks, anyway?'' Martha asked as she put away the cookie tin.

Isabel turned to face her all-knowing grandmother then. Too late to deny what was so obvious now. ''I've always cared about Dillon. And since we've been back together, well...''

''You love him, don't you?''

Wrapping her arms across her chest, Isabel lowered her head and nodded. ''I don't want to—but, yes, I guess I do. I think I've always loved him.''

''So you'll fight for him?''

''If he'll let me.''

''And who will you be fighting?''

''I don't know. Eli, mostly, I guess. I want Dillon to be happy again, but Eli disapproves of me so much. If I get involved, it's only going to make matters worse.''

''You might be getting into something you can't fix, child. We have to choose our battles very carefully.''

Isabel rushed to her grandmother's side then. ''Help me, Grammy. Tell me how to make those two stubborn men see that it's time to end this grudge.''

Martha patted Isabel's shoulder, then stood back.

"Does Dillon know Eli's been having some troubles?"

Shocked, Isabel let out a breath. "No, and how do you know that?"

"I hear things. This is a small town, Isabel. Rumors are grist for the mill around here."

Glad to be able to share this burden, Isabel nodded. "Susan told me about it. She thinks Dillon should stay here and help Eli out. I wanted to talk to Dillon about it, but he'll be so upset and bitter. I don't know what to do."

Martha hugged her close. "For now, go to bed and pray. The Lord will help you—even if it means you just have to stay out of it."

"I have to help Dillon."

"I don't think Dillon is ready for your help."

"Then I'll wait."

"You never were good at waiting."

Hugging her grandmother close, Isabel said, "Dillon was right about one thing. I never realized how blessed I was, living here. Why couldn't I see that, Grammy?"

"You had too many dreams, honey. Too many stars in your eyes."

Isabel watched as Martha headed down the tiny hallway toward the back of the creaking house. Then she turned to stare over at Wildwood, her heart breaking. Yes, she'd certainly had stars in her eyes. Maybe because she didn't even realize until she was around six years old that her father didn't own the land he worked. She didn't realize until she got to school and saw all the other children laughing and playing, that she was just a poor country bumpkin who got teased because of her homemade dresses and hand-me-down cast-off clothes. Soon, she'd discovered the world beyond Wildwood, and she'd promised herself she'd explore that world and conquer it. But was she any richer for having done so?

She should just pack up and leave right now. She'd told herself not to get involved, yet here she stood, worried and confused, and right in the thick of things between Dillon and Eli. But, she couldn't leave.

Because she was in love with Dillon Murdock.

"I'll wait," she whispered to the whining wind. "I'll wait right here, Lord, until You show me what to do."

Just then, a light flickered to life in an upstairs window of the mansion. Isabel watched as the shadowy silhouette of a man appeared at the window.

Dillon.

She watched as he stood there, his hands braced on the windowsill, looking out into the night. Was he looking for her? Was he thinking about her?

Dillon had come so close to telling her everything. But something kept holding him back, something kept him from being honest with her and maybe with himself. What kind of pain had Eli and their father inflicted on him? Why had he felt it so necessary to run away from his home? Somehow, she had to find a way to get inside his head, to understand why he was afraid to love her the way she loved him.

Until then, she'd have to be patient. She'd wait.

She watched his shadow, so still, so clear, so dark there against that single lamplight.

And then she knew. He was waiting, too.

Chapter Nine

Dillon was up at dawn the next day. Actually, he'd never really fallen asleep. Instead, he'd lain in bed listening as the thunder moved farther to the south. The rain had missed Wildwood, and Dillon now missed the rain.

He needed a good cloudburst to relieve some of the tension that had kept him awake all night. Today was his brother's wedding day, but that was the least of his worries.

He loved her.

And now, he wanted her to love him, too.

Isabel Landry had told him she wanted to stand by him, but could she ever return the love he felt for her?

Now he had to decide what he was going to do about this love he'd so long denied. His initial reaction had been pure joy. But, it was a joy born of long ago dreams and long forgotten hopes. Since leaving Wildwood, he'd tried to put Isabel out of his mind—

for her sake. She deserved better than him; she deserved so much more than he could ever give her.

Taking another sip of coffee, Dillon sat back on the ratty cane rocker he'd found in the attic and pulled onto the porch, wondering if he'd ever be capable of accepting love from any woman. Oh, he loved Isabel, knew that in his heart. But in his head, logic told him he shouldn't acknowledge that love. He couldn't ask her to take him on; he couldn't ask her to accept his family into her heart.

So here he sat, wishing, wondering if he should just leave soon after the wedding, or stay and pour his heart and soul into rebuilding this old house, and winning over the woman of his dreams. Could he actually have both?

Right now, that didn't seem possible. She'd promised to stand by him, to help him reconcile with his brother. But what Isabel didn't know was that she couldn't help him. She'd only make matters worse.

But Dillon couldn't tell her that. He couldn't tell Isabel that *she* was one of the main reasons he and his brother were no longer on speaking terms.

Throwing the dregs of his coffee out into the overgrown shrubbery, Dillon stood to go inside. That's when he saw Eli and two other men standing in Eli's front yard. All three were looking a little too keenly toward the old mansion. Stepping back out of view, Dillon watched as Eli talked in an animated fashion, his hands gesturing, his face flushed with anger.

"What are you up to, brother?" Dillon muttered. The men sure seemed interested in the old plantation house. Squinting toward the fresh rising eastern sun, Dillon recognized one of the men. Leland Burke. The president of Wildwood Bank and Trust, complete with suit, tie and a notebook. Dillon watched as Leland jotted down information. He didn't recognize the other man.

Now, what was so important that Eli would be standing out here on a Saturday morning, on his wedding day, at that?

Isabel glanced out the window over the kitchen sink, wondering what Eli was doing standing out in his front yard. From her vantage point, the three men were nearly obstructed by trees and bushes, and she had to crane her neck to even see them at all. But there was no doubt in her mind that one of them was Eli Murdock.

Shrugging, she guessed Eli had to conduct business, even on his wedding day. Running a huge plantation was a twenty-four hour job. She could remember lots of times when her father would stay out in the fields well past dark, then come home and collapse before rising with the dawn to get a head start on the next day's work. That grueling schedule had put him in an early grave. A few years later, it had also taken Eli and Dillon's father, Roy, to his grave.

She had to agree with Susan. If Eli didn't slow down, he might wind up the same way. He did look rather haggard. Of course, he had aged since Isabel had been away. They were all getter older. But after what Susan had told her, she supposed Eli's pallor had more to do with worry than age.

All the more reason to bring peace to the Murdock brothers, she mused as she finished washing the breakfast dishes. Looking out toward the rising sun, she sent up a prayer for help.

"Should I tell Dillon what I know about Eli's financial problems? Or should I do as Grammy says and keep praying about it?"

If she told Dillon, he might confront Eli, and Eli would only resent her even more for interfering. Yet, Dillon had a right to know that his home was in jeopardy.

Isabel didn't know how to approach this. Dillon was still struggling with his past, and after last night, she knew in her heart that underneath his tough guy veneer, there was a heart that longed to come home. Dillon needed to be accepted back into his family completely.

If he found out about Eli's financial woes, that acceptance would be shattered. Yet he was bound to hear about it sooner or later.

"After the wedding," she said on a breathless whisper. "Once Eli's away on his honeymoon, maybe I can talk to Dillon about this."

That would give him time to cool down before he confronted his brother. In the meantime, Isabel had a job to do. She had to be at the church early to capture the entire wedding party in various shots. Susan would be frantic if Isabel didn't arrive on time to photograph every aspect of this important day.

So much fuss over a mere wedding. Isabel had never given her own wedding day much thought, maybe because she'd never pictured herself as a beaming bride. Thinking of Dillon and how his kisses made her feel, she closed her eyes and had a fine little daydream of her own.

She was standing in the wildflowers in a creamy gown and Dillon was walking toward her with that sideways slant in his eyes, and that precious grin on his handsome face. He carried a bouquet of wildflowers—pinks and blues, yellows and whites—picked especially for her. Birds were singing, bees were buzzing and the sunset behind them was so brilliant it hurt her eyes. So brilliant—

"Too brilliant," she said now, snapping back to reality. "Just a silly dream, Issy. It can never happen, no matter how hard you wish it."

Chastising herself, she remembered her duties. This was Susan's big day, not hers. She wouldn't let her friend down.

But she hoped she didn't let Dillon down either.

Hours later, Isabel looked about at everyone who'd assembled at the church for the big event. And big it was. Looking around the sun-dappled sanctuary, she was amazed at the expense that had obviously been put into this wedding. The Murdocks never did anything second-rate, and while the Websters were comfortable financially, Isabel imagined they broke the bank trying to accommodate Eli and Cynthia Murdock's demands.

The theme was Victorian, about as delicate and dainty as a theme could get, complete with hearts, pearls, flowers and lace. Pinkish-white day lilies with rich burgundy centers, and pink roses in tight cotton-candy clusters, adorned the pews and the altar, while baby's breath and white satin ribbons scattered throughout complimented the fragrant flowers. Candles burned from exquisite silver candelabra, complimenting the bridesmaids' muted pink lace-trimmed dresses. Isabel had to admit the barely-there pink was pretty and a little more subtle than the bright teal Susan had originally picked. But she'd give Miss Cynthia more credit for that, than Eli's bullying Susan to change things.

Standing back in a corner, Isabel mentally went over her last-minute list. She'd taken the obligatory shots of the bride and her bridesmaids, and the groom and his best man. Eli had actually smiled into the camera, but his smile didn't hide the bright worry Isabel now recognized in his unforgiving eyes. She supposed it was her good fortune that Eli was so pre-occupied with his wedding and his debts that he didn't have the inclination to pick on her.

She could almost feel sorry for Eli. He seemed to really care about Susan, and Isabel believed he wanted to make his new bride happy by putting up a good front at this wedding. But the pressure had to be tremendous. She wondered how long he could keep all these balls in the air. So far, he'd done a passable job, other than refusing to welcome Dillon back home as his mother had requested. Obviously, Eli didn't want Dillon to find out about his troubles. He had way too much pride to ask for his brother's help.

At least Dillon was still part of the wedding party.

Because this was a Murdock wedding, and because the whole town was talking about the famous grudge between the two brothers, the turnout for today's nuptials had reached maximum capacity. It seemed as if everyone in town who'd been invited had made it a priority to attend. Dillon, along with the other ushers, had escorted a steady stream of well-heeled, curious guests to their seats.

Isabel watched now as he held the arm of an elderly woman wearing a bright floral ensemble complete with a yellow pillbox hat. His hand was steady on the woman's plump arm, his demeanor respectful and charming as he talked with the lady in quiet, animated tones. Isabel snapped a picture as Dillon walked by. She wanted to capture that not-so-innocent grin.

Putting her camera down, she took a deep breath. They hadn't spoken since last night. Things had been too hectic for more than a polite nod. But behind the nod and the quiet looks, she could see the darkness in Dillon's eyes. In spite of their new closeness, she believed he was still holding something back.

Wishing she could gain his complete trust, Isabel continued to watch him. He looked so handsome in his tuxedo—a paradox of a man, gentle and shy in some ways, bold and unyielding in others. To the manor born, but so down-to-earth and unassuming about his own success.

In many ways, Dillon had changed. In many ways, he was still the same. And she would always love him. Now that she'd accepted that, she felt a little more at peace. Underneath the turmoil, underneath the fear and worry, her center was settling into a nice contentment. She'd denied her feelings for Dillon for so long now, that she realized she'd been empty inside. But since coming back here, since seeing him again and accepting that she cared about him, that emptiness was gradually easing away. Grammy had always told her she'd find peace once she focused on what really mattered in life. And Dillon was what mattered in hers.

Soon, they'd both be leaving Wildwood. But somehow, after last night, Isabel didn't feel as strongly about leaving the place she'd once called home.

Wanting to understand why Dillon was still keeping her at arm's length, she continued to study him now. And again wondered if maybe Dillon didn't care about her in the same way she cared for him. Maybe he was trying to let her down gently. Maybe his flirtation *was* just that, a flirtation, a way to spend time while he was forced to be here. She'd certainly seen him tease many a young girl way back when, only to leave another broken heart in his wake. What if that part of him hadn't changed after all?

But, no, that couldn't be right. Last night, he'd opened up to her a little bit, at least. Dillon cared about her, he'd admitted that much. Yet, she knew in her soul he was fighting his feelings. Why?

Moaning, Isabel took a step back as the crowd continued to grow. Lifting her camera, she automatically clicked several shots of the various guests, making sure she got the most prominent ones, as Susan had suggested. The whole while, Isabel kept thinking what if she'd been wrong, hoping Dillon might actually feel something real for her. Sure, he'd kissed her with a tenderness that made her heart palpitate, but that was part of Dillon's charm. At times, he'd sought her out; other times, he'd sent her away. Had it all been a game, like the silly games they used to play when they were growing up?

She looked up then, to find Dillon's gray eyes centered on her with all the gentleness of a dove. As he came toward her, her heart picked up its tempo. The expression on his face told her he did care, and the look in his eyes changed from gentle to tumultuous within the fraction of a lazy blink.

"Hello, gorgeous," he said, his gaze moving across her face with unabashed intensity. "Why are you hiding in the corner?"

"Just doing my job," she quipped, the catch in her voice causing her to groan silently.

"Listen, about last night—"

"I thought we'd reached some sort of truce last night," she replied as she checked her camera. "Was I wrong?"

"No. You really got to me last night, Issy. I'm through running, but hey, I'm still a little skittish. Just give me some time. I promise, after this shindig is over, we're going to have a long talk."

Her heart soared with new hope. "I'll hold you to that." And maybe then, she could tell him about his brother's troubles.

He nodded, then his features relaxed into a grin. "You should be center stage; you look much prettier than the bride."

"How do you know—you haven't peeked into the bride's dressing room, now have you?"

"I don't have to see her. Susan's the cute cheerleader type, but she doesn't hold a candle to you. A bit too frilly for me, I'm afraid. I like *your* dress, Issy."

"You said that same thing at the rehearsal dinner, if I recall, and I also recall—you dated a lot of frilly cheerleaders in high school."

"You looked good at the rehearsal dinner, too, if I

recall, and yes, I went out with a few cheerleaders, but hey, none of them could handle having a cad like me for their steady.'' Lifting a dark brow, he said, ''Maybe because they all figured out I really preferred a tall, willowy artistic blonde with wild curls and not a spot of lace anywhere on her dress. I like all of your dresses, but this one is especially nice—green becomes you.''

Looking down at the flowing skirt of her tea-length crepe gown, Isabel pushed at the unruly curls he'd just complimented and shrugged. ''This old thing—plain and simple and very functional for a working girl.''

''That old thing brings out the green in your eyes, and you know it.'' Coming closer, he said in a low, gravelly tone, ''I'm sorry I left in such a huff last night.''

''Stop apologizing. I understand.''

His brow furrowed. ''Are you okay?''

She shook her head. ''I'm fine. I want to get through this, so we can talk.''

''I know the feeling. Remember, you promised me a dance at the reception.''

Her heart started the dance without her. ''I remember.''

''Okay. I've got to get back to ushering, or I might get fired.''

''See you later.''

He gave her his salute. ''Count on it.''

She would. And she hoped she could count on him. She'd wait for him, but she wouldn't force him into a relationship he might not be ready to accept. There were too many things brewing in the air, too much standing in the way of any happiness for Dillon and her. Her love for him had made her temporarily forget all the obstacles holding them apart, the same obstacles that had been there from the very beginning. Namely, his brother's intense disapproval of her.

Loving Dillon hadn't changed a thing, except she now realized she'd been waiting for him most of her life.

And, as her grandmother had pointed out, Isabel wasn't very good at waiting.

The wedding was lovely. Susan made a pretty bride in her beaded frock and elaborate veil. Eli was a handsome groom in spite of the occasional scowl he shot toward his brother. He did seem nervous and preoccupied to Isabel, though. As he promised to love, honor and cherish his bride, Isabel said a prayer for him—a first for her. She'd never considered including Eli Murdock in her prayers. But Susan had always been a good friend to her, in spite of their different positions in small-town society, and the romantic in Isabel wanted this marriage to work. She'd be wrong to hope for that without asking God to watch over both Susan and Eli. And Dillon, too.

Careful not to be intrusive, Isabel took a picture of the groom kissing his new bride. Automatically, she searched for Dillon and found him watching her with that unreadable, brooding look on his face. But when he lifted his gaze to her face, Isabel saw the darkness disappear. His eyes became bright with hope and longing.

Feeling silly over her earlier misgivings, she again reassured herself that he did care. But, something

wasn't quite right. It was as if Dillon wanted to return
her feelings, but he couldn't give himself permission
to do so just yet.

He said we'd talk after the wedding, she reminded
herself as she watched Eli and Susan walk back down
the aisle. This whole event had been a strain on everyone, as blessed as it was, but now it was just about
finished.

She'd use the few days Susan and Eli were away
to organize her pictures. She wanted to have a complete set of contact sheets ready for Susan when she
got home. And, she'd be able to spend time with Dillon, alone, without Eli's condemning eyes watching
over them. Maybe then, she could find out what exactly was on his mind, and what exactly was in his
heart.

And after that…she'd do whatever she could to
help Dillon mend his torn relationship with his
brother.

Because if Dillon and Eli could mend their fences,
there might be hope for Isabel and Dillon, at last.
Maybe that was what was holding Dillon back from
giving her his love.

"Did you get a lot of pictures of us at the altar?"
Susan asked much later at the reception.

The church social hall was decorated in the same
Victorian theme as the sanctuary had been, with
muted pinks and blues and roses, hearts, seed pearls
and baby's breath scattered among ribbons and lace.
The wedding cake carried the theme to new heights,
all five tiered layers of it.

"I promise, you'll have the biggest, best wedding

album of any woman in the state of Georgia," Isabel assured the fidgeting bride. "Now, relax. The wedding was so beautiful and you were the perfect bride."

Susan swiped at fresh tears. "I'm being so silly. I can't stop crying. Hope you didn't get any pictures of my puffy eyes."

"I got you in your very best light," Isabel again assured her. "I should have most of them developed by the time you get back from Saint Simons Island."

Susan frowned, then lowered her voice. "I'm just glad I was able to pull Eli away from this place for a few days. Have you talked to Dillon yet?"

Glancing around, Isabel saw Dillon talking to his mother. Eli was deep in a discussion with two other local farmers. "I've tried, Susan, but I'm afraid if I'm the one to bring it all up, Eli and Dillon both will resent me for interfering. I really would rather not get involved."

Susan touched Isabel's arm, her hand cold in spite of the warm day outside. "You've got to let him know, Isabel. Eli needs his brother's help."

"But do you realize how angry Eli might be? Having Dillon learn the plantation's in trouble can only make matters worse between him and Dillon."

"Tell him while we're away. He can watch over things while we're gone, and maybe by the time we get back, he'll be calmed down enough to talk to Eli and offer his help."

"You're sure optimistic."

"Just hopeful. I want those two to reconcile, too."

Before Isabel could reply, she turned to see Dillon coming across the room. He extended his hand to her as the ensemble of musicians began to play a beautiful classical waltz.

"It's Mozart," Dillon said into her ear, his eyes warm. "And I asked them to play it just for us." When Isabel hesitated, he added, "Hey, I asked you for a dance the night of my senior prom, remember? And you turned me down. You aren't going to do that to me again, are you, Issy?"

Isabel swallowed the lump in her throat. "No. I'll be happy to dance with you, Dillon."

He took her into his arms and whirled her around the dance floor. Isabel gazed up into his eyes, aware that the entire room, full of prominent Wildwood citizens, was watching them as they moved to the exquisite music. Her dress flared out behind her like green sea foam. Her hair lifted away from her damp neck. Her hand touched on the corded muscles of Dillon's arm, while her other hand held tightly to his. The dance became a breathless kind of wonder, a fantasy come true, a sweet memory that she'd lived and relived, and had now become a reality. She was dancing with Dillon Murdock.

"Why did you turn me down that night?" he asked now, his words lifting out over the strands of the music, his eyes centered on her with that brilliant intensity that took her breath away. "Why, Isabel?"

Isabel looked down at the neat black bow tie at his neck, afraid he'd see the truth there in her eyes.

"Tell me the truth," he said.

She met his eyes then, her face inches from his. How could she answer such a question. Should she just blurt it out? Because I was in love with you. No. Not yet. Hating the catch that clutched at her words, she said in what she hoped was a light tone, "I couldn't bear it, Dillon. I couldn't dance with *you*— the boy who'd chased me around with spiders and lizards, the boy who'd beat me too many times at baseball in the back pasture."

The music stopped then, but Dillon didn't let her go. Instead, he pulled her close, his hands moving over her hair as he stood there with her in the center of the hushed room. Isabel held her breath, thinking he was going to do something really stupid like kiss her. But he didn't. Instead, he just held her, his eyes, bright with regret, bright with need, searching her face.

"No more games," he said as he lifted a finger to touch a curl falling away from her temple. "We're adults now, remember? And I do believe the rules have changed. This is a little more challenging than backyard baseball, isn't it?"

She nodded. "We've changed, but some things are still the same. I guess, I've always felt that I don't deserve you, Dillon. Maybe that's the real reason I didn't dance with you at the prom."

She watched as he let that admission soak in.

Then he shook his head. "You've got that all backwards, Issy. *I* don't deserve you. Thanks for the dance, though. I've always wondered what it would be like to dance with you in my arms—it was wonderful."

With that, he turned and stalked across the room and out the door, leaving Isabel in the middle of the empty dance floor, with the roar of whispers in her ears as everyone there talked and pointed and smirked.

She looked up to find Eli watching her, the smug expression on his face like a hard slap across her flushed skin. Moving in on her, he said, "You just can't seem to understand, Isabel. Dillon will never settle down with one woman. Nothing will ever come of his pretty words, no matter how hard you try to cling to him. He'll be gone before sunrise, honey. Just like before. I can promise you that." His eyes flickered over her with a look close to disgust. "At least then, we'll all be rid of both of you and these embarrassing public displays."

Humiliated, Isabel managed to make her way to the ladies' room, her head held high. She didn't know what was going on here, but tomorrow morning, she intended to have it out with Dillon Murdock one way or another. And she'd tell him all about his brother in the process. Maybe if he knew the truth, he'd finally tell her what his problem was.

He didn't think he deserved her; well, she certainly didn't deserve to be held one moment, then pushed away the next. Each time she thought she and Dillon had grown closer, he retreated behind that distant, stony wall again.

She had to find out why. In the meantime, she'd go home and talk to Grammy. She needed someone to help her with her prayers. She needed all the prayers she and her grandmother could muster. And then some.

They all did.

Chapter Ten

Isabel went to church with her grandmother Sunday morning, then came home determined to find Dillon and get the air cleared between them. Even the preacher's sermon had seemed delivered just for her.

"Let all that you do be done with love."

That had been the Bible verse for the sermon, straight out of the first chapter of Corinthians. The preacher had talked about courage, strength, overcoming fear and obstacles. Well, she intended to overcome her fears and all the obstacles holding Dillon and her apart. Beginning with his thorny relationship with his brother. Dillon had to know the truth, and it looked as if she would have to be the one to tell him. It was wrong for Dillon to go on punishing himself for past deeds, when Eli was just as guilty of mismanaging the Murdock fortune as his brother seemed to think he'd been.

"Still worried?" Martha asked as they finished putting away the brunch dishes.

"Yes," Isabel had to admit. "And I really appreciate your listening to me whine last night, Grammy."

"That's part of a grandmother's job," Martha replied. Untying her apron, she yawned. "But all these late nights you young people keep have caught up with me. I'm going to take a long Sunday afternoon nap."

Isabel gave her grandmother a hug. "Good idea. And I'm going to go and find Dillon. Do you think I'm doing the right thing?"

Martha hung her apron on a nearby peg. "I'm beginning to think he needs to know—maybe he can help his brother out of this mess. Eli has just about reached the end of the road. Everything crumbles if the foundation isn't solid. Remember the parable, Isabel, the one about the sower and how some of the seeds fell on the wayside, but some fell on good ground?"

Isabel nodded.

"Well, Wildwood is good ground, honey. The best. And this land has belonged to the Murdocks for well over a century now. Eli means well, but his heart has hardened. He's lost his way."

"But how can we help him, if he doesn't want our help?" Isabel asked. "Eli is so stubborn, and he's a snob to boot!"

"Yes, but we have to be steadfast. We have to remember that we have always lived on this land, too."

"Eli doesn't care about us, Grammy. Why, he'd just as soon we were off this land for good, as let us help him."

"We can't stand by any longer, though," Martha

said, worry creasing her usually serene face. "In spite of our good intentions to stay out of Murdock business, we can't forget that Cynthia will certainly need us."

Isabel had to agree there. "Poor Miss Cynthia doesn't have a clue as to what's really going on. She's been rich and pampered for so long, she won't know how to handle things if they lose this place."

"Give her some credit, Isabel. Cynthia Murdock is made of strong stock. This will shock her, of course, and she'll be deeply humiliated and embarrassed, but if we offer her our support, she'll come through just fine. She'll survive and be a better woman for it."

"If you think so."

"You have to have faith, honey. Faith that this will work out for the best," Martha said.

"But…if they lose everything…Dillon will be devastated. I don't know if he and Eli will ever overcome their differences if that happens."

"Well, people go through these types of crises every day. Many a Georgia farmer has had to lay awake at night wondering how he was going to feed his family."

"Daddy sure did his share of worrying, didn't he?"

"He did, since his pay depended on how good the Murdock crop turned out each year. But he always took the high road. Remember that, Isabel."

"Yes, ma'am. I will."

Isabel watched as her grandmother shuffled off down the hall, wondering why Grammy always made such pointed remarks. There was so much she didn't understand about her gentle, caring parents. She needed answers, not just from Dillon, but from her grandmother, too.

Maybe then, she could find the same sense of peace Grammy seemed to possess. Maybe then, she could make her own peace with Wildwood, at last.

She found Dillon in the middle of the great old house, sitting on the floor against a wall, the portable stereo playing some jazzy instrumental tune. His head was back, his eyes closed while he swayed to the music.

Watching him from the open back door, in spite of her confusion and anger, Isabel once again felt that tug of love inside her heart. And once again, she reminded herself that she needed to keep that love guarded and hidden, until Dillon was ready to accept it.

Dillon seemed so far away, so lost in his thoughts, she hated to bring him the news about his brother's financial woes. He had all the doors and windows flung open so that a cross breeze could blow through the wide central hallway. But his skin held a fine sheen of sweat in spite of the humid afternoon breezes roaming at will through the empty house.

He looked so lost, sitting there.

She knocked, hesitant to interrupt. How she dreaded this confrontation. But this had to be done.

"Go away," he said, not even bothering to lift his head or open his eyes. "Whoever you are, just go away."

"It's me," she called as she stepped inside the squeaky screen door.

Dillon sat up away from the wall, his eyes centering on her. "I was just thinking about you."

"Yeah, well, I've been doing some thinking myself," she replied as she stopped a short distance away from him. "I don't like being left on the dance floor, Dillon."

"I was rude," he admitted. "It's just that...you caught me totally by surprise—saying you didn't think you deserved me."

"More like I scared you away. I just want you to understand that...that I care about you, but I don't expect anything more than friendship."

"You're being honest, or at least you *think* you're being honest."

"Is it so hard for you to believe that I care?" she asked, "or are you uncomfortable *because* of my honesty? Maybe you don't think you need my help or my friendship."

He glanced away, then back up at her, his gaze shrouded. "Honesty is a tricky thing. It takes away all of our defenses." Trying to explain, he said, "I told you, I don't want to hurt you."

"Well, you did last night."

"I didn't mean to." He tilted his head, staring up at her. "You know, Isabel, I'm not going to hold you to that offer you made the other night."

"Oh, and why not?"

"I don't expect you to stay here and help me reconcile with my brother. It was sweet of you, but I'll deal with Eli on my own terms."

She tugged her hands through her hair in frustration. "In other words, mind my own business? Is that why you've been acting so erratic?"

"In other words, I don't want you to get caught in the cross fire by trying to salvage me."

Isabel moved farther into the room, then sat down on the aged planked floor, forcing him to look her in the eye. "In other words, you really don't want me around. You don't want to accept my help, right, Dillon?" When he made a move to touch her, she held up a hand. "No, I've thought about this over and over again since you walked away from me last night. You wanted just one dance, and now, we can go back to our separate lives, no hard feelings, no regrets. I get it, all right. You tease me, flirt with me, make me believe things I don't need to believe, even thrill me with a dance and a kiss or two, yet you claim you don't want me to get hurt."

She paused, swallowed back the threatening tears. "Because you don't feel the same way about me. I understand, really I do, Dillon." She turned to stare out of an open window. "Can't you see—that's exactly what I was trying to tell you last night. I'm still not good enough for a Murdock."

He reached out a hand and pulled her in his arms before she could take her next breath. "Don't," he said, his face inches from hers. "Don't ever say that to me again. Don't ever think that again."

Isabel stared at him, wishing she could read all the emotions playing across those storm-tossed eyes of his. "It's the truth, isn't it? You always did get your kicks out of torturing me—teasing, flirting, spending time with me, but never really putting forth a real commitment. I thought you and I were friends, real friends, but I was wrong about that, too, apparently.

That's the way it was when we were growing up, and that's the way it is now.''

"You are wrong," he said, his hands clutching her arms. "You are so completely off base, it's laughable."

"I'm not in a laughing mood, Dillon," she said. "And I came here for some answers."

"You won't get any from me."

She glared at him, her nose inches from his. "I'm not leaving until I do."

He let her go then. "Suit yourself." Deliberately, he turned the music louder. "I'm kinda busy here."

Isabel marched to the stereo and turned it off. "No. That silent treatment isn't going to work anymore. We need to talk."

He glanced at the stereo. "I was listening to that."

"You're going to listen to me instead."

"Oh, really? You are one stubborn woman, Issy."

"Not as stubborn as you. You danced with me last night, then left me standing there, Dillon. It's just like all those years ago, when you left without telling me goodbye. And I'm not going to let that happen ever again. Talk to me, please?"

Clearly frustrated, he threw his hands up in defeat. "About what? About my brother? About my dreams for this house?"

"That's a start, yes."

He jumped up then, waving his hands in the air. "I couldn't sleep last night, so I got this wild idea— I want to redo this house. I'm going to rebuild Wildwood, just like we talked about."

"You what?" Shocked, Isabel realized he was doing the usual, avoiding the question. "How do you think Eli will take this news?'' Maybe now would be a good time to tell him what she'd heard from Susan.

"I really don't care what my brother thinks," Dillon replied hotly. "He has his side of the road, and I have mine."

"That sure sums it up," Isabel said. "But, Dillon, about Eli—"

He didn't let her finish, let alone begin. "How much longer will you be here, anyway?"

She shrugged. "A few days. I promised Susan I'd have her proofs ready when they get back from the honeymoon."

"I'm staying a few days longer, too," he said. "I think Mama needs me here—she's exhausted after the wedding."

"Okay, but what's all this got to do with us, with you really talking to me for a change?"

Taking her by the hand, he said, "Remember when you told me I needed to learn to trust again?" At her nod, he continued, "You've taught me to trust my faith, Issy. And since the other night, since I saw what real trust is, there with you and your grandmother, I've been giving that some serious consideration. I've actually prayed about it, a lot."

"That's good. You'll need lots of faith—taking on Eli and this old house again."

He leaned close then. "Well, I have to ask you to do the same for me. Isabel, I can't tell you everything you need to know—I'm still wrestling with all of this myself. I'm asking you to trust me, to have faith in me. You did say you were willing to help me, didn't you?"

"Yes, but—"

"So will you just hang on a little longer?"

"But, Dillon, there are some things I need to tell you, today."

"And I'm telling you, no, I'm asking you, to listen to me, Isabel. If I take on this project...it will be demanding. I'll have to fight Eli, I'll have to rearrange my schedule to find time to supervise things here—"

"And that means you'll have to put our relationship on hold?"

"No, that means I'll need you more than ever."

His words, spoken with complete honesty at last, captivated her. "I don't have a problem with that, Dillon."

"But there might be some problems," he tried to explain. "Eli will make our time together miserable."

"I can deal with Eli."

"I don't want you to have to deal with Eli, and I don't want you to have to deal with all the things I've done."

She stared at him, realization dawning. "So, that's why you think you don't deserve my help, my friendship, me?"

He nodded again. "That's my excuse. For wanting to be with you, then pushing you away. For flirting with you, then being rude last night. I'm just so afraid. So afraid I'll blow it all over again."

"But, Dillon—"

"Just tell me you'll trust me, Issy. Just tell me you'll try to understand why I'm the way I am."

"I'll try," she said, resignation taking over some of her earlier determination. "I am trying. But what about Eli?"

"Right now, Eli is faraway and occupied with his

new bride. Want a tour, to see what grand plans I have for fixing this place up?''

Isabel's heart soared, then sank. She really needed to talk to him about Eli, but Dillon obviously wasn't in a listening mood. And after what he'd just told her about this house, she couldn't bring herself to shatter his hope. In a way, this might work out. If Dillon put some money back into this place, things might turn around for Eli, too.

Turning to lift her gaze up to the winding staircase, she said, ''I used to bring things to your mama—sewing, laundry, fruit and vegetables that we'd been hired to pick and can, and I'd always stand in this hallway, wishing I could explore this house from top to bottom.'' Shrugging, she said, ''Of course, I never got any farther than that old settee that used to be against that wall.'' She pointed to the empty spot between the parlor and the formal dining room. ''Your mama would come out of one of those big rooms, all bright and dressed to the nines. She'd gush with pride and thank me for all my hard work. Then I'd hand over the finished product and hurry out the door.'' Her smile was bittersweet. ''I'd always turn about halfway up the lane, though, just to get one more look. I thought this place was a palace.''

Dillon lowered his head, his eyes falling across the hardwood floors. ''It wasn't a palace at all. In fact, it wasn't much of a home. Not in the real sense of the word. It took me years to figure out my family was totally dysfunctional—make that *still* totally dysfunctional.''

Surprised that he'd let her in on that obvious revelation, Isabel said, ''You always seemed like the perfect family to me. I used to watch you all in church, sitting up front on your family pew. Your mother, so pretty, so fashionable, your father, so debonair, but so intimidating, like a lion ruling over his domain. And of course, you and Eli, two handsome brothers with everything good in life going for them.''

He glanced up toward the high ceiling. ''If these old walls could talk. You know, Isabel, sitting on the front row in church doesn't necessarily mean you're guaranteed a spot in Heaven. You saw a whole different picture than the real one.''

He was right, of course. Grammy also said actions spoke louder than words or appearances. And the Murdock actions spoke volumes. ''I guess so. I believe we see what we want to see.''

Tugging her along, he said, ''Well, the whole town saw what my parents *wanted* them to see, that's for sure. We kept our secrets safe and our problems behind the walls of this house. That is, until Eli and I had our parting of the way.''

Thinking he was going to open up at last, she said, ''That is when everything changed, isn't it? I guess that's why your leaving was such a shock. It was so unexpected.''

''It was a long time coming,'' he replied, a contemplative frown crossing over his features. ''My father and I...we didn't see things eye to eye, and Eli and I had our share of problems long before I took off.''

He guided her up the stairs, his big hand holding tightly to hers as he easily tried to change the tone of the conversation. ''You're gonna love these big, old rooms.''

Refusing to let him sway her from her intent, Isabel said, "I'm sure I will. But tell me, what kind of problems did you and your brother have?"

He shook his head. "Sorry, that's not part of the tour package."

Isabel watched as the wall of blankness fell back across his face, shutting her out as effectively as the shuttered windows of the upstairs landing tried to shut out the sun. Just like this old house, Dillon didn't want to give up his secrets. He would fight her every step of the way. Maybe that was what Grammy was trying to make her see. She wouldn't be fighting against Eli if she got herself involved in this; she'd be fighting against Dillon's resistance, too.

How could she tell him Eli was in trouble, when he seemed so excited about drywall and paint, when he went on and on about antiques and family heirlooms. Dillon intended to bring it all back, in full glory. But she had to wonder if he was considering restoring this house because he wanted his home back, or because he wanted the home he'd never really had. Maybe it was all a facade, and maybe he was building his dreams on that facade—the sower throwing out seeds at random, mindless of where they would land.

She'd hate to see him try to restore something that had never been there in the first place, especially when he could easily lose it all again. If things had been as bad as he'd indicated, he was definitely sowing on ground that had not been as solid as everyone believed.

They finished the tour—five bedrooms, an upstairs sitting area and den, four bathrooms, and then back down the stairs to the central hallway with four huge open rooms on each side. There was an office just opposite of the long kitchen. Dillon had made that into his own temporary living quarters.

Within each room, he'd talked about what he hoped to accomplish. Restoring his great-grandmother's four-poster rice bed, the one that had been especially designed for her up in New England, which now stood empty and open, without even a feather mattress to grace its frames, finding antiques to match the ones Eli had sold off or given away, bringing this house back to life in a timeless fashion with respected memories and traditional treasures, both bought and borrowed—he was willing to put everything into making this house what he pictured in his mind.

Even though she knew she should, Isabel couldn't find it in her heart to bring up Eli's problems.

"Restoring this place will be a huge task," she said as they moved back down the stairs. "But you seem to know what you're talking about—antiques and heirlooms! I always remembered you as being only interested in fast cars."

He shook his head. "I was young, a rebel in the worst way. I've learned a lot since then." He gave her a look that touched her heart, yet revealed nothing. "I know what really matters now, Isabel."

His words and the look in his eyes caused her breath to flutter much in the same way as the faded lace curtains at a nearby floor-to-ceiling window.

"Such as this house, and rebuilding your life here," she said to deflect the warm sensations pouring over her. She had to remind herself he could never love her the way she loved him, no matter how he looked at her. She had to remember what really did matter the most to Dillon Murdock. "It should turn out beautifully," she told him. "I hope it does."

The intimacy was gone, replaced by that controlled, brooding mask...and doubt. "You don't sound so sure."

"It just seems like a huge undertaking for someone who didn't want to stick around."

"You don't believe I have sticking power?"

She stood on the last step of the curving stairs, with him down below her. Looking down at him, she prayed he did see this old house restored, and she prayed even harder that he'd find the restoration his tattered soul needed. "I believe in *you*, Dillon. I told you that. But I really wish you'd talk to Eli, try to patch things up before you spring this on him."

"And I told you, I'm not worried about Eli—except to protect you from him. I won't let him ruin what we have between us."

"Why would he even try? I mean, I know he's never liked me—he thinks I'm just some poor country girl. But, I'm not that girl anymore. I can stand up to Eli. And I will, just to prove to you that I'm stronger now."

Dillon looked over at her, forcing the old blankness to take over his expression and his emotions. He couldn't let her see the truth there in his eyes. He refused to open her up to that kind of pain. She might be stronger now, but in some ways she was still fragile. What they had together now, friendship or more, was too precious to him to squander in another fight with Eli. If she knew, if she even suspected, that he and Eli had quarreled about her and her family all those years ago, she'd bolt like a fawn and he'd never see her again.

Remembering all the old hurts Eli had inflicted on him, remembering his brother's dire warnings and malicious jeers, Dillon steeled his heart against loving Isabel. He didn't want to bring her into his family; she'd only wind up resenting him for loving her, for making her love him. Theirs could never be an easy coupling. Eli would make sure of that, just as he had once before. And no amount of praying or repentance could help this situation.

"Dillon?"

He heard the need in her voice, saw the hurt and confusion in her eyes. By trying to protect her, he was hurting her just as badly. Thinking he should just grab her by the hand and run away with her, Dillon shook his head. He was tired of running. And he was also tired of fighting his feelings for Isabel. He was no longer content with having her assume the worst of him. So he did the only thing he could do. He gave up.

"You want the truth, Issy?" he said now, his heart crystallizing and breaking like the aged paint on the walls. "You want to know what makes me the way I am?"

"I want you to be honest with me."

Coming close, he willed himself to find the strength to let her know his real feelings. "Okay, I'll tell you, but you might not like it."

Shaking her head, she said, "What do you mean?"

The war inside him shifting into a gentle surrender, he pulled her into his arms. "I mean, I think I'm falling for you. And I don't want that to happen, not yet. Not here on Wildwood. Maybe when we both get back to our own worlds, away from here, maybe I can think straight about all of this. You offer me friendship and support, but by doing that, you don't know what you're asking in return. I might not be able to give you everything you need in return.''

Filled with shock and joy at the same time, Isabel touched a hand to his face. "What if I told you I feel the same way—about the falling for you part, I mean.''

He swallowed, stared at her, touched a hand to her hair. "I'd say what I've already said—I don't deserve you.''

"Okay," she said at last. "I'm sorry. I'm sorry I threw myself at you, sorry I forced you to care about me. I'm sorry I've been hovering around…as Eli put it…chasing after you.''

He lifted his head then, his eyes flashing fire. "Eli? What did he say to you?''

Her head down, she whispered, "He told me you'd never settle for one woman. He told me you'd never change.''

A frustrated rage simmered beneath the deliberate calm Dillon tried so hard to maintain. "That's my big brother. He always did have me pegged.''

Tossing her hair back, Isabel gave him a pleading look. "Well, this time, he was wrong, *wasn't* he? You say you might be in love with me, yet you tell me you don't want to love me—you're afraid of something. You're hiding something deep inside. And you won't let me in. That hurts much worse than anything Eli could ever do to me. Much worse.''

She didn't have to convince him. He could see the

hurt in her beautiful eyes, in her defeated stance, in the frown marring her expression. But this hurt would go away; if he told her everything, it would be ten times worse.

"I'm truly sorry, Isabel," he managed to say. "But some habits die hard. I'm not very good at talking things out, and until you came along, I didn't think I was capable of loving anyone. It's scaring me."

Hearing the sound of tires on gravel and clay, Dillon pulled his gaze away from her to look out the open double doors at the front of the house. "We've got company."

Struggling somewhere between resentment and rejoicing, Isabel watched as Dillon headed up the hallway to see who'd come up the drive, then she took the time to get herself together.

Dillon loved her, but he didn't want to love her. Something was holding him back—maybe his own fear of making that final commitment, maybe his problems with his family, maybe their life-styles being too different, and too far apart. Whatever it was, Dillon still didn't trust her enough to tell her about it.

"Just leave," she told herself now. "Just tell him about his brother, then go before things get much, much worse."

But she'd waited too late. With Dillon's next heated words to the man out in his yard, things went from bad to worse in a matter of minutes. Rushing up the long, wide hallway, Isabel heard his shouts as she reached the front doors.

"I won't let you do this. I won't let Eli do this!"

Isabel hurried out onto the porch to see what the

two men were arguing about, but the sign in Leland Burke's hand told her everything she needed to know.

The Wildwood mansion and the surrounding land, was going to be put up for public auction, one week from today.

Dillon was going to lose the home he loved so much, the home he'd come back to, the home he had just decided to rebuild. And now, it was too late for Isabel to warn him, or to help him.

And it was too late for her to tell him that she'd known for days now that something like this might happen.

Chapter Eleven

"**M**other, you have to tell me what's going on!"

Dillon watched his mother's face, saw the confusion and shock that had changed her usually serene features into a mask of grief. It wasn't easy interrogating his mother this way, but someone had to explain why his brother would be willing to let the bank auction off part of Wildwood—the main part of Wildwood as far as Dillon was concerned.

Cynthia seemed to age right before his eyes. Swallowing back some of the rage he'd felt at seeing Leland Burke in his yard just over an hour ago, Dillon took a long breath then reached out a hand to take his mother's trembling fingers. "What's Eli done, Mother?"

"I honestly don't understand," Cynthia said weakly. "I just can't believe he'd stand for this—auctioning off the plantation house. Why, it's ridiculous to even think of such a thing."

"The sign's up on the front field, Mother," Dillon

reminded her. "I yanked it down, but Leland put it back up. According to him, Eli mortgaged that piece of property and now the mortgage is due. We'll lose it, Mama. We'll lose Wildwood. From the sound of things, we've already lost it."

Cynthia shook her head, disbelief evident in her misty eyes. "That house is over 150 years old. I shouldn't ever have left that old place."

Dillon tilted his head, his voice softening. "I know, Mama. I know. We should have taken better care. *I* should have taken better care of the place."

"I never wanted to move, you know," Cynthia said, her voice low and raspy. "I begged Eli to let me stay there. I wanted to live out my days in that old house—you know how I love my wildflowers. But he insisted I'd be more comfortable here with him."

"Why did you move in here if you knew you wouldn't be happy?" Dillon asked now, concern for his mother calming his earlier anger. He could understand Eli wanting to punish him, but it was cruel to do this to their mother.

Cynthia held his hand in hers, her eyes bright with tears. "I didn't want to be alone, and Eli insisted it would be easier on both of us. I didn't argue very much, because I missed your father so terribly, and you—oh, Dillon, how I longed for you to come home and make peace with your brother. I prayed for it and when you came back, I thought my prayers would be answered." She hushed, looked over at him, then reached up a hand to touch the spike of inky hair covering his forehead. "But now, it looks like that won't be possible. I can't believe we might actually have to give up Wildwood.''

"Not if I can help it," Dillon said, letting go of her hand to pace the length of the kitchen. "I might not be able to make peace with Eli, but I certainly don't intend to stand by and watch him destroy Wildwood.'' Whirling, he glared out the window at the sign now back on the grass in front of the old mansion. "I'll do whatever I have to, to save that piece of land.''

"It'll be another fight," Cynthia said. "I don't know if I can stand this.''

Dillon shot a hand through his hair, then looked at his mother. "I don't want another fight, but I won't run away this time, Mama. I came home hoping to find forgiveness and a fresh start with Eli, but since I've been here, he's done nothing but ridicule me and condemn me—it's not ever going to change.'' He turned back to the window, his mind made up.

"Well, I might as well live up to my reputation. If he wants a battle, I'll give him one. I'm older now, and stronger, and I won't let him do this to our family.''

Cynthia leaned her elbows on the table, then placed her head in her hands. "How can you stop this? I had no idea Eli had done this—mortgaging our land. Why, we've never owed a dime to that bank—we helped build that bank with our hard-earned money and our backing. How can Leland even be a party to something like this?''

"Leland is well within his rights," Dillon explained. "He wouldn't give me all the details, but apparently Eli is heavily in debt to the Wildwood

Bank and Trust. I intend to find out exactly what my brother's been up to. Starting right now.''

"What are you going to do?" Cynthia asked.

Dillon headed up the hallway toward Eli's elegant office and all the files and documents concerning the operation of Wildwood. "I'm going to do a little research—find out just how much money your elder son owes to the bank."

"Debt," Cynthia repeated, her mouth falling open. "We won't be able to hold our heads up in public. I'll be ashamed to walk down the street. Your father would turn over in his grave."

Dillon didn't reply. Answering to the fickle citizens of Wildwood was the least of his worries since he'd had plenty enough practice at that particular chore. But he hated seeing his mother this way. He didn't care what others thought of him or his brother, but Cynthia would have a hard time dealing with the public condemnation and scorn.

Theirs was one of the founding families of this town—the town had been named after the plantation. Wildwood, the town, was just an extension of the Murdock dynasty that had started with cotton long before the Civil War. This land had survived that war, and had continued to thrive and prosper with other crops and other ventures. Farming was in the Murdock blood. Which made it that much harder to accept what Eli had done.

Cynthia was used to everything being taken care of, everything tidy and in its place. She'd never had to deal with very much scandal. Dillon wanted to comfort her, but right now he was too anxious to find out all the sordid details of Eli's business ventures.

"You should call our lawyer," Cynthia suggested, her head popping up. "Fletcher Curtis will know what to do, since I certainly don't."

Dillon didn't trust the family lawyer enough to call him right now as Fletcher had been the other man standing with Eli and Leland yesterday morning. Well, he'd deal with all of those involved later. Now, he'd call Sanford—see if there was any way his business manager could arrange for Dillon to pay off the mortgage on Wildwood.

If he'd been more alert, Dillon thought, he could have tried to stop this sooner. But no, he'd been too caught up in his feelings for Isabel, too preoccupied with her honesty and his denial to notice anything out of the ordinary around here. And Eli had covered his tracks very well, apparently.

Now, he stomped up the hall, thinking his mother was right about one thing. Murdocks didn't fall into debt. They often bailed other people out of debt. Other people usually owed the Murdocks money. Isabel's own father, Leonard, had come to Roy Murdock, asking for a loan once. But Dillon didn't want to think of that fateful day right now, or what it had cost both him and Isabel.

Thoughts of Isabel reminded Dillon of how they'd left things earlier. After he'd practically attacked Leland in the front yard, Isabel had rushed out of the house, her face ashen, her eyes wide with shock and...and something else he couldn't quite put his finger on. Too distracted by this latest development, though, he'd ignored her to try to pin Leland down on the details of this upcoming auction.

After arguing with the man until they'd both lost

their tempers, Dillon had turned to see Isabel walking away, back toward her grandmother's house. Humiliated, and beyond reason, he'd let her go. What could he say to her now? How could he explain that he loved her so much it hurt with each breath he took, but that his family problems had once again gotten in the way of that love?

He'd go to her later and explain. He had just found her again—he wouldn't lose her now. His priority had to be saving Wildwood, and that meant concentrating on getting to the bottom of Eli's deceptions. Slinging his body down in Eli's burgundy leather office chair, Dillon clicked on the computer sitting on one corner of the executive-style desk. While he waited for the computer to boot up, he looked out the window, toward the little cottage where Isabel had spent her childhood.

Leonard Landry had spent his entire adult life on that little spot of land. Isabel's father had come to work for the Murdocks as a teenager, then continued working here after marrying Isabel's quiet, shy mother, Miriam. How could a man make that kind of sacrifice? How could he continue taking orders from someone else without some sort of resentment building up inside him?

Well, the resentment had been there, all right. But not in Leonard Landry. The resentment had become Isabel's legacy. It was now so deeply embedded inside her, Dillon doubted she herself even recognized it for what it really was. Which was why Dillon still found it hard to believe that she could possibly love him. She didn't know how much he loved her, and how hard he'd fought for her all those years ago. He'd fought then, and he'd lost. And he'd failed Isabel's family.

But Mr. Landry had accepted his lot in life and had worked as hard as any man could, trying to keep his family out of debt. And he'd done it on the meager wages Dillon's father paid out, without ever once questioning or demanding any changes.

Except for that one time.

Memories of that day and the horrible consequences of Dillon's interference came back to him now, capturing him like the blinking cursor light on the humming computer screen. Isabel was right; that was when everything had changed.

He wouldn't hurt Isabel with the ugliness of his father and brother's snobbery and prejudice. She'd never be able to face him again if she knew all about that terrible day so long ago.

Well, I won't lose you again, Issy, he thought now as he grimly started scrolling Eli's files, *and I won't lose Wildwood.* This was his opportunity to make things up to his mother, and he intended to take full advantage of it.

When this was all over, he'd tell Isabel everything. He prayed that she'd understand and not turn away in disgust. And he prayed for guidance; he needed God's help with this, and he hoped that the good Lord would give a sinner like him one more chance.

Since sleep was impossible, Isabel worked long into the night, developing roll after roll of film and several sheets of proof shots from the hundreds of pictures she'd taken since coming back to Wildwood. Most were of the wedding and the activities leading up to that event, but a lot of the pictures she now held in her hands were of Wildwood itself…and Dillon.

At least she'd have these memories to take back to Savannah with her. She'd have her own private album of their time together here on this land. It would have to be enough, she decided. Because Dillon had more important things on his mind now. His home was in jeopardy; he didn't have time to spend with a woman who'd never measure up to the Murdock standards.

Remembering how angry he'd been earlier that day, remembering her part in all of this, Isabel shook her head. Why hadn't she prepared Dillon for this? Why had she held back the information Susan had given her? If she'd gone to Dillon sooner, he might have confronted Eli before that auction sign had gone up. Now, Dillon was madder than ever and in shock over this latest turn of events.

Had Eli deliberately waited until after the wedding to drop this little bombshell? Why couldn't he have at least told Dillon what to expect. Because he probably thought Dillon would be long gone before the sign went up. Boy, would he be in for a surprise when he returned from his honeymoon and found Dillon still here and fighting harder than ever to keep his home.

Isabel leaned back in her chair by the window, wishing she'd had the courage to help Dillon. But she'd waited too long, hoping he'd trust her enough to share his past miseries with her.

"It was just wistful thinking, Lord," she said into the still summer night. "Just me being foolish again."

Her mother used to tell her not to wish too hard for things she could never have.

"You can't just go out and start snapping pictures and call yourself a photographer, honey. Best you get a job at the sewing factory in town and bring home an honest day's wages," her mother had told her years ago.

Well, she'd tried that, Isabel remembered now. It hadn't lasted because she couldn't conform to the work the way so many women living in the rural areas had. She wanted an honest day's work, but she also wanted more.

"No, Mama, I had to go out to prove you all wrong, didn't I?"

She'd enrolled at the local community college about thirty miles away from Wildwood, much to the dismay of her parents.

"Girls don't need that kind of education," her father had warned. "You just need to find a good man and settle down. How you gonna get back and forth to that fancy school anyway?"

Isabel had found a way. She'd worked at the sewing factory just long enough to buy a run-down used car. And she'd driven that car back and forth for two years, using the scholarship she'd earned through the help of a guidance counselor at Wildwood High to help pay her tuition.

Then, a few days after she'd graduated, two years after Dillon had left Wildwood, she'd told her parents she was moving away.

"And where do you think you're going?" her bewildered father had asked.

"I've found a job in Valdosta," she'd explained, afraid that they'd talk her right out of moving to the larger town a few miles north, if she gave them time to argue with her. "I'll be working for a newspaper there, as a secretary. I'll be able to take a few photographs here and there—"

"She's crazy," Leonard had told her mother. "Crazy, just plain crazy. Girls don't run off to Valdosta to work for a newspaper."

But this girl had. And from there, she'd transferred to Savannah and now, she was independent and stable, on her own and…still trying to prove herself.

Funny, when she looked back on things, she'd always thought she'd find Dillon somewhere out there. Isabel had never dreamed she'd have to return to Wildwood to find the one man she would always love.

Well, finding him was one thing. Spending the rest of her life with him was quite another. She'd waited; she'd tried to talk to him, to get him to talk to her. She'd come so close to telling him about Eli's problems.

And she'd failed at all those attempts.

Now, Dillon had a new battle to fight. And he didn't need her right in the thick of things. She'd just be a distraction now, no matter how willing she was to stay here and see him through this.

And yet, she couldn't just leave.

"You told me I wasn't very good at waiting, Grammy," she said now as she touched a finger to the first picture she'd taken of Dillon. Holding the black-and-white photograph close, she said, "Lord, I've been waiting most of my life for this man. I've prayed about this, longed for him to love me back— at times I didn't even know or understand what I was waiting for. Now, I do." She closed her eyes, the sweet memory of Dillon's kisses causing her to draw in her breath. "I thank You for bringing me home again, for letting me see that Dillon means so much to me, and he always will. I guess I'm going to have to leave it in Your hands from now on. We need Your help, Lord."

She'd finish the preliminary photographs of the wedding. She'd have everything in order for Susan so the bride could pick the best shots for her wedding album. Then Isabel could concentrate on Dillon.

Holding Dillon's picture away so that she could barely make out his features in the soft light from a nearby lamp, she whispered, "I made you a promise. I'll see it through."

When he'd left all those years ago, she'd been hurt that he hadn't told her goodbye.

This time, she wouldn't be able to tell him goodbye.

"He asked me to trust him," she reminded herself again as she turned out all the lights but one and sat there clutching Dillon's image close to her heart. "And that's what I intend to do."

From his spot in Eli's office, Dillon saw one soft yellow light burning in the Landry house down the road. It was late, so late, and everything about the countryside was quiet and still. Shadows loomed here and there, waiting, hushed, warm with the wind of a summer night. The sleeping land reached out to him, holding him close in its embrace.

His land.

Isabel's land.

They'd lived here, watched this land change and grow, shift and blossom. Apart, they'd lived a life together that few people could ever understand. And tonight, they'd each worked at their individual tasks, in individual, completely different homes. That, at least, brought Dillon some measure of comfort. Somehow, he knew Isabel was there in the dark, thinking of things, thinking of him maybe, just as he was thinking of things, and her, always her.

He sank back against the soft leather of the office chair, picturing Isabel hard at work in her makeshift darkroom, her green eyes bright with excitement and pride as she created her own special way with film and chemicals.

Dillon smiled now, proud of her gift, proud that she'd overcome all the obstacles holding her back, to move on with her life. She could have easily settled for living out her days in Wildwood, Georgia, but she'd had the courage to follow her heart.

He wished he had that kind of courage. Instead, he'd been a coward who'd run away from his home and his responsibilities. He'd followed nothing except his own stubborn pride, and he'd wasted so many years and so much time holding on to a grudge that didn't seem to matter very much right now.

As angry as he was with his brother, Dillon also felt some sympathy for Eli. With Dillon's defection and later, their father's death, Eli had been left with the tremendous responsibility of running the huge plantation. He'd done the best he could, under the circumstances. Granted, according to the files in front of him, Eli had made some bad decisions, but then he'd had no help, none at all.

Running his hands through his hair, Dillon fought exhaustion and regret. If he'd stayed here, this might not be happening now. If he'd stayed here, he and Isabel might have wound up together. But no, her life had turned out much better without him. He had to remember that, at least. She didn't have to deal with the mess he would have to face come morning. And he intended to keep her out of it, for her own sake.

His brother had really created a monster of tangled finances and bad business decisions. Apparently, Eli had a dream of reopening the old, long-idle cotton gin that had once been the mainstay of Wildwood. But before his brother had accomplished that particular feat, Eli had decided he needed a new house and a new car and new farm equipment.

In essence, his brother had robbed Peter to pay Paul.

In essence, not only the old plantation house, but most of the Wildwood land, was in danger of being sold or auctioned off. From everything he'd been able to decipher in the computer files, Dillon now understood that things were worse, much worse than anyone knew, probably even Eli himself.

With a groan of frustration, Dillon hung his head. He sat there, adding and subtracting, reworking the figures, trying to come up with a viable solution, trying to understand what had driven Eli to such extremes, but nothing worked.

Yet he would not give up. And in the back of his mind, a solution had started to form, a germ of an idea that was swiftly growing into the only way out of this whole ordeal. If Eli would go for it.

Tired, Dillon decided he'd go back to Wildwood and try to get some sleep. As he reached to turn off the single lamp splattering bright light across the cluttered desk, his hand struck a worn Bible sitting off to the side, on top of some battered, stuffed folders.

His father's Bible. Did Eli actually read the word of God?

Curious, Dillon picked up the leather-bound book and surveyed it. When was the last time he'd actually taken the time to read the Bible? When was the last time he'd turned to God, really turned to God, for help in his life?

He remembered a time when God was his only salvation, when he'd had no hope left and he'd reached out into the dark night. He'd found his salvation then, alone and lonely, and on his last shreds of dignity.

Would God listen to him one more time?

Without hesitation, Dillon opened the book to a passage that Eli had obviously marked with a torn piece of paper.

It was the book of Ecclesiastes. The first chapter was headed "The Vanity of Life."

Shocked, and even more curious, Dillon started reading.

"Vanity of vanities," said the Preacher; "Vanity of vanities, all is vanity."

"What profit has a man from all his labor, in which he toils under the sun? One generation passes away, and another generation comes; but the earth abides forever."

The earth abides forever. This land had survived in spite of everything that had happened. The winds of both fortune and bad luck had blown over Wildwood, and still this earth had withstood the test of time.

"What were you searching for, there in those passages, Eli?" Dillon wondered now. "Did you realize too late that you'd overstepped your bounds, that your vanity had cost you more than you were willing to pay?"

Dillon got up, placed the Bible back where he'd found it, then on second thought, picked it back up and clutched it underneath his arm. He had a lot of soul-searching to do and this particular book might help him find some of the answers he needed.

For the first time in many years, Dillon's heart went out to his older brother. How long had Eli carried the burdens of Wildwood on his shoulders, without any support or understanding, without any guidance, except what he could find in this worn book?

"I've been unfair to you, brother," Dillon whispered as he closed the kitchen door and walked through the gardens toward home.

He was still bitter, but he felt a new peace settling over the earlier fatigue that racked his body. He would try, really try, to understand why Eli had done the things he'd done.

And, he'd offer his help to his brother.

Holding the thick, worn Bible close, Dillon stared up at the house he loved so much. And he prayed his stubborn brother would be able to accept his help.

Together, they could keep this land.

Together, they too could abide forever.

Chapter Twelve

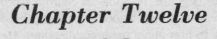

Dillon hesitated a few seconds, then knocked softly on the heavy wooden door of the Landry house. The information he had to tell Isabel and her grandmother weighed heavily in the pit of his stomach, choking him with a helpless despair. Better coming from him, though, than through official papers from the bank.

Martha opened the door and smiled brightly. "Dillon, what brings you to my doorstep on a humid Monday morning?"

"Hello, Mrs. Landry," he began, shifting his booted feet in an uncomfortable fidget. "I I need to talk to you."

"Sure, c'mon in," Martha replied, swinging an arm in invitation. "How about a cup of coffee and some apple cake?"

"Coffee sounds good," he said as he entered the small dining room. "I'll pass on the cake. I'm not very hungry, but thanks anyway."

"Suit yourself." Martha indicated a chair, then

turned to go into the kitchen for his coffee. "Isabel, as you might remember, has a rather large sweet tooth, so I always bake on the rare occasions she comes home. How that girl gets away with eating all that fattening stuff is beyond me. Guess she walks it all off, out on her photography excursions. She does have a talent for taking pictures, doesn't she?"

"Yes, ma'am." Dillon let Martha's proud chatter pour over him like a soothing balm. She didn't have to brag to him about her granddaughter. He was completely convinced of how special Isabel was. Which made his visit all the more difficult.

"Where is Isabel?" he asked now, glancing around after Martha handed him a steaming mug of coffee.

Martha gave him an indulgent look. "She's on the phone in the bedroom, talking to her agent. She was up to the wee hours again last night, working on those wedding layouts. Wants to get them in order, so she can have a few days to concentrate on...other things."

Dillon slammed his cup down, his head coming up. "She's not leaving, is she?"

Martha placed her hands on the back of her own chair. "I honestly don't know what her plans are. But she will eventually have to get back to Savannah, of course."

Worried, Dillon said, "She didn't mention anything about a new assignment—I thought she'd be staying a while. But then, I've been a bit preoccupied since the wedding."

Martha sat down, then patted his hand, a look of tenderness entering her eyes. "I sure am sorry it all had to come to this. Imagine, Wildwood being sold at auction.''

''Yeah, it's a raw deal.'' Dillon willed himself not to panic. Right now, he didn't really care so much about Wildwood. Surely, Isabel wasn't planning to leave yet?

He glanced at Martha, saw the sympathy in her eyes. It wouldn't take much more of her grandmotherly persuasion before he'd fall into the woman's arms like a baby and babble out all his fears and frustrations, namely that he was about to lose both his home and the woman he loved.

This was supposed to have been simple, he thought, his bitterness coming back to provide a nice warm cloak that effectively blocked out Martha's caring attitude. He should have been the same old cynical Dillon Murdock, well on his way back to Atlanta by now. But he was no longer that man.

Now, he was having to deal with all these new emotions, such as panic and pain, and a fierce need to go grab the phone away from Isabel and tell her agent to get lost.

''Why don't you relax, son?'' Martha said as she refreshed his coffee.

''I can't,'' he quipped. ''I'm a Murdock, remember? We have a hard time dealing with the truth.''

''And the truth is?'' Martha asked gently.

''I don't want her to leave,'' he blurted out. And immediately turned red with embarrassment at the admission.

But from the look of understanding and concern in Martha's eyes to the warmth of her hand covering his, Dillon knew he could tell this woman anything and she would neither condemn him nor judge him. Martha Landry was not self-righteous or full of overblown pride.

And she proved it with her next statement. "See there, that wasn't so bad, now, was it?"

He had to smile then. "No, I guess not." And he did relax, in spite of the news he had to tell them. Then he started talking. "You know, Mrs. Landry, I've never had this kind of stability, this kind of honesty in my life. In fact, my family's ability to hide the truth has been a carefully calculated form of denial. And the worst sort of hypocrisy."

"Because you all smoothed things over?"

He nodded. "Behind closed doors, that's where the real show started—the condemnation, the name-calling and the badges of shame, the humiliation of knowing I'd never be able to live up to Murdock standards—and Eli was usually the master of ceremonies."

Martha looked thoughtful. "Well, now *he's* going to be the brunt of scandal and rumors and condemnation."

Dillon took a sip of coffee, then lowered his head. "Yes, and at one time, I would have relished that. But now, it doesn't bring me any pleasure or peace. Instead, it makes me sick to my stomach."

"You look defeated, son," Martha said, giving him another gentle pat. "Is it as bad as it sounds?"

"Worse," he replied, impatient to get this part of the ugliness over. Taking a deep breath, he gave Martha a direct look. "Which is why I came by. I really need to talk to both you and Isabel."

"About what?" Isabel said as she entered the

room, clearly surprised to find Dillon sitting at her kitchen table.

Dillon stood up, a worried expression on his face. "Hi."

"Hi," she replied. "You don't look too hot."

"I don't feel too hot," he admitted as he slumped back in his chair. And he gained no satisfaction from noting the dark circles underneath her eyes. Although she looked as lovely as ever in her sleeveless khaki ankle-length shirtdress, with her long hair still damp and unruly from her shower, he could tell that she, too, had had another rough night.

Isabel watched him watching her. Unable to take the heat from his eyes, or the feeling being in the same room with him brought over her, she tried to stay rational. But he obviously had more bad news. Heading straight for the coffeepot, she asked over her shoulder, "Did you find out anything else about the auction?"

Dillon waited for her to join Martha and him at the table. "More than I want to know." Rubbing a hand over his unshaven face, he sent Isabel a beseeching look. "My brother has gone and got himself in one big mess."

Martha automatically handed Isabel a fat slice of warm brown apple cake. "Eat something, honey." Then, turning back to Dillon, she asked, "Is he really going to let the bank auction off part of Wildwood?"

Dillon looked down at his near empty coffee cup. "He doesn't have any choice. Technically, the bank now owns the land, since he defaulted on the loan they issued a few years back. If Leland doesn't get a good bid from the auction, he'll just slap a For Sale sign up and get rid of it that way.''

"But the auction's quicker," Martha stated, nodding her understanding.

"Yep." Dillon drummed his fingers on the table, his eyes never leaving Isabel's face. "I've gone over the books—took half the day and night just trying to decipher what all Eli *has* done. My brother's record-keeping is haphazard at best. I can't seem to find the title to this place."

Isabel's heart went out to Dillon. She could tell this was killing him inside. All his hopes had been dashed with a cruelty that must have felt like another slap in the face from his cold, condemning brother. Feeling guilt all the way to her soul for not at least warning Dillon about Eli's problems, she had to look away from his sharp, unrelenting gaze. She couldn't face him this morning. Especially when she knew he'd be so hurt and angry if he found out she'd kept this from him.

Changing the subject with lightning swift accuracy, Dillon gave her a pointed look. "Are you leaving, Issy?"

Looking up, Isabel ignored the knowing expression on her grandmother's quizzical face. Nervous, she rammed a fork into the aromatic cake sitting in front of her. Not that she was hungry, but she had to at least look natural and unaffected. "I called in to check with my agent about any upcoming bookings, and I've been offered a lucrative assignment from a southern lifestyle magazine. They want me to do some work on a few tourist spots around Georgia. The magazine's based in Atlanta and I'll have to go there to meet with the editors, but—''

She stopped as Dillon's dark brows shot up like twin question marks. "Oh, yeah? Well, I guess you have to do what you have to do, right?" Before she could explain, he rushed on "I understand. I have a business to run myself. Luckily, I've got very capable managers holding down the fort, but sooner or later, I'll have to make a quick trip back to Atlanta." As if he were talking to himself, he added, "And there's really no reason for you to stay here any longer, right?"

Isabel glanced at her grandmother and saw the questioning expression on Martha's face. Dillon thought she was leaving. And he didn't want her to go. Touched, she sat there looking across at his handsome, confused face.

But when she tried to speak, he only held up a hand. "Before you go, I think you ought to know something."

"Oh?" She gave him a look that spoke of both hope and regret. "What's that, Dillon?"

Dillon willed his drumming fingers to a shaky quiet. Then, glancing from Isabel's questioning eyes to her grandmother's curious stare, he said, "Well, there's no easy way to say this, but…it's about the auction."

"What?" Isabel said.

Dillon let out a defeated sigh. "The auction includes the plantation house, of course, and about fifty surrounding acres of land."

"The wildflower field," Isabel said, the sick feeling in her gut growing worse by the minute. Well, Eli might not have wanted the auction, but he'd be getting his revenge, anyway. If he couldn't wipe away the wildflowers with a mower, he'd watch them become trampled by the highest bidder.

"Yes, that, too." Dillon sat up, ran a hand through the straight, shiny locks mashed against his forehead, then plunged ahead. "And, well, it also includes something else—"

"This house," Isabel finished, her anguished gaze slowly lifting to his face.

Dillon nodded his head, his hand reaching across the table to grasp hers. "Yes, Isabel. The bank is going to auction off your home as part of the package." Giving Martha an apologetic glance, he added, "Leland tells me that once that happens, you'll have about thirty days to vacate the premises."

Isabel stomped up the path that wound through the wildflower field, with Dillon hot on her trail. "How could Eli let this happen? How, Dillon?"

Not waiting for a response, she paced back and forth, her eyes moving over the serene yellow faces of black-eyed Susans and the lush carpeting of blue phlox. Even the flowers looked wilted and dejected today, their fate sealed right along with Isabel's.

"I can't believe this is happening! What has my grandmother ever done to deserve this? She's worked for your family most of her life, and now this?"

"Isabel, stop," Dillon said as he stood in front of her to halt her pacing. When she tried to step around him, he reached his arms out to grab hold of her shoulders. "Stop."

"I can't stop," she shouted, her eyes bright with

bitter tears that she refused to let fall. "I've got to do something to help my grandmother. Dillon, she has no other place to go. She's lived in that house since my grandfather died over twenty years ago, since my parents died. I just can't—"

Dillon pulled her into his arms. "I know and I'm sorry. And I promise you this—I'm going to fight this with every breath in my body."

Isabel fell against him, drained and defeated. "I can't believe Eli has let it come to this."

Dillon patted a hand on her lush hair, then kissed the top of her head. "I intend to question him on it, believe me."

Pulling away, Isabel gave him a scrutinizing glare. "And what can you do, other than fight with him again? He wanted both of us gone, and now, because of his greed and mismanagement, my grandmother will have to leave, too."

Dillon held her by her arms, forcing her to listen to him. "I intend to do plenty. I've racked my brain all night and half the morning about this, and I've come up with some options."

She lifted her chin, her eyes widening. "Such as?"

"I'd rather not discuss it just yet. I want to talk to Eli first."

Pushing his hands away, she said, "Fine. That's just fine. You still can't trust me enough to level with me, can you, Dillon?"

"What?" He placed a hand on her bare arm, tugging her back around to face him. "What's that supposed to mean, anyway?"

Isabel gave him an openmouthed look of disbelief. "Isn't it obvious? You aren't ready to tell me how we're supposed to get out of this mess? How can I possibly stay calm when I don't even know what's going to happen to my grandmother? Why can't you just trust me and let me help you?''

Dillon plopped down on the ground, mindless of the buzzing bees and colorful butterflies he'd startled away from the fragrant flowers. ''It's not about trust, Isabel. I'm trying to keep you out of this. You shouldn't have to be involved in the ugly dealings of the Murdock clan.''

Glaring down at him, she said, ''But I am involved. I'm involved all the way around. I'm involved because of my grandmother, I'm involved because I came back here in the first place, and I'm especially involved because of…because of—''

''Because of me,'' he finished just as he lifted a hand to pull her down beside him, his expression daring her to try and get away.

No, she wanted to shout, *because of my own stupidity. Because I didn't listen to Susan and tell you the truth.* Dillon thought this was all his fault, but he was so wrong. And now, she didn't know how to be honest with him. She was so afraid she'd lose him forever.

So she stayed silent, then fell down on the soft cushion of flowers, scaring a pair of squawking blue jays out of a nearby camellia bush.

''I tried to warn you,'' he said on a low, husky voice. ''I tried to tell you that I'd only bring you misery.''

''*You* didn't do this,'' she retorted, her fingers busy plucking the petals off of an already crushed variegated petunia. *And I tried to warn you, but not in time.*

Dillon turned to her then, his eyes centering on her face, his expression softening with a tenderness that took her by surprise. "Stay here, Issy," he said, his voice low and vulnerable. "I'm not good at asking for help, but I could use yours right now."

Isabel shut her eyes, then sent up a quick prayer. He wouldn't want her help anymore if he knew the truth. But she could at least tell him that she'd never intended on leaving in the first place. "I am staying, Dillon," she said, her hand on his arm. "I turned down the assignment in Atlanta."

Dillon covered her hand with his own, then pressed it against his face, closing his eyes in apparent relief. "I thought—"

"You thought wrong," she whispered, tears pricking her eyes. "I told you I'd stay and I intend to do just that. Besides, I can't leave my grandmother now, can I?"

"No." He wrapped his other arm around her neck. "I shouldn't ask this of you, I know that. I should send you packing, get you away from this mess. But I'm being selfish—I don't want you to go."

Trying to be rational in spite of his lips grazing the palm of her hand, she said, "I'll probably just make things worse. I'm so angry right now, it's hard not to lash out at Eli."

"You let me take care of Eli," Dillon stated, the tenderness in his words and his gentle actions melting her fear and guilt. But she also sensed something else there. A warning?

Lifting her hand away, Isabel stared him down. "Just exactly how do you plan on doing that?"

He shrugged. "I'm learning patience, and I'm trying hard to forgive him. But…this isn't going to be easy.''

Isabel sighed and hugged him close. ''No, it's not. And I guess I need to get back inside and help Grammy decide what her options are. There aren't that many available houses around here, and she's on a fixed income. And I doubt she'd be willing to move to my cramped apartment in Savannah.''

''She's lucky to have you for a granddaughter,'' he told her, pride shining in his eyes.

''And what about you, Dillon?'' If he wouldn't say it, she'd say it for him. ''You say you could use my help, but do you need me here?''

Dillon sank back against the soft perfume of a thousand flowers, his heart thumping quicker than the spindly green grasshopper escaping across the denim covering his leg. What was he doing? And who was he trying to kid? If he wanted her to stay, if he wanted her to know him, truly know him, and to understand him, then he'd better start relying on trust and faith. As he looked up at her hopeful, beautiful face, and saw the awe and pain in her searching eyes, he acknowledged that he'd also have to rely on his own heart's yearnings, and The Good Lord's promise of hope and redemption.

''I think you know the answer to that question,'' he told her. ''Earlier, when I thought you might be going—I've never felt such panic.''

Reaching up to her, he sat up and took her back in his arms. ''You know, last night I found my father's Bible in Eli's office.'' He took a breath, then told her what was in his heart. ''I read some of the passages someone had marked—my mother probably, maybe even Eli, and…it helped me, Issy.'' He tightened his arms around her, urging her head to rest against the crook of his arm. ''There was this one passage about the value of friends. It said, 'Two are better than one.' It said that when one falls alone, he doesn't have anyone to lift him up.''

Isabel shifted in his arms, and he wondered if she felt the urgency of his grip, the beating of his heart like a trapped bird trying to escape its cage.

''Tell me, Dillon.''

Dillon swallowed, touched his lips to her hair, then continued. ''I was so alone after I left Wildwood. So alone. And when I fell, I fell hard and fast. I…I didn't have anyone there to lift me up.''

Isabel remained still, but he could see the tears glistening in her eyes when she looked up at him. ''Dillon,'' she said, his name muffled as he held her close. ''Dillon—''

His sigh was filled with a deep trembling. ''I *do* need you, Issy. I need you to be here in case I fall again. You always were the best friend I ever had, and that verse from Ecclesiastes is very true. Two are better than one.''

Isabel lifted her face then, the tears glistening and wet on her cheeks. He'd just told her he needed her, as a friend if nothing else. And oh, how he'd struggled with the telling. She could see it in his face, the pain, the pride, the weariness of someone who'd traveled a long road to find his way home again. And she also saw the longing to be held, just held, unconditionally. How many times had she felt that same longing in her own heart?

''I'll stay, Dillon,'' she said, tears making her

words shaky and broken. "I offered you my help once, remember? And I meant that with all my heart. We'll fight this, together."

He closed his eyes, then lifted his head up to the sun. "And will you be there when I fall?"

"You won't fall," she whispered. "But I promise, I'll be there, good or bad, to lift you up. You won't have to go through this alone."

Then she pulled his head back down to hers and sealed the deal with a kiss. For these few precious minutes, at least, Dillon could forget all about Eli and his problems. For now, just being here amid the wildflowers with Isabel in his arms was enough. And all the more proof for him to believe God had sent him home for a reason.

Tomorrow, they'd find a way to save the very land that had abided and held them together like a threefold cord all these years.

Gaining strength from Isabel's trust and willingness to help him, Dillon remembered another verse from Ecclesiastes. "A threefold cord is not quickly broken."

Chapter Thirteen

Isabel snapped another picture of the figure sitting on the floor in the middle of the empty room. With the early morning light pouring in from a nearby window, Dillon looked as natural and content as a man could look surrounded by open textbooks and crumpled farm manuals. Except when the camera caught his gaze. The turmoil and determination raging against each other in the depths of his eyes told the tale of the past few days. This was no common man; he wouldn't quit until he had this all sorted out and found a way to help his brother and save this land.

Watching him, Isabel knew she'd made the right decision by staying here with him. When Dillon looked up from studying the latest crop report, his eyes held hers in such an intimate gaze, she couldn't deny that she was glad for any excuse to be with him.

"You're frowning," he remarked as he dropped the folder and leaned back against the wall. "I thought that was my job."

"Just thinking," she told him. Placing her camera on the planked floor, she strolled across the empty parlor, enjoying the morning breeze that teased at the thrown-open floor-to-ceiling windows. Tugging at her haphazard ponytail, she focused on a peeling spot of rose-patterned wallpaper. "What else can I do to help?"

Dillon stretched his legs out, then crossed his booted feet at the ankles, his deceptively lazy gaze moving over her face. "You've already done more than enough. You didn't desert me." Then he asked, "How are things on your end?"

Memories of his words to her just yesterday washed over Isabel, making her flush with joy and hope. Attempting to waylay her optimistic feelings, she slid her hands in the back pockets of her jeans and said, "Well, I have to find out about possible places for my grandmother to move. So far, those places have been slim to none, unless we consider putting her into a nursing home in Valdosta or Albany."

"Not an option," Dillon said as he reached out a hand to her. "Martha is not nursing home material. Do you know your grandmother gets up at dawn every day to take a long walk?"

"She is pretty amazing." Laughing to hide her own fears, Isabel lifted a hand to accept the one he offered her, then settled down on the hardwood floor next to Dillon. Scanning the array of research books and disorganized files, she said, "I think you've checked out every book in the Wildwood library."

"Trying to get a handle on land management and cotton farming, sugar."

Isabel knew he already had a handle on the situation. He'd stayed up most of last night, going back over the records, calling bankers in the middle of the wee hours, talking with the family lawyer. Then, early this morning, he'd organized the workers, giving them irrigation, pesticide, and herbicide schedules to try to salvage the cotton crop. But basically, he was spinning his wheels. Short of a windfall, part of his heritage would still be going up on the auction block come Saturday.

"Do you think you can save this place?" she asked, her fingers still laced with his.

Dillon lifted his head, his gaze roaming around the big, empty room. In typical Dillon style, he ignored her question, choosing instead to admire his surroundings. "Look at these ceilings, will you? So grand and lofty. That ceiling medallion around the chandelier was hand-carved."

Isabel tilted her head to study the yellowed, rose-etched wooden pattern that formed a beautiful, ornate raised circle in the center of the ceiling. "How could Eli let something like this happen?" she wondered out loud.

Dillon dropped her hand then. Jabbing a fist against one of the crop manuals, he said, "I'll tell you how. It's like you said—greed and mismanagement. He overextended himself before he got a good handle on growing cotton. It's like he got the cart before the horse. He went out and bought all the right equipment, hired the best workers, built himself a fancy new house and a nice storage barn, then threw a few thousand cotton seeds in the ground and waited for them to bring him a profit."

"Will they?" she asked, her gaze drifting to the budding cotton bolls out in the distant fields. In spite of the heat outside, the sight looked like snowflakes against a blanket of green.

Dillon let out a huff of a breath. "It would be something. From everything I've found out from talking to the few remaining workers and studying his crop reports, he's done it all wrong. He's overfertilized, thinking to cause a growing spurt, he's overwatered way too early, which could bring on a fungus and possible boll rot, and in spite of the boll weevil eradication program, he's got some pest problems because he can't keep track of his herbicide schedule. It's all been hit-and-miss at best."

"And I always thought Eli was the farmer in the family," Isabel said, surprised.

Dillon looked away, as if he didn't want to continue this conversation. "He always tried to be. He wanted to be the best in order to please our father."

"But?"

He shook his head. "Don't make me talk about this, Isabel."

"I stayed to help you, remember?" She nudged at his muscular forearm. "Tell me, Dillon."

He sighed, then plunged ahead. "Most people around here don't realize this, but Eli never was very smart in school."

"Really? *I* certainly never knew that."

"Another Murdock secret. He always had trouble figuring things through. You know he waited a few years before he went to college, then when he was in college and I was in my first year of high school, I used to help him with his homework."

Amazed, Isabel shook her head. "I would have thought it was the other way around."

"Most people did. I mean, I was the wild child while he walked the straight and narrow. But he struggled all through school, only my mother's support and her hardheaded bullying of his teachers saved him. When I was old enough to understand, I helped him and covered for him. He got into college strictly on our father's name, and he came home on weekends so we could have study sessions together, but then after I left town...well, he never finished. He really wanted a degree in agriculture, to validate his dedication to being a farmer."

"I always wondered why he dropped out," Isabel said, remembering all the rumors she'd heard about Eli wanting to quit college to help his father run the plantation, the way he'd done right out of high school. "Everyone thought he was being noble—you know, taking some of the load off your father."

Dillon picked up a piece of paper he'd scribbled some notes on, then crushed it in his hands. Throwing the discarded wad across the room, he said, "Yeah, he was being noble all right, while I was out gallivanting and sewing my wild oats."

Noting the bitterness of his admission, Isabel touched a hand to his arm. "You still blame yourself for this, don't you?"

He didn't answer right away, but the guilty look he shot her told her she'd hit right on the mark. "If I'd stayed here to help him out, if I'd come home after our father died, things might be different now."

"You don't know that, Dillon."

"I abandoned him, Isabel. No wonder this place is in such an uproar."

"And look how he's always treated you," she reminded him. "He used to bully you and tell you you were worthless, or have you forgotten that?"

"I haven't forgotten anything," Dillon retorted hotly. "But he did always manage to bail me out of the tough spots, too. Can't you see, Eli wanted to make me look small and unworthy because that's the way our father made him feel all the time. And he came to my rescue just so he could rub my nose in it."

"What do you mean?"

Pulling his knees up, Dillon propped his elbows on his denim-clad legs. "Our father would tease Eli about his bad grades. He'd call him stupid and tell him he'd never amount to anything."

She shook her head. "I'm still amazed that this was happening and nobody knew. Your father always seemed so pleased with both of you. He'd brag and go on about his two handsome, smart sons, and now you're saying it was all a sham."

"I know it's hard to believe," Dillon agreed. "But that was just part of the punishment, almost like a cruel reminder to us of what we really were. In private, things would always turn nasty. If he wasn't badmouthing Eli, he'd turn to me and point out what a no-account I was. He told me over and over again how disappointed he was in me and that I'd better shape up, or he'd boot me out the door." He let out an irritated sigh. "Then, of course, he'd find a shred of conscience and forgive me of my transgressions. So that became the pattern. He wasn't so forgiving of

Eli, which is why Eli tried so hard to win his favor. Because of that, Eli also grew to resent me.''

Stunned, Isabel shifted and crossed her long legs. ''So Eli stopped defending you, and you turned against each other?''

Dillon glanced up then, the shame evident in his dark gaze. ''Yeah, then it became sort of a game to see which one of us could win Daddy's favor. Our father pitted us against one another. He'd get Eli going on my bad attributes, then step back to watch the fireworks. Sometimes, they'd gang up on me. Eli would have done anything to win my father's approval.''

Horrified, Isabel said, ''And your mother just turned a blind eye to all this?''

He looked out the window, as if remembering. ''She'd be in the kitchen, humming, or out at some country club function. And even if she had wanted to say something, she didn't dare try to defy my father. You have to remember, my mother comes from the old school that teaches women to stay in their place.''

Reaching out a hand, Isabel caught his hand in hers. ''All those days we ran around this place together, and I never knew. You never once told me.''

Dillon looked up to the ceiling, then pulled his hand away. In one fluid movement, he was up and stalking across the aged floor. ''This is why I don't like to talk about my past. I can't stand that pity I see in your eyes.''

Isabel hopped up to confront him. ''Pity? Is that what you think, that I pity you?''

He whirled, his eyes a dark, raging storm. ''Well, don't you?''

Aggravated, Isabel tossed a hand in the air. "I guess I feel some pity, only because it sounds as if you went through a horrible time back then," she admitted, "but mostly, I feel…I feel so proud of you, Dillon."

Clearly confounded, he put his hands in his pockets and rocked back on the scuffed heels of his boots. "How can you be proud of me after what I just told you?"

She came to stand by him, then touched his arm. "Because if I remember correctly, you never once inflicted that same kind of torment and pain on your brother. Sure, you and Eli fought all the time, but that was mostly because you felt you had to defend yourself, and you defended me a lot, too, back then. Dillon, you kept Eli's learning disability a secret, in spite of everything. All this time, you've protected your brother. Why would you do that, after what he put you through?"

Dillon looked down at her then, his eyes a misty pool of longing and tenderness. "That's simple, Issy. I love him."

Several hours later, Isabel strolled back up the wildflower path. She'd spent the entire day helping Dillon go over the records. Together, they'd managed to get them in some semblance of order, for the bankers and lawyers, if for nothing else. Behind her, the sun was hovering over the trees, its vanishing rays giving the entire sky a bluish pink shimmering cast. The weatherman was predicting rain over the next few days, but Isabel couldn't tell it from the brilliance of this sunset.

As she reached the small backyard, she heard someone humming a sweet tune, then recognized it as one of her favorite hymns—"Just A Closer Walk With Thee." Her grandmother, obviously. Walking around the house, Isabel spotted Martha sitting on a gardening stool in the middle of her prize tomatoes, cucumbers, and purple-hull peas.

Isabel's heart filled with an abundant love as she stood by the back steps, watching her grandmother lovingly tend to her small garden. Martha wore an old, men's work shirt and an Atlanta Braves baseball cap. She seemed perfectly content, as if she didn't have a care in the world.

Swallowing heavily, Isabel once again wondered how Eli Murdock could have let this happen. True, they'd never owned this land or this house but it was home. Well, this old rickety house might not belong to her, Isabel thought, but suddenly it seemed very precious to her, and worth any fight. And it had taken her too long to see that she'd had a good, stable home here, with loving parents who only wanted the best for her. Dillon had been right. Compared to his dysfunctional family, Isabel had had the things that really mattered, but had wished for all the things that really didn't count for much now.

Placing her camera equipment on the steps, she hurried over to her grandmother. "How's it going?"

Martha glanced up, squinting underneath the blue of her hat. "Hi, sweetie. Did you and Dillon get anything accomplished today?"

Falling down on her knees in the soft carpet of loam, Isabel automatically started pulling random weeds away from the tender tomato stalks. "Not much, I'm afraid. But he assures me he's got a Plan B in the back of his mind. By the way, thanks for bringing over those sandwiches.''

Martha gave her a playful wink. ''No problem. I walked over to see Cynthia and took her some apple cake. She's in a bad way. She's so distraught, she's canceling all her commitments and she's hardly answering the phone. This has completely thrown her out of kilter.''

''I can certainly understand that,'' Isabel replied as she sat back to stare off in the distance. ''How can *you* keep a smile on your face, Grammy? How can you sit here in your garden, humming a happy spiritual, when our whole world seems to be falling apart?''

Martha stopped her digging, then carefully put down her mud-caked spade. Turning to give her granddaughter a serene look, she said, ''Why, Isabel Landry, how can *you* ask me such questions?''

Isabel saw that spark of indignation in her grandmother's warm eyes. ''Well, look around,'' she said, swinging her arms wide. ''We could lose all this. I'm worried sick, Grammy, and I don't know what to do about it.''

''So you think I should just give up and mope around, wringing my hands in helpless frustration?''

Isabel tried to picture that particular image, then seeing the traces of amused indignity in her grandmother's eyes, managed to smile herself. ''Well, no, I've never seen you wringing your hands in any sort of frustration.''

''Nor will you ever,'' Martha replied with a

chuckle. "Child, I have complete faith in God's plan for me."

Isabel nodded. "Okay, I can buy that, but what if God's plan involves you having to find a new place to live?"

"Then I'll start looking."

"How can you be so calm about this?" Isabel questioned. "There aren't many available places to rent around here."

"I'll find something," Martha assured her as she turned back to her digging.

"The Lord will provide?"

"Yes, but The Good Lord also gave me a brain and enough sense to start looking in the classified section for rental property."

"And what if you don't find any?"

"I'll cross that bridge when I come to it."

"You amaze me," Isabel stated, shaking her head.

Martha looked back over at her. "Isabel, darling, I've lived on this earth a long time. And I've learned to take the bad with the good. I've buried your grandfather and both your parents, so I've known grief and despair, but I have also known happiness and joy. And I've learned to roll with the punches." Raising a hand to ward off any protests Isabel might voice, she added, "When your grandfather passed away all those years ago, I moved in here with you and your parents, remember?"

"Of course," Isabel said, smiling in spite of her worries. "I missed Grandpa, but I was happy you came to live with us."

"Yes, it turned out okay," Martha continued. "I was so afraid I'd be in the way, a burden on all of you. But your father and mother took me into their home with open arms. In the end, it worked out for the best because I had to take care of them—and you.''

''You sure did,'' Isabel said, her voice quieting. ''And you've also done your share of work for the Murdocks.'' Pointing toward the house, she added, ''Look at this place—paint peeling, porches leaning. Never once have they offered to fix things around here, and now, we're losing what little we have left.''

Martha finished her work, then took off her thick cotton gloves. Gathering her basket and spades, she sat back on her stool. ''Eli isn't doing this to get revenge on us, Isabel. He's become a very desperate man. He has no choice.''

''Hmmm. So desperate he waited until he was away on his honeymoon to spring this on everyone.''

''He's ashamed and he's hurting,'' Martha told her. ''And we need to pray for him.''

Isabel jumped up. ''I have prayed for Eli Murdock. But it's hard praying for someone who's only brought me misery.''

Martha placed her hands on her hips. ''Isn't that just a tad like the pot calling the kettle black?''

''What's that supposed to mean?''

''You're sure ready to forgive Dillon his past transgressions, but not his brother?''

Tugging at a particularly stubborn root of Johnson grass, Isabel said, ''I love Dillon, and I know in my heart he's changed. He came back here to make amends, but Eli has pushed him away at every turn.''

''Ah, but did Dillon ever once tell his brother how he felt?''

"No, of course he didn't. He was too...too ashamed."

Suddenly realizing she'd been backed into a corner of her own making, Isabel bit her lip, then rolled her eyes. "Okay, okay. Point taken. Dillon was too ashamed to approach Eli, and Eli was too ashamed to tell anyone he was about to lose Wildwood." Sitting back down, she gave her shrewd grandmother a small grin. "What is it with men and their stubborn pride, anyway? I guess they're both pretty hardheaded, aren't they?"

"Yes. And, they *both* need our prayers."

Reaching out to take her grandmother's hand, Isabel gave Martha a quick kiss on the cheek. "But how can *you* not be worried, Grammy?"

Martha patted Isabel's hand. "Psalm 46 tells me not to worry—'God is our refuge and strength, a very present help in trouble.'"

"Will God provide you with shelter?" Isabel had to ask.

Martha nodded. "Yes, if I'm smart enough to seek that shelter myself. Remember, the Bible says that in my father's house are many mansions. I guess it depends on how you look at things—some want a mansion here on earth, some just want the peace of knowing their soul is secure."

Isabel wanted that peace herself. "Your soul is secure, isn't it, Grammy?"

"I'm working toward it," Martha said. "Child, would you look at that glorious sunset." She reached out her wrinkled hand, as if to touch the very rays of the fading sun. "That right there is enough to make anyone feel secure."

Seeing the dancing sun and lace-edged clouds made Isabel suddenly miss watching the sun set over the Atlantic Ocean up in Savannah.

"My offer still stands. You could come and live with me in Savannah."

Martha chuckled. "And all those characters you allow to sublet your apartment?"

"I'll just explain to them that I have a new room-mate—or better yet, I'll find a new apartment, or maybe even a small house. You could go to the beach every day, if you wanted, and grow a garden. And you'd love Savannah. You could explore the old city to your heart's content and join the historical society. Lots to do there."

Martha stood up then, and Isabel followed suit. "Wouldn't you like that, Grammy?"

Tears formed in the depths of Martha's eyes. "I'd love that, honey. And we'll see if it has to come to that."

"I feel better now," Isabel said as, arm in arm, they strolled toward the house.

"I told you the Lord would give us the answer," Martha reminded her.

"Does that mean you're ready to go with me? We could leave whenever you say."

"What about your grand plan to help Dillon?"

"I mean, after we get this auction thing resolved."

"And where exactly will that leave things between the two of you—after you've fought the good fight?"

Isabel stopped to stare down at her grandmother's questioning face. "I don't know. I honestly don't know."

"C'mon in, honey," Martha said, tugging Isabel

up the steps. "I've got corn bread and a chicken pot-pie in the oven."

"Umm, sounds great."

Martha faced her before opening the screen door. "It will all work out, Isabel. You and Dillon have a special bond, and...the Lord has plans for you two."

"I'll keep that in mind," Isabel replied sagely.

When the sounds of wheels scraping across the rocks lining Eli's long drive caught their attention, Isabel craned her neck to see who was visiting Cynthia. Then her heart literally dropped to her toes.

Grabbing her grandmother's retreating shirttails, she said, "Grammy, look!"

"What on earth?" Martha came back out to the end of the porch, her eyes going wide as she glanced over at Isabel. "Well, I declare—"

"It's Eli and Susan," Isabel said, her hand flying to her heart. "They weren't scheduled home until Friday. I guess Susan's honeymoon got cut a little short."

Chapter Fourteen

Dillon heard his brother's car turn into the gravel driveway across the stretch of country road. So, Eli had come home early. That either meant he was worried about what he'd done, or he'd found out Dillon was still here. Wanting to get this over with, Dillon stomped across the wide porch and down the cracked steps, headed for a confrontation that had been a long time coming.

Just help me, Lord. Just give me the strength to face him without hurting him. Give me the courage to admit I was a part of all of this, the courage to help him.

Not bothering to knock, Dillon entered the back door of Eli's house, willing himself to stay calm. He had a lot riding on this, but he meant to end it here tonight, one way or another.

Eli was standing in the kitchen, with Susan on one side and Cynthia on the other. The tension in the room hit Dillon squarely in the face as the three of them turned to see who'd just rammed through the door. Susan had obviously been crying. The new bride looked tired and drained. And his mother looked old, her usually impeccable clothes now wrinkled and haphazard, her eyes red-rimmed and devoid of the heavy makeup she normally wore.

But it was the look on his brother's face that stopped Dillon in his tracks. Eli's expression ranged between despair and rage. He looked as if he'd aged overnight. Which suited Dillon just fine, since he felt the same way.

"Well, hello all," Dillon said as he closed the door with a bang. As he faced his brother, all charitable thoughts flew by the wayside. "Home so soon, brother? What's the matter, your conscience get the better of you?"

"Just shut up," Eli warned with a wagging finger. "I'm home because our poor mother called me in a crying fit, telling me you were going through all my files and records. What gives you the right to come into my home and rifle through my private documents?"

Dillon edged close, his hands on his hips, his expression grim. "I'll tell you what gives me the right— my name. I'm still a Murdock, and you should have discussed this financial problem with me, since I still have *the right* to know what goes on on this land."

Eli glared over at him. "You gave up your rights when you left here, brother."

"Maybe so, but I'm back now and I intend to stop this sale."

"How?" Eli asked, his dark eyes blazing with a dare, and maybe a little hope.

Seeing the genuine worry in his brother's eyes, Dillon took a long breath and silently asked God to help both of them. "I haven't figured out how yet, but...Eli, I'm willing to mortgage my business if I have to, to get the money to save this place."

"I don't want your money," Eli said. "You'll never have enough money to pay back what you owe, brother."

Susan began to cry again, softly at first, then in sobs that shook her entire body. Cynthia came around to take the woman in her arms, talking to her new daughter-in-law in hushed, fretful tones.

"See what you've caused with your meddling?" Eli said, waving a hand toward the two women. "Susi and I were supposed to be on our honeymoon, but you've managed to ruin that for us, too."

Indignation coloring his words, Dillon groaned. "You can't be serious? How could you even go on a honeymoon, knowing that you were about to lose part of our land? Did you really think you could let this happen simply by waiting until after the wedding? Did you think I'd leave, and that I'd never find out about this taking place?"

Eli's haggard expression filled with hurt. "Leland told me he'd wait a few days. And I didn't think you cared anymore, little brother."

"Why didn't you tell me, Eli?" Dillon said, his tone soft now. "I could have tried to help."

"Oh, sure. I relied on your help for a long, long time, but you left and I learned to do things on my own. I don't need your help now. I'm doing what has to be done. And there is no way you can stop it."

"Well, don't be so sure," Dillon warned. "I've got

my lawyers working on this, and I can promise you—I will do whatever it takes to end this thing. I can't let our home slip away, Eli.''

''What home?'' Eli said, bitterness cracking his voice. ''Why should I care? That house means nothing to me. I built my own house.'' Glancing over at Susan, he added, ''And I intend to raise my children here—not over there in that run-down white elephant.'' He hung his head. ''I didn't know it would come to this, though.''

For the first time, Dillon saw the torment in his brother's eyes. He'd never considered that Eli held only bad memories of their childhood home.

''I can understand your wanting your own life, your own home, Eli,'' he said now, ''but you went about it all wrong. If we can sit down and talk about this—''

Susan interjected then, her blue eyes wide and misty. ''I tried to tell Isabel. I tried to tell her that you needed to know about this.''

Dillon's heart lurched as her words hit him in the gut like pointed arrows. He must have heard her wrong. ''What did you say?''

Susan wiped her eyes and lifted her chin. ''I said, Isabel knew about this. She's known for days now. She didn't know about the auction—nobody but Eli knew about that. But she did know things were bad financially around here. I told her all about it before the wedding.''

Cynthia gave her daughter-in-law a harsh look. ''Susan, you shouldn't have gone around discussing this with other people.''

Flipping her blond curls, Susan said, ''I only told

Isabel that Eli was in financial trouble, and that he was so worried I was afraid we might have to change our wedding plans.'' Looking frantic, she hastily added, ''Well, I had to tell someone! I wanted her to talk to Dillon and see if he'd help out.''

Both Eli and Dillon stared over at her, but Eli spoke first, his tone full of disbelief and anger. ''You discussed my private affairs with that…that trash?''

Without thinking, Dillon bolted across the room, grabbing his brother by the collar. ''Don't you ever call Isabel that again, do you hear me? Isabel wouldn't do something like this—that's more your style.''

Trying to pull them apart, Susan shouted, ''Well, it's true. She knew this might happen, but she was afraid to discuss it with you, Dillon. If you don't believe me, talk to her yourself!''

''I will.'' Letting Eli go, he turned to the cordless phone sitting on the counter.

''Don't you call that woman over here,'' Eli warned. ''She doesn't have any business getting in the middle of our affairs.''

''Her grandmother could soon be out on the street,'' Dillon reminded him, his fingers jabbing the numbers. ''I think that makes it her business.''

Turning away from the scorn in his brother's eyes, he thought back over the last few days, a sick kind of dread pooling like a liquid heat in the bottom of his stomach. Had Isabel known all along? Then he remembered little fragments of conversation. *Eli could use a brother right now. Eli could use your help.* Had she tried to warn him?

Her voice, sweet and warm, came across the line, breaking into his thoughts. "Hello?"

Swallowing back disappointment, Dillon said, "Isabel, it's me. I'm at Eli's house. Could you and your grandmother come over here. We need to talk."

Eli broke the unbearable silence while they waited for Isabel and Martha to arrive. "I told you that girl was trouble—she always has been." With a smug shrug, he added, "I wonder why she didn't bother telling you—I would have thought she'd take pleasure in seeing me suffer."

"Maybe you misjudged her," Dillon retorted.

"I doubt it," Eli replied, but his gaze was wary. "She probably just decided none of this was worth her precious time. She's never cared about this land, but she's sure always wanted to get her hooks in you."

Dillon jabbed a finger in the air. "I told you to quit talking about Isabel that way."

"Still sweet on her, huh?" Eli teased. "Guess some people never learn."

"You certainly haven't," Dillon replied, the last shreds of his patience snapping. "We're all in this mess because *you* didn't tell any of us that the bank was taking over Wildwood."

"Isabel could have warned you," Susan repeated, her own smug look telling him that she would be loyal to her husband, friendship aside. "Apparently she didn't think it was important enough to bother you with, though."

Amazed, Dillon said, "Oh, so now it's convenient

to put all of the blame for this on Isabel? Why didn't either of you see fit to clue me in on this situation?''

"Because there's nothing you can do," Eli said.

"And because you've never cared what happens here," Susan added hotly.

Dillon shook his head. "You two were made for each other."

"Hey, watch it," Eli replied. "You'll show my wife the proper respect."

Dillon huffed a breath. "Oh, that's rich, coming from someone who's never shown the Landrys or anybody else in this town any respect."

"Don't start again," Cynthia said, the tone in her voice brooking no argument. "I mean it, boys. I won't have you two fighting over that girl again."

Curious, Susan whirled to glare at her husband. "What does she mean? Have you fought with him about Isabel before?"

"It was a long time ago, honey," Eli said, his hand touching her shoulder. "Nothing for you to worry about."

Susan crossed her arms over her chest. "You could have told me about it."

"We'll discuss it later," Eli said, his tone firm. "Right now, I've got more important things on my mind—like why you had to go and drag that woman into our business."

A knock at the door brought Susan's head up. Dillon didn't miss the streak of self-righteousness in her eyes. She had told him this deliberately, to take the heat off her husband.

Cynthia opened the door. "Please come in."

Isabel ushered her grandmother into the room, her

eyes moving from Dillon's stony face to Eli and Susan. Susan shot her a knowing look, then held fast to her husband's arm.

"What did you need to talk to us about, Dillon?" she asked, hoping they couldn't hear the tremble in her voice.

Before Dillon could respond, Eli spoke up. "Susan told us she shared some of my private concerns with you—without my knowledge—before the wedding. Seems she wanted you to talk to my little brother about my problems." His expression pleased as punch, he added, "But for whatever reasons, you didn't tell him anything and now…well, he's gone and got his feelings hurt."

"Shut up," Dillon warned his brother, his head down, his fists clenched against the counter.

Martha gave Eli a harsh look, then turned to Isabel. "What's he trying to say?"

Dillon looked up then, his face full of torment. "Yes, what is he trying to say, Issy?"

Isabel's gaze shifted from Eli's condemning expression to Dillon's demanding one. Feeling weak, she leaned against the same counter Dillon was holding on to. "It's true. Susan told me the night of the rehearsal supper that Eli was in some sort of financial trouble."

"And why didn't you tell me about this?" Dillon asked, shaking his head. "You've had plenty of opportunities."

Before Isabel could respond, Eli interrupted, "Because she's a conniving—"

"I told you to shut up," Dillon said, whirling to

glare at his brother. Spiking fingers through his hair, he faced Isabel again, silent and waiting.

Isabel swallowed back her own sorrow and humiliation. Seeing the disappointment in Dillon's eyes caused her heart to tighten inside her chest. She could take anything, but that look. "I didn't tell you... because I wasn't sure if it was my place—"

"You've got that right," Eli shouted. "You don't need to meddle in our business. You don't have any say-so here, little lady."

"I know that," Isabel countered, her indignant gaze never wavering. "You've always made very sure I knew exactly where I stood as far as Wildwood goes."

"Yeah," Eli continued, anger fueling his tongue, "and I saved my brother from making a big mistake. I told him all those years ago, that you were just out to move from the rental house to the big house. You wanted in on a piece of the pie, didn't you, *Issy?*"

"What on earth are you implying?" Martha said, her voice lifting out over the suddenly quiet room. "We've lived on this land for decades now, and we've never once asked for anything from you."

Pointing a finger at Isabel, Eli said, "She wanted more, though. She wanted Dillon. But me and Daddy, we nipped that little fling right in the bud."

Her eyes flying to Dillon's face, Isabel felt the heat of embarrassment rushing across her skin. Dillon looked up, his expression full of apology and...regret.

Humiliated, Isabel asked, "Is there something I should know? What happened back then, Dillon?"

"Yeah, why don't you tell her what happened the day you left Wildwood, little brother?" Eli's expression was dark and grim. "Tell her, then maybe she'll have the good sense to leave again. And this time, as far as I'm concerned, she can take you with her. I'm not happy about this auction; I tried to stop Leland from taking our land, but if this will get both of you out of my life, then I say let him have it."

Slamming a fist down on the counter, Dillon caused his mother to gasp as pots and pans rattled. "We're not talking about me or why I left, Eli. I'm trying to understand why Isabel—or any of the rest of you—didn't warn me about this auction."

"I didn't know about the auction," Isabel said in her own defense. "I only knew Eli was in trouble. And I *did* try to bring it up, several times. But we had to get through the wedding, and then when I came to the house on Sunday—"

"She didn't care either way," Susan said now, her eyes wide. "She didn't tell you, Dillon, because she was afraid it would distract you—take you away from her."

"That's not true," Isabel said, appalled that Susan could turn the tables on her. "Susan, you know that's not how I felt—I was trying to spare Dillon another fight with his brother. I honestly didn't know what to do."

Susan had the good grace to look sheepish, but then she said, "You told me—you said you didn't want to get caught in the middle of their problems."

"Yes, but…" Isabel stopped, her head lifting, her spine straightening. "You know, I don't owe any of you an explanation for what I did or didn't do. I don't belong here—I never did. I was perfectly happy with my life in Savannah, until you called me back."

"My mistake," Susan replied harshly. "If you'll just make sure my wedding pictures are delivered, I'll send you a check in the mail."

"Forget it," Isabel retorted. "You'll get your precious pictures, but I don't want your money."

"That's a hoot," Eli said. "I guess once you found out there might not be any money to be had, you decided to string my innocent little brother along just for fun. Of course, he has managed to eek out a living for himself with those fancy bookstores. Guess you'll have to settle for that."

"Is that really what you think of me?" Isabel said, her voice shaking with rage and sorrow. Turning to Dillon, she repeated her question. "Is that what you believe?"

"Right now, I don't know what to believe," he said on a weary voice. "It would have been nice if someone had warned me about this disaster, though."

The implications of his statement sealed things for Isabel. He would never trust her again; maybe he'd never trusted her at all. And he surely would never be able to love her, not with all of Eli's poison spouting through his mind. Her gaze moved over the worried, defensive faces of the people in the room. There was a quiet desperation here, between these brothers. And it would always be here, holding them at odds. Well, she refused to be a part of it, ever again.

Whirling back to Eli, she told him, "You contradict yourself. First, you tell me I'm just out to get Dillon, then you swear I'm out to get part of Wildwood. What are you so afraid of, Eli, that I'll wind up with both your brother *and* your heritage?"

"I'm not afraid of anything. I'm just protecting what's mine."

Isabel stared at him in awe. "Oh, so that's why you've let Wildwood go into debt?"

"Get out," Eli told her, his finger pointing toward the door. "Get off my land, and take your do-gooder grandmother there with you."

"Eli!" Disgusted, Dillon could only stare at his brother.

Cynthia gasped. "Eli, that kind of talk is uncalled-for. Martha Landry is my friend, and I won't tolerate you being disrespectful to her."

"Sorry," Eli replied, but his expression only grew more harsh. "Mama, there's not much I can do for Miss Martha, anyway. She's gonna have to move once this auction goes through."

Martha spoke up then. "You don't have to tell us twice, Eli. You're a sad, bitter man and you're lashing out, grasping at straws to try to justify your own self-ish actions. And right now, you're rejecting the very cornerstone that you need to be holding on to."

"Get out," Eli repeated. "Take your Bible quotes and get out."

"I'm so sorry," Cynthia said, tears streaming down her face. "He doesn't mean it, Martha. You know he doesn't mean it."

"Yes, he does," Martha replied, her own eyes watering up. "But you don't fret for Isabel and me. We'll be just fine."

Dillon had been standing as still as a statue, but now he raised his head. "Isabel, wait."

Isabel turned at the door. "No, Dillon. Eli is right about one thing." Her voice cracked, but she held the tears at bay. "I have always loved you. But tonight, you proved that isn't enough. You can't even trust me enough to tell me what happened so long ago, yet you have the audacity to stand there and judge me simply because I was trying to save you any further pain.

"I waited until after the wedding to talk to you, so I wouldn't be accused of ruining things for Susan and Eli. Then I listened and waited as you told me all your grand plans for Wildwood. I didn't want to be the one to have to tell you the bad news, Dillon. So I waited too long, too late, hoping you'd learn to trust me. And now, I've waited long enough. I'm done with the Murdocks, for good."

Lifting her head, she directed her gaze toward Eli. "Don't worry, we'll be gone by the end of the week, auction or no auction. And as for you two, I hope you don't let this grudge continue to fester. Because if you do, neither one of you will ever be truly happy." Then she looked back at Dillon. "I'm sorry you fought because of me. But whatever caused this rift, whatever part I inadvertently had in it, it stops here and now. I will not be a bone of contention between the two of you. Maybe with me out of the picture again, you can work together to save Wildwood. After all, that is what matters the most to both of you, right?"

Chapter Fifteen

"I didn't think it would matter to me so much, Grammy," Isabel said as they put the last of a set of old, chipped dishes into the large moving box. "I didn't realize how much I loved Wildwood or this old house, until it was too late."

All around them, the house sat still while a soft drizzle covered the surrounding countryside in a fine mist. In every corner, boxes sat marked for either storage or transfer. They'd reached a tentative plan. Martha would move to Savannah with Isabel for the rest of the summer.

As to where her grandmother would live permanently, a small house close to the unincorporated town of Wildwood proper was coming up for sale in the fall, and if Isabel could swing the financing, she intended to buy it for her grandmother. She'd already spoken to the man who owned it. Now, if she could just work out the details.

In the meantime, as Martha had pointed out, they'd

have some time together, then each get back to their own lives. But she refused to live indefinitely with her granddaughter—she thought it best if Isabel and she both continued to maintain their own space and independence.

"Oh, honey," Martha replied now, reaching across the box to give Isabel a hug, "we're going to be all right. We'll survive and we'll just chalk this up to a new adventure, a new path in our faith journey."

Isabel sat back on the footstool she'd pulled up to the deep box. "You amaze me, Grammy. You're dealing with all of this much better than I am."

Martha's soft chuckle filled the still morning. "That's because I don't have a vested interest in this place the way you do."

"You mean Dillon."

Martha nodded. "Still hasn't come around, huh?"

Isabel shook her head, her eyes automatically going to the window, her mind moving toward the looming presence of the house that Dillon had been holed up in since Eli had come home. "I can't blame him. It was wrong of me to keep all of this from him."

Martha took a sip of the hot tea she'd brewed earlier. "Your heart was in the right place. And you were right—you don't need to be at the center of those boys' troubles."

"Which apparently I have always been," Isabel reminded her. "But I guess that doesn't matter any more."

Martha stood up to stretch. "What say we take a little midmorning break? I've got chocolate chip cookies."

"Sounds good," Isabel said, her tone dull and absent. Standing herself, she dropped the stack of *Wildwood Weekly* newspapers she'd been using to wrap plates, then walked over to the open screen door.

The rain colored everything in shades of gray and blue, and gave the old mansion a melancholy look that tore through Isabel's consciousness with such a poignant tugging she had to suck in her breath. Why did this pain feel as if it would literally rip her body in two? Why did loving Dillon so much have to be so wrong?

Needing to feel the wind and water on her hot skin, Isabel grabbed a lightweight white-and-blue-striped rain slicker, then reached for the small, waterproof camera she kept for just such days. "Grammy, I want to get a few shots of the house in the rain. I'll be back in time to finish up these dishes before lunch."

"What about your cookies?" Martha asked from the kitchen.

"I'll eat them on the way."

With that, Isabel grabbed a couple of the fat, brown cookies from the tin her surprised grandmother was holding, and shoved them in the pocket of her slicker.

"All right," Martha said to herself, her eyes wide as she watched Isabel skip down the slippery steps. "Got to get that one last shot—of Dillon Murdock."

Then, smiling softly, she sat down and munched her own cookie, her eyes roaming around the sad remains of her life here on this beautiful piece of God's green earth.

"Help her, Lord," she said now, her eyes closed in a fervent attempt to intervene where her granddaughter's heart was concerned. "Help them both. Show them the life You envision for them, Dear Father. And while You're at it, how about sending a little inspiration my way, too.''

With that, she finished her cookie and tea, then sat back down to wrap up her memories, in shapes of round and square, some soft with age, others as fresh as the new rain falling outside. She'd never been more lonely, but Martha lifted her eyes to the cloudy sky, and smiled in spite of the ache in her heart.

Isabel snapped another round of black-and-whites, her mind centered on her art, her turmoil settling down a bit as she captured the essence of this land and the old, columned mansion. With the drooping wildflowers in front, and the rows of lush cotton growing in back, the house seemed caught in a time warp. Wildwood's history was tumultuous at best, but the house still held a timeless beauty.

Slaves had worked this land at one time, then once the Civil War had ended that horrid practice, share-croppers, both black and white, had taken their place. Her father had come from a long line of sharecrop-pers, and had continued that tradition. And all the while, the aloof, condescending Murdocks had ruled over the land.

Except for Dillon. For some reason, he had broken with tradition. He had rebelled. Why?

Isabel knew part of that answer. Dillon was a sen-sitive, caring man who couldn't tolerate bigotry or prejudice in anyone, including his own family. Cou-ple that with his hunger for knowledge, his need to educate himself and expand his own horizons and vi-sions, and the puzzle pieces started falling into place.

He'd obviously taken a stand against his father and his brother.

But how had she played a part in that?

Why had Dillon and Eli fought over her?

Probably because Dillon flirted with you one time too many and Eli pushed him into a fight about it.

That had to be it. Eli had probably taunted Dillon to no end, and Dillon had finally snapped. But to the point of leaving for good?

So many secrets, so much pain and resentment, shuttered behind the walls of that old, crumbling mansion. Would she ever know the real story?

The house stared back at her, its windows flung open to the rain, its many roofs and eaves dripping with a pretty tinkling melody of water against tin and shingle. The windows might be open to the outside world, but this house held to its secrets like a widow clinging to a faded family portrait.

Stopping at last, she wiped her small camera down on the inside pile lining of her coat, then dropped it into one of the slicker's large, long pockets. Rising up from her crouched position to wipe raindrops away from her brow, she stilled as memories of being here with Dillon fell all around her with the same gentleness as this endless summer rain.

Three days and not a word from him. He had shut down completely, reminding her of the old, brooding Dillon.

Had she hurt him that badly, or was this just an excuse for him to run away again?

She'd thought about confronting him, just having it out with him once and for all, but her pride wouldn't allow that. After all, she'd bared her soul to him, giving him promises as freely as she'd given him kisses. And he'd taken those promises and thrown them back in her face.

And, she reminded herself bitterly, he'd made no promises of his own. He'd asked her to stay, but now he didn't need her or her misguided help. Or her love.

Closing her eyes, Isabel held her head up to the rain and let the tears she'd held back for so long fall freely down her moist cheeks. "Is this my answer then, Lord? Is this the way it has to be?"

How could he live without her? Dillon asked himself as he stood at the huge, open parlor windows, watching Isabel through the sheer ancient curtains. How could he watch her without losing his heart all over again?

How could he forgive her?

Was there really anything to forgive?

He'd thought about her, day and night, since that terrible scene in Eli's kitchen. And he remembered every nuance, every fiber of *her*. He remembered the disbelief and the disappointment on her pretty face when he hadn't leapt to her defense. He remembered the hurt and the shock in her eyes when she'd realized that he and Eli had fought over her long ago. He remembered watching her go, and wanting to pull her back.

But, coward that he was, he hadn't done so. No, instead he'd buried himself in finding a way to stop this land auction, while he'd buried his feelings for Isabel behind a facade as fragile and torn as these decaying, moth-eaten curtains.

C'mon, Dillon, he told himself now, one hand on

the lace and the other on the window frame. *You know she didn't mean to deceive you. You know you told her to stay away. You could have at least listened to her explanation.*

He knew all of that, but still, it hurt. It hurt because he loved her. And, he'd come so close to telling her all his secrets and…he'd come so close to letting her really see inside his soul.

And all that time, she had been aware that something might happen, that Eli was up to something.

Why hadn't she just told him the truth?

And why haven't you just told her the truth? the voice inside his head echoed right back at him.

Because he'd wanted to protect her.

And maybe, blockhead, that's what she was trying to do for you.

What would happen if he did exactly that? he wondered now. What if he just told her the truth, and hoped for the best, on faith alone?

"Two are better than one."

The verse came into his head, reminding him of a need so great, he shook from the force of it. He needed Isabel. He loved Isabel. And he had been fighting for all the wrong reasons.

"For if they fall, one will lift up his companion. But woe to him who is alone when he falls, for he has no one to help him up."

Dropping the curtain, Dillon stepped back into the darkness of the house, then whirled, his boots clicking with purpose against the old hardwood floors. He knew that before Isabel left Wildwood, he owed her the truth, at least.

At last.

* * *

Isabel *felt* him moving toward her before she saw him. Dillon stalked through the wildflowers, his gray eyes centered on her, his whole body tense, his expression unreadable.

Her heart pounded against the warmth of her slicker as she watched him. Devoid of either coat or hat, he kept coming. Apparently, the man had something on his mind.

But she wasn't ready to hear it.

Not willing to bear the brunt of his wrath, Isabel turned back toward the lane leading to her house.

"Isabel, wait!"

She heard him calling, remembered he'd said those exact same words to her the last time she'd seen him. But still she walked toward home, willing herself to be strong.

"Issy, please!"

That stopped her. That note of despair, that hint of regret. That vulnerable quality she'd sensed in him so many times before.

She turned, her eyes touching on his face, her breath leaving her body in a soft sigh of defeat. "What is it, Dillon?"

He met up with her in the middle of the flowers, in the center of the lane where they'd first fallen amid the blossoms all those days ago.

Reaching out to touch her across the short distance, he took a long, shuddering breath. "I...I want to tell you, Issy. I want to tell you everything."

Thinking she'd heard him wrong, Isabel just stood there with her lips parted. Then, coming to her senses, she asked, "But what about…what about me keeping Eli's troubles from you?"

He shrugged, his hand still on her arm. "A minor technicality, all things considered."

Afraid to move, she whispered, "What made you change your mind?"

He moved his hand up the arm of her wet slicker, to coax a tangled mass of damp, heavy curls off her shoulder. "Yours was the lesser of two evils," he explained. "I figured you didn't owe me any explanations, since I had refused to ever give you any."

"So you thought I withheld what I knew deliberately?"

"No, I thought you did it strictly as a self-preservation tactic. And you were wise to stay out of things."

"Why?"

Placing his hands on her shoulders, he held her with an unflinching gaze. "It's a long, ugly story. But I want you to know, before I tell you everything—I love you, Issy."

She gulped, opened her mouth to speak, but he brought a finger up to touch her parted lips. "Just listen, and while you listen, remember that one thing, please?"

"Okay."

He dropped his hands away, and stepped back. "Eli and I were at the pond, fishing with our father. He and Eli were in one of their less charitable moods, so they started teasing me—about you."

At her hiss of breath, he held up a hand. "Just listen."

She nodded silently.

"Eli told my dad that I was hung up on you. Up until then, Dad had been just kinda ribbing me, but all of a sudden he turned nasty.

"Then my father turned to me and told me to drop that notion. He said Murdocks don't mess with girls like Isabel Landry. That I wouldn't want to wind up marrying beneath myself.

"And I asked if he meant we were better than the Landrys.

"Eli chimed in and said we'd always be better than that 'poor trash.' Then he turned to Dad, and grinned. He mentioned your father, how Leonard had had the nerve to want to buy a house in town. It seemed your father wanted to move off Wildwood. Eli couldn't believe that, considering everything we'd done for him."

Isabel interrupted. "What are you telling me? You knew about my father trying to move away?"

"I knew," Dillon replied, the bitterness choking his response. "Eli told me earlier that day, your father had come to speak with him and my father, asking for a loan to buy a house in town. He wanted to buy it for your mother as an anniversary gift, but of course, he didn't have enough money for the down payment."

He couldn't, wouldn't tell her that Eli had taken great pleasure in mimicking her father—his hat in his hand, his head down, his voice shaky.

"I remember when that all occurred," Isabel said, her tone so quiet Dillon could barely hear it above the drizzle. "He was so excited about that house. He told Mother and me it would be a new beginning, that they could at last retire in a home they truly owned."

She shrugged. "Then, he just changed completely. When I mentioned the house again, he told me we wouldn't be moving. And he told me to just forget about it. But I never did."

"Well, neither did I," Dillon replied. "When I asked Eli and Daddy if they'd given the loan to your father, they both laughed in my face.

"Dad said of course he didn't give your father the loan. He figured he'd never get the money back. He didn't feel Leonard Landry had an ounce of backbone. And if he allowed your dad to move into town, he'd start shirking his duties at Wildwood."

Isabel hitched a breath, seeing things in a whole new light. "So my father just gave up, didn't he?"

"He didn't have much choice. He couldn't afford to get fired. And that's exactly what Eli and Daddy threatened to do if he tried to buy that house."

A dark helpless rage coursed through Isabel. "He just wanted something to call his own, Dillon. Something for my mother and me to be proud of. How could anyone be so cruel?"

She hadn't realized she was pounding her fists against Dillon's chest until his hands halted hers.

"I wondered that myself, sweetheart." He swallowed, paused, then said, "And that day, I made the fatal mistake of questioning my father's authority. You see, I defended your father and begged my dad to reconsider. I told him it wasn't right. But he just laughed and said as long as he had people willing to work for room and board and a few acres of crop he'd never give it up.

"I'm telling you, Isabel, it sickened me, watching them make their snide jokes about a man who'd dedicated his life to this place. So I got angry and tried once again to reason with them.'' He stopped, his eyes lifting to hers. ''And that's when Eli started in on you again.

''Eli accused me of wanting to get on your good side. He said I was so busy chasing you around, that I'd forgotten who I was, and who you were. He said low-class girls like you were good for only one thing. Then he made a derogatory remark about you and I lost it. I went after him with both fists.''

Humiliation colored Isabel's words. ''Oh, Dillon, I'm so sorry.''

''Don't be.'' Lifting a hand to her face, he said, ''I told him flat out that I loved you.''

Shocked, Isabel raised her head, her gaze holding his. And then, she saw it there in his eyes. Dillon had *always* loved her, even back then.

''You fought against your brother and your father because you *loved* me?''

''Yeah.''

''I can't believe you did that, and I never knew.''

Dillon lowered his head to briefly touch her forehead. ''That's because my father got so mad. He told me that if I ever went near you again, he'd kick your family off this land and he'd make sure your father never found work in the state of Georgia.'' He swallowed again, then looked away, off in the distance. ''Then he told me if I didn't like the way he operated, I should get off Wildwood and never come back. I didn't give him time to take back those words. I knew I had to get away. I had to leave, or I'd become just like them.''

Isabel's hands were shaking. Reaching up for him,

she touched her fingers to his face. In a cry filled with anguish, she said, "Are you telling me you left Wildwood to protect my family? To protect me?"

"Yes," he said at last, the one word lifting a tremendous burden off his shoulders. Placing his hands over hers, he moved closer, his gaze holding her. "I loved you, Isabel. And I knew if I stayed here, I wouldn't be able to deny or control that love. So I left."

"I can't believe this," she said, tears falling down her face. "I can't believe a father would do this to a son, or a brother would be so cruel."

"Believe it. But don't feel guilty, honey. Like I told you once before, it had been a long time coming. I'd stood by too many times, watching the sickening way my family dealt with people they considered subordinates. I knew it was wrong, but I never spoke up because of my old need to be loved and accepted. Yet that day I realized I would never be able to stay here. And I knew in my heart that once I took a stand, I'd have a tough battle ahead, and worse, so would you."

"What…what did you do?"

"I walked back home, then I saw you sitting on the old swing that used to be out in your backyard. You had your legs curled up underneath you, and your nose buried in a book." He reached out now to pull at a strand of her soaked curls. "I remember your hair—it was so short and curling all around your head. I wanted to go to you and tell you how I felt, but instead I went to the bank, and with my mother's help, withdrew a large sum of money, and headed north. I enjoyed life to the fullest, soaking all my sorrows in a carefree life-style, partying away my pain, until the money ran out.''

Isabel pulled him close, sorrow evident in her eyes. ''Dillon—''

He hushed her. ''I woke up on a park bench in downtown Atlanta. There was an old man standing over me with a cup of coffee. He owned a bookstore on Peachtree Street, and after I poured out part of my sorry story to him, he hired me—on the condition that I get cleaned up and start going to church.''

''And?''

''And I did exactly that.'' His smile was wry and bittersweet. ''This man saw everything in me that my parents and brother hadn't. He let me read books to my heart's desire, never once calling me a bookworm or a sissy. He let me fiddle with the store, rearranging things to bring in more business. After a year or so, I asked him if I could become his partner. He co-signed a contract that allowed me to buy into the bookstore, and we were in business.'' Dillon's voice became soft then. ''He died five years ago, and his family sold his half of the business to me. I named the chain stores Rhyme and Reason, but that one downtown store will always remain Sweeney's Books.''

''Rhyme and Reason?'' Isabel shook her head, wondering if this man would ever stop surprising her. ''You own Rhyme and Reason and Sweeney's Books?'' Sweeney's was a legendary Atlanta land-mark, and Rhyme and Reason was very popular with book lovers all over the south.

''I own them so far, unless I mortgage the whole lot to save this place,'' he said to her. ''The day I left, I remember my father telling me there was no rhyme or reason to a son turning on his father the way I'd turned on him." He wiped the thickening mist off his forehead. "Well, I found my rhyme and reason."

Isabel started crying all over again. "And you did it because of me—"

"I did it because it was the right thing to do, and yes, because as I told you at the beginning of this sordid tale, I love you. But I was so afraid to tell you that, so afraid you'd be disgusted by what my family had done." He pulled her close. "But I promise you—I'll do whatever it takes to make it up to you and your grandmother. That is, if you'll still have me."

Running her fingers through his wet hair and tugging his head close, she laughed through her tears. "If I'll still have you? Dillon, I love you so much, I'm even willing to stay here at Wildwood and put up with Eli—that's how much I want you."

"We don't have to stay here," he said, hugging her. "I know it's asking a lot —I'm going to do everything I can to save this place, but I need you, Issy. Are you up for the fight?"

"Yes," she told him. "Yes,"

He kissed her with a gentle surrender, the last of his defenses shattered by a cloudburst of joy.

Still dazed, still deeply touched by all the sacrifices he'd made for her honor, Isabel pulled back to stare up at him. "I should have told you about Eli's problems, Dillon—"

"It doesn't matter. You couldn't have done anything, anyway." Looking up at the old house, he said,

"Let's face it. The Wildwood we knew is gone. And maybe it's for the best."

When footsteps sounded in the nearby mud, Isabel glanced up to find Susan standing there, tears falling down her face.

"It's not for the best, Dillon," the blonde said as she hiccuped and walked toward them. "You and Isabel love each other, and there's nothing wrong with that. And if you want to help rebuild this place, then I've got some information that will get things started, no matter what my husband thinks."

"What are you talking about?" Dillon asked, his tone wary.

"I'm talking about the deed the lawyers have managed to bury under all those files you've been searching," Susan replied after a loud sniff. "The deed that names *both* of Roy Murdock's sons as co-owners of this entire property."

Isabel's gasp echoed over the wet field. "What?"

"That's right," Susan affirmed, her tone laced with an apology. "Dillon, your name is on the title to this land—your father never did change his will. While I may be stupid in most things, I've heard enough talk between Eli and the lawyers to know that if that's the case—"

"If that's the case, the bank can't auction this land until I have a chance to buy it back!" Dillon said, a new hope rising in his words. "I can stop the auction."

"That is, if you're still interested," Susan said, one hand pushing through her drenched curls. "From the look of things, I'd say you've found what you came back here for—and I don't think it's an old house."

"You're right," Dillon quickly agreed, his hand squeezing Isabel's. "I came back for Isabel—she's more important than Wildwood—"

"But you have to try," Isabel told him. Then she turned to Susan. "Why are you doing this?"

Susan shot her a bittersweet smile. "I've learned a few things over the last few days." She pointed toward the old mansion. "For one—that's the real Wildwood. Eli built himself a showcase, and now he's trapped inside that showcase. When I got home today, I dreaded going inside to face him—he's so bitter and ashamed of what he's done, but he refuses to acknowledge that and take responsibility for his actions. Well, I'm speaking for him." She gave Dillon a pleading look. "He doesn't want to lose this land, but he thinks it's too late."

"We can help him," Dillon told her. "That's all I've ever wanted, for us to be a family again."

Susan nodded, then looked at Isabel. "I'm so sorry. I was wrong the other night, but I was so afraid Eli would hate me. I do love him and after watching you two together today, I can see that you deserve some happiness, too. Eli will spit nails when he hears I told you this, but…somebody had to stop all of this foolishness."

Dillon caught her arm. "He'll forgive you. He loves you." Then he surprised Susan by giving her a brotherly kiss. "Thank you. This means my father forgave me, too."

Susan laughed shakily. "I only hope we *can* forgive each other and find the faith you two seem to possess. I'm going to work on that, too."

"We'll work on Eli together," Isabel said, taking

Susan's hand. Now that she knew Dillon loved her, she could handle his stubborn brother.

"Thank you," Susan replied. With that, she turned to make her way through the mud back to Eli's house.

Isabel watched her go, then turned back to Dillon. "Are you sure we have that faith she's talking about?"

"Very sure. I have complete faith that Wildwood will be restored to its former glory, and I have absolute faith that I'm going to be a happily married man soon."

Isabel thought she couldn't possibly love him any more than she did right this minute. "So you're really going to buy it back from the bank?"

"Oh, I intend to buy it back," Dillon said, "but I don't intend to live in it. I've got a better idea."

"What?"

"You'll just have to wait and see," Dillon replied. "But first, I need to talk to my brother."

"And we probably should get out of the rain. I'm sure I look a mess."

Dillon's eyes filled with love. "No, even soaking wet, you look incredible."

Isabel wrapped her arms around his shoulders. "That's because I've finally found the perfect picture—the one of us together."

"We'll have lots of pictures. First, of our wedding, then our children and grandchildren," Dillon promised as his lips met hers. Raising his head, he said, "I'll always be there to catch you if you fall."

"Two are better than one," Isabel replied.

"Make that three," Dillon said, raising his gaze to the heavens. "A threefold cord is not quickly broken."

Isabel smiled. "Welcome home, prodigal son."

Epilogue

One year later

"Can you believe it's finally happening?"

Isabel turned from the window of the upstairs bedroom to smile at Susan Murdock. "It doesn't seem real, considering I've been in love with Dillon for half of my life, maybe all of my life. But, yes, on a perfect day like today, I can believe it's going to happen."

"You two really fought the odds, didn't you?"

"Yes, but we have more than good odds—we've been blessed, Susan. We all have."

Susan's smile disappeared as she fluffed the skirt of her floral print matron of honor dress. "I just wish Eli would change his mind and come to the wedding. Dillon really wanted him to be his best man."

Isabel looked back out the window, down on the new blooming field of wildflowers where in just a few minutes she would become Mrs. Dillon Murdock. "The day's young, Susan. He might show up yet.

He's come around on Dillon's new crop maintenance plan, and just about everything else we've thrown at him over the past year.''

Susan shook her head. Before she left the room, she said, ''Well, you're getting hitched, with or without my husband's blessings. And…you look so beautiful, Isabel.''

''Thank you.'' Isabel lifted her gaze to her reflection in the beveled mirror. The white linen sleeveless wedding dress was cool and simple, the full skirt falling out around her legs in yards and yards of frothy material that both her grandmother and Cynthia Murdock had worked to create. Her hat was simple, too. White straw with a tiny sprig of wildflowers tucked underneath the linen band. It sat at a jaunty angle over her long, loose curls. Touching a finger to the strand of pearls Dillon had given her, she decided she'd have to do. She didn't want to make a splash as a bride, she just wanted to be with Dillon.

And now that Wildwood was completely renovated and things were back in order, she would have that chance.

True to his word, Dillon had taken most of his savings, investments, and a loan against his business to pay the bank back for the debts owed on Wildwood. Eli had been furious at first, then resigned and humble. Since he no longer owned this part of the land, there was little he could do to protest the proceedings.

Isabel knew he was grateful, though, because he'd forgiven Susan right away. He truly loved his wife, and deep inside, he'd been glad that someone had found a way for him to save face and Wildwood at the same time. And Susan was learning how to handle her husband. She had him attending church each Sunday, granted with a scowl on his face. But Eli was changing. Isabel could tell.

And, this big old house was still in the family.

But it now belonged to the entire community. Dillon had turned the house into a museum. The entire first floor was open to the public each Monday through Saturday.

On the second floor, Cynthia Murdock and Martha Landry now shared twin suites—comfortable, elegant apartments with small kitchens and baths. Together, the two women had formed a partnership—they were the official curators of the Wildwood Foundation.

Martha had agreed to do it only as an *equal* partner. She'd take no more orders from a Murdock. Cynthia had agreed to do it only if both her sons would include her in all of their daily decisions regarding their holdings. She'd not be left in the dark ever again. Both women had been granted their stipulations.

Together, they'd worked to have the mansion registered as a historical landmark. They loved their work, and enjoyed getting paid equally for doing it. Together, they planned teas, showers, weddings and any and every other sort of gathering imaginable on the grounds and in the long, airy dining room located on one entire side of the bottom floor. By giving them this responsibility, Dillon had given them their spirit back. Those two would never be idle in their old age.

Cynthia now kept sharp tabs on both her sons, and kept the lawyers and bankers hopping as she called for updates on the now thriving cotton crop and the Wildwood Foundation.

Both Cynthia and Martha had worked hard to help

Dillon and Isabel renovate the house. While Dillon worked in Atlanta, and Isabel finished up her commitments in Savannah so she could join him there, the two women searched and researched everything it would take to get the house back to its original splendor.

And Isabel's childhood home...well...Isabel smiled and clasped her hands, tears of joy and love brimming over in her eyes. She'd come home one weekend, hoping to meet her future husband here for a few days of painting and scraping, only to find her wedding present waiting for her.

Dillon had completely renovated the shack she'd called home most of her life. It was now an official caretaker's cottage, complete with lacy white shutters and screened porches; white, shining walls and working bathrooms and sturdy floors; and beautiful antique furniture including his great-grandmother's beautiful rice bed which had been removed from the mansion and restored for his bride. No leaky roof, no dips and creaks, no bad memories.

"I told you I'd make it up to you," he'd explained as he'd held her in the cottage's garden. "This is our home, Issy. Yours and mine. We'll always have a place to come back to—we're the official caretakers of Wildwood."

And tonight, she'd be in his arms, there in their little house. Their home.

"Oh, Daddy," she said now as she looked up toward the heavens. "I never understood. I never knew about the sacrifices we have to make for those we love. But you did. And Dillon does, Daddy. He's a lot like you."

Just then a knock at the door brought her head around.

"Coming."

Isabel opened the door to find her grandmother standing before her in a mauve chiffon dress. "It's time, honey."

Grabbing her Bible, Isabel looked around. "Where's my bouquet?"

"Dillon has it."

"That's not traditional—I think I'm supposed to be the one who carries it."

"Dillon's not a traditional sort of man. He picked it fresh—wants to hand you your flowers the minute he sees you."

Touched, Isabel let out a lovesick sigh. "Have you ever known a sweeter, kinder man?"

"Oh, one or two," Martha said, her wink misty.

"Any sign of Eli?"

"No, but the Lord has brought us this far—He won't let us fall now."

They walked down the shining curved staircase, past the dining room where the small wedding cake sat in all of its white-and-yellow splendor, then out onto the front porch. The Wedding March began as Martha escorted her granddaughter down into the garden and onto the open path where the guests were seated just a few feet from the wildflower field. The wildflowers were spread out before Isabel like a wedding quilt, brilliant and dainty, delicate and strong, the perfect decoration for her wedding day.

Dillon stood there, his gray eyes bright with a bursting of emotions, his cream-colored summer suit crisp and dashing, his grin slanted and devastatingly charming. And in his hand, he held a fat bouquet of flowers, freshly picked just for her.

Martha chuckled as she gave Isabel over to him. "She's all yours, son."

"Thank you," he said, his eyes never leaving his bride. "I like the dress, Issy."

Isabel's words held a breathless quality. "You say that about all my dresses."

"But I especially like this one, sweetheart. You are the best-looking bride I've ever seen. And you're mine."

"You've got that right."

The ceremony progressed with the bride and groom completely absorbed in each other. Then the preacher got to the part that asked if anyone objected to this wedding.

"I do," came a bold, deep-throated voice from the back of the rows of white chairs.

A gasp went out over the crowd as Eli hurried up the path, wearing his own white linen suit. "I mean," he said in an even tone, his gaze moving from his wife's frozen expression to his surprised brother, "I object to this wedding taking place without me. I do believe I'm supposed to be the best man."

Dillon closed his eyes, clearly relieved. Then he turned to his brother and reached out a hand. "Thank you, Eli."

Eli accepted the handshake, his eyes brimming with pride and apology. "No, thank you, brother." Then, he began, "Dillon, I—"

"Don't," Dillon said in a soft voice. "We'll talk later, though. We've got a lot of catching up to do."

"Okay," Eli replied, bending his head sheepishly.

Then he turned to the confused preacher. "Well, what are you waiting for? I hear there's going to be a wedding at Wildwood today. Let's get things rolling."

"Amen," Cynthia Murdock said, her wide-brimmed pink hat bobbing in delight. Then she raised her camera and snapped a picture. Looking across at Martha, she wiped her eyes and said, "I just love weddings. Don't you?"

*   *   *   *   *

Dear Reader,

I grew up on a farm in south Georgia and lived in a house similar to the one described in Isabel's story. I couldn't wait to leave that house, but it has stayed with me all of these years. My memories are sometimes bittersweet, but I realize now that I loved my home and I often dream of my life there.

The story of the prodigal son has always fascinated me. Coming from a big Southern family, I've learned lots of lessons about forgiveness, but this parable teaches all of us that there is sometimes more to the story than what appears on the surface.

In this story, there were two prodigal sons. Dillon lost his way by running away, and Eli lost his way because he'd never learned true humility. Not only does the Bible teach us to forgive those we love, we also have to remember that as human beings, we are all God's children.

I'm glad Isabel and Dillon found each other again, and learned the lessons of forgiveness and acceptance. Hope you enjoyed their story.

Until the next time, may the angels watch over you while you sleep.

Lenora Worth

SILHOUETTE Romance®

From first love to forever, these love stories
are fairy tale romances for today's woman.

Silhouette® Desire®

Modern, passionate reads that are powerful and provocative.

Silhouette® SPECIAL EDITION™

Emotional, compelling stories that capture the intensity
of living, loving and creating a family in today's world.

Silhouette® INTIMATE MOMENTS™

A roller-coaster read that delivers romantic thrills
in a world of suspense, adventure and more.

ving room, continued to
andy and hugged her. "Mom, I just heard about
Philip's accident. I'm very sorry. How is he?"

"Not good."

"Where in the world was he going at that hour?"

Should she tell the girl? Why not? "He was returning from the coast," Andy said, "where he was
looking into a matter that concerns you."

"What matter?"

"Realm."

The chill reached Andy even before her daughter
dropped her hands and took a step back.

"What did Philip have to do with Realm?" the girl
asked, spitting out each word.

"There are things you don't know about the game,
Patty . . ."

Andy's voice trailed off as her daughter's jaw tightened and her gray eyes darkened.

"More than you'll ever know, Mother. . . ."

REALM SEVEN

REALM SE

Tony Chiu

BANTAM BOOKS

TORONTO • NEW YORK • LONDON • SYDNEY • AUCKLAN

To Bob Abel,
with thanks.

REALM SEVEN
A Bantam Book / August 1984

ISBN 0-553-23847-7

Published simultaneously in the United States and Canada

Bantam Books are published by Bantam Books, Inc. Its trademark, consisting of the words "Bantam Books" and the por-
trayal of a rooster, is Registered in U.S. Patent and Trademark
Office and in other countries. Marca Registrada. Bantam
Books, Inc. 666 Fifth Avenue, New York, New York 10103.

PRINTED IN THE UNITED STATES OF AMERICA
H   0 9 8 7 6 5 4 3 2 1

Book I
PROBE

One

The early March blizzard roared out of the north-
west on Wednesday. Though forecast, it had arrived a
full fourteen hours ahead of schedule, and even now,
on Saturday morning, the residents of Ann Arbor, Michigan, were still paying the price for unpreparedness.

Andrea Matteson sat behind the wheel of her
Honda Civic and surveyed the jammed traffic ahead of
her on slush-crimped State Street. She turned to her
daughter and asked, "Do you really need that book
today?"

Patty nodded. "Why?"

"I was thinking of making a U turn out of this mess
and going for some hot chocolate."

"Truly?" The teenager's face lit up for a second before falling again. "Mr. Feldkamp wants the report
Tuesday. But maybe if I hop out now and run ahead to
the store, we can still do it?"

Andy was about to reply when the cars ahead
began to move. She saw that the side street to her right
was clear, so she shifted into gear and turned down it.
The road conditions on central campus having discour-
aged most drivers, she was able to find a parking spot
near the Administration Building.

Mother and daughter began bundling up for the
cold.

Andy, at thirty-eight, was one of those women who
always seemed to others noticeably more attractive in
person than in photographs. Film, being two-dimen-
sional, could only record her offbeat features: an unusual face—high forehead, flaring cheekbones, incon-

3

gruously dainty chin—framed by straight, shoulder-length hair the color of aged oak; pellucid, deep-set gray eyes; a snub nose, and wide, full-lipped mouth. Yet in person, these same features informed by unmistakable intelligence, humor, and confidence, Andy was invariably the one on whom all eyes paused.

At first glance Patty, possessed also of a honeyed mane and gray eyes, seemed her mother's mirror image. Her nose, though, was not snubbed but patrician, like her father's. And she had definitely inherited Larry's strong chin.

When Andy and Patty stepped from the car, parkas zippered and scarves drawn across their lower faces, they could easily have been mistaken for sisters; the girl had just turned thirteen, but she'd already achieved a height that was approaching her mother's five-foot-eight.

They took the shortcut alongside Newberry Hall back to State Street. There, they saw coming toward them a wedge of University of Michigan football heroes. Thick-necked and bristling with machismo—on this subfreezing day they wore maize-and-blue letter jackets open over gray athletic department T-shirts, bermuda shorts, and jogging shoes sans socks—the young men reminded Andy of no less than the pampered cows from which Kobe beef is cleaved.

Knee-high mounds of snow had pinched the sidewalk to a lane and a half.

When the two groups neared each other, the jocks showed no sign of giving way. In fact, one of them, obviously the jester, leered at Andy and Patty and bellowed, "Well, fuckin'-A. Catch these foxes!"

Andy reflexively reached for her daughter's arm.

Another jock broke into a spastic dance: "Foxes! Let's get it on . . . hey, foxes, wanna party? We're just six wild and crazy guys!"

The rest of the group laughed immoderately.

Andy could sense Patty's commingled shame and exultation in the face of this crass attention. She could also sense her own anger coming to a head. Pulling the scarf down from over her mouth, she said, in as level a voice as she could muster, "Would you please let us by."

The jester guffawed lewdly. "Aw, come on, cupcake. All we want to do is make you two the sweethearts of Sigma Chi."

The chorus of "Right on"s and "You tell 'em, Denny"s was cut short by the unflinching gaze with which Andy riveted the jester.

Though this young man came in at six-four and two hundred and twenty-five pounds, he looked away nervously.

One of his mates whistled in amazement.

The jester forced himself to look back at Andy.

Her eyes still bore into his.

From the rear of the group now, a snicker. The jester flushed and then took a halting step back—right into a snowbank. Suddenly his arms were windmilling as he fought for balance, and then his free foot slipped on the treacherous sidewalk, and then he was toppling ass-first into the snow. As he spluttered violent obscenities and his buddies wiped tears of laughter from their eyes, Andy grabbed Patty and escorted her past.

When Andy felt herself calming down, she glanced at her daughter, curious about the girl's reaction. Patty's face remained half cloaked by the scarf, but her eyes were bright with excitement.

Follett's Bookstore was surprisingly crowded for a late Saturday afternoon. Patty headed straight for the paperback section.

"Hi, Andy."

Andy turned and recognized the mother of one of her daughter's friends. "Oh, hi, Jane."

"We haven't seen much of you this semester."

"I've just been buried," Andy said. "Sometimes I wonder what the hell could have been on my mind when I decided to finish my degree."

"Ginger said you did well the first semester."

Andy shrugged modestly. "By the way, where is Ginger? I want to say hi."

"Around here somewhere—oh. There, by the paperbacks."

Andy looked over—and frowned. Ginger and Patty were standing less than two feet apart, and yet they were studiously, and rather awkwardly, avoiding each other. Odd behavior, she thought, considering that Ginger had been her daughter's first friend in Ann Arbor.

". . . sometime soon," Jane was saying.

"I'm sorry, my mind was elsewhere. What did you say, Jane?"

"You and Patty must come over for dinner soon."

"For sure," Andy said. Then she spotted Patty making her way toward the cash register, so she excused herself.

On the way back to their car, Andy said, "What's going on between you and Ginger?"

"Nothing."

"I know 'nothing.' You didn't even say good-bye to her at the store. What's the matter?"

"Nothing, Mother. Okay?" Patty retorted.

Rather than press the point, Andy reminded herself that the girl was entering a most difficult age; that in addition to raging hormones and a dawning self-awareness of her own beauty, Patty had, lord knew, enough else to cope with. There had been the divorce. And then Andy's quitting of a challenging but ultimately dead-end job, as a senior associate with one of New York's premier corporate design firms, so that she could pursue the architectural degree she'd abandoned seventeen years earlier to the cause of matrimony. Hence, their move the previous summer from Manhattan to Ann Arbor. Patty's adjustment to the profoundly different tempos and values of heartland America hadn't been helped by a severe winter and its accompanying cabin fever.

The past several weeks, especially, had been hard. Yet mother and daughter had recently struck a quicksilver truce, and it would be best, Andy thought, to go out of her way to preserve it.

They reached the Honda and got in. As Andy started the car, she said, "Patty, I wasn't trying to nag."

"I know. Sorry I got so bitchy. Truly."

"Where shall we eat tonight?"

"Do we have enough money, Mom?"

Andy couldn't help but grin. "Yes, dear. Enough for dinner—and the movie I promised."

Patty's own smile widened.

The road to North Campus was, mercifully, lightly trafficked. Andy coasted across the bridge that spanned the river and swung into the complex. Though she spent most of her days up here, she held to her conviction that the starkly modern buildings were an abomination, that she would be happier taking her classes back on central campus.

The parking lot of the Art and Architecture Building was nearly deserted. Ironically, this structure, which had become Andy's second home, offended her aesthetic sensibilities the most: it was the epitome of "post-modern," which meant a squat, flat-roofed edifice that, instead of grace and humor, offered up acres of glass supported by files of concrete columns. Not that Andy considered herself a romantic in terms of architecture. But having lived and worked for fifteen years in the anonymous high-rises of Manhattan—and suffered modular floor plans, low ceilings, Sheetrock walls, and, in her offices, hermetically sealed windows—she had come to the conclusion that architects could no longer emphasize form over function.

This belief was one factor impelling her back into academia at an age when most adults had either found themselves or given up the search. But whether her viewpoint, which was heretical in a school that bowed low to Bauhaus, would survive the grading system remained to be seen.

Andy and Patty entered the Art and Architecture

Building and made their way through the silent corridors to the faculty offices. They stopped in front of a door bearing the nameplate Prof. Wesley Aldrich. Andy looked at the closed door and then at her watch. It was 5:27. Aldrich was never late, but then he was never early, either. She led her daughter over to a window, where they perched on the sill.

Two and a half minutes later, the door was opened by a tall, middle-aged man puffing on a pipe. In his free hand were a number of manila packets. Aldrich, seeing Andy, acknowledged her presence with a curt nod. Then he quickly began taping the packets to his door. When he was through, he ducked back into his office without a word; the door closed and the lock snicked home.

Patty saw her mother's lips tighten. Finally Andy stood. She walked to the door, found the packet marked with her name, and tugged it free.

Down the corridor two students, one male and one female, emerged from the elevator and started toward Aldrich's office.

Andy opened the packet. Inside were several sheets of balsa wood and a small tube, which she guessed held glue. Her attention, though, was fixed on the single sheet of paper within. She pulled it out and skimmed it. Because she knew that Aldrich was most likely hovering on the other side of the door, Andy stifled her groan.

"What is it, Mom?"

"Come on," Andy said, starting toward the elevator.

Patty, confused, was still trying to catch up when Andy neared her classmates.

"What's the news?" one of them asked.

"Grim."

Their faces sagged.

"What the hell's grim, Mom?"

"This project. I'm afraid my weekend stops here."

"But what about dinner and the movie tonight? You promised."

Andy shrugged lamely. She reached for Patty. The girl's body was stiff with disappointment.

Two

The room was desperately overheated, yet they sat, Andy and the six others, frozen in dreadful anticipation. They stared at the ceiling or the floor or out the large picture windows, but not at each other.

Part of it owed to Monday morning funk. More of it owed to the worktable at the front of the room on which stood seven structures, hopelessly spindly, and the brutish instruments by which they would be judged: calipers, an old-fashioned set of scales, and a can of Campbell's Tomato Soup.

The four men and three women were all master's candidates at the University of Michigan's College of Architecture and Urban Planning. Their considerable academic experiences, however, did little to lessen the stomach-churning panic induced by a complicated assignment that had to be crashed through in too short a time. Further, it had to pass the muster of a sarcastic martinet—Professor Wesley Aldrich, who taught their course, Materials in Building. Design Application.

This project's materials, which the students had collected from Aldrich's office door on Saturday, consisted of a half-dozen sheets of eight- by ten-inch balsa wood and a small tube of alaphetic rosin glue.

The design application, which had caused Andy to wince, was, simply put, a bitch. With only the supplies provided, each student was to design and build a structure that stood at least nineteen inches tall but weighed no more than one and a half ounces. Yet this structure—by necessity frail—had to be sturdy enough to support an unopened can of Campbell's soup, which weighed fourteen ounces.

It was a difficult stunt to pull off on forty hours' notice. Aldrich had chosen to load the dice even more by making the packets unavailable until five-thirty on Saturday. At that hour Ann Arbor's hobby shops, the only sources for replacement balsa sheets, had closed for the weekend.

Only the most confident of students would dare test his creation, for if it broke there would not be enough material to construct another; in fact, none of the seven sitting there that Monday morning had assumed that risk.

One of the women restlessly lit up a fresh cigarette from her old butt.

A radiator pipe rattled.

Andy sipped coffee from a container and let her fatigued mind wander. She had assumed that school would get easier once she rediscovered the academic rhythm. Yet, though no stranger to hard work, here she was in her second semester, feeling very vincible in general and very drained in particular by her weekend on Project Balsa. Would she be any perkier right now were she as young as most of her classmates?

One of the men in the room noticed the wall clock at the front of the class and began to fold his newspaper.

As if on cue, the rest of the students began snapping out of their reveries.

Andy swallowed the last of the coffee and wedged the container into her bookbag.

At fifteen seconds before nine, the woman who was smoking took one last drag before snuffing out her fresh cigarette.

So habitually prompt was their professor that all eyes turned to the door.

It remained closed.

*   *   *

The man who should have entered, Wesley Aldrich, was standing in a nearby stairwell, puffing idly on his meerschaum. In his early fifties, he had been on the Michigan faculty for sixteen years, since being passed over yet again for a partnership in a medium-sized Chicago architectural firm.

Aldrich no longer resented teaching. To be sure, the pay was less, but so was the pressure. He had even discovered a silver lining: within the arena of the classroom, he could act every bit the autocrat without fear of challenge.

When his pipe began to burn a trifle hot, Aldrich consulted his watch: 9:07. They should be good and nervous. He ruffled the hair that he'd taken to wearing long as soon as it had started to gray, then buttoned the tweed jacket that sat well on his lanky frame. Tapping the ashes from his pipe, he left the stairwell, and strode around the corner to his waiting students.

"Good morning, ladies and gentlemen."

The tense faces that greeted Aldrich made him feel good. As he sauntered toward the worktable, his eyes flicked from one balsa wood structure to the next. The fact that at least five would snap like kindling made him feel even better. He took his station behind the table and began to work fresh tobacco into his meerschaum. Without looking up he said, "Did we have a pleasant weekend?"

There were a few titters.

Aldrich packed the tobacco, lit a match, and drew noisily on the pipe. Then he peered through the smoke. "Come, come, our simple little exercise shouldn't have taken that much out of us. Or if it did, perhaps we should ask Mrs. Matteson her secret."

Andy felt herself coming under scrutiny and became suddenly self-conscious for having uncharacteristically worn makeup, nail polish, and a tailored flannel suit from Bergdorf Goodman. She also sensed in Aldrich the return of a hostility that had lain dormant for several weeks.

"Very fetching outfit, Mrs. Matteson," he continued. "A welcome change from our customary denim attire. . . . Are we pledging Tri-Delts today?"

When the class laughed, Andy flashed a wan grin.

As if tiring of the sport, Aldrich turned his attention to the seven structures before him. "Some of these look very fetching, too, not to mention ingenious. Shall we see which of them work?" He withdrew a pair of half-spectacles he didn't really need and began fiddling with the calipers. "What did we say the height ought to be this semester? Nineteen inches?" He slid the caliper's upper arm up a fraction. Next he zeroed the scales and opened a box of weights. "And the avoirdupois? Twenty grams?"

One of the students blurted, "No, sir, thirty grams."

Aldrich chuckled condescendingly. "Quite so, Mr. Gruson, quite so." He selected a tiny weight, made a production of inspecting its marking, and then placed it on one arm of the scale. The arm pivoted downward, bottoming with a sharp *clunk*. Aldrich smiled frostily.

Ignoring the five structures that he knew would break under the weight of the soup can, he regarded the pair that appeared the flimsiest, yet in fact stood a good chance of surviving. Both resembled miniature oil wells and consisted of spidery networks of interlaced X members.

The nearest bore the name tag Andrea Matteson. Aldrich's lips tightened around his pipe stem.

The other, by Chang Su-tung, seemed less well constructed. He picked it up. Chang had used a prodigious amount of glue on the lower joints, so much so that he must have run out, for the upper joints had been fastened with some other adhesive. From the milky shine, it looked like airplane glue—which was meant for plastic, not wood. Aldrich suppressed a smile. There was still a way to fix that Matteson bitch's wagon.

"Mr. Chang, our theory behind this design?"

"Uh, well sir, I calculated that the multiple X members would, uh, would allow the structure to displace downward stress through progressive flexing."

"Quite so."

Aldrich measured the structure, weighed it, and set the soup can atop it. Then he took his hand away.

As it should have, the structure sagged. As it shouldn't have, two of the upper joints, secured with an improper adhesive, separated; the can began tilting, more joints blew out, and then Chang's creation was crumpling.

Even as the soup can slammed onto the table, Aldrich sneaked a peek at Andy. She looked stricken. Finish her off now or let her sweat? Let her sweat.

Aldrich turned next to the most amusing of the failures. It consisted of three cylinders, each formed by a curled sheet of balsa, stacked in order of diminishing circumference. They look like goddamned hatboxes for Papa Bear, Mama Bear, and Baby Bear, he thought sourly as he measured and weighed the structure. Aldrich lifted the can atop the smallest cylinder; before removing his hand, though, he said, "Such an extravagant use of materials, Miss Dobie. Do we aspire to practice our calling in the Soviet Union?"

There were a few guffaws. Dobie blushed.

"Design overkill has its place, but we must be sure of our materials. Question: is the alaphetic rosin glue strong enough to keep our cylinders cylindrical? Question: does balsa wood, when curved and thus placed under stress, retain enough plasticity to support a significant downward force?"

Answers were not long in coming. Aldrich took his hand from around the can. The glue was strong enough, but not the wood. Under downward pressure the top sheet—the most tightly curled and, therefore, the most severely stressed—split along the length of the grain. Once asunder, the sheet uncurled and literally sprang sideways. The can seemed to hang in midair for a heartbeat; then it plummeted straight down, smashing through the centers of the remaining two cylinders before thwacking against the table.

Aldrich started to pick up a rather grossly constructed pyramid, then stopped. "Mrs. Matteson, having seen the fate of Mr. Chang's project of similar design, we must be in terrible suspense. Perhaps we should end that suspense?"

Andy sat up straighter.

As Aldrich turned to her structure, he scanned its joints. They looked disgustingly sound. Well, then, he'd just have to change the ground rules, wouldn't he?

In his own mind, his animus was well founded. It had been at a faculty tea the previous semester, Matteson's first on campus, that Aldrich had met her. How refreshing she had seemed, attractive and poised—unlike the shrew he was married to, unlike the other desiccated faculty wives, unlike the callow young bunnies all too willing to share his warren for a passing grade. And since she was divorced, surely she would come to see how much he could help her, both professionally and personally.

But the first time he'd asked her out, her daughter had some junior high function. The second time, it was a crash project for another course. The third time, she had told him—coldly and with unearned arrogance, he thought—that her agenda called for study, not men. Especially married men. The crowning insult had come when he learned that she had recently begun seeing another member of the faculty. Not even permanent faculty, mind you, but a visiting professor who was both entirely too slick for his own good and also at least five years her junior.

Yes, he decided, a little humiliation was in order.

Aldrich sized Andy's structure against the calipers and weighed it. Damn, but it was built well, certainly well enough to support the soup can. If, that is, he placed the can gently atop it. There was, however, a trick he could pull that should result in a pile of balsa toothpicks.

"Mrs. Matteson, have we any predictions about whether this construction will succeed where Mr. Chang's failed?"

Something in Aldrich's tone cued Andy; all those years in the New York business world had instilled in her an early-warning system that sounded whenever someone was about to jerk her around. Just as quickly, she realized that whatever his game, she was powerless to stop it. Andy made herself return his gaze: "For the sake of my grades, I can only hope so. Sir."

A couple of nervous chuckles; Aldrich's eyes narrowed imperceptibly.

The can was in his right hand. As he raised it, he snuggled his pinky below the bottom rim. This had the effect of raising the can a quarter-inch above the platform of Andy's structure; the momentum gained from even this slight height would make the can "weigh" much more than fourteen ounces at impact.

Aldrich straightened his pinky. And released.

The can struck with a soft but audible *thunk*.

Andy's tower quivered as the X members compressed, sponging up the shock—and, it seemed, all the attention in the room as well.

Except for Andy and Aldrich's.

Their eyes remained locked. Finally, when a smattering of applause broke out, Aldrich looked away and snatched the can of Campbell's Tomato Soup from Andy's still-standing balsa fortress.

Three

Mondays in general were so tough for Andy that she spent them entirely on campus, relying on her daughter to fix dinner.

This Monday in particular had proven brutal. The

high that she'd carried from Aldrich's class had lasted through lunch; that meal was taken with a partner of a local architectural firm, and hence the smart business suit that had been the butt of Aldrich's sarcasm. Although Andy's classes ended in less than nine weeks, she had been too harried to make plans for the summer. As a result of the lunch, she had another option—staying in Ann Arbor as an architectural apprentice. Andy reckoned she could easily double the proffered salary by returning to Manhattan and pinch-hitting at her old corporate design firm. As much as money mattered, though, and as much as returning East would please her daughter Patty, she already knew what her decision would be.

In mid-afternoon the strain of the interview, and of the around-the-clock weekend on Aldrich's assignment, finally caught up with a vengeance. By the time her last class broke, she felt as though elephants had been dancing on her retinas.

Andy paused in the lobby of the Art and Architecture Building. She had intended to do the grocery shopping preempted by Project Balsa. But peering out into the late winter dusk, she realized she didn't have the stomach for the supermarket—or, for that matter, the frozen casserole Patty should be sticking into the oven right about now.

She swung into a phone booth, dropped in a dime, and dialed.

No answer.

Anger flared like a flashbulb. The one day a week the girl was asked to show a little goddamned responsibility, and she was off doing—doing what? Just as suddenly, Andy was swept by remorse. She closed her eyes and leaned back against the booth. Fatigue was no excuse for being so ready to unilaterally shatter the quicksilver truce.

There was a gentle tap on the door of the booth. Elaine, a classmate from the just-concluded course, was standing there, a look of concern on her face. Andy pulled the door open.

"You okay?"

Andy nodded, then noticed that Elaine was holding a cigarette. "Would you have an extra one of those that I could bum? I'm kind of spaced out—four classes and a job interview, on top of a weekend balsaing for Aldrich."

Elaine clucked sympathetically, then dug into her purse and came up with a pack. "Did your thingamajig survive?"

Andy accepted a cigarette before flashing a wide grin.

Elaine laughed and returned the pack to her purse. Then she reached to the bottom of the bag, reemerging with a clenched hand. "Congratulations," she said, and opened her fist.

Andy looked at the joint. Her grin grew even wider. "Thanks," she said, stashing it in the pocket of her suit jacket.

Outside, a custom car horn—the kind that went *aahh-oouu-gah*—belched. Elaine sighed. "That's Charlie. Only a yo-yo would buy a horn like that, right? And only a yo-yo that glowed in the dark would put a horn like that on a Ferrari, right? Well, got to run. . . ."

Andy left the booth feeling buoyed. Patty had done yeomanlike service during the brutal weekend just passed, and what better time to start returning the favor than tonight? She fished out matches, lit her cigarette, and inhaled with pleasure. If her daughter wasn't home yet, then the casserole wasn't started yet, either. Andy would do her shopping, and the two of them would go out for dinner. She buttoned her coat and plunged into the chilly night.

It was almost seven-thirty when she swung the Honda into the driveway of the two-family house out beyond the stadium. Andy glanced automatically up to

her apartment on the second floor. In disbelief, she saw
that all the windows were dark.

Upstairs, her morning note to Patty still lay on the
kitchen table. Andy's resolve to be more understanding
toward her daughter started to disintegrate; by the
time she had collected the day's mail and carried the
groceries upstairs, it had all but disappeared. In fact, she
worked herself into such a state that she dropped not
one, but two eggs as she transferred them to the refrigerator door.

Seven forty-five. She had better start calling
around. But to whom—Ginger's parents? Sally's? Neither girl had been around much since—since early January. Then who was Patty hanging around with now?

Andy began to shake. Had she been so intent on
holding the perimeters of her own chaotic life, so obsessed with remastering the academic grind, that she
was losing touch with her daughter?

She unpocketed the joint and studied it. No, it
wasn't what she needed or wanted at this moment. She
tossed it on the kitchen table and went to the liquor cabinet. The bottles, purchased the previous fall, were
dusty. Andy's hand hovered over the sherry before pulling out the scotch. She poured a double and carried the
drink and the mail into the living room.

Andy turned on a pair of lights. Tonight the bulbs
seemed all to be of twenty-five watts, so she turned on
two more. To cheer herself she punched up a cassette
of Galway playing Vivaldi.

As the clean notes of the flute chased away the silence, she slumped into an armchair. It, like the rest of
the furniture that came with the apartment, was cheap
but durable and student-proof: fake maple-and-calico
Americana seating from Sears Roebuck, coffee and end
tables laminated to withstand molten lava, lamps from
K-mart. Her former husband, Larry, had offered Andy
their furniture. She had declined, unwilling to drag in-
animate pieces of the past to first Ann Arbor and then
who knew where? Thus, the apartment fairly shouted

the transitory nature of its tenants, and she had done little to silence it outside of redecorating the two bedrooms, hanging her own collection of lithographs in place of the standard-issue, framed Woolworth seascapes, and installing a drafting table in a corner of the living room.

The scotch seemed to rush through the lining of her empty stomach and into the bloodstream, anesthetizing, tranquilizing.

She leafed through the day's mail. Bill, bill, charity solicitation, advertisement, bill. And a letter from Patty's school.

It was the principal writing to say that her daughter's performance was growing perplexingly erratic. In several courses that demanded concentration, such as math, she was doing fine. But in two others, English and social studies, she was not preparing her lessons and was inattentive in class. In fact, Patty was in danger of flunking both.

Anxiety and doubt engulfed Andy like a wave. The previous semester she had kept her daughter on a relatively short leash; the girl responded with three As and two B-pluses, super work considering the emotional turmoil of adjusting to a new town. This semester, as Andy's own workload grew, she'd relaxed her supervision of Patty.

With dire results, apparently.

Suddenly Andy longed for a hug. Second choice was a friendly voice. She stared at the phone but settled for another sip of scotch.

Of course she should call Larry, who as Patty's father had the right to know about her progress—or lack of it. But she knew she wouldn't, at least not that night.

Larry was a journalist who, at forty-one, was already the third-in-command of a newsmagazine. In a trade notorious for its obsessive and arrogant practitioners, he had risen so rapidly because he could back up his self-confidence with talent, charm, and what seemed to be an encyclopedia implanted in his brain.

On five seconds' notice Larry could ad lib a brilliant five-minute discourse on Reaganomics or Mideast political currents; on the fossils of Olduvai Gorge or the discoveries of Voyager II; on Bach or Boy George. What Andy needed least at this moment was his five minutes on child rearing—especially if what he said happened to be right.

Why had she married him? More important, why had the last of the tenuous filaments that bind any two adults together snapped, after so many years?

Which led Andy to consider calling the only adult to whom she currently had an emotional lifeline rigged. Where would Philip Hunt be at this hour? In his office or at the biochemistry lab; she smiled ruefully as she recognized her predilection for brainy, driven men.

They had met shortly before the intersession break. Andy most definitely had not been looking for someone. Even if she were, she would not have been able to conceive a more unlikely candidate. At thirty-two, Philip was six years her junior, and his field, biochemistry, was one that she had always associated with white lab coats and wristwatches that doubled as calculators.

Several coffee dates later, though, Andy had to admit that her liberal-arts prejudice against scientists was ill-founded: like Larry, Philip had a stunning breadth of knowledge, which, unlike Larry, he rarely showed off. Yet the major reason that, shortly after classes recommenced, Andy had taken Philip as her first steady lover since the divorce was that their liaison seemed by definition finite. Philip was in Ann Arbor on a visiting professorship and would soon have to decide whether to continue his research in academia or on the payroll of one of the large pharmaceutical companies bidding for his services.

Andy remembered Larry telling her, some years ago, about a famous movie actress who referred to her string of on-location lovers as "bed warmers." Philip was much more than that—but far less than a surrogate father. Of course if she wanted to talk about Patty, he would listen attentively and offer sympathy and perhaps even constructive ideas. Yet she knew that this was not the time to make those demands.

No, she would solve this one herself. Andy took another sip of scotch and felt a strange emotion coming unbottled, a mixture of pride and wistfulness. She had been the one tough enough to pronounce her marriage beyond retrieval. She had been the one tough enough to quit a job that had its moments, though not nearly enough of them, in favor of returning to school. But what would the replacement realities be? What had she turned three lives inside-out to pursue—personal fulfillment? And how much heavier would the price grow?

Andy glanced at her watch. It was past eight-fifteen. Had Patty ever been this late before? Yes, she realized with a start, the girl had come home even later two Mondays ago. And beginning—when was it, late January?—her daughter had taken to straggling back just in time for dinner once, and then several nights, a week. Andy had chalked all of this, as well as Patty's long hours on the telephone, to a fuller social life.

It was time to reevaluate. Where the hell was the girl? Andy thought of making some calls, or at least fixing herself something to eat. But the flute music was so soothing. . . . Why was she suddenly so weary? Stress, and the damned drink. Andy blinked her eyes and tried to stifle a yawn.

The key in the lock woke her.

"Patty?" The voice, thick with sleep, emerged as a croak. "Patty?"

"Yes, Mom."

Andy's system seemed filled with a fluid far more viscous than blood as she struggled up out of the armchair and headed toward the vestibule.

Patty was hanging up her parka. The girl's ensemble—turtleneck, jumper, and knee socks—accentuated coltish legs that augured more growth to come. She turned. Her cheeks were flushed from the cold—or was it guilt?

"Well?"

Patty met her mother's gaze and held it. A bad sign; like Larry, the girl grew defiantly quiet when there was something to hide.

"I asked you a question. Do you know what time it is?"

"Late."

"Damn straight it's late, young lady, it's—it's nine forty-five!"

"I tried to call—"

"Like hell."

"Mother!" Patty's mouth opened again, but she held the retort that was brewing and stalked into the kitchen.

"Don't you walk away from me," Andy said, following her in, the last of her goodwill gone.

Patty wheeled. "I was studying. Truly. I tried to call, but you weren't home. And then I tried again, and then Rolf's parents asked me to stay for dinner, and then we had this one last section to go over, and here I am! I tried to call, Mom."

Andy stared at her daughter for five seconds before saying, "That's not good enough. I got a letter today from Mr. Strick. It was about your grades—"

"I can explain," Patty interrupted.

"—and until you improve them, you're grounded."

Patty's jaw dropped. Tears started to well, but she fought them back.

"That means home before six on weekdays and no parties on weekends."

"But, Mom," Patty said plaintively, "this weekend's the overnight ski trip!"

Andy wavered. It was an outing run by one of the junior high's extracurricular clubs. "Okay, but that's the one exception until I hear from Mr. Strick that your grades are better."

As the message sunk in, the self-pitying look on

Patty's face dissolved. "You don't believe me! Here, call the Schmidts, they'll tell you where I spent the afternoon."

Andy started to turn away.

"You're the one who's never home!" Patty shouted accusingly. "Like tonight . . ." Her voice trailed off as she spotted the joint lying on the kitchen table. She picked it up and darted around to intercept her mother. "Where were you tonight," she said sarcastically, brandishing the joint, "out scoring with dear Philip?"

The right hand that slapped, hard, against Patty's cheek stunned both mother and daughter.

Patty's lower lip began to tremble.

Andy knew that she had until the next heartbeat either to console the girl or walk away. Patty didn't avoid the hug— nor did she return it with a lot of enthusiasm.

"That was unfair, Patty."

The girl dropped her head and nodded.

"I—I know this hasn't been a fun year. I'm sorry. But we've both got to keep pushing so that it'll get better." Andy began to steer Patty toward the living room. "You did so well last semester, and you know both your father and I are proud of you. What's been happening?"

"Mr. Strick's letter's a bum rap, Mom."

"Oh?"

"Truly. Miss Jordan, the English teacher, she's had some kind of nervous breakdown, and there's this real assh—there's this real jerky substitute who's had the class for more than a month now, and no one can stand him. You can check it out."

"Is the same substitute also teaching social studies?"

Patty turned and looked Andy in the eye. "No, that one's my fault. I got bent out of shape by a project he assigned. As a matter of fact, the boy I was studying with tonight, Rolf, he's from that class."

Andy nodded, even though the built-in Geiger counter that all parents possess was registering way off scale. Patty was lying. But about what—her problem with the teacher? This boy Rolf? Or how she spent the after-school hours with him?

Four

On Thursday afternoon, at an hour when she should have been hiking homeward, Patty Matteson stood in a phone booth on a corner in downtown Ann Arbor. For the last ten minutes she'd held the handset to her ear even though the line was dead, thanks to the cardboard shim she'd inserted to keep the plunger in the down position.

The girl fidgeted less from the cold than from nerves. If she wasn't inside the apartment in twenty minutes, there would be a replay of Monday's argument with her mother.

But she couldn't leave until the call came. And she couldn't even phone home with some excuse because this line had to be kept free. Standard operating procedure dictated that if the caller got a busy signal, he would switch to a fallback number; this in turn meant she would have to proceed to another booth and begin her vigil anew.

Patty's toes were getting stiff, so she wiggled them. She tried to focus on the call that would come soon. But her mind began wandering again, and soon she had resumed her brooding.

She had seen the Monday showdown coming and had had plenty of time to steel herself for it. Instead, she had blown it; she had lashed out at her mother and hurt her, for no purpose.

But there was no way to explain what was going on without hurting her mother even more. At stake was trust—trust that the girl knew what she was doing.

Patty couldn't expect it from her mother, or from any other grown-up. They just wouldn't understand.

A sharp rap on the glass door of the booth. Patty glanced up to see a middle-aged man gesturing toward the phone; she bit her lip, shook her head, and began chattering into the dead line. The man glared at her, then moved away.

Patty was mortified by her discourteousness. She would never have had the nerve to do that before—before the day her childhood ended.

Events, words, moods, textures, all these were frozen in her memory, like facets of a mental Rubik's Cube, a puzzle to be worried at and explored—but never solved.

A Saturday in May of her eleventh year; her parents oddly at peace; the ritual of accompanying her dad to their special place, a Village coffee house where he would drink bitter double espressos while she would indulge in a wickedly delicious chocolate rum cake; and then the unexpected monologue, delivered with casual intensity, about why mom and dad weren't getting along ("Maybe you'll understand it better as you grow older") and the announcement that he was moving to another apartment ("It's just a few minutes away, you'll have your own keys, and you can come by as often as you want"). The following day her mother had taken Patty to visit friends in the country. When they got home after dinner, her dad and all his belongings were gone.

Patty's childhood had ended, but not her world. Like all only children she was naturally reserved. She was also unusually suspicious of those who seemed attracted to her because of her looks and thus was slow to commit to friendships. Yet to fill the inexplicable vacuum in her life, Patty had begun hanging out for the sake of hanging out those last eighteen months in New York and the first half-year in Ann Arbor.

And then had come the reprieve from the banality

of sweet simps who nattered about such concerns as rock stars, trendy clothes, and their first periods.

During her first semester at the new junior high, she had gradually become aware of a small clique that kept tantalizingly to itself. Shortly after New Year's one of them, Rolf, had approached her. As she listened, Patty's initial skepticism dissolved. They were interested in her *mind*, a realization that had made her heart soar.

Of course, there were initiation rites to pass. These were tough. They might also seem to outsiders—especially grown-ups—irresponsible and reckless, but Patty knew two things: that she could distinguish between right and wrong and that never before had she felt so alive.

Even now, standing in the numbing cold, waiting, sure beat watching a *Laverne and Shirley* rerun.

The dusk deepened. The girl moved about the booth restlessly, beginning to feel naked under the ceiling light.

Out of the corner of her eye, Patty noticed a patrol car braking to a stop at the corner. She sensed one of the cops looking her way. They were nosier here than in New York, especially about kids out once it started to get dark; it was a good thing she was tall for her age. Once more Patty began talking into the dead line.

The traffic signal finally changed, and the patrol car eased into gear.

How soon before it cruised by again? And would she still be standing in the booth? Patty looked at the telephone and willed it to ring.

Much to her astonishment, it did.

Once.

She clamped the handset between ear and shoulder and pulled back the left sleeve of her parka so she could see her watch. Concentrating on the sweep-second hand, she began to count.

The phone rang again when she reached twenty-two. Patty reached up and removed the cardboard shim; the plunger sprang up, and the connection was established.

A youthful male voice asked, "What time is it?"

Patty calculated quickly: double the time elapsed between calls was forty-four, and because today's date was an even number, the forty-four should be *added* to the correct time. She said, "It's six twenty-six."

"How can I help you?"

"Is it arranged?"

"Yeah," he replied nonchalantly.

"Quantity?"

"As much as you want. The rates we discussed are acceptable."

Patty suppressed a sigh of relief and said, "Good work."

"Look, are you really going to go through with it?"

"Yes. And jewelry is still acceptable, right?"

"Right."

"Okay, then when's it on for?"

"What's the rush?"

"No rush."

He laughed.

"Listen, creep," Patty said, "you think you're the only game in town?"

"Like hey, I was only joking, okay?"

Patty noted the defensiveness and decided to measure his insecurity.

After ten seconds of silence he surrendered. "How's Sunday?"

"No good," she said, remembering her ski trip.

"Tuesday, then."

"Where?"

"The A & P out on Packard. Near the yogurt. Three-thirty."

"Standard rendezvous rules?"

He sighed. "Of course. But I'll be there way before three-forty."

"Likewise." Patty broke the connection, drew a few deep breaths to calm herself, and then called home.

"Hi, Mom. I'm leaving the library right now. Can I pick up anything on the way home? Butter? Okay. See you soon." She had managed to placate her mother, and by 4:00 P.M. on Tuesday she'd be solid with Conchis. All in all, not a bad afternoon, she thought as she stepped from the booth.

Five

That Saturday Andy and Patty were stowing the girl's overnight gear in the back of the Honda when the phone rang upstairs.

"I got it, Mom," Patty said as she bolted for the door.

A minute later, she was hoisting open a window. "It's for you," she called, a sour expression on her face. "Philip."

"Tell him we're running late and that I'll call him later."

Patty slammed the window shut a bit emphatically for Andy's taste.

The car was idling by the time the girl returned downstairs. She swung into the passenger seat and said, "Philip has to go to Detroit this morning, so he asked me to give you a message."

Andy glanced over.

"He'll be by at six-thirty. But you don't have to cook him dinner, he's taking you out tonight. Lucky you."

Andy started to say something. Instead, she rammed the car into reverse and popped the clutch; the squeal of tires startled her daughter.

When they pulled up in front of the junior high school, the chartered bus was already loading. The teachers chaperoning the expedition came over to introduce themselves and to help with Patty's bag. By the time Andy was ready to leave, Patty was deep in conversation with a lanky, blond teenage boy.

As she approached them, they both looked up.

"Mom, I don't think you've met Rolf. Rolf, my mother."

"Nice to meet you, Mrs. Matteson."

He was tall, one of the few boys Patty's age who was also her height. There was a light growth of wispy blond stubble on Rolf's chin, but he was otherwise impeccably groomed in a style she thought of as post-preppy.

"Rolf's the one who's helping me with my social studies," Patty said.

"That's very kind of you, Rolf."

He flashed a wide and appealing grin. "It's a two way street. I'm a spastic when it comes to numbers, so I'm making her help me with my math."

Just then the bus engine kicked over.

"See you tomorrow night, Mom," Patty said, giving Andy a hug.

"Good-bye, Mrs. Matteson," Rolf added as he followed her aboard.

Andy walked back to the car. What was it about Rolf that didn't sit quite right? Perhaps he was too clean-cut—but then she was unfairly remembering her own junior high days, during an era when scruffiness was a welcome antidote to conformity. Perhaps he was too mannerly—but then she was unfairly remembering all those courteous youngsters who used their sharpshooting merit badges to gun down bystanders and even politicians. No, she was showing her age and her New York provincialism. Patty should always bring home young men this presentable.

Andy was firing the Honda into life when she finally hit upon what was bothering her. Rolf's eyes—were they always so watery and distant, or was it just the cold?

*   *   *

At 6:00 P.M. the alarm clock that Andy used to ration her short supply of time rang. She shut her textbook on the tensile strengths of various construction materials and stretched. Looking at the tome, Andy shook her head. Perhaps she should make her fortune writing textbooks that could be comprehended by mere Ph.D.'s.

She was at the refrigerator pouring herself a white wine when she decided to ice a martini for Philip.

The vodka wasn't in the front row of the liquor cabinet. Had it been that long since he'd been over? Quite possibly; the one ground rule she'd established at the beginning of their relationship was that she would not entertain him overnight when Patty was home.

Andy frowned. For several months her daughter had averaged a sleepover a week. But lately, even before her grounding, Patty hadn't been staying over with friends much. Why had those invitations stopped? Screw it, she shrugged, too bushed to worry about her daughter tonight.

Andy found the vodka at the back of the cabinet. When she pulled it out, she stared at the bottle in disbelief; it was half empty. She had bought it the night Philip was last over, and he was the only one who drank vodka. Patty? Or was it one of her friends?

She fretted about it all through her shower, and it was still on her mind when Philip arrived.

He was, physically, a man of seeming paradoxes. His narrow face, dominated by thick brows over piercing brown eyes, and his wiry body, that of a runner's though he didn't run, gave him an aura of great angular intensity. Yet Andy had come to think of Philip as anything but hard. She approved of the way he wore his dark, curly hair shaggy; she approved of his casual attire—denims never bearing a designer's label and never pressed, for instance—and most of all, she approved of the quick, lopsided grin that he flashed often.

As soon as Philip stepped into the apartment, he reached down and folded her into an embrace.

She returned it distractedly.

"Andy?"

"Hmmm? Oh. I, uh, my head's somewhere else. I'm sorry." She gave him a peck and headed for the freezer to get his drink. On returning, she noticed that under his coat Philip wore a suit. "Uh-oh, we're going someplace fancy tonight."

"Didn't Patty tell you? A faculty sherry blast, but only for a few minutes. My old doctoral adviser popped into town to do some recruiting, and I haven't seen him in, oh, four years."

"I'd better change into something dressier."

"Nonsense. You look fine. In fact, more than fine."

Andy laughed. "Flattery will get you everywhere."

He held open his arms again, and she slipped between them.

"Hey," he said softly, "is everything okay? Patty sounded a little weird this morning."

She kept her head pressed to his chest, savoring the contact and the warmth. "We've been in some heavy traffic for about a week. But things'll work themselves out." Then she leaned back and looked up at him. "You're very sweet to ask. Are you always so sweet?"

"That's what all my women tell me," he said, smirking.

When they arrived at the reception, the guest of honor was already surrounded three-deep by well-wishers and supplicants.

Philip handed Andy a sherry, took a sip of his own, and winced. "Brother Timothy must have aged this batch in his lower intestines."

"They save the good stuff for us liberal arts types," she said.

"Well, my dear, how does that explain me?"

"I'm slumming."

Philip laughed. Then he hailed one of the waitresses circulating with drink trays. Was any other beverage being served? She shook her head, so he said to Andy, "Let's go pay my respects and then get out of here."

As they circled the periphery of the clot around the guest of honor, Andy studied him. He was a dapper, robust man in his late forties.

"His name's Merle Vaughan," Philip said. "You wouldn't know it to look at him now, but he's a brilliant theoretician who might well have been on the verge of a major breakthrough in viral research."

"What happened?" Andy asked, surprised at the strange tone in Philip's voice.

"Mammon. He let himself be coopted by what's known as 'the private sector.' "

Just at that instant, Vaughan spotted his former protégé. "Philip! You live! Come come, my boy, don't be bashful, I shan't rescind your doctorate."

Philip blushed, took Andy's hand, and pressed through the bodies toward Vaughan. The two men traded bear hugs.

"Andy, Merle Vaughan. Merle, Andy Matteson."

"My pleasure, Mrs. Matteson."

"Please call me Andy."

"Young lady, I should call you a fool for spending time with this lout," Vaughan said. "The dear boy is very sweet, but his prospects are most dim. What a life it must be, wandering from campus to campus, shoving a mendicant's bowl in front of foundations near and far. Philip, I hear there's a group in North Dakota that will grant a stipend to any biochemist willing to study the incidence of venereal disease among sheep."

Philip laughed. "Ah, yes, North Dakota—where men are men and sheep are nervous." He turned to Andy. "I think this is a prelude to a recruiting pitch. Merle works for SOTA, a bunch of—"

"A bunch of dedicated scientists committed to improving the lot of common man through genetic research, and you should join us, my boy."

"—a bunch of white coats who live for science but who die for the old Dow Jones. Right?"

Vaughan shrugged modestly; he was enjoying himself hugely.

"SOTA's one of those research boutiques," Philip explained. "Wall Street developed a crush on them in the late seventies—Cetus, Genentech, Biogen. SOTA's the trendiest of them all. In some circles they're known as the Calvin Klein of genes."

Vaughan roared with glee. "Penury sharpens your wit, my boy."

Philip regarded him with mock wariness. "Every time this man brings up my financial status, he follows up with an offer. What bonus are you offering these days?"

"For top-notch scientists, a choice of a condominium or a Saab Turbo. For you"—Vaughan fingered Philip's lapel like a tailor—"for you, maybe something in a worsted."

Philip patted Vaughan's cheek affectionately. "We have to run. Join us later for dinner?"

"I'm afraid not, my boy," he said ruefully. "The chairman of your department has graciously invited me to break bread with him."

"Tomorrow?"

Vaughan brightened. "No, I'll be on the ten o'clock flight to Pittsburgh to have lunch with the top student at Carnegie, and then on to Columbia, MIT, and Harvard."

"Cradle robber," Philip said with mock disdain.

"Dreadful, aren't I? But we're a progressive company, and we do consider elderly candidates. Why don't I send you tickets to visit me on the Coast?"

Philip pretended to consider the offer. "Sure. But route it through San Francisco. There's a visiting chair at Stanford that's still vacant."

"Dreamer."

"Sellout."

The two men hugged again.

By the time Philip and Andy reached the door, Vaughan was again besieged by scientists angling for the chance that Philip had spurned.

Andy's gasps quickened.

Philip coyly slowed his tempo.

She intensified her grip and raised her hips hard against his, and his movements lost their coyness. Bodies rocked in exquisitely timed counter-thrusts, each seemingly deeper and wider; ears sang with the rhythmic flow of coursing blood; minds grappled with sensations that were at once more concentrated and more diffuse, duller and more vivid.

She felt the spasm pass through him, heard his muffled cry, and then she was calling his name and shuddering with gratification and relief and fighting back the mists that swam up to envelop her.

Philip was still panting when he craned his neck downward to allow his mouth to seek out her thickened and feverish nipples. At the touch of his moist tongue, her breath caught; little after-tremors surged through her body. He was like a kitten, licking gently at her breasts and then up the side of her neck. Finally his mouth found hers.

"Mmmmmmmmm." Andy kissed back deeply but softly, greed having given way to languorous contentment.

Finally Philip started to shift his weight off her.

"No, no," she whispered, placing a staying hand across his buttocks. "Please. Just a little longer."

He readjusted his balance and buried his face in her hair.

After a while, she murmured, "You were in a rare mood tonight."

"At the reception?"

She nodded.

"Merle and I go back a long way."

"It was nice to see. You've rarely seemed so—so lighthearted in public."

"That's the price we men pay for chastity."

Andy laughed. "We women, too."

Philip pushed up on his elbows and began rotating his pelvis in almost imperceptible circles. Seeing Andy's face draw tight, he whispered, "Chastity's a bitch, isn't it?"

Suddenly she reached up and clung to him with ferocious intensity. But when she released him, she turned her head away.

Philip disengaged himself and placed a hand lightly on her cheek. "What is it, Andy?"

She shook her head.

"Come on, something's been bothering you all night."

Andy hesitated. All these months she had shielded her frustrations from Philip; why lay them on him now?

As if reading her mind, he said, "You know what happens to brave little soldiers? They get their asses blown off."

"People shouldn't bring their problems to bed."

"People shouldn't go to bed with people they can't bring their problems to."

Andy looked away again. "I don't think I'm being fair to you, or to myself."

"Bullshit. I've got no complaints, and you're handling yourself just fine."

"No, I'm not!"

Andy's vehemence startled Philip, but he continued stroking her cheek.

After a few moments, she snuggled closer. After a few moments more she said, in a low voice, "Ever since I left Larry, I've been going through life like a bulldozer. What for? Oh, I'll get my degree, but my courses are all looney tunes—they're not preparing me one damn bit for real-life architecture."

He considered his reply. "True, but you've always known that. What's really the matter?"

Andy blinked her eyes rapidly but couldn't suppress a snuffle. Finally she said, "Patty. She's moody and irresponsible, her schoolwork's going to hell, she's testing me at every turn. The worst of it is, I didn't really notice until this past week."

When Philip didn't react, she reached over and touched his face.

He cleared his throat. "This is kind of hard for me to say, but is Patty's behavior all that unusual for a girl her age?"

Andy thought back over what she had just said and realized how normal her daughter sounded. But there was so much more; should she tell him? If not Philip, who? "Perhaps it's all relative to last semester," she said, "when Patty seemed to adjust so well. She made some friends who were nice. Dull, but nice. She doesn't seem to see them anymore. I think I can understand it—she's a city girl, and kids who grow up on the streets, those who are smart, they like to live close to the edge. Only I don't know exactly what that means in Ann Arbor, and it scares me. Today I found—I found about half a bottle of vodka gone."

"But you let her have wine and beer at the table," Philip observed. "I can't claim to know her well, but Patty doesn't strike me as the kind to haul off and get blasted for kicks."

Andy nodded morosely. "But something's going on. Her hours have become irregular. And I got a note that said she's in danger of flunking two courses. *Two*. The girl's never gotten below a B in her life."

"Like my two cents' worth?"

Andy's eyes traveled down the length of their naked bodies, which were still silky with sweat; she was both touched and amused by the formality of Philip's question. Giving out a tired laugh, she replied, "Yes, my dear, I would."

"I think Patty's unhappiness involves a guy. And I have two suspects. Didn't you mention some boy named Rolf over dinner? Couldn't it be a case of puppy love?"

Andy mulled this over for a moment. "Your second suspect?"

"Yours truly."

"You?"

"Sure. Hey, look, Andy, you can't get much more discreet than us. But Patty sees me over here, she knows we talk a lot on the phone, she's old enough to figure out that we might be going to bed together. The question she must be asking herself is, 'Is this turkey going to become my mom's new husband?' Not to mention the fact that she might see every minute you spend with me as another minute you're not spending with her."

Andy closed her eyes. Her lower lip began to tremble. Then she buried her face in his chest and said, "It's not fair." He remained silent, so she continued, "Don't you see the bind I'm in? I'm not giving her enough, not nearly enough, because I have to charge so damned hard at my own private windmill. But if I don't, I'll screw up, and then what's it all been for? Oh, shit, it's a no-win game."

He gently hooked a finger beneath her chin and tilted her face up. A tear was slanting across her cheek. He wiped it away. When she finally opened her eyes, Philip knitted his brow and said sternly, "You're right—you're a bad mommy."

"Oh, you!" Andy rolled on top of him, then dissolved into a fit of giggling, which she stopped by smothering him with a long, probing kiss.

Slowly, he began to stiffen.

Later, drained and savoring a most comforting ache in her loins and thighs, she was in the twilight zone when images of the reception they had attended earlier in the evening flitted through her mind. Andy knew she was repeating herself, but she murmured, "You certainly were in a rare mood tonight." She lifted heavy lids and looked at Philip. His eyes were closed, his face calm in repose, and his breathing regular. She smiled dreamily and curled tighter against him. The damp spots had cooled, but she didn't mind, not tonight. Perhaps she had been selling their relationship short; perhaps there was life for them after Ann Arbor. Again an image of the reception, of Philip and Merle Vaughan, and then Andy remembered a question she had meant to ask about Vaughan. Was it important enough to wake Philip? Before she could decide, she had joined him in sleep.

Six

On the following afternoon the alarm clock went off as she worked through a problem in structural engineering. She absently reached over to punch it off, then finished writing a tentative solution.

Andy looked at the clock—4:08—and scowled. She had less than two hours to start dinner and clean the apartment. And, of course, she was behind in her work, in part because Philip hadn't left until after brunch—not that she regretted the morning.

As she began rinsing the chicken, she found herself wondering, once again, whether she had been too quick to dismiss their romance as one of mutual convenience. How did he feel about it? The previous night Philip had mentioned, rather offhandedly she thought, that his department head was making noises about extending the visiting professorship. Should she phone the architectural firm that she interviewed and accept their offer? How would Patty feel about spending the summer in Ann Arbor—especially if Philip was around? How would Larry feel about taking Patty for a month? Why was life so fucking difficult?

Andy sighed and packed the chicken and the peeled vegetables into a roasting pan.

Then she went to the hall closet for the vacuum cleaner.

Out of habit, she started with Patty's room. Among other bad traits, she noted disapprovingly, her daughter had grown sloppy in recent months. Andy sorted quickly through the piles of clothes and straightened the books and record albums. Then she started to make the bed.

As Andy tucked the sheets between mattress and box springs, her fingers jammed against something. Curious, she lifted one edge of the mattress and pulled out a dark brown object.

It was a diary. Funny, she hadn't known that Patty was keeping one. The volume was bulky and bound in imitation leather. In an inset along the spine, the girl had written "January to   ." That meant she'd started it about the time her behavior and attitude had begun to change. The lock looked flimsy. Andy turned the diary on end: judging by the way the pages at the front of the book were crinkled, Patty had been writing a lot. She reexamined the lock. It was indeed flimsy; what did they use in the movies, a hairpin?

Andy's heart was beating too loudly.

She pursed her lips. Suspicion versus trust, the need to know versus privacy, hypocrisy versus honor, parent versus child—her head spun with conflicts that defy easy answer. All the while, the diary grew heavier and heavier in her hand. No, she finally told herself, Patty must be presumed innocent until she proved herself guilty. Andy pointedly ignored the follow-up question—guilty of what?—and snapped out of her reverie. She started to lay the volume on the desk, then realized her daughter obviously wanted its existence kept a secret. Andy lifted the mattress again and slid it all the way to the center of the bed.

By the time she finished cleaning the apartment, she had just about convinced herself that she had behaved properly.

Why then the double scotch?

Seven

The A & P on Packard was less than a mile from Patty's school.

The girl had planned to be casual about it, to walk slowly and arrive at 3:30 sharp. Anxiety, though, has a way of quickening the pace; when she got to the parking lot, it was only 3:12. Patty looked around for a place to lounge unobtrusively. Just then a carload of smart-ass high school boys, flaunting quarts of beer, roared into the lot.

Patty wasn't afraid for her own safety: New York was a guaranteed education in survival. But the one hundred and fifty dollars in birthday money and the pilfered antique cameo, the one engraved "Andy/Love, Larry," that were stashed in her handbag made her uneasy, so she ran a gauntlet of wolf whistles and lewd suggestions and entered the store.

It was, to her relief, crowded. She took a shopping cart and joined the hair-curlers-and-whiny-brats set in a minuet to Muzak, up and down the linoleumed aisles. So that she wouldn't draw attention, Patty began to place items into her shopping basket.

Time dragged. The number of items in her cart increased.

At 3:27 she was at the opposite end of the store from the dairy section. As she pivoted the basket around, the Muzak stopped suddenly.

"Attention shoppers, your attention please. Our meat manager is happy to announce a special on center-cut pork chops. Our meat manager has priced these succulent center-cut pork chops at only a dollar twenty-nine a pound. This is an unadvertised special, quantities are limited, so first come first served."

A metallic click, and it was back to 101 Strings playing "The Sounds of Silence."

Patty rounded the corner and ran smack into grid-lock in front of the pork chops display. She quickly circled back and traversed the length of the store, negotiating this detour so fast that she almost ran over the assistant manager of the store. But at 3:30 sharp she was in position, overlooking the yogurt section.

Not her contact, though.

So into her cart went milk. And cottage cheese. And yogurt—will one carton be enough? No, make it three. And swiss cheese. And muenster. Oops, almost forgot the eggs. And cream—heavy or light? She looked at her watch: 3:34. In disbelief, she held the timepiece to her ear; it was still ticking.

Where the hell was he?

And wasn't that the assistant manager regarding her with more than a passing interest?

Patty moved on to the cereals section and passed a few more minutes unit-pricing various sizes of Cheerios. Then, she started reluctantly down the next aisle. Wait: there was a large convex mirror, part of the store's antishoplifting arsenal, in which she could monitor the dairy cases. Patty stopped in front of the canned juices and nervously began to pull down beverages. Prune juice; V-8; apple juice, but maybe in the six-pack instead of the quart. . . .

Damn it, where the hell was he?

She checked her watch again. Time was up. But unable to make herself leave, she slid down to the canned fruit section: pears; fruit cocktail; peaches, both freestone and cling. . . .

Three fifty-two. Quivering from tension and numb from the awful realization that he wasn't going to show, she started her cart in motion. Seeing a pay phone in the corner up ahead, Patty's anger came to a sudden boil; anger at the little blowhard for standing her up, anger at herself for waiting around long past the cutoff time. The girl knew that what she was about to do violated all procedures, but she marched to the phone, dug a dime out of her handbag, consulted her address book, picked up the handset, and dialed.

On the third ring, he answered: "Yes?"

"What the hell *happened*?"

"I been home all day. I got the flu. Didn't you get the message?"

"What message?"

"That I got the flu."

"No."

He blew his nose. "Yeah, well, I got the flu. Anyway, you shouldn't be calling me at home, it's against the—"

Patty's exasperated growl cut him short.

"Hey, you okay? You sound hassled."

"I . . . oh, listen, penis-breath, go soak your head in orange juice!" She banged the handset down and without thinking returned to her shopping basket. Just as she reached it, something made her look up.

The assistant manager was walking briskly up the aisle toward her, his suspicious gaze riveted on her cart.

She glanced down. It was piled with enough groceries to feed a family of six for a week. Her eyes darted back to the assistant manager.

His pace was quickening.

Reflexively, she grabbed the handle and leaned her weight against the basket; for a split second it remained rooted, and then inertia gave way. Patty had taken barely three steps when she considered stopping and brazening her way through the dilemma. But, no, it was too late; she had behaved furtively for more than half an hour, and now, in panic, she had turned her heels.

Without having to look back, she knew the assistant manager was overtaking her.

The girl redoubled her efforts. The cart picked up speed. At the end of the aisle Patty made a left, almost colliding with an old man studying cat foods, and then another left, the growing momentum of the overburdened cart almost swinging her into the shelves that held soup. She wrestled the cart back under control and hurried down the long straightaway that led to the front of the store—and freedom.

Behind her, the footsteps were gaining.

The cart was now rolling at full tilt. Ahead were the checkout counters. Which way was the exit, right or left?

The girl was so engrossed in planning her next move that she never saw the patch of recently mopped linoleum in her path.

She may as well have been sprinting across ice. Even as Patty's legs began to skid out from under her, the shopping basket pulled from her grasp. She managed to throw out both arms to cushion her fall; then she was scrambling for balance, and then she was back on her feet, lunging after the runaway cart.

It was too late.

Behind her, the assistant manager let out a strangled yell.

A few shoppers in the checkout lanes turned.

Now Patty began shouting, "Look out, look out!"

More heads snapped around. The sight of this moving mountain of groceries lumbering toward them caused slack-jawed wonderment—until the out-of-control basket clipped a pyramid of soda bottles, at which time the shoppers started ducking for safety.

"Stop! Stop her!"

Patty dashed past the toppling pyramid—some falling bottles glancing off her legs, others exploding at her feet—and sensing the exit to her left, made for it.

By this time her cart had ricocheted down a line of quickly abandoned shopping baskets and squashed into a wire bin that contained light bulbs, which in turn was caroming into a tall wire rack that held jars of strawberry preserves.

At that instant the Muzak died.

The sudden silence was more than filled, though, by an assortment of odd sounds: the muffled crunch of several hundred light bulbs imploding within their cardboard sleeves; the screech of the wire rack wrenching free of its mountings; the bellows of the assistant manager, which were cut short by a heavy thud as he went down among the fallen soda bottles.

Screams started to rise, but these were drowned by the thunderous clatter of the strawberry preserves pitching sideways and pushing a conveyer-beltful of groceries to the floor.

And then the Muzak kicked back on—with a disco version of "Hawaiian War Chant"—and up ahead an office door opened to reveal the store manager and a cashier with a beehive hairdo. Their lascivious grins turned into astonishment as the chaos before them registered.

The man reacted instinctively by grabbing at Patty.

She swivel-hipped past him and out the exit and across the parking lot; she ran until her lungs felt like pincushions and her eyes teared and her shins were on fire and her feet ached, and then she ran some more, finally reaching a small park where, ascertaining that no one was following, she collapsed to the frozen turf.

Patty had not yet recovered her wind when the laughter started. A mixture of hysteria and jubilation, it continued unabated until she reached for her handbag. And realized that it—with the one hundred fifty dollars, the antique cameo, her special key chain and, worst of all, her identification papers—still lay somewhere back there, amidst the devastation she had wrought.

Five minutes into dinner that evening, Andy gave up her attempts at conversations with her daughter.

The girl was washing the dishes when the phone rang. As Andy picked up, she heard a glass shatter in the kitchen.

"Oh, hi, Jane. Hold on a minute, will you?" Andy cupped the mouthpiece and said, "Patty, you okay?"

"Uh, yes, Mom. Who is it?"

Andy frowned at the strained pitch in her daughter's voice. "For me. It's Ginger's mother." She uncupped the mouthpiece. "Sorry, Jane, we had an accident in the kitchen. No, it's okay." But what Andy heard wasn't okay; soon, her brows had furrowed again. "I see. Of course . . . Where, the junior high? Thursday? Let me just make sure I don't have something due Friday. . . . Nope, sign me up."

She replaced the handset and stared blankly at the telephone for a few moments. Then she walked down the hall to the kitchen.

Patty, her back to the door, was squatting near the sink, sweeping up shards of glass.

"That was Ginger's mother."

"Oh?" The girl stood and carried the dustpan to the garbage can.

"There's an emergency parents' meeting on Thursday. It seems there's a drug problem at your school."

Patty carefully emptied the broken glass into the garbage can. Without turning, she said, "What else is new?"

"What do you know about it?"

The girl shrugged. "Grass is a little easier to score here than it was back in New York."

"The problem doesn't seem to be marijuana."

Patty hung up the dustpan under the sink and finally turned to face her mother.

Andy studied the carefully composed mask that was her daughter's face. Then she noticed one of Patty's neck veins pulsing. Finally she said, "Are any of your friends doing coke?"

"Nope."

Andy shifted her weight uneasily. Had the answer come too quickly? Did the fact that Patty was returning her gaze so levelly mean she was hiding something? The silence began to grow uncomfortable.

Just then, the doorbell rang.

Patty's expression remained impassive, but her eyes flicked first to the door, then to the floor.

Andy stared at her for another few seconds before going to the vestibule and peering through the peephole.

The man standing on the landing wore a uniform.

As Andy opened the door, the cop took off his cap. "Mrs. Matteson?"

"Yes?"

"Sorry to disturb you, ma'am, but we found something of your daughter's." He held up Patty's handbag.

"Oh. Won't you please come in?"

As the cop stepped forward, Andy called, "Patty?"

Only half the girl's face was visible from around the corner.

"This be yours?" the cop asked.

Patty nodded mutely.

"A bus driver turned it in. How's about checking it to see if anything's missing?"

Patty's expression was still impassive, but to Andy's practiced eye, her daughter's face seemed to sag in relief, and as she came around the corner and reached for the bag, her hand seemed to tremble ever so slightly.

The girl clutched the bag to her chest and riffled through it. The antique cameo was safe, as well as her special keychain, the one with the leather sac. The money seemed intact, too, but she wasn't about to count it just then. Patty smiled wanly at the cop. "Everything's here, officer. Thank you."

His expression appeared quizzical. At last he sighed and said, "You ought to take more care when you carry so many valuables around, young lady."

Andy was closing the door after him when she saw Patty start for her room. "Patricia."

The girl stopped and turned.

"Why didn't you tell me you lost your handbag? And what are these valuables he was talking about?"

Patty chewed her lower lip.

"Don't make me empty your handbag."

Tears suddenly welled in Patty's eyes. "There's twenty-five dollars from my savings account and the antique cameo Dad gave you, and I was taking a bus downtown to that store that sells antique jewelry because I know how much you like the cameo and because your birthday's coming up and—" A shudder went through her slender frame. "And I got careless, and now everything's spoiled!" Patty wheeled, ran to her room, and slammed the door after her.

Andy was stunned by the outburst. But not too stunned to take note of the churning in her gut, a peculiar churning she always associated with suspicion.

Half an hour later, when Patty heard the cassette deck begin to play the baroque music that her mother always studied to, she picked up the extension phone in her room and quickly dialed a number.

"Hello?"

"Good evening. May I speak to Rolf, please?"

"Just a second. Rolf, honey, for you. I think it's Patty."

"Hello."

"Hi. Hey—thanks. Truly."

He chuckled. "Sleep well."

Eight

When Andy returned to the apartment late Thursday afternoon, she was still preoccupied by a problem raised in her last class, so it took her awhile to spot the note from Patty saying that the girl was at Rolf's house, studying for a test.

But this was the night Andy had to be at the junior high so, note in hand, she went to the phone.

Her call was answered by Rolf's mother. "It's so nice to speak to you, Mrs. Matteson. I can't tell you how much my husband and I think of Patty. She's a young lady anyone would be proud to know."

"Why, thank you," Andy replied, disarmed.

"Would you like to talk to her?"

"Please. We seemed to have crossed signals about tonight. I have a meeting later, and I need her home for dinner."

"Oh, my. We had promised to run Patty home, but my husband's taken the car on an errand, and he's not due back for at least another half hour."

"No problem," Andy said. "I can swing by."

"I can't tell you how awful I feel, Mrs. Matteson. Here it is almost six already, and you with a meal to cook. How would it be if Patty took dinner with us?"

"Oh, I couldn't—"

"Come, come, it's no trouble at all," Rolf's mother said soothingly. "And we guarantee that we'll have Patty home no later than eight."

When Andy hung up she recalled Philip's supposition that her daughter was in the throes of puppy love. Patty certainly had been spending a lot of time lately with Rolf. Andy smiled softly, thinking back to her own first crush. Watery eyes or no, the girl could do worse than Rolf. And the young couple—if they were indeed a couple—seemed to be well chaperoned.

She went to the kitchen to fix herself a snack. As Andy was discarding some waxed paper, she noticed that the bag in the garbage can was piled dangerously high. Damn, but Patty was getting irresponsible; if she could come home to leave the note, she could take out the garbage. Muttering to herself, Andy compacted the trash as best she could and carried it downstairs.

Dusk had become night. She flipped on a spotlight and went to the two large plastic containers next to the garage. The right one was for the Boleys, their landlords, and the left for the Mattesons.

Andy lifted the left lid and started to hoist the bag in.

Her eye caught on something bright at the bottom

of the can. She frowned; there had been a collection that morning, and the can should have been empty. It was a plastic bag imprinted with the name of a store. But not any store that she patronized. Curious, she reached down for it.

The bag was from a local camera shop. Inside were: an empty pint flask of vodka; a small box that once held 35-mm film; an empty pack of Polaroid film; a batch of discarded black Polaroid backing sheets.

Andy's head swam. Where had the flask come from? And why the type of Polaroid film where you had to peel apart print and negative, when she owned a camera that spat out a finished picture? It must be a mistake; the Boleys must have thrown the bag in here because their own receptacle was full. But even as she lifted the adjacent lid, Andy knew what she would find: an empty container.

She began to shiver. Would her mind be leaping to such sickening conclusions had her daughter's behavior not undergone such a noticeable change lately?

Andy considered dropping Pandora's bag back into the container, but it had already been opened. She started back upstairs, the lightweight contents dragging like a millstone.

The Polaroid negatives numbered eight. By slanting them against the light, she could discern images.

The ghostly silhouettes were unmistakable: a naked female, probably young. In one of the shots the girl's head was thrown back as her hands clutched her budding breasts. The others concentrated on the juncture of her wide-spread thighs. In two of them, she was probing herself with her hand. In a third, she was grasping a long, tubular object. In the final frame, she was inserting the object.

Andy felt like throwing up.

Why? Why, Patty, why?

She started for her coat, psyching herself for the confrontation in which she would force the truth out of her daughter.

Then she stopped and reconsidered the sickening negatives. The lean form and coltish legs were without doubt those of a teenager, but could she be positive they belonged to Patty? She looked closely at the shot in which the girl's head was thrown back. Andy realized that even if she could pull another print from the negative, she still wouldn't know for sure.

Yet it had to be Patty. If it wasn't, what was this bag doing in their garbage container?

On a hunch Andy went to the girl's room. She flinched when she snapped on the light, so intense was its glare. She flicked it off, dragged over a chair, and unfastened the ceiling fixture. What the hell had Patty needed a two-hundred-watt bulb if not for photography?

Suddenly she remembered the empty box of 35-mm film. She rushed out to the hall and dug it out of the plastic bag. Kodachrome. Which called for a lot of light. And which yielded slides that could be reproduced in magazines.

Andy went to the hall closet and pushed aside the overcoats. Her heart sank further. She always hung the Nikon on the right-hand peg. Now it dangled from the center hook.

With a trembling hand, she took it down and unsnapped the cover. The film counter read empty, as it should have; the last time she'd used the camera was to photograph her balsa-wood project for Aldrich, and that roll had been developed. But then why had the Nikon been hanging from the wrong hook?

She was snapping the cover shut when she remembered that she had photographed her project in black-and-white Tri-X, which had an ASA rating of 400. She checked the camera's ASA meter. It rested between 80 and 64; someone had definitely used the Nikon since. Steeling herself, she checked the ASA rating on the side of the Kodachrome box: 64.

Andy sank slowly onto her haunches and balanced herself against the wall.

She was still squatting there, head bowed, trying to fathom the unfathomable, when the phone rang.

The caller gave up after eight rings.

Ten seconds later, it started again.

Andy struggled to her feet and answered it with a leaden "Hello."

"Hi, Tits."

On hearing the familiar breezy voice, fear and anger gave way to irritation; she slammed the receiver down.

The next time the phone rang, she picked up immediately and barked, "Retire that act, Larry."

"Sorry," her former husband said, though he didn't sound it. "You okay?"

"No, I'm not okay. What do you want?"

"Hey, I said I was sorry. I'm calling about Patty's Easter vacation. Like, is she coming to New York?"

"I don't know, and she's not here right now."

"Oh. Well, look, you got a second?"

"Just about."

Larry, thrown by her hostility, hesitated. "Maybe we ought to talk some other time."

"Come on, Larry, what's on your mind?"

"Patty. I'm getting worried about her."

Andy recoiled. What did he know?

"Ever since she was out here over Christmas," Larry continued, "she's seemed lost in another world. For instance, she used to write me long, chatty letters. I haven't gotten anything for three weeks."

Andy felt her irritation turning into guilt, and it was guilt that made her lash back. "When's the last time you dropped *her* a note? She's going to grow up thinking the whole damn world's one big tie-line."

Larry was silent for several seconds, but he came out swinging. "Listen, Tits, don't tell me nothing's wrong. Our kid's got an answer for everything. Always has, since the day she could talk. I haven't mentioned this before, but the last time she was out here she was very moody and uncommunicative. And it hasn't gotten any better."

"What are you talking about?"

"How about last Tuesday? I asked her if she was coming East for Easter. She said maybe not. I asked her why. She danced around the question and never answered it."

"Maybe Patty has a paper due," Andy said. "So she'll visit an extra week this summer."

"Goddamn it, that's not the point! She's become vague about everything. How are things going? Oh, fine. What are you up to? Oh, just things."

"It's nice to see you're finally paying attention to your daughter," Andy said acidly.

"What the fuck are you so goddamned defensive about?" he shouted. "What the hell is going on out there?"

"Nothing!"

Larry took a deep breath and exhaled it noisily. When he finally spoke, his voice was calmer. "Hey, look, I didn't call to start an argument. I'm sorry."

"Me too. I guess school's making me squirrelly."

Another pause, and then Larry said, "Andy, I'd like very much to see Patty over Easter. I miss her. Ask her to call me tonight—I'll be at the office until about three."

"Right."

"And will you try to find out what's bothering her? I know I'm six hundred miles away, but somehow I sense that she's going through some pretty heavy number."

Andy bit her lower lip. "You'll be the second to know. Promise."

When she hung up, her fingers ached from the death hold by which she had grasped the handset. Why hadn't she shared her concerns with Larry? Because she wanted to confirm her suspicions first? Because she didn't want to admit that she had been too lax and inat-

tentive? Or became some irrational part of her continued to hope that everything was in fact okay?

More than a few of Ann Arbor's parents were concerned about drugs; by the time Andy got to the junior
high auditorium at 7:25, she was fortunate to snare a
seat. As she took off her coat, she looked around and recognized a few faces. Were Rolf's parents among them?

Up on stage the movie screen had been lowered.
Two men stood off to one side, engaging in fitful conversation. The prissy fellow who kept fidgeting with his
eyeglasses was the principal, Strick. He appeared torn
between gratification at the enormous turnout and humiliation at the fact this meeting was necessary. The
other was a short, burly but athletic-looking man in his
late twenties.

Finally Strick rechecked his watch, nodded to the
other man, and stepped forward.

The audience quieted in nervous anticipation.

"Good evening, mothers and fathers, and thank
you for coming here on such short notice." Strick
paused to readjust his glasses. "Uh, as you no doubt
know, this school has had a drug education program
since the early nineteen-seventies.

"Do we think it's effective? Yes, very, all things
considered. I will concede that there is marijuana abuse
at this school. Do we prohibit it on school grounds? Yes.
Do we discourage your children from smoking it? Absolutely. Do we search and confiscate? Here the answer
is unfortunately no, and that's because we feel our
hands are tied. The city council, in its wisdom, has
deemed possession of marijuana to be no more serious
an offense than jaywalking. If you parents believe that
this narcotic should be punished by more than a
two-dollar summons, let city hall know it.

"Despite this handicap, we do intervene if a student shows pronounced abuse—that is, if he or she wan-
ders through the day absolutely zonked."

A few titters greeted Strick's uncharacteristic lapse into the vernacular.

"I wish the purpose of tonight's meeting," he continued, "were to discuss marijuana. It's not. At this point, I'd like to introduce you to Sergeant Henry Wilhite. Sergeant Wilhite is with the narcotics division of the Ann Arbor Police Department. Sergeant?"

The cop stepped forward.

"Thanks, Mr. Strick. I'm afraid what I've got for you parents is bad news. Maybe you've read in the *News* or the *Free Press* about the gangs battling for turf in Detroit. It used to be that the mob kept their mitts off Ann Arbor. They figured, this being an open city for grass, on which they turn a pretty penny, why look for trouble on hard stuff? Only today's young turks don't quite see it that way.

"Ladies and gentlemen, since the first of the year there's enough heavy stuff coming into town to make Eli Lilly look like a mom-and-pop shop."

A shocked buzz swept through the audience.

Wilhite held up his hands for quiet. "Now I'm going to get down to specifics, but first I want you to sit through a short movie. It was made by the National Institute on Drug Abuse. As a movie, it stinks. But it spells out the ABCs of narcotics real clear, and I think it'll make the rest of our meeting a lot more useful." With that, he waved to the projectionist; the house lights began to dim.

As a critic Wilhite couldn't have been more perceptive. The camerawork was wooden, the editing full of visual non sequiturs, the narration pompous. Yet the audience paid the documentary an unwavering attention that would have made even George Lucas envious; when the lights came back up eighteen minutes later, the parents had absorbed a chilling overview of the contemporary parmacopoeia from marijuana to cocaine to heroin, from uppers to downers to angel dust. They had also come to learn about the bewildering array of head-shop paraphernalia that surrounded drugdom:

empty soda cans with screw-off tops to hide stashes, roach clips, bongs, spoons, hypodermics.

Wilhite resumed his position at stage center and surveyed the subdued audience. "Luckily the Motown *paisanos* haven't started running in heroin. But they've built up a real nice market in two real middle-class favorites, cocaine and Quaaludes.

"The movie spelled out some of the tip-offs to drug abuse. Why don't we review them?"

Andy studied her clasped hands. She didn't need the review, having already committed the tip-offs to heart.

"Okay, here goes," Wilhite said. "One—a change in personality. A bright, cheery kid turns sullen. He stops hanging around with his pals, he mopes a lot.

"Two—a change in appetite. Tough, I know, because what kid doesn't load up on junk food ten minutes before dinner? But Mr. Strick and his teachers have agreed to keep an eye out in the cafeteria to see who doesn't have much use for lunch. If your child doesn't have much use for dinner, either, maybe you want to think about letting Mr. Strick or me know. We'll try to see if one and one make two.

"Three—a change in schoolwork. Grades have got to suffer if a kid's flying around blasted all afternoon and all night.

"Four—a change in health. Now we're still smack in the middle of the flu season, but drugs lower resistance. Is your kid usually healthy as a horse? Is he suddenly coming down with a couple too many runny noses? Think about the other changes—together, they may add up to something.

"Five—a change in behavior. A kid doing drugs's got something to hide. This usually means lies. About where they spent the afternoon. Or their allowances.

"Which brings me to the final point—theft. Grass is cheap. In fact, the most expensive way to buy is by the joint, and the most expensive joint in town is only a buck and a quarter, down by the Greyhound depot. Good stuff, too."

A few people chuckled, but Wilhite cut them short with his next words: "Ludes, on the other hand, go for six bucks a copy. Call it three ludes to get a good buzz going, plus whatever you pay for the wine or the vodka, and you're talking a twenty-five-buck night on the town. Coke comes even higher. This week the price tag for a gram is a hundred thirty-five. A gram'll carry a light user a week, a moderate user three or four days. A couple of pals out for a heavy evening can finish a fresh gram by one in the morning.

"So how do they come up with that kind of scratch? The easiest way is to steal it from mommy and daddy. Hey, this is an awful thing to ask, but if you suspect your child may be abusing drugs, won't you take stock of your valuables? Especially the little items, like jewelry?

"You should know that the pawn shops in the area have been put on alert. Anybody who's not an adult comes in, we know about it. But there's a limit to how much kids'll boost out of their own homes, and our merchants are learning that the hard way. Shoplifting is up maybe twenty percent in the last two months. Fancy clothing, expensive pens, pocket calculators, transistor radios, records and tapes. If the D.A. gets tough, like he says he's going to, I'm afraid a lot of kids are going to get yellow sheets—unless we can all stop the problem before it gains momentum."

Wilhite felt badly about laying it on so thick, and yet his department couldn't hope to staunch the epidemic without the help of the parents. So he had to leave them between a rock and a hard place—had to force them to uncover and reevaluate their children's quirks and foibles.

Not that Andy had far to search.

The question-and-answer session was proceeding desultorily when a woman asked, "Sergeant, it seems to me that a lot of the symptoms you describe are pretty common to adolescents who aren't on drugs."

"Yes, ma'am, they are. Adolescents don't need much to throw them off stride. If yours is having a bad time with his teacher or suddenly can't stand the sight of red meat, I wouldn't worry about it too much. But if there's a whole range of changes—then I'd do some hard thinking."

Next a man rose. "All these things you say are being stolen—how do they get rid of them?"

"The perpetrators sell them to fences."

"Do you know who these fences are?"

"Knowing and proving are two separate matters, sir. We're working on it."

"It still doesn't add up," the man persisted. "You talk about twenty-percent increases in shoplifting. This town has a lot of well-stocked shops, but not enough, I wouldn't think, to finance the kind of drug wave you've described."

Until this moment, Wilhite had been remarkably self-assured. Now he seemed discomfited.

"Sergeant?"

The cop massaged his jaw for a few moments before answering. "I didn't want to bring this up unless I was pressed, because we're still checking out the information, but, uh, there's evidence that a group of local kids is making money by participating in a teenage pornography ring."

Around the auditorium, loud gasps, and then everyone seemed to be talking at once. Not Andy, though. She just sat, eyes unfocused, listening to the roar that was growing inside her skull.

An hour after the meeting broke up, Andy found herself in her car, whizzing along at sixty miles per hour. She had no idea where she was, having spent the time correlating Patty's behavior to the cop's checklist—and making herself accept the awful implications.

The sign up ahead indicated that she'd driven almost to Toledo. Just beyond it was an exit ramp. She turned onto it, made a left, and got back on I-23 headed the other way. Ann Arbor lay an hour north; she would need at least that much time to decide on her next step.

It was well past eleven when Andy finally arrived home.

She looked under her daughter's door. It was dark. She eased the door open.

The soft light that flooded in from the hall illuminated the sleeping girl. Patty looked like a nineteenth century painting commemorating that magical window in life called adolescence: her face in repose was clearly not that of an adult, while her body, draped in a white nightgown whose hem was bunched high on her thigh, was clearly not that of a child.

Her daughter's leg twitched slightly. At the same moment, a dream slid across her face, clouding her features. Then she sighed gently, smacked her lips several times, and swallowed—and innocence reigned once more.

Andy was still debating the wisdom of waking her and having it out on the spot when she remembered the diary sandwiched between mattress and box springs.

That's it, she thought; that's where the secrets are confided, and that's where I'll start in the morning.

Nine

The day broke raw, with brooding gray clouds obscuring the sun and carrying the threat of a marrow-chilling drizzle.

Shortly after nine, reckoning that Patty was safely in school, Andy entered her daughter's room.

When she switched on the overhead light, she was surprised at the dimness of the bulb. Andy checked and discovered that the two-hundred-watt from the previous evening had been replaced. Was Patty belatedly trying to cover her tracks?

She began her search.

In the center desk drawer lay a tiny key—was it for the diary? In another drawer, wedged casually next to a packet of letters from Larry, was a vial. The pharmacy label on it indicated that the medication within was for Patty's allergy. Andy snapped off the cap, removed the cotton wadding, and shook out a pill. The capsule, which bore the Upjohn label, certainly was not a Quaalude. She pulled the two halves open and dumped the contents into her palm. The granules were definitely not cocaine.

The rest of the room contained neither pills nor powders.

But behind a stack of record albums, Andy found a Pepsi can. It felt empty; indeed, its flip-up tab had been popped. She peered into its dark recess and then tried to unscrew the top. It didn't turn. She placed the can back behind the albums.

Unable to postpone her awful mission any longer, Andy took a deep breath, stooped, and dug out her daughter's diary. She took it to the living room and sat down. When she set the volume on the coffee table, she noticed a couple of moist spots on the imitation leather cover. Andy stared at her palms and then dried them on her jeans.

The tiny key from the center drawer fit. She turned it; the lock snicked free. Andy thumbed the clasp aside and opened the volume.

The first entry was dated January 1. Patty's year had not started joyously. The previous night, Larry had taken her as his date to a small New Year's Eve dinner. One of the women there had paid him undue attention, and, in Patty's eyes, he had flirted back shamelessly. The girl had passed most of the night hunched before a television, wondering if her dad and the woman had met by prearrangement. When she wasn't brooding, that is, about her suspicion that her mom was most probably spending the evening with that yucky new guy, Philip Hunt.

So Philip had been right about Patty's animosity; Andy found herself thinking back to that happy evening, which at this moment gave her no pleasure.

She turned the page.

It soon became clear that Patty's main concerns were two. The first was how to reunite her parents. The second was her growing unhappiness in Ann Arbor. The more acquaintances she made, the lonelier she seemed to feel. Almost as proof that she was a slick journalist's daughter, Patty dismissed her newfound pals with the cruel pun "Close Encounters of the Nerd Kind."

Andy suddenly thought back to her own adolescent diaries. She hadn't read them in almost a quarter of a century. Were they still in her parents' attic? Undoubtedly. Were they similarly filled with woes and imagined calamities? She couldn't be sure.

Late in the second week of January, this passage:

> I've been approached by Conchis! He swore me to secrecy—I can't tell even you, dear diary—but the next few days, or weeks, or months, should be interesting! For a change!

Andy frowned. Had Patty ever mentioned a boy by that name? She went to her own room and opened the file folder containing all the papers relating to her daughter's junior high. The letter from Strick about the girl's grades should have been at the front. It wasn't. She started to riffle through the file, then gave it up as unimportant and pulled out the class list.

There was no student named Conchis.

Next she fetched the Ann Arbor telephone directory. No family by that name was listed.

Andy's foreboding intensified when she resumed reading the diary. The long, moping, self-analytical passages quickly gave way to what could only be a code:

Jan. 16. Urfe at rdvz late (B = +) and betrayed Caulfield. Surmise Urfe = Facet 2. But is Caulfield playing straight? Called Conchis. He said work it out before R2b.

Andy flipped forward until she found the notation "R2b":

Challenged Urfe. His defense—Section 3—was lame. Goodbye Urfe. Conchis said he was a weakling anyway.

Andy looked at the dates again. No doubt about it, this was when Patty's behavior had begun to change. She read on in chilled fascination. The notations grew even more cryptic, the strange names more numerous. Finally, in an attempt to keep things straight, she took out a pad and began taking notes.

She was two-thirds of the way through when her alarm clock rang; it was time to leave for her eleven o'clock lecture. She continued reading.

When Andy finally finished the diary, she got up and paced the living room.

It was obviously a conspiracy. By whom, and to achieve what, she could not tell; yet there was a group of people, presumably children her daughter's age, who had formed a gang. They'd started with many participants, but through bizarre initiation rites that seemed to involve spying, lying, and an unfathomable form of personal confrontation, the group had been ruthlessly weeded down to a nucleus of—Andy picked up her note pad—eight.

She couldn't help but think of what Sergeant Wilhite had said about the efficient distribution of drugs in Ann Arbor.

Andy studied the columns she had made on her pad.

The first listed every name appearing in Patty's diary since mid-January. In all, there were nineteen.

But during the past ten days, only eight had appeared, of which two dated back to the very beginning. Andy transferred these eight names to a separate sheet: Baggins; Conchis; Hankshaw; McMurphy; Muad'Dib; Ravenwood; Trumper; Zuko. Several sounded hauntingly familiar, but no matter how much she racked her brains, no associations came forth.

Second was a list of two dozen phone numbers. These hadn't appeared in the diary itself, but rather on a sheet of paper wedged into the volume.

Third was a list of dates involving a place code-named 206. Andy consulted a calendar and discovered these meetings occurred every Monday, Wednesday, and Friday. But where was 206? And what happened there?

The fourth column was devoted to activities—apparently, meetings and phone calls—that did not involve a rendezvous at 206. Andy had given up on this list after five days, so numerous were the entries. Small wonder her girl was doing poorly in school, she thought; Patty's absorption in this gang seemed total.

But wait: what about the girl's life outside this most suspicious cabal? For instance, the previous night she had studied with Rolf. Andy turned to the last entry in the diary. There were notations of two meetings and a slew of phone calls—but no study date, no dinner.

Andy resumed her pacing.

Finally, she gritted her teeth and picked up the telephone directory again. Baggins, negative. Conchis, she knew. Hankshaw, negative. Three minutes later, she had finished checking out her short list, with uniform results.

If the names yielded no clues, what about the phone numbers?

She dialed the first and let it ring eight times before hanging up.

The second number was answered on the fourth ring: "Yeah?" It was a man of at least forty; in the background, Andy could hear machinery running.

"Who is this, please?" she asked.

The man sighed noisily. "Aw, come on, lady, it's cold out here! Who do you want?"

"What number have I reached, please?"

"The one you dialed, for Christ's sake! The pay phone outside the Amoco station on Washtenaw, town of Ann Arbor, state of Michigan, U.S. of A. Now, you got eighteen questions left, lady."

"I, uh, I'm sorry, I seem to have the wrong—"

Andy heard the phone slammed down.

The third number she tried picked up instantly: "Safeway Supermarket."

The fourth number was a pay phone in a shopping center on Packard.

The fifth was another no-answer.

The sixth was an A & P on Main Street.

Andy put a halt to her dial-a-farce by calling a number jotted down the previous evening and saying, "Hello, may I please speak with Sergeant Wilhite?"

The headquarters of the Ann Arbor Police Department was relentlessly cinder-block nouveau. Andy was directed through a maze of linoleumed corridors to the narcotics bureau.

Wilhite was alone in a small, windowless office that contained two desks. Embers still glowed in the ashtray on the other desk; Wilhite must have told his partner that this parent was tightly strung. As the cop drew up a chair for her, he said, "Mrs. Matteson, you were at the junior high last night."

She nodded.

"Did you have any reason to suspect your child—by the way, boy or girl?"

"Girl. She's thirteen."

"Did you have any reason to suspect your daughter's messing around with drugs?"

Andy shook her head, then blurted, defensively, "I don't know for a fact that she is—"

Wilhite flashed a disarming smile. "Believe me,

ma'am, your coming here doesn't say to me that she is. But it does say you're worried about something."

Andy spotted a pack of cigarettes on his desk and asked for one. He passed the pack over, then reached across with his lighter. She took a deep drag and quickly tapped it against his ashtray; flakes of fresh ash fell away.

Wilhite noticed her nervousness, of course, but he discreetly busied himself with lighting his own smoke.

Finally she said, "For a couple of weeks now, I've been—apprehensive. I was divorced last year, and my daughter and I moved here so I could finish up a degree at the university. I thought she was doing fine. Better than me, in fact. But since the first of the year, she's been exhibiting a lot of the—the symptoms you talked about last night."

"Remember, I said most teenagers go through at least some of them."

Andy nodded and played with her cigarette again. "But there were a couple of other things. . . ." Her voice trailed off as she thought of the incriminating Polaroids. Yet, could she be sure? She dropped her gaze. "Things I'd prefer not to go into right now."

"No need to, Mrs. Matteson," Wilhite said reassuringly. "This meeting's strictly off the record. No notes, no dossier."

Andy tried to get comfortable in her chair but couldn't. "I guess that last night made me reconsider my daughter's behavior in a new light. This morning, I read her diary." She hesitated again; the next step, if taken, could prove irrevocable. "She seems to have begun associating with a bunch of people, kids, I guess, whom she's never mentioned to me. I've copied down some of the names. Are any familiar to you?"

Wilhite looked from Andy's distraught face to the piece of paper she had taken from her coat pocket. He stubbed out his cigarette and accepted the sheet.

Andy watched Wilhite's eyes flick down the page. His expression remained neutral. Then he returned his eyes to the top of the sheet and worked his way through again, only much more slowly. Halfway down, he leaned back in his chair and frowned, but in concentration rather than disapproval.

At last Wilhite looked up. "These aren't any of our active targets."

Andy's eyes closed in relief.

"But—"

Her eyes popped open again.

Wilhite was massaging his jaw. "But a couple of them ring a bell way back somewhere."

"Odd, I had that feeling, too, so I checked Patty's class list and the phone book. Nothing."

Wilhite lit up another cigarette. "I'd like to run the names through some channels."

Andy shifted uneasily in her chair.

"Off the record, of course," he added quickly. "I want to see if any of the guys on the street know them, if Detroit knows them, or if these are aliases. I don't think anything'll turn up, but we might as well be sure, right?"

It wasn't until Andy left Wilhite's office that she remembered her lunch date with Philip. She glanced at a wall clock. It was almost two. Still, she swung into a pay booth and called his office. No answer. She looked at the clock again. There was still time to retrieve one class from this lost day. But it was also Friday—which meant Patty was due to go to this mysterious 206.

Twenty minutes later, Andy was parking the Honda as close as she dared to the junior high school, in a row of cars catercorner to the main entrance. Would she be able to spot her daughter from fifty yards away? Would her daughter be able to spot the car? Andy tilted the seat back so she could hunker down lower.

The gray clouds that had hovered all day finally sighed; a light rain began to fall.

At 3:02 the doors to the junior high burst open.

Andy's eyes fanned the stream of kids that flowed out. Damn, every other girl seemed to be wearing a powder-blue parka. . . .

When the first wave subsided, Andy was reasonably certain Patty had not been in it. Now the students were emerging in smaller bunches. A few began to gather beneath the portico.

At the far end of the building, several cars pulled out of the driveway that ran back to the faculty parking lot.

The drizzle grew harder.

The group beneath the portico now numbered a half-dozen. These boys and girls carried, rather than wore, their coats. Andy didn't recognize any of them.

She glanced at her watch: 3:20. A solid line of cars was edging out of the faculty lot, and some of those parked around the Honda were being driven away.

At 3:27 Patty, wearing her parka, came out of the door. She said something to the group beneath the portico. A few of them laughed as they began shrugging into their coats. Andy was wondering if starting up the car might draw Patty's attention when, to her surprise, the group clumped back into the building. Why had they put on their coats to go inside?

The drizzle slackened but would not stop. An air of quietude settled over the school, broken only by a few stray vehicles—two cars, then a van—pulling out of the faculty parking lot. Andy drew her coat more snugly around herself; the interminable rain seemed to leach warmth from the air.

At 3:48 a chubby girl came out of the school and started down the walkway. Andy started the car, made a U-turn, and pulled up at the foot of the walkway just in time to intercept her. Leaning over, she rolled down the passenger-side window and said, "Hi, Ginger."

The chubby girl blinked in surprise. "Oh, hi, Mrs. Matteson."

"Have you seen Patty this afternoon?"

Ginger ducked her head and stared at her boots. "Uh, no, I haven't, Mrs. Matteson."

Why was the girl lying? "I thought the two of you were in some extracurricular program together," Andy said.

"That was last semester," Ginger replied, her head still down.

"Oh." Andy was about to try another line of questioning when she noticed the raindrops dripping off the girl's parka. She took pity and offered Ginger a ride home. To her relief, the offer was refused. "Hope to see you again soon, Ginger."

"Sure thing, Mrs. Matteson," the girl said disconsolately as she turned and trudged away.

Andy knew she could continue waiting—but for how long? Or she could return to the apartment. Or she could go inside the junior high and if not confront Patty, at least locate her. Choosing the third option, she flipped the car into gear and headed into the faculty parking lot.

By now, the school was virtually deserted. Did 206 mean room 206? Andy's footsteps echoed hollowly as she climbed the stairs and headed for the classroom.

A janitor was mopping the corridor. When he saw her, he frowned. "You got a pass to be up here?"

"Uh, I was supposed to pick up my daughter about ten minutes ago, but she didn't show up. I think she said she'd be in room two-oh-six."

"Ain't nobody there now, lady." When Andy hesitated, he shook his head in resignation and said, "Go check it yourself if you want."

Unable to help herself, Andy strode across the fresh-mopped floor to room 206 and peered through the open door. Empty. Then she turned to the janitor, who was waiting impatiently to remop her footprints, and asked, "What other rooms might be open at this hour?"

He shrugged. "The gym. The library until

four-thirty. Maybe the computer room, maybe the language room. It's Friday afternoon, lady."

Back downstairs, Andy hiked over to the new wing. The basketball team was scrimmaging in the gym; a cluster of girls watched with adoration, but Patty was not among them. Andy continued to the computer room. Most of the consoles were idle; those that weren't were all manned by boys.

She was back in the main building, on the way to the library, when she passed a stairwell.

There was a sudden "shush" and a giggle from the other side of the fire door. At the same moment, Andy smelled the unmistakable sweet aroma of marijuana. Her footsteps faltered. Dead silence, and then from the other side the scrape of shoes on stairs. Heading—upward.

Andy spotted another stairwell on the other side of the hall, perhaps fifteen yards away. Instinctively she leaned over, whipped off her boots, and in stockinged feet sprinted silently for the stairwell and up the steps to the second-flood landing.

There, she sucked in air through her nose in an effort to quiet her gasps. Then she cracked open the fire door.

Twenty seconds later, the door to the other stairwell burst open. The two kids that bolted through it were both boys.

Andy wiped perspiration from her forehead. She also had trouble slipping her boots back on because her legs seemed made of jelly.

Descending again to the first floor, Andy proceeded to the library and stuck her head in. She didn't recognize any of the half-dozen bookworms. She was about to check out the language lab when she remembered that Patty wasn't taking French that semester.

When Andy returned to her car, she was still shaking. No longer from her exertion, though; now, it was from anxiety. Half an hour ago, her daughter had gone back into the junior high school with a group of at least a half-dozen others. Where had they all disappeared?

Ten

Patty, head down and laden with schoolbooks, passed beneath a streetlight as she made her way toward home. Andy, who was standing at the apartment window, saw that her daughter was alone and let the curtain fall back in place.

She was seated in her armchair, textbook in hand, when the front door opened.

"Hi, Mom."

"Hi."

A thump as the girl dropped her books on the table in the vestibule, then the rustle of fabric as she slipped out of her parka. Then footsteps.

Andy's hands were trembling, so she set the textbook on her lap.

Holding a sheaf of papers, Patty entered the living room. She eyed the opened volume and said, "How's it going?"

Andy shrugged, then forced a smile.

Patty frowned. "You look whipped, Mom. Truly. You ought to lighten up a little, you know?"

Andy's eyes flashed, but she bit back an angry retort. Though in her mind the battle lines were drawn, this didn't seem the time nor the place to fire the first salvo; not quite yet.

Patty, taken aback by her mother's radiating tension, fiddled nervously with the papers in her hand. Finally she asked, "Do we have some extra poster board?"

"What size?"

"Oh, maybe this big," she replied, stretching her arms.

Andy gestured to the supplies alongside her drafting board near the window. "Check there. Or in my closet—back near where I keep the camera."

The word "camera" slid right by Patty. The girl went to the stack of poster boards and began to rummage through them.

What are you waiting for? Andy asked herself. Come on, start the dialogue. Force it into the open. Lance the boil. But a terrible inertia was at work; she remembered the months of painful avoidance that had preceded her showdown with Larry. This confrontation was, of course, for stakes even higher than a marriage—it was for her daughter's future. Yet when Andy finally opened her mouth, the silence remained unbroken.

Patty rose, holding a piece three feet by four. "Okay if I take this?"

Andy nodded.

The girl started to leave the room. "Oh, what's for dinner?"

"Carbonara."

"Oh."

The downward inflection of the single syllable forecast to Andy an entire meal: dinner would be, as had become the distressing habit of late, hellish.

She was right. Patty smothered the pasta with grated parmesan cheese; but after only a couple of mouthfuls, she began separating out the pieces of bacon.

Andy was watching the girl pile these to one side of her plate when she felt her skull about to achieve lift-off. She said in a voice taut with control, "You don't seem very hungry."

"Unh-unh," Patty replied, without looking up.

"I've asked you not to eat before dinner."

"I didn't. I'm just not hungry tonight, okay?"

"No, it is not okay. Not tonight, not last night, not

the night before last. If I go to the trouble of putting food on the table, I want you to eat it."

Patty sensed her mother was walking an emotional tightrope—and despite herself, couldn't resist giving it a pluck. She looked heavenward and groaned melodramatically, "Mother, I do not need your starving Indians lecture tonight!"

"Patricia!"

"Look, Mom, can we drop it?"

"No, we cannot drop it. It's more than your eating habits, it's your entire attitude. Such as toward chores."

"Oh, Mom . . ."

"But that's probably because you're out roaming around every afternoon," Andy continued. "God knows, you'd still be out there right now if I hadn't grounded you."

The girl made an exasperated sound but said nothing.

Andy leaned back in her chair. The churning in her stomach would not stop. This is it, she thought; Patty's recalcitrance was an inauspicious sign, but she could no longer bottle up her suspicions. She forced herself to look into her daughter's sullen eyes. "Patty, I want to talk to you about your friends—"

"My friends?" the girl replied, surprised.

"Who are they? I haven't seen Ginger over here in months."

"I have new ones. And you've met Rolf."

"By chance, in a parking lot. Have you ever asked him, or any of the others, over to the house when I'm here?"

Patty dropped her eyes. "No."

"You wouldn't be ashamed of me, would you?"

"Moth-er," the girl said plaintively.

"What else am I to think? If it's not me that you're hiding, what is it? Or are you the one who's hiding? When you do remember to come home, you spend most of your time on the telephone. How many calls should a girl your age make? No wonder your grades have gone to hell."

Patty started to stand.

"Sit down."

"I have something to—"

"Sit down."

The fury in her mother's voice seemed to buckle Patty's knees. She plopped back heavily into her chair and, staring at her plate, mumbled something.

"What?"

"I said, what is this, an interrogation?"

"Something like that," Andy replied icily.

Patty looked up, startled.

Andy was considering her next words when the phone rang. She glared at the extension in the kitchen, as if willing it to stop. It didn't. Finally she flung her napkin on the table, rose, and strode angrily to it.

"Hello!"

A stunned silence, and then Philip said, "Hey, you okay?"

"No. And I can't talk now."

"Fair enough. But the message on my machine said it was urgent."

"It was." Andy looked at Patty, who clearly wanted to be somewhere else. Then she sighed. "Where will you be later?"

"My apartment."

"I'll call." Andy replaced the receiver, leaned against the kitchen counter, and crossed her arms. "Patty, do you know where I went last night?"

"To my school."

"Why."

"To hear some nark talk . . ." Suddenly the girl's eyes widened, her mouth dropped open, the blood drained out of her face. "No! Mother—you don't think I—" As the shock of realization wore off and the implications sank in, her face contorted in grief. Patty buried her head in her arms and began to cry.

Andy's heart shattered like dropped crystalware. Her fingers dug into her biceps with such force that knuckles whitened. But as badly as she wanted to comfort her daughter, she had to know if this time the tears were for real.

The girl's body was racked by deep shudders as she fought her way back from the edge of hysteria. When she finally raised her head, her cheeks were glistening and swollen, her eyes those of one who has just visited the blackest reaches of the soul.

At that instant, Andy knew; she rushed to Patty and pressed the girl's face to her own chest. Her daughter responded by pressing tight, as a trembling fawn nestles against its doe.

Patty sniffled and then said, in a strained voice, "How could you think that about me?"

Andy continued stroking the girl's hair. Did it matter? Yes; the catharsis should be total enough to leave no unanswered questions. "The policeman last night was very specific about the problem's symptoms," she said softly.

Trapped in weeping's aftermath, Patty tried to gain control of her breathing.

"He told us several things to watch out for," Andy continued. "Changes in eating habits. In friends. In schoolwork. And in moods. You can't tell me you haven't behaved differently this semester, dear. I've been worried for several weeks, and last night—last night brought it all to a flash point."

Patty relaxed her grip on Andy, leaned back, and looked up. Her face was a wreck, yet nothing a night's sleep wouldn't repair. "Would you wait here a minute, Mom?"

"Wh—"

"Please?" Patty stood and walked on shaky legs from the kitchen. Andy heard the footsteps continue to her daughter's room. Next, she heard a nose being blown. A dark thought—might Patty be destroying evidence?—streaked through her mind, but then the girl's footsteps were coming nearer again.

Patty returned holding a sheaf of papers. "I was going to show you this when I got home, but . . ."

It was a report, written for her English class, on Emily Dickinson.

"The last page, Mom."

Andy flipped to it. At the bottom was a handwritten evaluation: "Incisive analysis, well-written presentation. But please be more careful with your syntax in future papers. A—." Andy looked up at Patty, who was studying her boots.

The girl said, "I think my social study grades are better, too. The test today was pretty easy." She paused, then added, "You're right, I've been into something this semester, but it isn't drugs. It's—" Patty looked up. "It's something that's real hard for me to explain without sounding like a sap. Could we talk about it in my room?"

Puzzled, Andy nodded and followed Patty out of the kitchen.

When she entered her daughter's room, she noticed the poster board that had been appropriated before dinner. On it, Patty had begun to Magic Marker blocks of words. "What's that for, dear?"

"Science class. Those ratty old plants by the window, my experiment? They're to demonstrate how different amounts of fertilizer affect growth." Patty picked up a plastic Fotomat bag lying on her desk. "I got these back today."

Andy reached into the bag and took out a packet of photographs. It held thirty-six color prints. There were a dozen plants; Patty had taken three shots of each, methodically bracketing her exposures. Suddenly, a two-hundred-watt bulb lit up in Andy's head. Plus, the film Patty had used was print-producing Ektachrome, not the slide-producing Kodachrome she had found in the bag. But then who put that bag of Polaroid filth in their garbage receptacle? She turned to her daughter and said, "Pretty good photography without a flash."

"Pretty good camera we have," the girl answered with a shy smile.

"But you didn't ask me in here to see this."

"No. I—I have a confession to make. About why I seem so out of it, I mean. I know this sounds crazy, Mom, but I've been obsessed with this game."

"Game? You mean one of those electronic things at the arcade?"

Patty sighed. "Oh, really, Mother. Do I look like some button-pushing nerd? No, I mean a role-playing game like D and D, only—"

"D and D?"

"Dungeons and Dragons. It's where the players take on identities, and go off on these quests for hidden treasures."

Andy cocked her head as she searched her memory. "Isn't that for college kids? I seem to recall that a couple of years ago, a boy up at Michigan State disappeared while playing some game like that—in the steam tunnels under the dormitory, wasn't it?"

"Yeah, that was D and D," Patty said. "And some lady wrote a really drippy novel about it. But not too many college kids play it. The game's basically for infantiles who get off on things like killer worms and nasty elves."

Patty's obvious scorn—and the intelligence that informed it—amused Andy. "Obviously, your game doesn't have killer worms and nasty elves."

The girl curled her lip in disgust. In that heartbeat, seeing Patty flying good humor, enthusiasm, and self-confidence like flags at full mast, Andy wanted to hug her daughter to pieces. Instead, she waited for a description of that on which the girl had become fixated.

"No way," Patty said. "D and D is sort of out of Tolkien. But ours is based on reality! You see, the players each have different Characteristic Matrices, which the Maestro assigns us, and we have Configurations to defend. So we issue Challenges that can be doubled and then—"

"Patty, Patty, Patty."

The girl blushed.

"From the top. Slowly. Pretend—pretend I'm an infantile."

Patty hesitated. "There's a real simple way to do this. . . . It's against the rules, but then, you *are* my mother." She went to her desk, opened a drawer, and pulled out a file folder. Andy noticed that written on the folder were the words "Realm: Intro and Levels 1–3." Patty opened the folder and handed the booklet in it to her mother.

Andy read the cover legend—"Warning! For Authorized Eyes Only!"—and suppressed a grin. Of all the parental apprehensions she might have spun herself into a tizzy over, none could be as harmless as this self-important game.

"This is just the introduction, to give you the idea," Patty said gravely. "Naturally, it gets more elaborate as you progress."

"Naturally."

"If you don't mind, maybe I can guide you through the highlights?"

Patty took the book back and perched on the edge of her bed. Andy sat down alongside her daughter.

"Okay," Patty said. "The game's called Realm. It has seven Levels. You start at Realm One and work your way upward. Players who can't hack it at the lower Levels don't get to continue."

"Where are you, dear?"

"Realm Seven," Patty replied proudly.

Andy couldn't help but give her daughter an affectionate squeeze.

"Oh, Mother." But then Patty giggled as she opened the book. "Now, these are the Configurations. The circle and ellipsis for Realms One and Two don't count because those are just warm-up Levels. But look here. Realm Three's Configuration is a triangle; Level Four, a square; Level Five's a pentagon, and so on. Each leg of your Configuration's a border, with another player on the other side. So in Realm Three, there are four players—one on each leg of the triangle, which makes three, plus you. Get it?"

Andy nodded.

"At the start of each game, the Maestro hands out computer-generated Characteristic Matrices. These list the strengths and weaknesses of all the players. For instance, maybe one character always has to be late. We use the Characteristic Matrices to try to figure out who's who."

"You mean," Andy interrupted, "that when you start one of these Realm games, you know who the other players are, but not their roles?"

"Right. You have to puzzle it out. You get points for guessing right, but that's sort of secondary. The real object of Realm is strengthening your Configuration.

"To do that, you use your Arsenal Points. We each start out with the same number and then try to win the other players' points. What you do is study the Characteristic Matrices. Then you try to guess who's on which border. Then you fire off a Challenge you hope he can't meet. For instance, the character who's always late? One Challenge would be to arrange a meeting and then insist that he show up early "

Patty pulled a sheet of paper from the file folder. "Here, Mom. This might help."

Andy looked at the heading: "Realmlog/Level Three." Under it were the names of four players: Diver, Glass, Patimkin, and Wing. She frowned. "This is your handwriting, but I don't see—"

"Oh, you mean the names." Patty laughed. "We agreed it'd be fun to take pseudonyms from fictional characters we admire. I'm Diver—Nicole from *Tender Is the Night*. Glass is from Salinger, Patimkin from *Goodbye, Columbus*—"

"And Isadora Wing from *Fear of Flying*," Andy finished. "Not exactly a book for junior high students, is it?"

Patty had the good grace to blush.

Andy's mind drifted in wonderment. Of course;

that's why the names on the list she'd taken to Sergeant Wilhite had sounded vaguely familiar to both of them. Baggins—that was Frodo's surname in *Lord of the Rings.* And she should have recognized Conchis, having recently completed John Fowles's revised *The Magus.* Several of the names remained beyond her grasp, but McMurphy was surely from *One Flew Over the Cuckoo's Nest,* and Ravenwood—Marian Ravenwood from *Raiders of the Lost Ark?*

". . . with different degrees of difficulty."

Andy looked at her daughter blankly. "I'm sorry, Patty, I missed that."

"I said, the real key to Realm isn't even the Challenges, but how you defend against them. You can shift Arsenal Points from one border to another, issue a Counter-Challenge with a greater degree of difficulty, stuff like that."

"Sounds complicated."

The girl shrugged nonchalantly. "Truly. I told you this wasn't for infantiles. In fact, we resolve all Challenges by die and computer."

She reached into her pocket and pulled out a key chain. At the end where an astrological symbol or auto marque or rabbit's foot would ordinarily dangle was a little leather sac. Patty pulled open the drawstring and dumped into her palm an elongated, off-white object the size of a quail's egg, which she handed to her mother.

The object seemed to be made of ivory, yet its weight was too light unless it was hollow—an unlikely possibility. Nor was it truly ovoid; Andy could feel tiny ridges and corners. She raised it for closer inspection. There were numerous flat surfaces. Each had seven sides, and each was shallowly incised with a number. Andy looked still closer. One of the facets facing the ceiling seemed brighter than the rest.

What it was, was a die the likes of which she had never seen.

"There're forty-nine sides, Mom," Patty said. "Pretty neat, huh? And watch this." She stood and flipped off the overhead light.

In the gloom the topmost facet glowed softly so that Andy could clearly read the number, 31. She tilted her hand slightly. Another number lit up.

Patty switched the overhead light back on. "With so many sides, it had to be made with sensors so that you'd always know which side was really up."

Andy couldn't take her eyes off the die. The technology involved was awesome, the craftsmanship impeccable. "How many weeks' allowance did this set you back?"

Her daughter laughed. "You're not going to believe this, Mom. When you first start Realm, you give them a ten-dollar deposit. If you get bounced at Level Five or below, you have to give the die back, and they return your money. But if you go on to Level Six, it's yours to keep. Forever."

"What's the punch line?"

"What do you mean?"

"How much more do you owe them?"

"Nothing! It's like a prize for doing well. Isn't that something?"

"Truly," Andy replied, trying to fathom who would sell for ten dollars a little high-tech jewel costing at least fifty to manufacture.

"Anyway," Patty continued, "you can see that with two players rolling forty-nine-sided dice, the combinations are out of sight. Like, for any one roll there are two thousand three hundred and seventy-one possible outcomes. And that's not factoring in relative strengths, degree of difficulty, and Arsenal Points. So the judge is a computer."

Andy arched an eyebrow. "It doesn't sound like something from Atari or Radio Shack."

"No way. We use the high school's. They have a computer club that's also open to really good junior high math students. One of the requirements for playing Realm is math grades high enough to get you into the club."

Andy recalled the letter from Patty's principal and his puzzlement over how the girl could let easier subjects slide while excelling in math. Then she remembered the mysterious 206—could that rendezvous be the high school's computer room? "Do you kids have a terminal at the junior high?"

"Nope. We go to the high school every Monday, Wednesday, and Friday."

"That's a long hike."

Patty nodded. "Sometimes we get lucky and hitch a ride. Like today? You know how it was pouring? Well, a couple of teachers agreed to drop us off."

Andy had a mental picture of the vehicles flowing from the faculty parking lot even as she huddled miserably in her parked Honda. Served her right, she thought ruefully.

"That's about it, Mom."

"Not quite. You're obviously spending a lot of time with these other Realm players. How come you never seem to go to their homes or invite them here?"

Patty turned her palms skyward. "It's kind of hard to explain. We're friends, see, but until the game's over, we're also kind of like enemies. I mean, it's always a matter of getting the edge on someone else. I think it's natural that no one feels like really palling around until the end."

"Which is?"

"Well, like I said, I'm on Realm Seven, the final Level. Our last session's in a week and a half."

"I don't know," Andy said. "You've answered most of my questions, but your grades . . ."

"Oh, Mother, really. You were right to get on my case a couple of weeks ago, but I'm pulling them up. Truly."

Andy was at a loss for words. In less than twenty minutes, Patty had punctured a month's accumulated anxieties.

As if reading her mother's mind, the girl said playfully, "Realm isn't quite the addiction you thought, is it?"

Andy laughed and hugged her daughter. "Would you like an apology?"

"Nah. Just another squeeze would be fine."

"My pleasure," Andy said, giving her another.

As Andy stood she felt suddenly giddy, as if waking from a fever dream. "How's about going out for a sundae?"

"I'm really wiped, Mom," Patty said, yawning, the experience having obviously drained her, too. "Can we do a rain check?"

"Of course."

Andy left Patty's room and headed for the liquor cabinet. Then she decided she needed to share her relief and exultation, so she picked up the phone. "Hi, it's me. No, I'm fine now. In fact, more than fine." She laughed coyly. "Buy me a drink at the P Bell, and I'll be glad to tell you. Thirty minutes? Fine."

She returned to Patty's door, tapped gently on it, and opened it. The girl, stretched out on her bed, gazed up with drowsy eyes.

"Patty, I'm going out for a while. Sure you won't change your mind?"

She shook her head.

"Okay. In case you need me, I'll be at the P Bell with Philip. But I'll be home before ten."

Patty nodded and yawned again.

Fifteen minutes later, when Andy left the house, her daughter was still lying in bed, fighting the fog of an emotional fatigue she had never felt before. But as soon as she heard the Honda pull out of the driveway, Patty forced herself to her feet.

She went to her desk and opened the drawer containing all her Realmlogs. The girl realized guiltily that she shouldn't have shown her mother the booklet and the game sheet. Yet how else could she have allayed Andy's raging fears about drug abuse? Luckily, though, Patty had contained the damage. The Characteristic Matrices for the lower Realms were simplistic: "Secur-

ing Realm from Outsiders"; "Promptness"; "Willingness to Tell the Truth." And because the Characteristics
were tame, so were the types of Challenges.

But the greatness of Realm lay in its escalating nature; each ascending Level drew the players that much
closer to the edge.

For instance, in Realm Four the new factor had
been classwork. Patty, challenged to perform so poorly
that her school would notify Andy, had Count-
er-Challenged, then almost failed two courses. By
bringing in a Xerox of Strick's letter to her mother,
she'd destroyed the cretin who'd issued the Challenge.

Now the girl retrieved her files for Levels Four
through Seven and reviewed the additional Characteristics. Level Five: "Willingness to Shoplift." Level Six:
"Willingness to Purchase Drugs." Level Seven: "Willingness to Engage in Sex."

She pulled out a manila envelope and inserted
these Realmlogs into it. Then she licked the flap and
glued it tight. Her mother housecleaned on weekends.
Where could she hide the material until Monday, when
she could stash it in her locker at school?

Weariness seemed to sap the gray matter from her
brains, making decisions almost impossible. Her desk?
The closet? Under the rug? Finally she gave in to the
stupor, changed into her nightgown, and tucked the envelope inside her pillowcase. Tomorrow morning,
when her mind was once more alert, she would find a
safer place, she decided. Meanwhile, it would remain
undisturbed beneath her head.

Though the girl sank swiftly toward sleep, shoplifting and drugs and sex flickered through her dimming
consciousness. In terms of the game, these areas were
both more—and less—than they seemed. Realm was
nothing if not full of surprises. But Patty knew what her
mother's immediate reaction would be. She wouldn't
understand. Nope, no parent could; because what it all
boiled down to was a matter of trust.

Book II
QUARRY

Eleven

The sun streaming through the living room windows felt splendid after the week of drear skies and intermittent rain. Andy sat at her drafting table soaking up the warming rays. The book she was trying to concentrate on was a contract-law manual for the course Professional Practice II. A yawn escaped.

It was late Saturday morning. Patty had already dashed out, brimming with plans to hit the library, lunch with friends, go to a matinee—and, Andy thought wryly, no doubt devote a few hours to Realm.

The telephone rang.

Andy set the textbook down gratefully, stretched like a kitten, and padded over to answer it.

"Mrs. Matteson? Henry Wilhite."

"Oh. Uh, good morning."

"Sorry to be calling on a Saturday, but I thought you'd want to know. Whoever your girl's pals are, they're not dealing. The names turned up clean."

"Sergeant, you can call me with news like that any day of the week," she said in a voice suddenly bright with relief. "Thank you—and sorry to have put you to the trouble. Truly."

Andy blushed as she caught herself using her daughter's favorite catch phrase. When she hung up, she looked at the contracts manual, eyed a pile of unread *New Yorkers*, and decided a break was in order. She headed into the kitchen for a cup of coffee.

On the way back, she happened to glance into Patty's room. The bed had been made, she noted with amusement, sloppily but without any nagging on her part. In the girl's haste to leave, though, she'd left underwear and socks piled on the floor beneath the nightstand. Obeying a maternal instinct, Andy went in and picked them up. She was turning to leave when she noted that one of the desk drawers lay half-open. It was the one in which Patty kept her Realm material. And on top, in full view, rested the file folder marked "Realm—Intro and Levels 1–3."

When Andy had skimmed the rules booklet and game sheet the previous evening, they'd seemed as bafflingly abstruse as some of her own textbooks. Might they be more comprehensible under less emotional circumstances?

She reached for the folder but stopped. Her guilt over violating Patty's diary was still fresh. Wouldn't this compound her prying? Yet her daughter had voluntarily shared it last night and besides, the drawer was already open. The more Andy found herself rationalizing it, the more uneasy she felt. But her hand, instead of retracting, continued forward until the folder was in its grasp.

She detoured to drop the laundry in the hamper and then returned to her drafting table. Opening the folder, she extracted the booklet whose cover read, "Warning! For Authorized Eyes Only!"

She took a sip of her fresh coffee, and began to read.

By the time she thought to pick up the coffee again, it was stone cold.

Andy set the mug down and stared blankly at the booklet. A vein in her neck throbbed. Her stomach felt queasy. The sun had moved, so she stood and walked over to the window through which it now tumbled. The rays were as intense as before, but they no longer seemed to carry warmth or comfort.

The night before, Patty had painted Realm as a territorial game in which players used deductive reasoning, shrewd ploys, and the luck of the die to strengthen their own spaces. That description, Andy now realized, was unimpeachable. It was also like insinuating that poker was merely a game of chance or Scrabble merely a game of spelling.

It had taken Andy awhile to puzzle through the booklet's turgid prose, which appeared to have been written by a computer or by someone to whom English was a third language. Yet she had finally understood that the barrage of buzzwords, as well as the high-tech die that glowed, were only Realm's skeleton.

The game's flesh? A philosophy of dishonor that was frighteningly amoral.

Despite the mumbo jumbo, any person of average brightness could master basic strategy and, with a few fortunate tosses, emerge victorious. But in Realm, the end meant nothing compared to the means. The game was set up so that its thrills lay in tactics that were the mental equivalents of pulling wings off flies.

Patty had alluded to employing indirection to learn another player's identity. The booklet put greater store in eavesdropping, lying, and "trading" information to a third party—which in some circles was known as "selling out."

Patty had stated that once the identities of the opponents started to become obvious, Realm was won by the player most adept at Challenges and Counter-Challenges. The booklet suggested a more efficient method—forming secret pacts for the purpose of ganging up on one hapless participant and blitzkrieging his Configuration into oblivion. According to this perverse social Darwinism, it was best to first clear the field of weaklings so that the strong could either go head-to-head by themselves or divvy up a shrunken universe.

Most chilling of all was a factor that Patty hadn't even raised. The booklet benignly called it Majority Rule. It was, however, the antithesis of democratic fair play. Majority Rule meant that if a majority of participants agreed that black was white—or John was a liar or Susan ought to lose a turn—then by Realm, that's the way it was. In short, a coalition of players could define their own reality. How to form a coalition sufficiently strong to impose its will? Persuasion. Or cajolery. Or barter. Or even blackmail.

Andy couldn't help but think of all the weeks—no, the months—that her daughter had spent buzzing around town and over the phone. Patty must be very accomplished at the more warped edges of wheeling and dealing; after all, hadn't the girl achieved Realm Seven?

Andy was familiar with the works of Bruno Bettelheim. She understood and agreed with the behavioralist's belief that as long as there are children, there will be Darth Vaders. Evil incarnate, be it space-age Hessians or the wicked stepmothers of the Brothers Grimm, was a necessary focal point around which the young could work out their dark fantasies on the way to a mature view of the world.

But the contents of this booklet were no fairy tale. Rather, Realm was a sadistic exploitation of adolescent fears and weaknesses. And though on the surface highly individualistic, the game was in fact a clarion call for conformity, for mob—not majority—rule.

Suddenly Andy shivered. The parallel image that came to mind was of the Third Reich's Youth Corps, those children brainwashed to inform on any German harboring anti-Hitlerian sentiments—even their own parents.

Then something else that had been floating at the back of her mind crystallized: the booklet's tactics seemed like overkill for the type of games that Patty had shown her the previous evening.

Andy walked back to the drafting table and spread out the Realmlogs for Levels One, Two, and Three. The Characteristic Matrices for Realm One were "Securing Realm from Outsiders" and "Promptness." The next Level added "Ability to Bluff Via a White Lie." For Realm Three, the new Characteristic was "Willingness to Tell the Truth."

All in all, these seemed about the speed she would have expected for kids Patty's age. But what were the additional Characteristics for the remaining four Levels?

Andy thumbed through the introductory booklet. Nothing.

She marched down the hall and into Patty's room and unhesitatingly searched the drawer, then the entire desk, and then the bureau and the bookshelf and the closet. Nothing.

Why the hell would anyone want to play with young, half-formed minds in such an aberrant way? And then Andy recognized the real question: *who* would perpetrate such a sick joke?

She returned to the living room and picked up the introductory booklet again. Odd, but it didn't list an author. She pored over the title page and then the front and back covers. The booklet also didn't list a copyright holder, nor was any publisher claiming responsibility.

This is absurd, Andy thought. Someone was obviously masterminding Realm; how else to explain the fifty-dollar die that sold for ten?

She pulled out the Ann Arbor telephone directory and turned to the Yellow Pages section devoted to stores that sold toys and games. Eight were listed. Fifteen minutes later, she had spoken to each of them. None had heard of a game called Realm, much less carried it. Three even asked her to let them know if she succeeded in tracking down the manufacturer.

Had it not been for the malevolent booklet in front of her, Andy would have pinched herself. Instead, she picked up the phone again.

Philip's home number was on machine.

She dialed the lab. He sounded surprised by her call. He sounded even more surprised when she said she'd be at his office in twenty minutes.

The standard-issue cubicle looked larger than its nine-by-twelve size because Philip didn't believe in desks. The guts of the office—a work station featuring a computer terminal with a display screen the size of a large portable television's—brooded in one corner. But he had added a splash of color with a small Turkish kilim and softened the room with an antique coffee table and a pair of comfortable upholstered reading chairs.

It was in these chairs that they sat as Andy related her fears.

But when she finished, Philip appeared less distressed than perturbed: "It doesn't sound like the Realm I know."

"You know about the game?"

He gestured toward the computer terminal. "I know it's on the Double-Z directory, and I'm pretty sure I've seen it played. Come on, let's have a look." As they stood he added, "Aren't you taking a computer course?"

"Yeah. An undergrad introduction I need to get into computer modeling."

"You don't sound thrilled."

"I just can't make myself focus on it. It seems—I don't know, Philip, it seems like a Mickey Mouse approach to something that'll always be beyond me."

"There's nothing mysterious about computers. I take that back—how one works is mysterious, even to me. But that's not the point." Philip rolled up a chair for her and then sat himself at the work station. "For instance, can you accurately describe the workings of an internal combustion engine? Or airflow over a plane's wings? Yet those things make life easier, and so does the computer."

He switched on the terminal.

In the middle of the screen flashed:

Log on please.

"This model's sophisticated by anyone's standards, but it isn't much harder to use than one of those automated bank machines," Philip said. He placed his hands over the keyboard, which resembled a typewriter's except for the extra rows of keys at the top and both sides. As he began to tap, asterisks floated on-screen. When five were up, Philip stopped and pushed a button marked Execute.

In the middle of the screen flashed:

Proceed.

Philip began typing again. This time, letters appeared on-screen:

DIR/ZZ

He hit Execute:

DIR/ZZ password please.

"This is an unauthorized, limited-access directory," he explained as he resumed typing. When seven new asterisks were on-screen, he hit Execute again.

Flashing on-screen was a list of some two dozen games, starting with Asteroids, ranging through six entries for chess and ending with Hangman.

"There's more," Philip said, pressing a button marked Scroll Down. The names on-screen began to crawl upward, like the credits at the end of a television show. He shifted to the Scroll Up button and reverse-crawled until Asteroids was in view again. Then, using a cluster of Up/Down/Right/Left buttons, he maneuvered the bright on-screen blip called the cursor until it was alongside that first game. Finally, he pushed a button marked Fetch.

In a twinkling this terminal in a biochemist's office was transformed into a video arcade game. There in the center was a triangular spaceship, toward which irregularly shaped asteroids hurtled at various speeds. By using the four cursor controls, he could pivot the spaceship in any direction. Philip placed a finger on the Fetch button. Every time he pressed it, the spaceship fired off a rocket, and when a rocket hit an asteroid, the asteroid exploded.

"It's good for hand-eye coordination," he remarked as he casually scored several hits, "but it's not as much fun without the sound effects."

He pushed the button marked Send, and the game vanished.

Then Philip called up the Double-Z directory again.

"Why are there so many chess games?" Andy asked.

"Different degrees of difficulty. For instance, Chess Four means you need at least forty master points to stand a chance." He began scrolling up.

"What's Fuck You?"

Philip laughed. "The dirty version of Hangman. Oh, here's something clever. Most games pit you against the computer. If there's more than one player, it's to see who does better against the machine. But watch this."

He moved the cursor alongside Monopoly I and hit Fetch.

Flashing on-screen was the familiar game board. Four markers rested on the Go square, and lined up at the top were four insets, each showing the sum of $1,500.

"This is the solitaire version," he said. "Only it's programmed so that you're not playing against the computer, you're playing three mythical opponents."

"But that's the computer," Andy protested.

"Yes and no. The computer plays the three dummies competitively against each other, as well as against you."

"Schizzy."

"Very," Philip agreed. He scrolled up until the game board disappeared. Now on-screen were instructions on how to roll the dice, buy property, build hotels, and the rest. After she studied them, he retrieved the game board.

Andy hit the dice-roll button. In the top right-hand corner appeared the number 8. At the same instant, the marker bearing the letter *A* hopped out of the Go square and down the board to Vermont Avenue.

"Care to buy?" Philip asked.

"Of course."

He pressed the transaction button. A ghostly *A* superimposed itself over Vermont Avenue, and the inset showing Andy's bankroll dropped by the correct purchase amount, to $1,400.

Even as the computer began to make Player B's move, she shook her head ruefully.

"What's the matter, Andy?"

"Very bright people spent a hell of a lot of time figuring out this program. Doesn't it strike you as pretty goddamned frivolous?"

"As opposed to mowing the lawn? Or cocktail parties? Or reading thrillers? Whoever did this was probably a NASA programmer or someone in a wind tunnel in Detroit or in a back room on Wall Street. He or she was just trying to unwind. What's wrong with that?"

Andy shrugged, unable to express her uneasiness.

Philip rolled his chair back a bit so he could prop his feet on the work station. "Anyway, this is the work of amateurs—kids' stuff."

"You mean there are more complicated computer games?"

He nodded. "Three whizzes up in Wisconsin have just about nailed down a chess program that can rip Bobby Fischer to shreds. And then there's this game for math Ph.D.'s—remember that old Steve McQueen movie, *The Blob?* Well, they've used a topographical system, like the kind you have in architecture school, to create a three-dimensional blob. It's set loose in a town, where it oozes about swallowing things and growing bigger. The only way to contain it is by applying exotic laws of mathematics and physics."

Philip had been speaking recitatively. Then, in some subtle way that Andy recognized but couldn't place, he grew more excited.

"The penultimate program is probably the Pentagon's," he continued. "Simply put, the game is war. You name the level, they've got it, from guerrilla to all-out, and in every conceivable operational theater. The data is updated continuously. Is the Red Army on maneuvers near the Black Sea? What's the Sixth Fleet's fuel status? How far will the jet stream carry fallout?"

Andy stared out the window. The sun seemed to be dying. Finally she said, "All that effort, all that money, all that creativity—for a game."

"It helps keep us alive," he replied quietly. "The Pentagon program is the twentieth century's real-life bogeyman. That and the one in the Kremlin. The generals play it all the time, Andy. And the results scare the shit out of them."

She stood and began to pace. Philip tracked her with his eyes but did not break the silence. At last she cleared her throat. "You said that's the penultimate program. What's the ultimate?"

"Maybe just a legend."

Andy stopped and propped herself on the arm of one of the reading chairs.

Philip glanced down at the bright kilim on the floor, a faraway look invading his eyes. "Supposedly, it came out of the San Francisco area in the mid-seventies, invented by three men: a math freak from Silicon Valley, a Berkeley psychohistorian, a theology professor from Stanford. It's called Ergo Est—a variation on Descartes's *Cogito, ergo sum*, or 'I think, therefore I am.'

"Supposedly, they piggybacked it onto the world's most powerful computer, the National Security Agency's Loadstone. Supposedly, everybody knows about it, but nobody can track it down. And supposedly, only two dozen people—certifiable geniuses and super-achievers—are allowed access to the game."

"And what is the game?"

Philip shrugged. "Incredibly complex, filled with the hardest options imaginable. Rhythmical, yet dazzlingly unpredictable. Finite yet never ending, like life itself. Or so they say. Who knows?"

Andy shivered. "A surrogate reality—why? Why would such brilliant minds choose to pass time in an artificial world when the real world needs them so much?"

"Did Einstein really live in the real world? Galileo? Plato?"

"But can't you see that at least they were—they were humanists? They lived in the mind, not in the world of chips and wire and memory bubbles. Computers have become the new icons, the new gods, and it scares me."

"Come on, Andy," Philip said impatiently "Your fear is of the unknown. The whole human race used to fear animals, but now that we've studied them, we anthropomorphize them into cuteness. Machines—not just computers, all machines—remain the unknown, so we still fear them. Outside of R2-D2 and C-3PO, name me a lovable machine. Didn't Spielberg make E.T. a being rather than a thing?"

When she didn't respond, he added, "Remember, when you train an animal, it can always turn on you. When you program a computer, that's it. It only knows what humans put in, and we're never going to be able to program evil."

"Or love," Andy said quietly.

Philip's face softened. "No, we'll keep that one for ourselves."

The tension broken, she smiled and returned to the work station.

On-screen was Monopoly. The computer had long since made her opponents' moves, and Andy found her marker blinking on and off. She pressed the dice-roll button: 9. Her marker hopped forward and landed on Community Chest. Inside a previously blank rectangle on the game board, words began to form: "Proceed Di-

rectly to Jail. Do Not Pass Go—Do Not Collect $200."
Before her marker reached the pokey, Philip hit Send,
and the game disappeared.

He called up the directory again, scrolled until he
reached Realm, and fetched it. "Look familiar?"

Andy nodded. The Configuration was a triangle.
Above it were four insets showing each player's Arsenal
Points. Below it were the Characteristic Matrices. But
when she studied these, she frowned. "Philip, the Characteristics are different. This version's much too
namby-pamby. All the players have to do is screw up
math problems and deliberately misspell words. In
Patty's game they have to do things like tell white lies
and be late for meetings."

"Some games really get flattened out when they go
on computer," he said. "It's the nature of the beast. You
can't really program being late."

"Nor, you say, evil." Andy stood and began pacing
again. "But Patty's Realm isn't on computer, and I think
that its programming is in fact evil. Yet I don't know
how to begin checking it out."

"Like me to look into it?"

Andy stopped. Socially acceptable demurrers—
"Do you have the time?"; "Only if it wouldn't be a bother"; "Oh, no, I couldn't ask that"—flitted through her
mind. But when she finally spoke, she said, "Yes, please.
And thank you."

Philip bowed his head with mock gravity, then
smiled. "Lunch?"

"I don't know, Philip—my appetite's off."

"Then permit me to restore it."

Andy kept looking at him until her own smile widened into a grin.

Intertwined on his bed, mostly undressed, they
sparred lazily with their tongues. Slowly, body temper-
atures climbed. The touch of his sinewy hand was as
light as a feather as it passed down her neck, down over
her collarbone, around a breast and down a flank, then

finally back up to a breast, around which it began to trace concentrically diminishing circles. Suddenly thumb grazed wine-dark nipple; Andy grimaced in delight.

Mouths separated. Philip's head swung first to her silken throat and then to her chest. Languid and liquid, each lap triggered in her a streak of pleasure like a jagged bolt of lightning. Then lips smothered a nipple, and rapid-fire flicks of the tongue began alternating with gentle sucks, the two contrasting sensations seeming to draw her sweet essences right from the very marrow of her soul. Her breathing rapid and shallow, her mind a skewed gyroscope on a storm-tossed sea, she felt a new sensation: his hand was gliding down her taut and trembling belly and inside her underpants, and she was raising her pelvis so he could push the garment away—the air impossibly cold on her glisteningly moist privacy—and then she kicked clear the panties. As his hand meandered back up her calves, Andy's legs anticipated its approach by inching open. His hand was at her knee; then above her knee, caressing and soothing; and then oh-so-gentle kneads of the soft muscles between the straining tendons of her innermost thighs.

Her skin was on fire; Andy gripped the back of his neck, hard.

Now Philip's fingers spidered teasingly through her matted pubic hair. At the source, a hesitation, and then they began to tentatively lower; at first touch she gasped and jerked her long neck tight. Tenderly, his digits slid around and then around again and again until, homage paid, they stole deftly into the temple.

At that instant her clenched mouth shot open, and her back arched, and her forehead crimsoned. Her moans and his fell into quickening step as she thrust her pelvis upward in search of more. He obliged. But not for long. Suddenly he withdrew his hand, leaving Andy cruelly frozen in prerelease, hips in midair, breath coming in short sobs.

And then weight shifted, as did warmth and densi-

ty; the galaxy cartwheeled, and when the stars resettled, so had Philip.

His face was buried between her thighs. And in
that safest of harbors his lips nibbled and plucked, his
tongue stroked and probed; now mongoose, now cobra,
his mouth became the palpitating levee against which
her eroticism dammed. There wasn't enough air in the
room, in the world, to fill her tortured lungs, and yet
she continued to inhale.

"Philip," she whispered coarsely, "please . . ."

Slowly his tongue targeted the locus of pleasure in-
sensate. It seemed to simultaneously fill her and con-
sume her, both of which should have been impossible,
for was it not she who was swallowing his entire being?
Licks grew into riffs, the tempo shifting into acceleran-
do, the pressure increasing with the rhythm. Andy's
tousled head thrashed from side to side, her body shook
and shivered; her consciousness was dominated by his
tongue. She filled her hands with his hair and began to
utter his name, like a ritual incantation, until words
were replaced by whimpers that emerged from deep
in her throat and that grew and grew and grew until
they bunched into a ululating scream.

At the epicenter lava flowed, the spasms radiating
outward, and then an icy breath was leaching the very
heat from her pores—my god, I'm cold—and ringing
down a seamless curtain of blackest velvet.

Warmth. His warmth. The warmth of his body covered her like a quilt, the warmth of his kisses dried her
clammy cheeks.

Early afternoon sunlight flooded the bedroom,
glinting off glass and metal, backlighting the motes that
danced in the air.

Andy raised her hands and clasped them behind his
neck and drew his mouth to hers. His wet hardness
throbbed against one of her thighs. She freed a hand
and stroked it down his muscled back, raked it upward—did his groan precede his shudder, or was it the

other way round?—and then down again. He propped himself on his elbows as she snuggled her head beneath his chest; his nipples tasted salty. At the same time she reached between their abdomens and circled his slippery member.

Philip sobbed from the exquisite tension.

On two fronts Andy sought his liberation, and when it was at hand, she squinched herself back up the mattress and opened her thighs once more.

Like a key entering a lock, like a sword returning to its scabbard, he slid home.

Philip's excitement was contagious. Soon she was clinging to him, moving with and then against, their thrusts alternately savage and sweet but always deeper, the room shaking off the scale, the sunlight so bright that it hurt to keep her eyes open, so bright that when they were closed the universe ran red, blood red shifting to rose and then to plum. They took themselves and each other to the outer limits of fleshly tolerance and then beyond, a cacophony of sounds from both within the skull and without, until at last he froze, like a suicidee with one foot over the ledge, and then he was hurtling toward climax. And then she felt herself on the same ledge, felt herself slipping off, the tumble this time quieter, mellower. And then their two bodies were still except for an occasional twitch or quiver as, spent, they drifted in each other's arms across a calm but fathomless sea, drifted toward the far horizon.

Andy awoke to love's unmistakable smell: It was on the sheets, it was in her nostrils; indeed, it seemed to saturate the room's very air.

Philip dozed lightly.

She tried to blink away her lassitude. A yawn started. She drowsily covered mouth with hand—and suddenly catching his strong scent on her fingers, began wetting those fingers with her tongue. A complicated emotion surged through Andy. She wanted to thrill Philip, sadden him, nurse him, fuck him, hold him for

a moment, hold him forever; she felt at once slut and
mother, chaste and carnal.

She lifted the sheet gingerly and beheld his limp
and shrunken member. Such a silly-looking thing, so
crudely designed in so many ways—yet so much fun.
Now, a gentle touch. His breath caught, but he did not
awake. Andy bent down and ran the tip of her tongue
along the underside of his shaft, tasting him and tasting
herself.

A muffled grunt of surprise and satisfaction; Philip
was awake.

Her tongue extended in length and in range. He
reached a hand to her back. She rebalanced herself and,
gently grasping the stiffened rod, began a slow, smooth,
easy stroke while her tongue turned into a butterfly, flit-
ting between the several sweet spots, landing there and
teasing here.

"Oh . . ."

A musky aroma accompanied the clear droplets
that began to tremble out. Andy lowered her mouth
over him. He seemed to grow harder and wider and
longer. Her tongue and mouth and hand worked con-
trapuntally but toward a common goal. His hand, which
had been on her back, slid around and not so much
cupped as grabbed a breast. Now so many juices issued
from the both of them that her tongue could not retrieve them all, the wet sliding down his shaft, covering
him, covering her fingers, covering her hand, and still
it spilled over, drooling down onto the sheets. Seconds?
Minutes? Hours? But then, what was time? The pace
and pressure of her hand and her bobbing head increased inexorably.

His breathing plateaued and a supertautness suffused his very being.

Andy had an instant to steel herself. Still she
flinched as his ejaculate drummed against the back of
her mouth. Her gorge rose, but then she was simultaneously swallowing the saline cream and playing with
this flopping fish within her mouth. She sucked greedily

until Philip seemed dry, sucked until one last dribble spilled forth, sucked until it shrank back into limpness, and then she bestowed on its tip a gentle kiss.

Arms that had refound their strength pulled her up and atop him. Their lips met. He probed her mouth.

And suddenly stabbed several fingers into her.

Andy's startled gasp was felt rather than heard. Then she settled back, impaling herself on his hand, riding until her stomach somersaulted with sensual nausea and giddiness, riding until she reached the convulsive contractions, and then she dismounted and floated through the viscous air until she landed spread-eagled on him, there to lie panting and wordless.

"Hey." There was a tremor in Philip's voice.

Andy opened her eyes. Tears welled in his.

"Hey," he said again. "You know I adore you."

She nodded and kissed away the tears. Then she drew the sheet up over them both, snuggled her head on his shoulder, and closed her eyes again.

While buttoning her sleeves, Andy finished off the last of the cheese and crackers and giggled.

Philip looked up expectantly.

She gestured at the kitchen clock, which read five-twenty. "I was supposed to put a roast for dinner. I guess Patty'll have to settle for pizza."

"Why not? We did."

She groaned and laughed at the same time, then stood.

"How do you feel?" he asked.

Impulsively she crossed her eyes and let her tongue loll out of one corner of her mouth.

He swatted her on the rump and walked her to her coat. Before he could help her on with it, she wrapped him up in an affectionate hug. "Thank you."

"For what?"

"For always seeming to be there. For—for being you."

"*Nada,*" he said gruffly. Then he hooked a finger under her chin and tilted it upward.

"See you around campus," she whispered.

He gave her a gentle peck and whispered back, "Take care of yourself, Andy."

As Andy drove home, she found herself wondering whether Philip's unexpected emotional epiphanies—in bed, with tears in his eyes, and at her leaving—were due to the same rush of insight that was forcing open door after door within her.

Twelve

Wednesday night, an unseasonably late cold snap moved down from Canada and settled into the valley in which Ann Arbor lay. When Andy dashed out the next morning to warm up the Honda, she discovered the battery was dead.

So, evidently, were many others in town. It took seven calls to find a garage that could get a truck to her before noon. Andy decided to cut her lecture—she was seriously behind in another course, and had to attend an obligatory dinner that evening—so she quickly arranged a lift for Patty. When she hung up, she realized the sudden freeze must also be affecting Michigan Bell's equipment, for her line was plagued by an odd assortment of squeaks, echoes, and clicks. She dialed the service number. It was busy. To hell with it, she thought; they must be aware of the problem.

Shortly before one in the afternoon, Andy was sitting in the kitchen, textbook on the table and a bowl of soup in front of her, when the phone rang. It was Patty. The friend whom she was visiting after school had asked her to stay for dinner. Andy, remembering her own party that night, gave permission and then took down from her daughter a number where she could be reached.

The line was still full of static, but Michigan Bell was still busy. Andy finished her light lunch and went down for the mail.

One letter was from Strick, the junior high principal. He was pleased to report that Patty seemed to have found herself in English and social studies. Andy smiled. Whatever reservations she harbored about Realm, her confidence in the girl was firmly reestablished.

She went to her room and opened the drawer in which she kept the junior high file. Odd: at the front of the file was Strick's previous letter, which had been missing the last time she looked. Who except Patty could have taken it? But what on earth would she have wanted it for?

Valets waited at the foot of the walk to take her car. Inside the spacious vestibule, with its hand-quarried Mexican tile floor, stood commercial coat racks already filled with winter outerwear. In the living room were large crystal bowls of mulled wine and champagne cocktail, as well as an open bar. Rent-a-maids circulated with trays of hors d'oeuvres. In the formal dining room, Andy glimpsed serving tables groaning under chafing dishes; carving boards spiked with roasts; platters of fish, of vegetables, of pilaf, and *pommes Anna;* and tureens of sauces and gravies.

Ostensibly, Roger and Muriel Gentry had invited one hundred junior high parents to their house in the fashionable Woods section to organize the eighth-grade class gift. In fact Roger, a rising young attorney with political aspirations, wanted his name in the society page of *The Ann Arbor News*—and wanted to gather support for his candidacy for the school board presidency.

Andy begrudged the time away from her books, hated herself for accepting such a transparent invitation. Yet, transient though she and Patty may have been in this community, they had more than a year left to live in it; a few hours of cordiality had seemed the better part of valor.

She made her way slowly to the bar. A double scotch would have braced her nicely for the evening ahead, but she had three hours of studying awaiting her at home: "A white wine spritzer, please."

The decibel count was already near maximum, most faces vaguely familiar but worth no more than a nod or a quick smile. And then suddenly, through the press of bodies, Andy spied Jane and Gordon Brockman, Ginger's parents. She made for them as a capsized boater for a buoy.

An hour later, Roger Gentry's speech having been endured, Andy sat with Jane and Gordon in a corner of the den, dinner plates on their laps.

"The trouble is," Gordon was saying, "the school board's going to be run by an asshole, no matter who wins. Gentry, you already know. But you ought to catch his opponents."

"One's the wife of the owner of a store on Main Street," Jane said. "Moral Majority. Her platform is, fire the degenerates and burn the books they assign."

"The minority candidate's a real winner, too," Gordon said. "A black doctor under investigation for Medicaid fraud."

"What's his platform?" Andy asked.

"Honky persecution," Gordon snapped.

"And I thought we had problems back in New York," Andy said.

He snorted, drained his wineglass, and stood. "Can I get either of you another drink?"

Jane shook her head. Andy looked at the almost finished spritzer she'd been nursing since she arrived, thought of the studying that remained, and asked for a Perrier or club soda with a twist.

When Gordon left she turned to Jane. "How's Ginger been? I haven't seen her in ages."

Surprisingly, Jane averted her eyes. "Still crushed. Still bitter."

"About what?" Andy said, visions of adolescent traumas dancing through her head.

"You don't know?"

"No."

"Realm."

"Realm?" Andy repeated, in disbelief.

Jane drew a deep breath. "Ginger wasn't allowed to play."

"My god, why? She's great at math. . . ."

"You really don't know, do you? But of course, why should you? It seems that when they organized the god-damned game early this year, the only kids they allowed to play were—were those with extraordinary good looks to go with their math skills." Jane's face hardened. "But even if Ginger looked like Patty—even if she looked like fucking Cheryl Tiegs—she'd still be on the outside looking in. You see, they don't seem to want Jews playing Realm."

Philip was not at his apartment or the lab. Andy hung up the phone in the room that Roger Gentry used for an office, bade her host and hostess good night, then fetched her coat. As she waited for a valet to bring the Honda, she couldn't take her mind off the implications of what Jane had told her. Andy's dominant impression on reading the Realm booklet the previous weekend had been one of neo-Naziism. Add to that now a bias toward attractive, high-IQ Aryans—and a streak of anti-Semitism.

She got into the car and began driving the several miles back to her apartment. Because traffic was light and because she was preoccupied, she paid less than her customary attention to the road.

On Packard, less than two miles from home, she heard the sudden bleat of a siren. Andy glanced in the rearview and saw the stroboscopic lights of a fast-approaching emergency vehicle. She flipped on her turn indicator and eased toward the curb.

One last blast on the siren and then rubber squealing on macadam, and then a dark mass was hurtling eccentrically past on the left; the police car slued halfway across her lane, as if cutting off escape, and before the vehicle had rocked to a standstill, both front doors were flying open and a pair of cops were springing out.

She hadn't been speeding, Andy thought in confusion. Were her taillights out? Or was it some sort of emergency?

Even as she began rolling down her window, one of the men planted himself in front of the Honda and flicked a powerful flashlight on her face. She recoiled from the glare.

"Okay, ma'am, gonna have to ask you to get out," the other cop commanded. He had positioned himself by the driver's side door, but just beyond its arc.

Dazed, Andy opened the door and stepped out. Instantly, the cop strode up to her. He was big. And young. And the disdain on his face seeped into his voice: "Driving kind of wobbly, weren't you, ma'am?"

"I beg your pardon?"

"Side to side, switching lanes without signaling, speed varying between twenty and fifty-two—"

"There must be some mistake."

"License and registration, please."

"What?"

He sighed condescendingly. "Those little bitty pieces of paper, ma'am? The ones from the motor vehicle department?"

As Andy leaned back into the car to retrieve her purse, her head suddenly cleared. And replacing confusion was anger: "I thought you boys only had quotas on parking tickets."

"Just your papers, ma'am," he said levelly.

She opened her purse and fished out her wallet. By now the cold was getting to her. Fingers that were numbing had difficulty withdrawing the documents from their plastic sleeves; as she started to hand them over, the registration dropped out of her grasp.

"I'd say this lady has a coordination problem," the cop shouted to his partner. He bent down, picked it up, and turned back to Andy. "Had a lot to drink tonight, did you, ma'am?"

"One white wine, cut with soda," she replied between clenched teeth.

He sighed again. "Fraid I'm gonna have to ask you to take a Breathalyzer, ma'am."

"Now wait a minute—"

"Course you don't have to," he continued blandly, "but in the state of Michigan refusal to submit to a Breathalyzer constitutes admission of operating a motor vehicle while under the influence."

"Then give me the goddamned thing," Andy said angrily.

The cop unzipped one pocket of his lined nylon jacket and pulled out a plastic envelope, which he popped open. The Breathalyzer looked like a party favor—a balloon affixed to one end of a short tube. "Blow on this end of the tube, ma'am, and inflate that there balloon. If the chemicals inside remain white, you're just fine. If they turn pink, though, I'd say you had a problem on your hands. Ma'am."

Glaring at him, Andy took the gizmo and began to blow.

He trained his flashlight on the balloon. As it inflated it turned—*pink*.

"Whoo-whee!" the cop guffawed. "Drunk as a skunk!"

"But—"

He snatched the Breathalyzer from her hand, shoved it and her papers back into the plastic bag, and crimped the bag shut. Then he took her arm. "Come on, ma'am, we are going to take us a ride."

Andy, stunned, allowed herself to be led unprotestingly toward the police car. By the time they got there, the other cop had opened the back door.

"Ma'am?" the first cop said. "Keys still in the Honda? Okay, my partner here'll drive your vehicle to headquarters." He motioned for Andy to get in.

The back compartment was partitioned from the front by a heavy metal grill. When the cop slammed the door shut, she noticed there were no handles on the inside. He walked around the front, swung himself in, and picked up the radio mike. As he began jabbering in that semi-intelligible CB slang, the gravity of her situation finally began to sink in.

The drive to headquarters took less than five minutes. During it, though, Andy mapped out her strategy. She knew only one lawyer in Ann Arbor; she'd met him earlier that evening, on attending the party at his house. Not that Roger Gentry would be thrilled to hear from her, but he should be more than anxious to convince the police—perhaps with the help of some of his parking-lot valets—that no guest of his had been permitted to drive off in an alcoholic stupor.

The cop escorted Andy inside. When did one request the permitted phone call, she wondered, before or after the booking? The cop stopped at the big, high desk over which the duty officer presided and asked, "The chief in?"

The duty officer nodded.

"Come on, ma'am," the cop said, gesturing for Andy to follow. Surprised, she trailed him through the maze of linoleumed corridors to a walnut-veneered door marked Chief Eric Schmidt. He rapped briskly on the door, then opened it.

The office was quintessential American Legion: flags and pennants on staffs topped by gilded eagles; a wall of stiffly posed photographs depicting the chief with this celebrity and that group; trophies and awards celebrating long-forgotten honors; bookshelves piled high with stacks of law enforcement journals; and, on the wall behind his desk, a collection of antique firearms.

The only thing out of place in the room was

Schmidt himself. He was a small, ferrety man dressed in a neatly tailored three-piece suit that Andy doubted could have been purchased in Ann Arbor. Schmidt sat ramrod straight at his desk, studying a computer printout with great intensity.

Obviously the cop beside her was used to his superior's ways, for he shifted into the "at-ease" stance.

Andy began to stew as Schmidt backtracked through the printout, doublechecking numbers with the precision of an accountant. Finally he accordianed the sheets back in order and placed the stack off to one side. Only then did he look up at the cop.

The cop passed over the plastic bag containing the Breathalyzer. "Stopped her on Packard, sir."

"Thank you, Keresey," Schmidt said in a voice so low that Andy had to cock her head to hear him. "Would you please wait outside."

As Keresey about-faced and left the room, Schmidt opened the bag and eased its contents onto his desk. He picked up her license and registration. Without looking up he said, "What do you do, Mrs. Matteson."

"I'm in the graduate program at Michigan."

When he finally looked up, his unblinking eyes held no curiosity. "Have a seat, Mrs. Matteson."

Andy wavered. "Chief Schmidt," she blurted, "I'd like to make a call to my lawyer, and I demand the right to take another Breathalyzer test. This one must've been defect—"

"Have a seat, Mrs. Matteson."

She flushed but sat.

"Have you been in Ann Arbor long, Mrs. Matteson."

"Since September."

He nodded, as if that explained everything. "We are a city in transition, Mrs. Matteson. Socially, politically, economically. But the one thing that will never change, that we do not wish to change, is the relationship between the community and the university. Students at the university are our guests. If our guests transgress on occasion, we try to make allowances.

"Those fortunate enough to attend our great university are faced with enormous pressures. We know that, Mrs. Matteson." Schmidt paused and lowered his eyes to his desk. "A small percentage of students even manage to cope with their academic work while raising children. I personally find that truly remarkable. Because being a parent is not easy, is it, Mrs. Matteson."

Andy tried to hide her shock. How did he know she was a parent? From that nark Wilhite? But her visit was supposed to be off the record. And where was this oblique soliloquy leading?

"I am myself a parent," Schmidt continued. "Fortunately, I have lived in this community for the past twenty-two years. I know it. I know its strengths, its flaws. On balance, it is a good community, one that gives me great pride to live in and serve.

"Yet, I understand the apprehension an outsider who is also a parent might feel in moving here. Our children are affluent. They are mobile. They are bright. A potentially dangerous combination, wouldn't you agree, Mrs. Matteson.

"Well, it worries me, too. But as I said, I am fortunate. I know the children who my child associates with—I know that they are not phantomlike purveyors of evil. And if there were phantoms, which there are not, I would have enough faith in this community to let it solve its own problems. I would definitely not get a lot of good people all stirred up. Not over phantoms that do not exist."

Andy's eyes widened in disbelief. The bastard was not only alluding to her meeting with Wilhite, but he was also telling her to stay out of it.

"But then, as we have agreed, being a parent is not easy," Schmidt said in his low monotone. "For example, tonight I faced a difficult decision. I was to have attended a dinner party. However, in late afternoon my deputy fell ill. I wanted very much to attend the party, for it was given by a good friend of mine, Rog Gentry. In addition, it was to honor educational excellence in our community, which is a subject that is very important to me. So my choice, Mrs. Matteson, was, do I attend the party, or do I come to the office."

He fixed her once more with those unblinking eyes. "I am glad that I made the decision that I did. Had I not, we would not have met, and I would not have had the chance to welcome you to Ann Arbor."

Schmidt pitched the Breathalyzer balloon into his wastebasket. Then he gathered up Andy's license and registration and handed them to her. "I hope that in the months to come you will feel more comfortable here, more trusting of the community and of its institutions. In the meantime, I do hope that you will not combat the many pressures you face with alcohol—certainly not if you plan to drive." He pressed a button on his desk. "Officer Keresey will see you safely home. Good evening, Mrs. Matteson."

The door was opening behind her, and Schmidt was again fussing with his computer printouts. Andy stood. She wanted to say something—but what? And then Keresey was alongside her, so she turned and quietly left the office.

When he heard their footsteps fading down the linoleumed corridor, Eric Schmidt got up and bolted his door. Returning to his desk, he unlocked a drawer and took out a red telephone. This private line's routing bypassed the headquarters' switchboard.

Schmidt dialed 1 to access long distance, followed by area code 408 and then a number. He let it ring twice and hung up. Then he redialed and waited one ring. Finally he dialed it once again and stayed on.

After the third ring, his call was answered by a male obviously speaking through some sort of electronic filter: "Yes?"

"Double-A Six," Schmidt replied.

"How did it go?"

"As you said it would."

"Does she suspect?"

"Yes."

There was a click and then the dial tone. Schmidt hung up.

Ninety seconds later, the phone in a shabby Ann Arbor rooming house began to ring. There were two men in the room. Both were in their mid-thirties and possessed the hard-faced, hard-bodied look associated with career servicemen or veterans of Grade-C action movies. The leader had mismatched eyes: one pupil was brown while the other, permanently dilated by a childhood accident, was jet black. This man wore a set of earphones as he hunched over an expensive tape recording rig. His beefy partner hovered over the phone, which had fallen silent after two rings. It rang again, once. Another pause, then one ring, two rings, three rings. He picked up but did not speak.

"Report, please." The male voice was electronically filtered.

"The operational transfer is complete."

"Does it go well?"

"Affirmative." Then the beefy man hesitated.

"Is something the matter?" the electronically filtered voice asked.

"Our access equipment. It's junk, and it's producing a lot of feedback—static, squeals, echoes. The target might suspect something."

"Proceed with the equipment that is in place. Status of Rover One, please."

"Vehicle secured and repainted, as per orders. Is surveillance to commence?"

"Negative."

A click and the dial tone; the beefy man shrugged, then replaced the handset.

Why the elaborate frame-up and why Schmidt's thinly veiled warning? Did it have to do with drug traffic in Ann Arbor? But that no longer concerned Andy. What was of concern was Realm—yet, how could Schmidt possibly know that? And even if he did, what possible connection could he have to the sinister game?

Andy stepped back into her apartment in a volatile mood that was equal parts fury and humiliation. Patty was still out.

It was not yet ten o'clock. Where would Philip be? Probably home. Andy picked up the handset and flinched at the piercing squeals it emitted. Damn the phone company, she thought. She jiggled the plungers until the squeal was replaced by mere static and then dialed. Philip was on machine; Andy left a message to call immediately. Next she tried his office; no answer.

She was just about to hang up when she caught a peculiar sound that made her nape bristle: an echoey whisper not at all like a crossed line. She pressed the handset tighter against her ear, as if willing herself into the instrument. There it was again.

Andy broke the connection.

Silence.

She took her finger away. The plungers popped up, the dial tone hummed—and the ghostly whispers returned. This must be some systemic freak, she thought, or a bad dream. Andy depressed the plungers again.

And let out a yelp when the phone rang.

"Uh, hello?"

"Mrs. Matteson?" a male voice asked.

"Yes?" she answered warily.

"Perry Chalmers—Melissa's father."

"Oh," Andy said. It was the Chalmerses' home that Patty had gone to for dinner. "Hi. Sorry I sounded so startled. I, uh, I happened to be holding the phone in my hand when it rang."

Chalmers chuckled sympathetically. "I'm calling because we just noticed how late it was. The girls are still engrossed in what they're doing, and we were wondering if it'd be okay for Patty to stay over."

"Well . . ."

"I can run her home right now," he added quickly. "But I'm sure they'd both appreciate it if you said okay. My wife and I promise that they'll be in bed by ten-thirty."

Andy hesitated and then said, "It appears I'm outvoted. I hope that what they're engrossed in is their books."

"They got a little studying done," Chalmers said. "Mostly, though, it's been—"

Another screech drowned out his words.

"I'm sorry," Andy said, "I've been having trouble with my line all day. I didn't quite catch that."

"I said, mostly they've been playing Realm."

It seemed to take a month for Andy's breath to return. She prayed that her voice sounded normal when she finally said, "Oh, Melissa's in the game, too."

"Yup," Chalmers replied proudly. "Best damn thing that's happened to her. You know how some of those highfalutin' experts say that fantasy games are bad for kids because it lets them create their own reality? I say, poppycock."

"Oh?"

"My little girl's imagination has been stretched for the first time. Realm's given her a sense of purpose, a reason to learn self-discipline. Don't you feel that Patty's benefited, too?"

"I—I suppose so," Andy said. "It's just that sometimes I worry because the game seems so all-absorbing."

"Exactly! Think of all those hours of TV unwatched. All those junk records unlistened to."

On a hunch Andy asked, "Would you know how Realm got started in Ann Arbor?"

"Sure. Rolf."

"Rolf?" Andy said weakly, her blood running cold at the memory of the tall, mannerly blond boy with the watery blue eyes.

"Melissa told us Rolf learned it out West somewhere, when he was bouncing around foster homes.

Can you imagine anybody not wanting to adopt a nice kid like that?"

Andy cleared her throat. "I didn't realize Rolf was adopted."

"I don't think it's a secret. Yes, about eighteen months ago."

"Who are his parents? I don't think I've met them."

Just at that instant, another burst of static overwhelmed the line.

"I'm sorry," Andy said, hearing her own voice echoing. "This phone is driving me nuts."

"I said, Eric and Heidi Schmidt," Chalmers repeated. "You know, the chief of police. . . ."

Time had long ceased to have meaning, so lost was Andy in her mental labyrinth. When the phone rang, she looked at the luminescent face of her alarm clock and was surprised that it was only twelve forty-five. She switched on a light and picked up.

"I have a collect call for anyone from Philip Hunt," an operator said.

Andy jerked upright. "I'll accept, operator."

"Go ahead," the operator said.

"Andy?"

"Philip! Where are you?"

"On the Coast," he said breathlessly. "Listen, time's short, so—"

"Philip!"

"Sorry, but my chartered plane's coming in any minute, and if I can connect with the red-eye, I'll be at your place before nine, okay?"

"What's going on? For god's sake, Philip, what's going on?"

"Realm! I've got answers! Documented answers, answers on paper!" But suddenly his exultant voice turned cautious. "Look, uh, it's better if I go over them with you in person. See you in about eight hours, okay? And, Andy—I love you. Uh-oh, the plane's landing. Got to run. Bye!"

Stunned, she held on to the dead handset. And then broke into a cold sweat as the mysterious echoes reasserted themselves.

Thirteen

When her eyes popped open, it was pitch black in the bedroom. It was also so still that the loudest sounds were the trip-hammer thuds of her racing heart.

Andy's head rested on the mattress, the pillow having been muscled onto the floor during her uneasy sleep. Her feet, too, were cold, the sheet and blanket having twisted loose.

She glanced at the glowing clock face. It was 5:52. What had woken her? Slowly, the residual memory of receiving a shot to the solar plexus, but try as she might she could not recapture the strands of the nightmare that had surrounded the imagined trauma. Andy jackknifed her feet under the rumpled covers. She feared she was too wound up to fall back to sleep. She was wrong.

At nine o'clock Andy called the telephone company to report the strange sounds on her line. The harried service operator said the cold snap was affecting the switching system; in fact, an entire neighborhood had gone down. Andy insisted that her line be checked, and thoroughly. The operator finally took down the information, though she concluded, snippily, that Andy would have to wait until the emergency crews had restored all lost service.

Andy returned to her seat by the front window to watch for the familiar sight of Philip's tan Alfa Romeo convertible.

The seconds grew into a minute, which grew into

ten, which grew into half an hour. The fact that he was by habit prompt did not allay her growing alarm.

She was reluctant to use the telephone, but finally she called his apartment. He was still on machine.

The red-eye; Philip had said he'd be catching the red-eye east. But from which city—Los Angeles? San Francisco? And on which airline? And into which airport—nearby Willow Run? Detroit? Or suppose at that early hour he'd been forced to fly into Chicago; would he puddle-jump in on a commuter flight or rent a car for the four-hour drive? What if he'd just plain missed the red-eye? But then wouldn't he have phoned again?

Andy gulped another cup of coffee.

Ten twenty-three. Surely Philip should have gotten to a phone by now to explain the delay. She dialed his apartment again and got the tape again. Then his office. No answer. Then the university switchboard, in order to get the departmental secretary, but that line was busy. Andy waited two minutes and tried again. Damn it, what could that woman possibly be yakking about?

Ten twenty-nine. With the semester drawing to a close, Andy's eleven o'clock Design Elective class was critical. She knew her concentration level would be that of a four-year-old's, but the professor had announced that he would begin reviewing all the topics to be covered on the finals.

Torn, she finally called Philip's apartment again and left another message—he was to summon her out of class the minute he got in—and scribbled a note to the same effect. Andy taped the note to her door and dashed down the stairs.

The cold snap continued unabated. The sky was cloudless but a dull gray, as if the chill had taken with warmth all color. She shivered uncontrollably. Come on, come on, she muttered, urging the Honda's heater to kick in; yet when it did, her teeth would not stop chattering.

Traffic was heavy, the parking lot jammed. Andy was already late when she finally found a space.

She dashed from the car into the Art and Architecture Building. Halfway to the elevators she suddenly slammed to a halt, her attention having snagged on something in the outer lobby. She turned back. It had been a newspaper headline.

As if in a trance, Andy began retracing her steps toward the metal-and-plastic newspaper vending machine. She was twelve feet away when her eyes darted to the bold headline that dominated the front page of *The Ann Arbor News:*

TENSIONS ESCALATE
IN ARGENTINA.

Under this was a large photograph of tanks trundling down Buenos Aires' streets.

She drew nearer, her attention shifting to the smaller headline in the upper left-hand corner.

For the second time in six hours, Andy felt as though a cosmic fist had slammed her breath away. She tottered the remaining few steps to the vending machine and clutched it to keep from collapsing. Slowly, her lungs started to work again. But something was wrong with her vision; little blips crisscrossed her eyeballs like tracers, and every image had at least two ghosts.

Finally the world snapped back into focus. She looked through the plastic casing. The awful words had not changed:

VISITING UM PROF
CRITICALLY HURT.

Underneath the headline, two photographs: a larger one of a crushed car, a light-colored Alfa Romeo convertible, and next to it a small portrait, like the type found in school yearbooks, of Philip Hunt.

She hunched lower and peered more closely, but still she couldn't seem to make out the words of the article; maybe the print was too small or the plastic casing too thick, or maybe it was her eyes, which felt as if they were underwater.

Andy took the change purse from her handbag and opened it: a bunch of pennies and two dimes. Not enough, so she placed the purse atop the machine and paid it no heed as it slid off the slanting surface and spilled onto the floor; she was too busy pulling items from the handbag—there must be more change somewhere in there, she needed change because it was important to have the right change—and keys and tissues and makeup and letters and bills began gathering at her feet. Incredulous passersby were stopping to watch. Andy ignored them, as she ignored the tears coursing down her cheeks. Instead she continued rummaging until, arriving at handbag's bottom and finding no more change, she let out a single violent sob.

Andy dropped her handbag and regarded the vending machine. Stare turned to glare.

And then she was accosting it, kicking, shaking, hitting, finally grabbing the metal handle and yanking upward and outward with all her might. A sharp *snap!* as the plastic cover splintered, its sudden unhinging throwing her back several steps.

Andy regained her balance and rushed the machine with hands outstretched. As she wrestled a copy of the newspaper free of the retaining bar, the broken cover swung back down; one jagged edge raked the back of her hand, splitting the flesh. She absently wiped away the blood and squinted at the article. Damn, but her eyes were going to hell, she'd better see someone soon. . . .

A biochemist completing a year as a visiting professor at The University of Michigan was critically injured early this morning in a one-car crash on Interstate 94. The predawn accident occurred two miles east of the State Street exit.

Reported in critical condition in the intensive

care unit of University Hospital in Ann Arbor is Philip L. Hunt, 32, a native of Van Nuys, Calif.

Hunt, who earned his Ph.d. in Biochemistry at the California Institute of Technology, suffered massive head and internal injuries and a broken leg.

According to the Washtenaw County Sheriff's Department, Hunt was proceeding west on I-94 when the accident occurred. His car left the road at a speed that authorities estimate, on the basis of skid marks, to have been 60 mph.

The vehicle, a foreign-made sports car, struck a light stanchion and rolled over several times.

Hunt was cut free of the wreckage by the Washtenaw Sheriff's Department Emergency Rescue Unit and rushed to University Hospital.

The sheriff's department states that there were no witnesses to the accident, which occurred shortly before 6:00 A.M.

Shortly before 6:00 A.M.
When had she awoken with the sensation of having her solar plexus stepped on? And then Andy remembered, and then, clutching the newspaper, she began running, trying to reach the women's room before she threw up.

In the cold white light his skin looked like gray wax. Philip's closed eyes were about the only visible parts of his face: his head was bandaged, and clear plastic tubes snaked up his nostrils.

An I.V. tube dripped a clear liquid into an arm taped to a splint. His left leg, too, was rigid, entombed in a cast and raised in traction.

Wires trailed from beneath his white hospital nightgown out to an electronic gizmo on a shelf over the head of the bed. The spidery contrails on the gizmo's screen, a nurse had explained, were his vital signs.

What did a goddamned machine know about vital

signs? About the five senses, about delight and passion and love? Had it really been less than a week since this now-mangled body had been fused to hers, robust and responsive, giving and taking? But now . . .

It had taken Andy more than twenty minutes to track down the resident in charge of Philip's case. The outlook, he had said, was not optimistic; before they could even conduct exploratory surgery, they had to stabilize his condition, and that was going to be a near thing.

When Andy pulled her face away from the window that allowed the outside world to peer into intensive care, the plate glass was streaked with tears. She took one last look at her comatose lover and headed for a pay phone.

Philip had said he'd obtained documents that concerned Realm. She had to retrieve them to ensure that his agony would not be in vain.

Luckily, the crash had been investigated by the county sheriff's department—and not by the men in blue of Chief Eric Schmidt. Andy was connected quickly to the investigating deputy. No, ma'am, no briefcase. Yes, ma'am, there was luggage, a carry-on suitcase. What was in it? Why, clothing. No ma'am, no papers inside the suitcase. In desperation, she asked for the name of the garage to which the wreck had been towed.

It was located out on State Street, near the I-94 interchange.

The Alfa was clearly beyond salvage. The right fender had been ripped off, most probably in collision with the light stanchion. The sides were stoved in from when it had rolled. The windshield was shattered and its frame, as well as the struts that supported the fabric top, bent down toward the chassis, as if crushed by a clumsy and very oversize child.

"Ain't no papers in that there car," the mechanic was saying. "After it was towed in, me and two cops gave it a final search."

"Cops? I thought the sheriff's department handled it."

The mechanic scratched his head. "Maybe so, it being out on the Interstate. But they'd be Ann Arbor cops that I searched it with, lady." He turned to spit and thus missed the flash of fear that danced across Andy's face. "Some kind of wreck, weren't it? No sir, lady, you can't get me inside one of these here Eyetalian toy cars, no way." Shaking his head, he moseyed off.

Morbid curiosity got the better of Andy's distress. She moved closer and began to circle what remained of the Alfa. The bent steering wheel caused her to avert her eyes, as did the blood-spattered windshield.

She was on the verge of leaving when something about the left rear fender caught her attention. Everywhere else on the car, the metalwork had been caved in. Here, it was punctured. And around these holes, in stark contrast to the Alfa's tan skin, were splotches of a most unusual hue: dark green and metallic.

Andy knelt to examine the torn metal. No rust, no weathering; the gashes were very, very fresh.

What—or who—had caused them?

"Larry Matteson's wire."

"This is the operator, and I have a collect call for Larry Matteson from Andy Matteson."

"Operator, this is his assistant. I'll accept the charges."

"Very well, go ahead, please."

"Hi, Andy, Marcia. Larry's down in layout working on the cover story. Can I have him call you when he gets out?"

Andy looked at her watch. The afternoon was still young, but if the cover story was what she thought it was—Argentina—she knew from bitter experience that he could be tied up for hours. "I'm sorry, Marcia, this is urgent. Would you transfer me over."

Marcia hesitated protectively, then said, "Let me put you on hold a sec."

Half a minute later, she was back. "Andy, he'll take the call in his office. How're you doing—oh, shit, there goes the other phone. Give him about two minutes, okay?"

Andy gazed out of the phone booth at the cars entering and leaving the shopping plaza. The rest of the world was going about its business while her life was being torn apart—a daughter ensnared in a diabolical game, a lover near death because he dared investigate that game, and here she was, spooked by her own phone, calling for help collect.

"Yeah," Larry said, sounding a little winded.

"Larry, there's trouble—"

"Patty," he blurted. "Is Patty okay?"

"Yes, for the moment, but—but I think she's involved in something terribly dangerous." In that millisecond before Andy continued, she thought she could hear Larry's brain printing out all the various parental phobias. "She's tied up in this game called Realm, and I'm scared. It's—"

"Jesus Christ!" Larry shouted. "It's fucking Friday afternoon, Argentina's exploding, and you're dragging me out of meetings because of a fucking game? I don't believe it! What are you, fucking crazy?"

"I'm sorry," she said quietly in the voice she always used to deflect his anger. "But you must listen to me. Patty isn't Argentina, but Argentina isn't your daughter."

Larry blew out his breath noisily but curbed his retort.

"She's been playing Realm most of this semester," Andy said. "The game's scary, Larry, it's like a neo-Na—"

"I know all about it. We did four columns on Realm last—last October. Relax, Andy. It's just another fantasy game that's the fad among bright but spoiled middle-class kids."

"Who happen to all have near-genius ratings, look

like the embodiment of the Aryan fantasy—and can't be Jewish."

"What?"

"And you can't buy the game of Realm in any store, Larry, and the instruction booklet carries no copyright, lists no publisher."

Larry's silence meant that his curiosity was whetted.

Andy continued. "I asked a—a friend to look into it. He ended up on the Coast. Last night he called me, all excited, saying he'd uncovered some evidence and would show me it this morning.

"But when he was coming in from Detroit or Ypsilanti, his car ran off the highway—he's in a coma and may not make it. The cops say it was a one-car accident. But I saw his car—there are fresh paint scrapes on the back end, the kind another vehicle would make if it pushed him off the road."

Larry absorbed this, then asked, "What this guy was going to show you—it's disappeared?"

"Yes. How did you know?"

"Oklahoma City, Kerr-McGee, Karen Silkwood. Sounds like an instant replay."

She was about to say something angry when she realized that he wasn't being sarcastic, he was just thinking aloud.

"Andy, have you gone to the cops?"

"It's—it's too complicated to explain, except that the police chief's son seems to be the ringleader of Realm."

Larry whistled in amazement.

"Will you do something about it, Larry? Patty's safe for now, but after this morning—after this morning, the game's gotten violent."

"Leave it to me, Tits," he said breezily. "I might not be able to get to it until tomorrow, after the cover's closed, but I'll check around. Listen, give Patty a hug and a kiss, okay? And don't worry—everything has a rational explanation. Even Realm."

* * *

Key in the lock, and then Patty was calling out "Mom? Mom?" and hurrying down the hallway. She burst into the living room, continued to Andy, and hugged her. "Mom, I just heard about Philip. I'm very sorry. How is he?"

"Not good."

"Where in the world was he going at that hour?"

Should she tell the girl? Why not? "He was returning from the Coast," Andy said, "where he was looking into a matter that concerns you."

"What matter?"

"Realm."

The chill hit Andy even before her daughter dropped her hands and took a step back.

"What did Philip have to do with Realm?" the girl asked, spitting out each word.

"There are things you don't know about the game, Patty. . . ."

Andy's voice trailed off as her daughter's jaw tightened and her gray eyes darkened. Patty struggled visibly to formulate the correct response. Finally she said, "More than you'll ever know, Mother." And then she turned and stalked off.

Fourteen

Tensions between mother and daughter remained high the next morning. As Andy prepared the shopping list, though, Patty entered the kitchen.

"Mom? I'm sorry."

"About what?"

"About last night. I—I had no right to jump on you. Truly."

"Apology accepted."

But Patty wasn't through. She stayed there, shifting her weight and clearing her throat several times before finally saying, "Maybe you guys're right to look into Realm. Maybe it isn't all that I thought it was."

Andy managed to both hide her surprise and remain silent.

"The reason I spent so much time with Melissa the other night," Patty continued, "was because I needed to talk it out. You see, I thought I was doing real well in Realm Seven. But on Wednesday Conch—on Wednesday Rolf told me I was next-to-last. I didn't understand it. That's why I had to talk to Melissa."

"And?"

"And so we reviewed my Realmlog. Mom, I should be second or third right now, with a shot at Number One. But—but I've been jobbed. The computer's lying."

Again Andy fought her instincts and kept quiet.

"Yesterday, at the game, I asked for an Arsenal Points summation," Patty said darkly. "What's in the computer isn't what it should've been."

"What did you do?"

"I wanted to walk out. But you and Dad have always made such a big thing about not quitting, so I stayed. Only you know how sometimes you're someplace doing something, but part of you is far away and watching everything, including yourself? Well, that's how it was."

"What did you observe, Patty?"

She shrugged. "I can't explain it, but I didn't like it. It was like—it was like everyone in the room had on those things they put on horses—"

"Blinders?"

Patty nodded. "Everyone had blinders on, and all they could see was how to screw someone else. All for the glory of being Number One."

Andy approached her daughter and drew the girl into her arms.

"The scary part, Mom, was when I realized that I

was like that, too. And if Rolf hadn't blasted me out of the water, I might never've known it."

"It's okay, Patty, it's okay," Andy soothed, even as her mind tried vainly to correlate her daughter's humiliation with Philip's accident. Finally she said, "Want to join me at the market?"

"I'd like to, very much."

"Good. Go get ready."

Just then the phone rang. Patty, who was nearer, answered. "It's Dad," she said. "He wants to talk to me. Okay if I take it in my room?" When Andy nodded, the girl put the handset down and went to her own extension. Andy waited until she heard two voices on the line and then hung up.

Fifteen minutes later, Patty emerged. "Dad wants to talk to you, Mom. And you ought to have our phone checked out, there're a lot of weird noises on it. Truly."

Fresh pangs of anxiety shot through Andy as she picked up. Sure enough, clicks and whistles reverberated down the line. Should she tell Larry of her suspicions that someone was listening in—or might that provoke some additional unforeseen action? Maybe she should wait until the telephone company—

"Andy? You there?"

"Yeah."

"Listen, you were right. This game Realm's more than a little strange."

Last chance to fire a warning shot, she thought.

And then the moment was gone: "I came into the office a while ago and pulled the files," Larry said. "When we set the piece up, we shotgunned the correspondents. Most of them replied—we got about sixty pages' worth. Lots of interviews, and several even sat in on games-in-progress. But catch this. In all those files, not a single word about who invented the game."

"How the hell did it get into the magazine without the name of the inventor?" Andy asked.

Larry's blush was almost audible. "The story was scheduled for a later issue. Something else fell apart at the last second, so it was rushed through. Davis was pinch-hitting as back-of-the-book top edit, and he decided to wing it—he okayed it as, quote, an underground game of scrambled parentage, unquote. The ignorant asshole."

Andy thought for a moment. "No indication of who started it, or where?"

"Nope. Just that it's played mostly in upper middle-class suburbs. Fairfield, Chicago North Shore, Webster's Grove, Marin County—you get the drift."

"Anything about who's allowed to play and who's not?"

"Not directly," Larry replied. "In fact, if you hadn't mentioned it, I never would have noticed."

"Notice what?"

"That in almost twenty separate and independent files, all the interviewees are without fail described as 'attractive' or 'all-American.' And not a single one of them had an obviously Jewish surname."

The silence that grew was punctuated only by a sibilant echo.

Finally he said, "I had a long chat with Patty, during which I approached Realm obliquely. Seems she's disenchanted with the game."

"Yeah."

"Anyway, I asked her about it. Her description's almost identical to the ones in our files. But she has no idea of who started it. It began for her when some boy named Rolf asked her to play."

"Rolf Schmidt. The police chief's adopted son."

"Oh."

"Exactly."

Larry sighed heavily. "Look, I'm sorry I yelled at you yesterday. You were right to be concerned. I think I'd better start some heavy digging on this end. The original story was a low-priority, back-of-the-book special. A lot of queries were routed to stringers. I'd like to see what the A-team, the bureaus, can turn up."

"Larry? This sounds crazy, but be careful."

"Right. That guy in the hospital, how is he?"

"Visiting hours are after lunch."

"Oh. Listen, I'll get back to you in a day or two. Promise. And get your phone checked out, will you? The feedback's driving me crazy."

In a shabby rooming house nearby, the man with the mismatched eyes was hunched over the tape-recording rig. Upon hearing the connection being broken, he quickly flipped off the recorder. He wedged a slip of paper into the feed reel, transferred the reels to a smaller machine, and placed fresh reels on the big deck, which he switched back on. Then he woke his napping partner.

His partner began the elaborate ritual of dialing the number in area code 408. The man with the mismatched eyes finished rewinding Andy's conversation with Larry just as his partner completed dialing and passed over the handset.

The electronically filtered male voice: "Yes?"

"Limpet One."

"Report, please."

Limpet One placed the handset in a cradle that was hooked to the smaller machine and switched the machine on.

When the tape played to the slip of paper he'd wedged in, he picked up the telephone. The line was dead.

Six minutes later, the phone started its pattern of coded rings. On the third trill of series three, Limpet One picked up.

The electronically filtered voice: "Your directive is to commence surveillance with Rover One. *Overt* surveillance. Questions?"

"The target is to be made aware of our presence."

"Affirmative. Very aware."

"The target is now fully cognizant of the old equipment on her line. She's demanded an inspection. That would blow the ta—the equipment."

"No inspection will take place before Tuesday. However, permission is granted to upgrade the equipment. Check that, remove it all. You and Limpet Two will confine yourselves to overt surveillance. Questions?"

"Negative."

A click and the dial tone; Limpet One hung up, looked at his partner, and smirked. "Come on," he said. "Our ears get a break, but our asses don't."

Andy's eyes frantically traveled the cold, white room on the other side of the plate glass window, disbelief turning into wide-eyed panic: Philip's bed was occupied by an emaciated elderly woman.

The nurse at the nearest station was chatting on the telephone and made it clear that she did not wish to be interrupted. As soon as Andy caught the gist of her conversation, she reached over and broke the connection.

The nurse simultaneously stood and wheeled, the dead handset gripped like a club. Her face was tight with rage as she barked, "What's so goddamned important, lady?"

"Philip Hunt."

"Who?"

"Philip Hunt. The car crash victim they brought into intensive care yesterday."

"What about him?"

"Where is he?"

The nurse's eyes narrowed as she appraised Andy. "You a relative?"

"Friend."

"Sorry, lady." She turned to walk away.

In a whisper as hard as titanium, Andy said, "I'm not through yet."

The nurse froze.

"Is Philip Hunt dead?"

The nurse shook her head and stammered, "Unh-unh. He—he was transferred this morning—"

"Transferred! But the doctor said yesterday he was too critically injured to even operate on."

The nurse, calculating that she was regaining the upper hand, said, "They weren't my orders, lady. I ain't no doctor."

"Where is he?"

"Who?"

"The doctor."

"Off-duty for seventy-two hours." Growing surer of herself, the nurse added, "And you can threaten all you want, bitch, I'm not giving out his phone number."

Andy's body sagged.

"Now you get the hell out of here before I call the guards."

Andy nodded numbly and started to leave. Then she turned back. "Were you on duty when the transfer took place? Yes? Was it—was it done by a medical team?"

"Of course! You think we turn patients in his condition over to civilians?"

"Would you happen know which hospital they took him to?"

The nurse continued to glare at Andy, but as her injured dignity reknitted itself, her hostility melted. She picked up a clipboard and thumbed through the forms. "Florida. That's all I got here, some hospital in Florida. The release is signed by a Mrs. Carol Fitzpatrick."

Andy stared unseeingly at the floor. Near the beginning of their romance, Philip had mentioned that his widowed mother had remarried and moved from California, where he'd been born. To Florida? Where in Florida? How many Fitzpatricks could there be in Florida? She looked up and said, softly, "Thank you. And I'm sorry for giving you a hard time."

As Andy departed, the nurse shook her head in bemusement. And then she began redialing her boyfriend.

*　　*　　*

Saturday afternoon; the biochemistry department would be closed. Who else might know Philip well enough to tell her where his mother now lived? Andy tried to recall his friends in Ann Arbor. She'd met several, but only at large parties, the kind at which last names are unimportant. But wait, there was someone: Philip's old doctoral adviser. What was his name, and what company did he work for? She closed her eyes and tried to summon up that sherry party. SOTA—that was the name of the biogenetic research firm that Philip had joked was run by "the Calvin Klein of genes." And the man's name? Vaughan. Mike Vaughan? Mark Vaughan? *Merle* Vaughan!

Andy dashed into the hospital gift shop and emerged with five dollars' worth of change. She had no idea where SOTA was headquartered, but she knew where to get the answer fast: the editorial reference department of Larry's magazine, which was staffed seven days a week. Andy ducked into a phone booth and dialed one number forever branded in her memory, that of the magazine's central switchboard. When she got a research librarian, she pretended to be a staffer. A minute later, the fact was hers—SOTA was located in the Southern California town of Point Concepcion. A fast call to California directory assistance, and two more facts were hers—SOTA's number, in the area code 805 zone, as well as Merle Vaughan's in the nearby community of Jalama.

But there her winning streak stopped. Vaughan was not at his office—it was, after all, Saturday—and his home phone went unanswered.

Out in the darkening parking lot, Andy walked, head down, toward the Honda. She was unlocking the door when an unusual beep, like the noise made by a doctor's remote pager, drifted across the chill late afternoon air. Something caused her to turn toward it. Out of the corner of one eye she saw a van pulling out of a space. And then the double-take: in the fading light it was impossible to be certain, but the vehicle appeared to be painted a distinctive metallic shade of dark green—the same color she'd found on the rear end of Philip's crushed Alfa.

Fifteen

"Would we agree with that observation, Mrs. Matteson?" Professor Wesley Aldrich asked.

"I'm sorry, I wasn't following the discussion," Andy replied.

"Obviously." He gave her a pitying look before redirecting his attention, and his sarcasm, elsewhere.

It was Monday morning, and Andy's preoccupation—no, her obsession—continued to grow like the web of a spider. Philip, presumably in Florida, remained unlocated. So did Merle Vaughan, whom she had phoned at least two dozen times in the past forty hours. And so, bafflingly, did Larry, whom she'd tried at least as many times.

There was more.

The previous morning, as she and Patty left the house, Andy had caught a glimpse of metallic dark green several blocks away. By the time she could jockey the Honda down the street, though, whatever had been there was gone. But the fact that a vehicle had been parked, most likely with its motor idling, was unmistakable. On the cold, dry macadam there steamed a circle of moisture—drippings from an exhaust pipe.

That circle soon evaporated, but not the metallic dark green van. It was lurking at the perimeter of the parking lot when mother and daughter emerged from the discount department store. It was down the street again when they left the house for dinner. Andy hadn't spotted it when she and Patty walked from the pizza parlor to the movie theater; but after the show, as she unlocked her car, the van had roared to life on a side street. And as it cruised past the Honda, its skin had glistened coldly and malevolently, like a prowling shark's.

"What is it, Mom?"

"Oh, uh, nothing, Patty. I turned my ankle in a pothole."

This morning, her street had been clear. So, too, her rearview mirror during the drive to North Campus. But, swinging into the Arts and Architecture parking lot, she had happened to glance at the building eighty yards away. There in the parking lot sat the metallic dark green van, as if in wait.

As soon as Aldrich's class broke, Andy hurried out to her car. A three-hundred-sixty-degree scan failed to turn up any trace of her accursed shadow. She got into the Honda and sped across North Campus to the building in which Philip worked.

The secretary in the dean's office recognized Andy as soon as she entered. "Hi, you're Doctor Hunt's friend, aren't you? I'm terribly sorry."

Andy nodded. "I'd like to ask a favor. Philip was transferred out of University Hospital at his mother's request. He's somewhere in Florida, but I don't have her address."

"No problem," the secretary said. She went to a filing cabinet and pulled out a folder. Then she frowned. "Did you say Doctor Hunt's mother?"

"Yes."

"There must be some mistake. According to this, both his parents are deceased."

"That's impossible! The nurse even gave me his mother's name—Carol Fitzpatrick."

"Carol Fitzpatrick?"

"She remarried. In fact, I remember Philip mentioning that she'd remarried and moved from California."

The secretary peered more closely at the file. "She

did. But Doctor Hunt's mother died two years ago—in Phoenix. And her first name wasn't Carol, it was Diana."

Andy leaned on the desk to steady herself.

The secretary turned the sheet over and let out a great sigh of relief. "There *is* a Carol Fitzpatrick—a sister!"

Andy drew a deep breath and picked up a pencil. "Do you have an address?"

"Ireland."

"What city?"

"I'm sorry, it just says Ireland."

On her way from the building, Andy stopped to call Larry. His assistant, Marcia, sounded puzzled. Upon arriving at the office that morning, she'd found a note, dated Saturday, saying Larry was pursuing some leads out of town. No, Marcia said, there was no hint as to what story and no details other than the fact he would be in touch Tuesday or Wednesday at the latest.

Next Andy called SOTA. Vaughan's secretary said he was on a recruiting trip somewhere back East. No, she hadn't heard about Philip Hunt's accident, but she would of course tell her boss the next time he checked in and have him contact Andy immediately.

Damn it, Andy thought, she was taking all the right steps, but they were leading nowhere. She pushed through the glass exit doors—and stopped dead.

Directly in front of her, in a no-parking zone less than twenty-five yards away, idled the metallic dark green van.

She stared at the passenger-side window. Inside, two men, both burly; but try as she might she couldn't make out their features because of the reflective glare on the glass.

Without thinking, Andy started running for the van.

She was halfway there when the man nearest her opened his mouth, as if in laughter, and then the squeal of tires and the van was peeling away from the curb.

Though she knew her chase was futile, Andy continued to run for another sixty yards before she pulled up, panting.

The hour was late, but sleep would not come. Andy turned on a light, slipped into her robe, and padded out to the living room. Scotch, two fingers, neat. The town had become her zoo, the apartment her cage. She paced it restlessly as she sipped the scotch. Where the hell was Larry, and when would he be back? She drained the last of her drink.

Why was her bedroom so stuffy? She crossed to open a window. Andy was parting the curtains when she saw, two stories below and across the street, a parked van. She regripped the curtains, but this time the eyes were faster than the hands. Color of vehicle: indeterminable. Occupants, if any: indeter—

A match flared—in its glow, two men, both staring her way—and then her hands came together, and the drapes slid mercifully between Andy and her tormentors.

She glanced at the phone. But even if it was untapped, whom could she call for help except the department that reported to Eric Schmidt?

Sixteen

At some point during the tortured night, the brain began to fight back. It sifted the information overload of the previous few weeks. It discarded the irrelevant and correlated the relevant with the experience of thirty-eight years. It placed into perspective various traumas and fears. It made certain suppositions.

Most important of all, it formulated a plan of action. So it was that when Andy awoke, she knew that no more would she wait for her suspect telephone to be inspected.

No more would she wait for Schmidt to drop another shoe.

No more would she wait for the men in the van to further tighten the screws.

No more would she wait for Larry and Vaughan to return her calls.

Whoever her tormentors were, they would violate her privacy no more; they would violate her sanity no more. They might not know it yet, but they were in for one hell of a fight.

Andy left the house with a steely calm that belied the game face she wore.

The men in the van were growing bolder. Before, they had been content to lurk at a distance; now, they planted their metallic dark green vehicle squarely in her rearview. Before, Andy would have been rattled; now, she began to scheme.

She pulled in alongside the Art and Architecture Building a full twenty minutes before the start of her class. The van eased into a space thirty yards away. Neither man made a move to follow her into the building.

Andy crossed through the lobby and ducked up the nearest stairs to the second floor. There, keeping carefully to the shadows, she edged over to a window that looked onto the parking lot.

The driver of the van was sipping from a Styrofoam container, and his partner had a newspaper opened.

Andy turned and walked quickly to the bank of phone booths at the far end of the building.

First order of business: Michigan Bell. Five days earlier, she told a service representative, she had accepted a collect call. Where had it been placed? In the time it took to punch up her records on a video terminal, she had the answer—from a public telephone in Lucia, California. The area code? Four-oh-eight, the service representative replied.

Second order of business: directory assistance for area code 408. Did Lucia boast a Chamber of Commerce? No ma'am, Lucia didn't boast much of anything. Would she like the hamlet's major listing, the Lucia Lodge?

Third order of business: the Lucia Lodge. Hamlet, it turned out, was an overstatement. The lodge was situated on California's scenic, coast-hugging Highway One, fifty miles below Carmel and forty miles above Hearst's San Simeon. Other businesses in the area? Why, there was the Halfway Inn, where you could gas up, about thirteen miles south. . . .

What the hell had Philip been doing in such an unlikely pit stop?

Fourth order of business: the resident who had handled Philip's case. The emergency room roster had been juggled at the last minute, Andy was told; she might try calling back after midnight.

Andy glanced at her watch. She still had time for another call.

It was to *The Ann Arbor News*, which would be pleased to accommodate a U of M graduate student researching a criminology paper. She was welcome to look at clippings from the newspaper's morgue as long as she didn't interfere with the staff's operations.

In early afternoon, the van tagged Andy from North Campus across the river to Main Street.

She parked the Honda in a municipal lot. The van pulled in, too. Once again, the men remained in the vehicle.

As a test she entered a luncheonette, bought a magazine, and ordered a cup of coffee, over which she dawdled.

Nobody came in looking for her.

To make doubly sure, she went next to a clothing store situated on a corner of Main Street. She browsed a few minutes and then ducked behind a tall rack, from where she could look through the plate glass windows back onto Main. No lurkers. She quickly exited the door that opened onto the cross street.

Four minutes later, Andy was striding into the *News* office on East Huron.

The file on Eric Schmidt was thick, but then he'd been chief of police for more than a decade. She began to weed through it. Several clips gave her pause. In the mid-seventies, Schmidt had been elected an officer of the International Association of Chiefs of Police. When that term was up, he ran for a vice-presidency and won. Schmidt was clearly tapped into the old cops network; how far did his influence extend? And why had he suddenly dropped out of the organization's hierarchy?

The answer to the second question was not long in coming.

In the summer of 1978, during the last year of his IACP vice-presidency, Eric and Heidi Schmidt's only son, Dolph, attended a summer camp on Michigan's Upper Peninsula. On August 11, a predawn fire swept through one of the dormitories. Counselors rescued every camper—except twelve-year-old Dolph.

That explained the Schmidts, but not Rolf. From what little she knew about adoption in America, Andy realized that blond, blue-eyed youngsters of superior intelligence were at a premium. Who was this Rolf, and what was his background?

She turned over a few more clips—and found herself staring at a photograph of the boy sitting on a couch between his new parents.

The article was dated twenty-one months earlier. If its writer was aware of the Schmidts' fortune in adopting someone like Rolf, she hid it well from her readers. The piece proved mostly puffery, filled not with information but with what Larry always sneeringly referred to as "thrill" quotes: Eric Schmidt was "thrilled" by his new son, as was good wife Heidi, and Rolf was "thrilled" by his new parents. The more Andy read, the more her heart sank; even bad reporters knew enough to put their best material near the top.

And then, in the last two paragraphs, serendipity:

As for young Rolf, the youth said he was relieved to find a permanent home. "After so many
years of shifting around," he said, "it sure feels good
to have a permanent home. And with such nice people as Mr. and Mrs. Schmidt."

The newest addition to the Schmidt family is
also looking forward to living in Ann Arbor. "The
last place I lived was in Omaha, and it is a nice place,
but nowhere near as exciting as Ann Arbor. I'm really looking forward to Ann Arbor because I think
it will really help prepare me for the future."

Welcome to Ann Arbor, Rolf, and we sincerely
hope that your future is bright!

Omaha, Nebraska. Lucia, California. Lucia, California; Omaha, Nebraska. Omaha, Lucia, Lucia, Omaha.
If there was a connection, Andy failed to grasp it.

Though absorbed in her newfound clues, she had
the presence of mind to walk out of her way so that she
approached the parking lot from a different direction.

As Andy fired up the Honda, the van kicked into
life, too. It didn't matter anymore. Surely by tomorrow
she would reach the resident, and through him track
down Philip. Or surely by tomorrow Merle Vaughan
would be in touch with his office, and he could help her
track down Philip's sister, Carol Fitzpatrick. And surely
by tomorrow Larry would be returning to New York,
and he'd not only be interested in Omaha and in Lucia,
but he'd be clever enough to make something of them.

Lips pliable, warm and wet; teeth nibbling; tongue
flicking; the fire in her breasts burned downward,
lower, ever lower—and then the phone, the phone was
ringing. He paused and looked up. Let's ignore it, his
eyes said, and then his head was dropping again. But
the fucking phone wouldn't quit. . . .

With a gasp, Andy awoke.

She looked through squinted eyes at the alarm clock—4:18—as she groped for the receiver. Her voice was clotted with sleep when she said "Hello?"

"Andrea." The woman was under great strain, but her voice was nonetheless familiar; it was her former sister-in-law.

"Cynthia? What is it? What's wrong?"

"Larry. He's—he's dead."

Andy felt as though she were plunging naked into a bathtub of shaved ice.

"It happened in New York a couple of hours ago," Cynthia said. "We—we don't have much information yet, but it happened on Fifth Avenue, in front of the magazine. A car went out of control and hopped the curb." She began to cry. "He died instantly. Oh, god, Andrea, what the hell was Larry going to his office for at two in the morning?"

Andy remained silent, her aching sense of loss suddenly replaced by raging guilt. She had become a mantis, sending the males she'd loved to maimings and deaths. Why had she involved them in her problems? Why had she talked openly on a phone she suspected? Why why why why . . .

"We'll be on the first available flight," Cynthia was saying.

"So will Patty and I."

"Why don't you two use the apartment? If it's not too painful, that is. We need more space, and Bob's already made reservations for us and for Mom and Dad."

"That'd be fine, Cynthia. Thank you. Listen, I hope this won't offend you, but I'd like very much to help with arrangements, to help settle Larry's affairs."

"No, it doesn't offend me. He would have wanted that because—because he still adored you." Another huge sob escaped, and then she said, "We'll be at the Park Lane by late afternoon. It's going to be hell, but let's check in with each other by dinner time."

After Cynthia rang off, Andy remained perched on the edge of her bed as eighteen years of mental snapshots flipped through the carousel of the brain: Patty's birth. Courtship. Europe, summer of sixty-seven. Wedding. The sandbox in Riverside Park. And then the projector shorted out. . . .

Finally, Andy realized she could no longer put off telling Patty.

She looked at the handset still in her hand and frowned. There had been something peculiar about the call from Cynthia, but what? And then she had it: for the first time in almost a week, the line had been free of squeals and echoes. Andy raised the receiver to her ear. The dial tone hummed strongly and without interference. She dialed a number she knew would go unanswered—Philip's—and listened closely to the connection and the rings. They were loud and clear.

Andy hung up and pulled out a tissue to dry her eyes. Why now? Why had the listeners stopped listening now? On impulse, she moved to the window and whipped the curtains aside. The metallic dark green van was no longer parked across the street, either.

Seventeen

When the doorbell rang, her eyes opened and registered comforting impressions. The windows were as ever to her right, and sunlight tumbled through them, turning that same patch of yellow wall golden; the same portraits and paintings hung in the same places; the television sat in the same far corner; the handwoven bedspread was the same one acquired that rainy Tuesday in Dublin so many years ago. The utter familiarity of it all teased the beginnings of a smile from Andy's lips.

And then she realized she was curled in a bed she

had left almost two years ago, a bed that would never bear its rightful owner to sleep again.

A knock on the door, followed by Patty's head ducking in. "Mom, Aunt Cynthia's here."

"I'll be right out, dear." Andy swung her legs to the floor and experienced that peculiar dizziness that follows a sleep that is both overdue and overlong.

The day before had been devoted to generating enough motion to keep pain at bay. There was Patty to wake, inform, console—and shield at all costs the fact her father probably died investigating Realm; that was one guilt the girl must never be allowed to assume. There were Andy's parents to call in Connecticut. There were airline reservations to make. There were schools, both Andy's and Patty's, to notify. There were arrangements to make with the Boleys, their landlords, concerning messages and important mail. There was the flight to New York to endure. There was an emotional reunion, Andy's first since the divorce, with her former in-laws. There was the private visit to the funeral home; surely Larry would rouse himself any minute from his peaceful sleep and step, like Sarah Bernhardt, from that silly casket . . . There were dinner reservations to cancel, followed by the strained and largely untasted room service meal up in the Mattesons' hotel suite.

And then, with Patty too distraught to sleep, there had been drinks late into the evening, the adults finally standing down from ceremony and openly trying to come to terms with their terrible loss. It had been well past midnight before Andy cabbed her daughter to the apartment on the Upper West Side and half carried the girl to bed. She had thereupon herself collapsed on the sofa, awakening toward dawn with a start and staggering into Larry's bed.

"Good morning, Cynthia."

"Hello, Andrea. How do you feel?"

Andy shrugged.

"Dad called the precinct this morning and told them you'd be handling things over there."

Patty came out of her room carrying her parka. She looked pale. Andy went over and gave her a hug.

"Bob and the kids are waiting downstairs in a cab," Cynthia continued. "It looks like a decent day, and we thought we'd take Patty with us on that cruise around Manhattan."

"That sounds like a nice idea," Andy said, looking at her daughter.

Patty nodded mutely.

"Then we're going to meet Mom and Dad for a late lunch back at the hotel," Cynthia said.

"Cynthia—thanks."

"Don't be silly. We should thank you for—for looking after Larry's effects. We'll meet at the funeral home at three-thirty?"

"Three-thirty."

When Patty and Cynthia left, Andy padded into the kitchen. The previous day's *New York Times* still lay on the table, open to the all-too-familiar headline on the first page of the Metropolitan section:

NEWSMAGAZINE EDITOR
KILLED IN ACCIDENT

Suddenly Andy was gripped by a hallucination common to any adult returning to his grammar school: the rooms looked too small.

Was this the same kitchen in which she'd managed to finesse sit-down dinners for twelve? She looked at the vials of lovingly collected spices that stood in neat rows on the shelf over the butcher block. Spotlessly clean, thanks no doubt to the ever efficient Pearl, who came in once a week, but Andy could tell they hadn't been used in months. And Patty's room, though stripped of her prized possessions—the artifacts and memorabilia of adolescence—retained the girl's imprint. In the other bedroom the large portrait of Andy was no longer up, but otherwise the sense of sameness was strong enough to trigger this morning's déjà vu.

She poured herself a cup of coffee and went out into the living room. Here, too, the furniture that she'd refused to take to Michigan waited silently in their familiar places. She sank onto the couch.

Why hadn't Larry rearranged things when he regained possession of the apartment upon Andy and Patty's move to Ann Arbor? Surely he could have found time in his brutal schedule to make at least cosmetic changes. Hadn't he been haunted by certain memories whenever he invited someone over? Or had he been, as Cynthia suggested, still nurturing the flame?

A full day of being brave finally caught up, and with a vengeance. Tears welled. And then she was hugging herself, rocking with the grief that shook her body.

It had never occurred to Andy that she might be mourning Larry. Not because they had been through a divorce, for two factors—Patty and their nearly two decades in common—would forever link them in friendship. Rather, it was because he had seemed so indestructible. Long after age had begun to atrophy the cells of the body corporeal, Andy had always thought, Larry's mind would remain diamond-hard, and thus imperishable.

That vision, and Larry, had been snuffed by the wheels of a runaway car.

And Philip lay in a bed, God knew where, fighting for his life.

Thanks to her. Andy's repressed guilt surmounted the dikes and washed over her like acid. If only she'd paid more attention to Patty. . . . If only she'd confided her worries earlier to Larry. . . . If only she'd been more alert to the noises on her phone and warned Philip of them. . . . If only she'd taken the time to tell Larry *everything*.

But what terrible secret had she threatened? Why had those who created Realm lashed back with such cold-blooded violence? If she stopped probing, would their anger be slaked?

The hopelessness of her situation—her isolation, her seeming lack of recourse—triggered a fresh round of tears. Gradually, when Andy's sobs subsided, she noticed the time. Her appointment with the cops was less than an hour off. She felt so drained that she considered postponing it, but in the end she stood and headed for the shower.

The Midtown North precinct house was a hulking pile of weathered stones on West Fifty-fourth Street. Its interior made the *Barney Miller* squad room look good. Though the outside temperature had climbed into the high forties, the radiators in the building continued to spew heat.

Detective Mario Ricci sat across from Andy holding a file folder tattered from its many reuses. "The vehicle was a seventy-seven Chevy Malibu," he said. "It was reported stolen in Trenton last week. The driver was gone when our car arrived at the scene of the accident."

"How do you know it was an accident?"

Ricci looked up sharply. "You got reason to think it wasn't, Mrs. Matteson?"

She pointed to the accident report in the folder. "According to that, it was a clear, dry night. Yet this car veers off the avenue without slowing—no skid marks, right? Then it crosses a sidewalk. Then it hits the only pedestrian for blocks around. Conveniently, the car is stolen. Conveniently, no driver. Conveniently, no witnesses."

Andy paused, trying to work out how best to phrase the next part. "My—my former husband handled a lot of sensitive stories. If you check with his magazine, you might find that he was in the middle of some investigation or another."

"The lack of skid marks bothered us, too," Ricci conceded. "We had the vehicle checked out. The brakes were shot. Whoever was driving probably couldn't have stopped if he wanted to."

"But he could make it all the way up from Trenton."

The cop shot her another glare before plucking a sheet from the folder. "We contacted your husband's magazine. It seems he was onto something. Only it was so hush-hush nobody knew what it was."

Andy frowned. "Larry might not say anything until he had enough facts, but he was the damnedest note taker and receipt collector you ever met. Whenever the IRS saw him coming, they'd just groan and call off the audit."

Ricci shrugged. "I personally went through his desk and files. Nothing."

To break the ensuing silence, he stood and went to a locker. From it he withdrew what looked like a large plastic garbage bag. He brought it back to his desk, opened the closure, and emptied out the contents.

Andy looked from the overnighter to the small, clear plastic bag containing Larry's personal effects and asked, "Where's his pouch?"

"Pouch?"

"A leather pouch the size of a briefcase. Larry never went anywhere without it. It held his wallet and diary, stories he was editing, reading material—it was the only way he could organize his universe."

"There wasn't any pouch, Mrs. Matteson. And his wallet's in that bag there."

Andy opened the clear plastic bag. It also held change and tokens; keys; his watch. She fished this latter out and winced when she saw the shattered crystal and the hands stopped forever at two-eleven. Then she removed his wallet and opened it. Inside were over three hundred dollars in cash, his credit cards, several of his business cards, and three laundry tickets.

"Detective, where did you find this wallet?"

He consulted the notes. "Sports jacket, inside left breast pocket."

"Larry never carried his wallet there. Someone took it out of his pouch and put it there."

Ricci wiped his mouth with his hand. The thought of this open-and-shut case popping back open did not please him.

Andy unzipped the overnighter. Toiletry kit; two shirts, soiled; two changes of underwear and socks, used; a pair of jeans; bathrobe and slippers. But not a single scrap of paper to show where he'd been. She zipped the bag closed.

"Larry was obviously returning from a trip," Andy said. "Whoever took his pouch got all his travel receipts, too. But he must've left tracks. He didn't walk to his office at that hour—some cab must have picked him up from one of the airports, or one of the train stations.

"That means tickets—airline or Amtrak. And he must have stayed somewhere when he was away, which means a hotel or a motel. Larry was in the habit of charging bills over one hundred dollars on a credit card, usually American Express. Records, Detective Ricci, there must be records."

He studied her for several seconds before saying, "This might seem like a stupid question, Mrs. Matteson, but why? What are we busting our chops for?"

"The place Larry went to. That might tell us what—or who—he was investigating."

Ricci began to take great interest in the condition of his cuticles. Finally he said, without looking up, "We'll play it one step at a time, Mrs. Matteson."

"Thank you."

As Andy left the precinct house, she suddenly realized what she'd done; she'd resumed her pursuit of Realm. Obeying a reflex that was almost Pavlovian, she nervously scanned the streets around her. The only hard-faced, hard-bodied men in sight wore blue uniforms, and none of the vehicles in motion or parked was painted metallic dark green.

* * *

Andy reached for the remote control wand and punched off Carson in mid-monologue. It normally put her to sleep, but not this night. Receiving mourners at the funeral home, many of them friends not seen since she quit New York, had left her exhausted yet strangely overrevved. And when she did manage to shunt the faces from her consciousness, her mind filled with dread questions that promised no answers.

She turned to the night table where Larry stacked the paperback thrillers that were his bedtime snacks. A couple of Le Carrés, Adam Hall, a Ludlum. The next book down was by an author she'd never heard of. She looked at the bright maroon cover, considered the cover blurbs, and decided to give it a try. When her eyes drooped mercifully shut, it was well past two.

Eighteen

As they got out of the cab at the corner of Fifth Avenue and Fiftieth Street, Andy sensed her daughter hesitating. She followed the girl's stare to the entrance of the building. The masonry to the left of the revolving doors sported a fresh coat of paint that denied the recent concrete patches. Accident? Death? Here? Andy gave Patty a hug and then guided her inside.

They rode the elevator up to Larry's floor. His assistant, Marcia, greeted them with forced cheerfulness and led the way to his corner office.

Patty drifted automatically to the south windows. Twenty-nine stories down, ice skaters pirouetted on the Rockefeller Center rink.

Marcia finished unlocking the desk and file cabinets. "I've ordered up some Transfiles, Andy. Would you like a hand? I mean, in case you're not sure if something's personal or work-related?"

"No. No, thanks, Marcia. Whatever we leave behind that's personal, you can—you can throw out."

Marcia nodded. "Can I get you coffee? Or a soft drink for Patty?"

Patty turned and asked for a Coke.

Marcia paused at the door. "Ed and some of the others wanted me to let them know when you arrived. They'd like to drop by."

"That'd be nice. But give us fifteen minutes alone, okay?"

"Sure thing, Andy."

Andy went to the window and wrapped her arms around Patty.

The girl continued to gaze down at the rink. "Mom? I can't not remember looking out these windows. Truly. Skaters in winter, those bright yellow restaurant umbrellas in the summer. And all those tourists taking pictures, and me way up here, thinking I was the luckiest girl in the world."

Patty wheeled and buried her face in her mother's shoulder, and as she began to cry softly, Andy's eyes misted, too.

All those hours they had spent here: her daughter usually on weekends, when she could bang away at the typewriter while her dad sorted out the debris of another late closing; she herself mostly on week nights, waiting impatiently while he fielded that one last call from the Coast before they dashed out for a quick bite and a screening or a play or a publication party. It had been a standing, though occasionally bitter, joke that with a mistress like the magazine, Larry didn't need other women. But as much as Andy sometimes hated the magazine and the intense commitment it demanded from Larry, she always felt comfortable here. It wasn't exactly "family," but it had been much, much more than a job.

Finally Andy leaned back and, in a voice still thick

with emotion, said, "All the big shots'll be by soon. We'd better get started. Why don't you collect the paintings?"

Patty wiped her eyes and began to take the artwork off the walls. "Look at this, Mom. From when I was still at the Brownstone. Yuck. Why would Dad keep paintings from nursery school?"

Andy started in on the desk. She was taking a few items from its top when she noticed a pair of Edit Ref "Subject" folders. These collected the stories published by the magazine on a particular subject, as well as correspondent and researcher files used in preparing them and newspaper clippings.

The top folder was marked "Computer Games, U.S. (see also: Video Games)." Because the topic was relatively new, she found inside only three articles from the magazine: on a computer that played chess; on an Eastern business school's simulation course in which MBA candidates "managed" *Fortune* 500 companies; and on the cost, in computer time, to Big Business of unauthorized programs that employees install for their own amusement. Skimming this last article, Andy thought back to the morning in Philip's office and to the directory he'd punched up, the one brimming with games like Asteroids, Hangman, Monopoly—and Realm.

She flipped through a clutch of newspaper clippings, mostly from *The New York Times* and *Wall Street Journal,* and then came to several cables in which correspondents were suggesting stories.

Two queries caught her attention. One was from San Francisco, the other Washington, D.C. Both proposed stories on Ergo Est, the legendary "ultimate computer game." On each occasion New York had shown interest and asked for further details. None was forthcoming; neither correspondent could substantiate the rumors and whispers. They should have interviewed Philip, she thought. Not that he could have provided proof, but he knew more than these journalists had been able to uncover.

Andy placed the papers back in the folder and turned to the second file.

Its heading was "Fantasy Games, U.S.—Realm."

Suddenly her adrenaline flowed. But as soon as she picked the folder up, she realized something was amiss. Larry had said he'd pored over sixty-plus pages of correspondents' files; the folder in her hand wasn't nearly thick enough. She slid out the contents. There was the story on Realm as it had appeared in the magazine, the annotated researcher's copy of the top-edited draft—and not a single correspondent's file. Could these have been in Larry's missing pouch? No, she decided. He had always scrupulously observed the company's injunction against removing research material from the building; if he'd needed a copy, he would have Xeroxed one. Andy shivered. Unless some of the files had found their way into cross-referenced folders, all of the magazine's raw data on Realm was gone.

There was a knock on the door, and Marcia entered with a Coke.

"Thanks, Marcia," Patty said. "Mom, could you help me with the books? I don't know which ones are Dad's."

Andy looked up and said, "Marcia, is your offer to help still good?"

Marcia smiled and joined Patty by the bookcase.

Andy began to search the drawers methodically. As she looked for something—anything—that might relate to Realm, she piled Larry's personal papers on the floor. One folder had no heading. She opened it. Upon seeing that the "Dear Larry" letter on top was written in a woman's hand, she closed the folder gently and returned it to the drawer.

The first file cabinet contained Larry's business calendar. Detective Ricci had been through the book, in which Larry recorded calls, meetings, expenses, and thoughts. Still, Andy opened it to the first week of April.

What day had she initially called him about the game? He'd been on deadline, which meant Friday. She flipped to the previous Friday's entries and found "A. re: Realm (?)" Larry had phoned her back the next day. Andy's eyes went to the right-hand page. It was blank. Odd; Larry had been referring to certain files, so he probably called from the office. It wasn't like him not to have jotted it down.

And then she noticed the blank page's heading: "Monday."

What the hell happened to Saturday and Sunday?

She drew the calendar closer. Once again a cold hand clutched her spine—the thin sliver of paper at the base of the binding bore mute testimony to the efficient work of a razor blade.

"Hello, Patty. We're all terribly sorry about your father." Andy looked up. It was Ed, the managing editor of the magazine. He was at the door, agonizing between the inadequacy of a handshake and the overfamiliarity of a hug; he settled for taking the girl's hands in both of his.

He met Andy, though, with a reassuring embrace. As she returned it, thoughts of enlisting his considerable power in her aid flitted through her mind. But was he powerful enough? That thought—as well as the fates of Larry and Philip—stayed her tongue.

Striving for equilibrium and unwilling to take another somber meal at a restaurant, Andy insisted on having her former in-laws, assorted nephews and nieces, and her own parents to the apartment for dinner. The mindless mechanics of shopping with Patty in their old neighborhood helped. So did cooking for eleven. And so, as the evening progressed, did the healing ritual of good old-fashioned talk. Bygones were interred. Details of the forthcoming service were ironed out. Memories were rekindled and shared. Good will and humor were rediscovered.

The adults were over brandy, and the kids were

washing dishes, when it struck Andy with sledgehammer force—

The journal.

Larry kept a secret journal in the apartment. It was partly an adjunct to his office calendar, a place to record professional problems too sensitive to leave at work even behind locks; but it also served as his personal confessional, receiving uncensored his hopes and his fears.

Andy's eyes darted involuntarily to the living room wall that was covered with books. Then she settled back in her chair and began biding her time.

Her parents were the last to leave. Patty had gone to bed a half hour earlier, but still Andy went into the girl's room; she was fast asleep.

She returned to the living room and studied the book-lined wall. If she let it rest, would they let her rest? Having maimed and killed the two men in her life, what more could they want?

Patty.

On that thought, Andy strode directly to the shelves on which Larry kept the classics.

The six-volume Simon and Schuster boxed set of *The London Shakespeare* had seen much wear. The gold lettering on the spines was mostly rubbed away, the cloth itself cracking. Andy pulled out Volume IV, which contained histories and poems. She consulted its table of contents. The poems started on page 1279.

She turned to page 1279 and read, in Larry's handwriting:

1 Jan. Patty is unhappy, and it's my fault because of last night. . . .

Once, long before Patty was born, Larry had taken a course in bookbinding. That skill enabled him to each year substitute in place of Shakespeare's early poems a fresh folio of blank pages, these to use as his secret journal. The theory was not unlike Hawthorne's *The Purloined Letter*—since the most obvious objects in the room were books, why not hide the journal in the midst of what now amounted to almost one thousand volumes?

Andy skipped ahead to the previous Friday. The few entries all dealt with office matters. She continued to Saturday:

> Andy called yest. re: Patty and game called Realm. She painted a lurid and sinister picture suggesting a real-life *Boys from Brazil*. Sent for files today and found them disturbing. Too many players adopted, inc. statistically improbable 5 from one city, Omaha.

> Omaha—where Rolf Schmidt had lived!

> Asked Fergie for a fast read.

Fergie. Barry Ferguson, a colleague since both were rookie correspondents working out of Los Angeles. Fergie was now chief of the Chicago bureau—and thus responsible for the plains states.

Andy turned the page. It was blank. Larry's last entry was atypically incomplete; what had interrupted him?

She went to his desk and located a list of the magazine's correspondents. It was just past eleven in New York, which made it just past ten in Chicago, so she dialed Fergie's number. When a babysitter answered, Andy left a message asking him to call her the next day. The matter, she added, was urgent.

Nineteen

"Andy? Fergie. I've been wrecked ever since I got the news. He was a good man."

"Yeah," she said, hoping her feigned nonchalance would disguise the quaver in her voice.

"I was going to call you today anyway. Julie and I are flying in for the service tomorrow, and if you're up to it, maybe we can get together for a little while."

"Best offer I've had this week, Fergie."

"Is there anything we can do? I mean, did you call about something specific last night?"

"Actually, yes. Larry was, uh, Larry was helping me with a problem, and it's important that I know how far he got on it. I know you two spoke Saturday. He was still in New York, right? Well, that was the last time anyone knew his whereabouts. I'm just playing a long shot, Fergie, hoping that what you guys discussed had a bearing on my problem."

Ferguson was silent for a few moments. "I doubt it, but for what it's worth, he called me about adoption agencies in Omaha." When she didn't stop him, he added, "Larry wanted the name of the most successful agency and who owns it. I flagged down a stringer who covers city hall for one of the local stations. She came back at me in less than an hour. I called Larry at home, relayed the answers, and that was that."

"About what time, Fergie?"

"That I called him? I had the Cubbies on, so it must've been before three-thirty."

"And what were the answers?"

She could almost hear him frown, but then he said "Hold on." Next she heard the rustle of papers. "The Hewes Service. That's H—E—W—E—S. It's been around less than two years, but it seems to've gained a national rep."

"The owner?"

"This gets kind of strange. It's a corporation called OvS Enterprises/N.A., Inc. That's capital *O*, small *v*, capital *S*, with no spaces, then 'Enterprises', slash, *N*, period, *A*, period, comma, Inc."

"What's strange about it?"

"It's a New York incorporation. Most adoption agencies are locally owned."

"I see. Thanks, Fergie, this helps a lot."

His hesitation was electric with curiosity, but when Andy didn't volunteer any further information he said, "Glad to be of service. Listen, we'll see you tomorrow, okay? And love to Patty."

Andy rang off and turned to her notes. Fergie's call to Larry was undoubtedly at three-thirty Chicago time, which meant four-thirty in New York. She fetched the Yellow Pages and turned to "Travel Agencies." Four minutes later she knew that on Saturdays there was a 5:55 flight to Omaha out of Kennedy. Larry would have had to hustle to catch it—which might explain why he hadn't recorded Fergie's information in his journal.

Next she called Midtown North. Detective Ricci was off-duty until Monday morning. She left her number.

Finally she pulled out her address book and looked up a friend who had become a partner in a large corporate law firm. He was out with his kids, but his wife was glad to take a message. Andy asked if he would research a corporation named OvS Enterprises/N.A., Inc. first thing Monday.

In a high-rise across the street from Larry's, the man with the mismatched eyes who called himself Limpet One sat in a sublet apartment, hunched over a tape recording rig. He heard the connection being broken. Patience being his second nature, he allowed a full five minutes to pass before deciding that the target was through with her calls for now. As he transferred the reels to a smaller machine, his partner began the ritual dialing of the area code 408 number.

An electronically filtered male voice: "Yes?"

"Limpet One."

"Report, please."

"Shift to ultraspeed," Limpet One replied. He placed the handset in a cradle hooked to the recorder, advanced the tape-speed knob so that the lengthy passage would play faster, and then switched the machine on.

When the tape reached the slip of paper wedged in the feed reel, he switched the machine off and picked up the receiver. The line was dead.

Twenty-five minutes later the phone commenced its coded ring.

On ring three of the third series Limpet One picked up.

The electronically filtered male voice: "Any further calls?"

"Negative."

"Your directive is to resume overt surveillance. Questions?"

"Negative."

A click and then the dial tone.

At dusk on Saturday night in Manhattan, cabs were hard to come by. Andy and Patty stood on the corner of West End Avenue searching for a taxi with a lit roof light. She began waving, then stopped when she saw the Off Duty sign.

Andy looked at her watch. "It's getting late, Patty. Maybe we'd better take the subway."

A vehicle approached from behind her. It was a cab coming up from Riverside, but it was already occupied. She started to turn back to her daughter.

What was that over there?

An Oldsmobile, parked and empty; her heart started beating again. Yet its dark hue seemed more than a little familiar. . . . Andy squinted, but the harsh glow of the mercury vapor street lamps played tricks with color perception.

She had taken a few tentative steps back down the block when suddenly Patty was calling out, "Mom! Come on, I got one!"

Andy wavered. She finally started for the waiting

cab—and found herself wondering if it was a case of hoping that ignorance would be bliss.

When they got home three hours later, the dark Oldsmobile was gone.

Twenty

The gray skies began to weep while they were still on the Major Deegan Expressway. The driver flipped on his windshield wipers.

The limousine carrying Andy, Patty, and the girl's three cousins north to the cemetery was the third car of a short procession. Larry would undoubtedly have wanted it even shorter, but the decision was no longer his. Still, Andy thought, he wouldn't have been displeased by the way the day was progressing.

The service had been held at Riverside Church because they needed a place large enough to accommodate all the mourners. Many had asked to be allowed to remember Larry publically, but only one request had been granted. His closest friend since childhood, Taylor Wall, had remained in Illinois to practice law; he was now a U.S. attorney. He'd been best man at their wedding, but Andy hadn't seen him since the separation.

Taylor's eulogy went a long way toward capturing his late friend's complexities. There were silly tales from school days; droll reflections on a young man from Middle America tackling New York; sharp insights into a driven professional who remained committed to family. He ended on the most moving note of all. From the thousands of stories his friend had written and edited during his career, Taylor had unerringly chosen to read from the one that Larry considered his best piece of work.

It had been a cover story for his magazine as the

sixties flickered to a merciful end. Less journalism than essay, its theme was the individual in contemporary America. Larry was then in his late twenties, shifting into the passing lane both personally, with the imminent birth of his first child, and professionally, at one of the bastions of groupthink. Yet somehow he had gotten outside of himself to address the issues of conformity and rebellion; sacrifice and selfishness; sharing and loneliness. It was a mature and haunting profile of a society redefining its concept of happiness, of a culture transforming itself into what would later be dubbed the "Me Generation."

"Larry had always promised himself a shot at a novel," Taylor concluded. "All writers do. He never got around to taking that shot, but not because he had nothing to say. We all know that to be a lie. And that leaves us with the most bittersweet consolation of all—our dreams of what might have been."

The limousine swung off the Saw Mill River Parkway and traversed the hills of western Westchester County to the cemetery. As the cars pulled to a stop, Andy counted them: eight. They were beginning to remove the casket from the hearse, so she stepped from the limousine, taking the waiting umbrella in one hand and Patty's arm in the other.

The unremitting drizzle had scrubbed the air and left behind a lucid landscape from the softest of palettes. Grass green, fresh-turned earth rich brown, buds breaking out on the branches of the trees; spring was coming.

The other mourners began emerging from their cars. Larry's parents with Cynthia and Bob. Her folks with the Fergusons. A small delegation from the magazine. Taylor and his wife with two of Larry's writer cronies. A television producer, two musicians, and an actor. Andy looked to the eighth car. It was parked a little distance away. Its doors remained closed. The wipers were off, but through the rain-splattered windshield, she could see a woman crying. The writer of the "Dear Larry" letters she'd found in his office?

The gathered relatives and friends followed the casket across the springy lawn to the open grave.

The site was at the base of a gentle hill. A breeze swept down off the hill, slanting the drizzle, causing the mourners to tilt their umbrellas as the casket was lowered to its final rest.

By consent, no more words were spoken; each was to remember Larry in his or her private fashion. The stillness was punctuated by only the buzz from the distant parkway. Andy felt a stinging sensation at the tip of her nose, followed by tears. She drew Patty tighter to her.

"Amen," Taylor finally said. His wife stepped forward with a cluster of lilies. There was just the right number for blood kin.

Larry's mother was the first to toss hers onto the casket, the flower hitting the polished mahogany with an audible *thunk*. His father followed, then Patty . . .

Andy looked away. The valley below stirred with a life unfelt in the cemetery up here. The woman in the eighth car was still sobbing. Andy's gaze continued to the hill above the grave.

Where it stopped.

At the summit, silhouetted against the leaden skies, stood two men. They seemed impervious to the weather, standing unprotected by either umbrella or raincoat. The drizzle in her eyes obscured Andy's vision, but not enough to hide the fact that the men were looking down on the funeral party. And that the one on the right held a camera fitted with a telephoto lens. And that the lens was trained on her. And that although the men wore no raincoats, they had on jackets of metallic dark green.

The madness that had not stopped with Philip's crippling was obviously not stopping with Larry's death. Andy climbed into the back of her limousine without bothering to check the hilltop again, for if the men were no longer on the summit, it could only mean that they were maneuvering to continue their surveillance.

Rather than shock or dismay, she seemed to be suffused with insights.

Supposition: Philip and Larry had gotten too close to Realm's secret.

Supposition: she was being watched to see how close she came.

Supposition: if she came too close, they would have no qualms about making Patty an orphan.

Just then the girl reached over to clutch Andy's arm. She folded Patty's hand into hers and gave it a squeeze.

At the gates of the cemetery, the cars that had come up from New York in procession headed their separate ways. When Andy's limousine turned onto the Saw Mill, she reached her free hand into her purse and pulled out the compact. She flicked the cover open and raised it to eye level. In its mirror: an Oldsmobile painted a metallic dark green.

Supposition: Larry's phone was tapped, because only after she'd called Fergie yesterday had the men reappeared.

Supposition: they would continue to monitor her until—

Until when? Even if she dropped all her inquiries, how could she prove to them that she wasn't a threat? Knowledge wasn't returnable; wouldn't they always worry that she might luck across something that would unravel their machinations? But if she were to pursue Realm, how could she hope to succeed where two very savvy men failed?

The driver of the Olds was good. All the way down the Saw Mill, the Deegan, and the West Side Highway, he kept his car precisely eight lengths behind the limousine. As they began to negotiate the streets of mid-Manhattan, Andy looked into the mirror of her compact yet again. In the the thickening traffic, the Olds had closed to a more cautious four carlengths.

The limousine pulled up to the Park Lane Hotel. The entire Matteson clan was leaving later that afternoon, so Andy asked the driver to wait. Then she and Patty went upstairs to say their good-byes.

When they came back down ten minutes later, Andy scanned both sides of Central Park South. The fact that the Olds had vanished, though, was no relief because she intuitively knew where it would next turn up.

She was right. When the limousine stopped in front of Larry's apartment, the Oldsmobile was parked brazenly in front of a hydrant directly across the street. It was so near that she could easily make out the two men in it. She paused to study their hard, blank faces, particularly the one with the curiously mismatched eyes. Both men stared back with disdain.

Realization: they were flaunting their faces, heretofore carefully concealed, because their identities no longer mattered.

Conclusion: their identities no longer mattered because Realm permitted no unilateral surrenders.

Andy thought back to the previous week and to the moment she'd emerged from the biochemistry building. Her wild dash after the van had been triggered by both panic and the irrational hope that she could somehow make its occupants reveal what was going on. But now, though five strides would carry her to the Olds, she recognized that the goons inside it were merely the muscles—and not the brains—of Realm. Plus now, knowing what had to be done, she was no longer panicky.

Which was why she took a last good look at the men, turned, and went into her building.

And why upon reaching the apartment she immediately called Fergie and begged off their dinner date that evening.

And why, after telling Patty she was going shopping for a few items, she went back downstairs, back past the Olds, and to a supermarket on Broadway. There she made a beeline for a pay phone that would be secure from prying ears.

"Hi, Dad. No, I'm okay, thanks. Listen, do you think your department could survive without you for another week? Well, it's because I just realized how many things I have to do to settle Larry's affairs. I'm not sure it'll be that pleasant for Patty, and I certainly don't want to send her back to Ann Arbor by herself. Anyway, I don't think she's going to feel much like school next week."

As she waited for her parents to consult, Andy found herself automatically twisting around to monitor the store's entrance.

"Bermuda? Gee, you and Mom don't have to do that. Are you sure you're up for it? Then great. How about reservations? Right. Listen, Dad, uh, you won't be able to call us tonight because we're going out for a woman-to-woman dinner. So why don't I call you? About nine? Talk to you then."

The thought of dressing up and going to a name-brand restaurant seemed inappropriate, so they dined at McBell's in the West Village. This cozy pub, which served excellent drinks and more than decent food, had for some reason always been Patty's idea of blasé New York chic. There was a bonus, too. McBell's was only three blocks from the girl's favorite coffeehouse.

Andy sipped a cappuccino as she watched her daughter dig into the Peacock Caffé's wickedly delicious chocolate rum cake. The meal had gone well. The main topic had been, naturally, Larry. It would take months—no, years—for the hurt to scab over, but it appeared to Andy as though Patty were willing to confront her loss openly, rather than from inside her shell.

The girl had also probed Andy for her reactions to

Larry's death. She was listening, of course, for signs that her mother regretted the divorce.

Andy gently but firmly disabused Patty of that idea. She began by talking about herself with unflinching honesty. And then, as if realizing that she was in a sense putting her house in order—as if compelled by visions of the uphill task that lay ahead—she talked about Larry with honesty and about their marriage with honesty.

Finally Andy deflected the conversation from herself back to Patty. And then, drawing a deep mental breath, she said, "You told me how disillusioned you are by Realm. Did anything good come out of it?"

Patty started to take another bite of her second chocolate rum delight but pushed the plate away. "I guess so. It taught me to think fast."

"What do you mean?"

The girl shrugged. "It's kind of hard to give examples. Oh, I know. At the sessions when we'd do our Challenges and Counter-Challenges? Well, everyone tries to pressure you, to make you mess up. But you know what you can always do? You can always ask for an Arsenal Point summation. It's like a time-out in football. Truly—it gives you a chance to regroup, to make last-second Arsenal Point changes. Well, if you forget that you can demand a summation, you might let yourself be hassled into blowing it."

Andy found herself tuning out. Obviously Patty had not yet thought through the game sufficiently to yield useful information.

Later, when Patty went to the bathroom, Andy phoned her parents. All was arranged: they were booked on the morning flight out of Kennedy, they had a week's reservation at the Bermuda Princess, and yes, they'd buy bathing suits and warm weather clothing when they arrived.

Not unexpectedly, Patty was too excited by her windfall vacation to go to bed early.

It was well past midnight when Andy took out a notebook and listed the disparate and paltry Realm facts at her disposal:

Vehicles painted, and men wardrobed, in metallic dark green.

The Hewes Service, Omaha, Nebraska.

OvS Enterprises/N.A., Inc., New York, New York. Next to this Andy jotted a reminder to call her friend the lawyer in the morning.

A public telephone, Lucia, California.

Chief Eric Schmidt, Ann Arbor, Michigan.

Philip Hunt, Florida. Next to this Andy jotted a reminder to try Merle Vaughan again in the morning.

She reviewed the entries. Not very promising. Unless her friend turned up something on OvS Enterprises, her only hard lead was The Hewes Service. But how to get to Omaha undetected? Those two men in the Olds had obviously been instructed to follow her much more closely than in Ann Arbor. And even if she could elude them, which seemed doubtful, there were still two thousand miles to travel.

Suddenly Andy remembered the paperback thriller she'd been reading. Its hero, forced to circle the world one step ahead of paid killers, had employed a bedazzling array of evasive manuevers. Had the author made those up, or had he done research—in short, would the tactics work in real life?

She went to the bedroom, found the novel, and began rereading it.

When dawn's first light snuck into the bedroom, Andy was still feverishly scribbling notes. Yes, she thought, not only could she take the battle to them, but she actually stood a chance—however slim—of winning.

Book III
RECOIL

The First Day

"Now remember, do as Grannie and Grandpa tell you."

"Yes, Mom."

"And be sure to use plenty of sunscreen the first few days. You wouldn't want to ruin your vacation with a burn."

"No, Mom."

"What else? Oh. The bathing suit. You'll be wearing it in Michigan, too, so don't buy anything too immodest, okay?"

"*Moth*-er!"

As her parents laughed at this uncharacteristic display of fussbudgetism, Andy blushed. But it was almost as if she couldn't stop prattling—as if she couldn't let Patty leave. This was, in fact, her last chance to call it off, to brake the headlong momentum that was separating her—perhaps permanently—from her daughter. Yet it had to be done. If the goons would go so far as to reveal their faces, their next move figured to be even more chilling. And she refused to wait for that move like the proverbial sitting duck.

Andy turned to her mother. "I'll be on the go the next few days. You might have a hard time reaching me, but I'll check in Wednesday at the latest."

Her father, who was helping Patty into her parka, said, "If you finish up early, dear, fly out. You look like you could use some time in the sun."

Andy walked her parents out to the elevator and hugged them. Then she embraced her daughter with unusual fervor. "Have a great time," she whispered. "I love you very much."

Patty sensed something amiss and tilted her head back slightly. The trace of moisture gathering on her mother's lower lids brought on a concerned frown. The girl raised a gentle hand to Andy's cheek. Their eyes locked.

Just then the elevator doors opened.

Mother and daughter remained rooted in the hallway, gazing at each other with palpable intensity; the air seemed to crackle with silent communications, the messages transmitted quarter-formed but the emotions full-blown.

Finally Andy blinked the mist clear from her eyes.

Patty lowered her hand and said softly, "I love you, too—truly." Then she planted a quick kiss on her mother's cheek and joined her grandparents on the elevator.

So the first crop of lies had taken root, Andy thought bitterly as the doors closed. And god knew but there were plenty more to plant.

Back in the apartment, she collected her notes and plopped onto the sofa. Andy was reviewing them when she was overtaken by a tiredness that had nothing to do with her meager two hours' sleep. No, she recognized the source of her lassitude: anxiety. Or more correctly, given the circumstances: fear.

The enormity of her quest seemed crushing. And suppose she could navigate her way around the force that was ingenious enough to follow her every conversation and track her every move, powerful enough to maim and kill with impunity; suppose she could reach the center of the maze. Whom would she tell? In what court would justice—and vengeance—be hers?

Andy wanted badly to lie down and nap. Instead, she made herself stand and head for her second shower of this young morning.

Limpet One had the mobile telephone in his hand

when Patty and her grandparents emerged from the building and walked past the Oldsmobile.

"It's the girl and the old people," he said. "They're getting into a taxi."

The electronically filtered male voice: "Any sign of the target?"

"Negative. The taxi is pulling away. Do you wish us to follow?"

"Negative. Your directive is to continue overt surveillance of the target. Questions?"

"Affirmative. We, uh, we resubmit our request for backups."

"Request denied. Questions?"

"No. But—"

A click and then the dial tone.

Limpet One glared at the dead handset before slamming it back in its cradle.

"Relax, good buddy," his partner said.

Limpet One took a deep breath but was unable to; something about this job was souring rapidly.

Not the pay, to be sure. Two hours after the client had first telephoned their agency in Houston with a priority surveillance assignment—one month's wages and expenses guaranteed—a bonded courier had arrived with the agreed-upon retainer of five thousand dollars. Every day since, no matter the city, other couriers had found them and delivered three envelopes. The ones bearing their names contained each man's day rate of two hundred fifty dollars, plus another fifty for per diem. The third envelope held expense money; this sum had ranged from two hundred dollars to slightly over nine thousand when they'd purchased and repainted the Olds.

Limpet One glanced at the gadgetry on the dashboard and front seat. There was the mobile telephone. There was the black box that connected them to the elaborate tap running upstairs in their sublet apartment. There were state-of-the-art walkie-talkies complete with solid-state earplug receivers, lapel microphones no more conspicuous than a fraternal pin, and wireless power sources smaller than a Zippo lighter. No, the problem certainly wasn't money, Limpet One thought. He stubbed out his cigarette and lit a fresh one.

"Come on, lighten up," his partner said. "You're getting on my nerves."

"Fuck off," Limpet One growled. "You know what the matter is. This job's getting too wet. First the bozo in the car back in Ann Arbor, and now the broad's old man buys it."

His partner shifted uncomfortably in the driver's seat. When he answered, his voice was both soft and defensive. "Look, we're clean. Did we cream that Alfa? Did we run over that Matteson guy?"

"So what the hell have we been doing? I mean, what are we tailing her for? Does this feel like a matrimonial? A child custody?" Limpet One glanced over and added sarcastically, "Oh, I know. Industrial espionage, right?"

His partner sighed and reached under the seat for his thermos of coffee.

"And you want to tell me how thrilled you are about our directives?" Limpet One continued. "You heard that cock-sucker just now—no backups. What the hell are we, Batman and Robin?"

"The guy thinks we're good," his partner replied weakly. "We delivered in Ann Arbor."

"Shit, Stevie Wonder could've delivered in Ann Arbor. What do we do if she puts us through a subway drill or decides to play games in Macy's at high noon?"

His partner busied himself screwing the top back onto the thermos and sipping his lukewarm coffee. "Listen, drop it, okay?"

"How'd you like to be on the receiving end of what we've been dishing out?" Limpet One continued. "The World War Two equipment back in Ann Arbor—hell, Beethoven would have known he was being tapped. And then we launch overt surveillance, which is usually end game. But no, after five days, we get pulled off. Only in New York we're put back on, at her old man's funeral, yet." He crushed out his fresh cigarette. "You see any end game in sight, good buddy? I tell you, the cock-sucker cutting our orders is one sadistic son of a bitch."

The silence in the Olds grew. Finally his partner said, "I don't see you returning the money."

Limpet One reached for another cigarette, stopped himself, and then, feeling suddenly claustrophobic, rolled down his window several inches.

Twelve minutes later, the black box sitting on the dashboard began to beep: the target was using her phone. Limpet One grabbed the earphones of the radio-remote unit and switched on a cassette recorder. "Busy signal," he reported, leaving the earphones on.

Two minutes later the black box beeped again.

Limpet One listened for a few moments and then checked the voice-level gauge of the recorder. When the call was over he said, "Passport office. She wanted to know how fast she could replace hers." And then, because he was a patient man and because he knew by now that the target usually placed calls in clusters, Limpet One kept listening.

Ten minutes passed.

He was about to dial the client when his partner said, "Here she comes."

The target emerged from the apartment building wearing a teal blue trenchcoat and carrying her purse. Without glancing at the Olds, she began to walk briskly toward Broadway.

"Call the cock-sucker but don't bother with the tape," Limpet One said. "Just tell him she's going for a passport." The target was already thirty yards up the block, so he picked up his walkie-talkie, hopped out of the car, and hastened after her.

She continued east to Broadway, where she turned downtown.

A burst of static on Limpet One's headset, followed

by the thin voice of his partner: "Message through, good buddy, and I'm a block behind you."

"Roger. She passed up an empty cab, and she's beyond the bus stop. Looks like the subway."

His partner sighed. "Roger. See you there."

The target neared the subway entrance. Limpet One sidestepped two elderly ladies and began digging for a token. When he looked up, she was gone.

Stay cool, he told himself; she didn't have time to get underground. Up ahead now, his partner was wheeling the Olds onto Broadway and jamming it in front of a hydrant. Limpet One, realizing they had her bracketed, stopped dead.

In less than a minute, the target came out of a head shop with a pack of chewing gum and continued toward the subway.

Limpet One and his partner faced a hard decision. The Olds gave them flexibility. But the walkie-talkie couldn't transmit from underground, so the car was also a trap; his partner would have to blindly pace the train until Limpet One could give him a fix from aboveground. Was it possible to pull off what would in essence be a one-man tail in the maze that is New York's subway system?

It was his partner who resolved the dilemma. Recognizing that the long lines extending back up to street level meant it was still the morning rush hour—during which even two men could easily lose a target—his partner bailed out of the Olds and ducked down the steps.

The station was crowded. As the target edged her way toward the head of the platform, Limpet One's partner positioned himself ahead of her so that he in turn lagged slightly behind, serving as the second bookend.

A train screeched in. It was as tightly packed as a sardine can, but the people on the platform surged toward the opening doors.

A moment of panic as he lost sight of her again, but

then Limpet One caught a glimpse of teal blue. Still, fresh beads of sweat popped onto his forehead. They weren't out of the woods yet; he and his partner had to be the last aboard, just in case she decided to dart off at the last second.

When the doors began to trundle shut, Limpet One insinuated his body into the closing gap. The mass of passengers proved unyielding. He snuck a glance up the platform: his partner was inside. Encouraged, he gave one last shove. The counter-pressure eased, and he squeezed all the way in, and the doors closed behind him.

The ride downtown was uneventful.

At the fourth stop, Limpet One and his partner followed the target off the train and up the stairs. She started east on Fiftieth Street; while his partner remained in her wake, Limpet One crossed to the downtown side.

Across Broadway now, approaching Seventh Avenue and the red Don't Walk signs were blinking. Limpet One tensed. Would the target dash across oncoming traffic in an attempt to lose them? Then he relaxed as she waited patiently on the curb for the light to turn.

Eastward still they continued until, at the corner of Fiftieth Street and Fifth Avenue, she entered the TWA ticket office.

His partner peered through the plate glass window before speaking into his walkie-talkie. "Listen, good buddy, there's a lobby entrance, too. I'm going to swing inside and cover it."

Limpet One acknowledged. He remained on the far side of the street, backing into a shallow niche of the nearest building.

From that vantage point he could see that the ticket office was crowded. The target took a queue number, grabbed a fistful of brochures, and settled into a seat. Ten minutes passed before her number was called; it took another seven for her to purchase tickets.

Limpet One prepared himself for action.

She turned from the counter and headed not back onto the street, but into the lobby.

Limpet One said into his mike, "She's headed your way. I'll be coming through the Fifth Avenue entrance." He crossed the street quickly, half ran up the block to the revolving doors, and pushed through them.

A scan of the lobby turned up neither partner nor target. "Limpet Two, do you read?"

"Loud and clear, good buddy. Escalator down to the concourse and hang a right."

The escalator was directly ahead. Limpet One hurried down it.

His partner stood in front of a passport photo studio.

The target was inside, near the cash register, collecting her change. Next she went to the back of the studio to get her photos. As she came through the door and climbed onto the ascending escalator, she pointedly ignored the two men.

How could she remain so calm in the face of their pressure? Limpet One wondered, stepping on the escalator after her.

At the lobby level the target turned left and continued to the escalator to the mezzanine.

Limpet One reached out to touch his partner. "The passport bureau's up there. I'll go up, too, just in case. You wait here. . . . Oh, and let the client know she's booked herself on TWA, destination unknown."

On the mezzanine Limpet One took up station at the head of the corridor leading to the passport bureau. He noted the length of the line the target was joining and groaned inwardly; it would be a long wait.

One hour and thirty-five minutes later, Andy emerged from the bedlam. It had taken a lot of fast talking to convince an agent that her passport was back in Ann Arbor and that she needed a replacement, fast, to join her brother, who'd been badly injured in a boating mishap near London.

The fact that she possessed a seat on TWA to London the next day turned the tide; the replacement would be ready the following morning.

As she walked down the corridor toward the escalator, she spotted the hard-faced man with the mismatched eyes. He was leaning against the balcony railing, watching her approach.

Andy fought back her feeling of revulsion. The psychic cost of pretending to ignore them all morning had been immense but worth it, for she had left the apartment hoping to ascertain three facts:

First, how good were they? By the way they'd clung to her through the subway at rush hour, very good.

Second, were these two operating alone? She couldn't be positive, but she thought so. Several times—like at the head shop—she had made an unexpected move in hopes of flushing out backups. None had appeared.

Third, though these two were obviously crack professionals, could she shake them? Probably yes. But she had to be patient; only after her entire escape network was in place would she make her break.

Andy steeled herself and swept imperiously past the man with the mismatched eyes and onto the down escalator. The other man was gazing up at her from a corner of the lobby. She ignored him, too, and made straight for a bank of pay phones, selecting one on the end.

She dug out a fistful of change, which she spread out on the shallow metal ledge. Then she opened her notebook.

The first call was to the Midtown North precinct house. Detective Ricci had both good news and bad. The good news was that he'd located the cabbie who had dropped Larry in front of his office; the pickup had been made at the American terminal at Kennedy Airport. The bad news was that no American manifest for the flights arriving in the two hours prior to the pickup had listed a passenger named Larry Matteson.

"Did you check the other airlines?" Andy asked.

"Now why would your husband have landed at some other terminal and then gone to American to catch a cab?"

Having no ready answer, she remained silent.

Finally Ricci said, "Look, I'm sorry, ma'am, I think we're dead-ended on this one. I know there're some odd wrinkles to it, and I discussed the case with my supervisor this morning. He told me to close it down. If you want to take it up with him, I'll give you his name."

"No, that's okay, Detective Ricci. Thank you anyway."

Andy hung up, consulted her notes, and punched the number of the lawyer who was researching OvS Enterprises/N.A., Inc.

"Hello, Frank? Andy Matteson."

"Andy. Hi. Linda and I were stunned to hear about Larry. Our condolences to both you and Patty."

"Thanks."

"How've you been holding up?"

"It's tough, Frank. Larry and I managed to remain friends."

"Patty?"

"Still in shock. It's good of you to ask."

"Not at all. Linda gave me your message, and I put an associate on it first thing this morning. Let me see if she's come up with anything. I'm going to put you on hold. . . ."

Frank was back on the line within two minutes. "Andy, I've got her report in front of me," he said, a note of concern creeping into his voice. "Some things about this company aren't kosher."

"Like what?"

"At least two things, and that's just from a fast read. One, judging by the incorporation papers, OvS is a front. The company was registered almost three years ago as a wholly owned subsidiary of Midcontinental

Placements, which is located in Freeport, the Bahamas."

"Why does that make it a front?"

"Well, I've never heard of Midcontinental, but I recognize its address. You'll find it on the letterheads of a lot of shell companies that specialize in offshore tax scams."

"Are you sure Midcontinental's one of them?"

"If you lie down with dogs, you get up with fleas. No legitimate business would think of setting up shop at that address."

"What else feels wrong, Frank?"

"Midcontinental's officer of record. His name's Eduardo Stroessel Betancourt."

Andy frowned. "That name sounds vaguely familiar."

"Stroessel's been in and out of the news for the last two decades," Frank said. "He's real slime, a Paraguayan lawyer who's a distant relative of the dictator down there. Reputedly, the guy earns his keep stitching together investment deals for some of his country's most famous visitors—the surviving brass of the Third Reich."

Andy's nape crawled. Her mind flashed back to her initial reaction upon reading the Realm instruction booklet; to Ginger's mother telling her about the game's ban on Jews; to Realm ringleader Rolf and his father, Eric Schmidt, ringleader of Ann Arbor's brownshirts. And most chillingly, she recalled the phrase from Larry's secret journal: "a real-life *Boys From Brazil*."

When she rang off, Andy couldn't help but stare at the two hard-faced men across the lobby. How old were they, early forties? They must have been young boys on V-E Day. Then how could they be tied up in this—unless their native tongue was Paraguayan?

Wait, she thought. This was New York City, and the time was the nineteen-eighties. Neo-Nazis working to build the Fourth Reich existed only in the feverish minds of thriller writers, right?

Andy's head felt light as her mind groped through a surrealistic fog. Then she blinked her eyes and focused them on the next call on her list.

Yes, she was told, seats were available on the United flight in question. Andy booked a ticket and arranged to pick it up at the airport no later than ten forty-five the following morning.

The following call was to another airline, with which she made another reservation. That ticket, too, would be paid for tomorrow, when she picked it up.

The important legs of her itinerary arranged, Andy punched up Chicago directory assistance.

She was about to dial her number when she looked out of the corner of her eye at the two hard-faced men; they were close enough to be able to note, by the number of coins she plugged into the phone, whether she was calling local or long-distance. Andy denied them that information by dropping in a dime and hitting the button marked *O*.

"Operator. How may I help you?"

"I'd like to charge this call to my home phone," Andy replied. To play it totally safe—if they could tap Larry's phone, they could probably check his billings, too—she gave the number of the phone in his office. Though his was a direct-dial line, she knew it was billed to the magazine's central switchboard; thus her call was the proverbial needle in a haystack.

Once Andy reached her party, it took just forty-five seconds to get the information she needed.

Two more calls to go, she thought.

Naturally, she began with the easier one. "Good morning. What's your schedule to Kennedy tomorrow morning, at about a quarter to ten?"

"We've got a direct flight at nine-forty," the agent replied.

"How long does it take?"

"Twelve minutes, ma'am."

Which would get her to the airport at about nine

fifty-five; too early, she thought. "And your next flight?" she asked.

"Ten-twenty. That's via LaGuardia, so it'll take seventeen minutes instead of twelve."

Which meant landing at about ten-forty; too late. "How much is a charter to Kennedy?" she asked.

"What size craft do you need, ma'am?"

"The smallest."

"Let's see. Our four seater'll run you one hundred and seventy-five dollars."

"Fine. I'd like to book one."

The agent switched her to the charter manager. It took Andy four minutes to complete the arrangements.

One call—the most important—remained.

Suddenly Andy wished she had a cigarette. She glanced at the newsstand just across the way. No, she wouldn't give those bastards the satisfaction of knowing she was nervous; she drew a deep breath and picked up the handset once more.

The final number was again long-distance, so again she had the operator charge it to Larry's office phone.

"The Hewes Service, good morning."

"Good morning," Andy said. "I'm calling to inquire about your services."

"Certainly. Are you seeking to adopt a child?"

"Yes, we are."

"I see. And how did you learn about The Hewes Service?"

"A neighbor of ours," Andy replied. "Part of his law practice is in the area of adoptions."

"I see. If you'll wait a moment, I'll connect you with our director, Mrs. Larissa Hewes. May I tell Mrs. Hewes who's calling?"

"Mrs. Robert Lyall," Andy said, giving her mother's name. She covered the mouthpiece and cleared her throat.

A few moments later an older woman came on the line. "Mrs. Lyall? This is Larissa Hewes. How may we help you?"

"My husband I have been thinking about adopting a child for some time now. The problem has been one of age—I'm forty-two, and Robert is fifty-one."

"That certainly shouldn't be a limiting factor," Mrs. Hewes interjected.

"Oh, I didn't mean that way," Andy said. "The problem is, we don't feel we should adopt an infant. By the time he or she is a teenager, Robert will be on the verge of retirement. The age gap really wouldn't be fair to the child."

"Mrs. Lyall, if more older prospective parents shared your sensibilities, we would have far fewer heartbreaks."

"We're just trying to be realistic, Mrs. Hewes. To make a long story short, we've been visiting adoption agencies in Connecticut, where we live, as well as in New York. As I'm sure you know, children in the seven-to-ten range who are—how can I put it, 'suitable'?—well, they're difficult to come across. But a close friend of ours is a lawyer who's experienced in the field. He mentioned that your agency has an outstanding record of placing youngsters of this age."

"I'm flattered that our reputation has reached the East Coast," Mrs. Hewes said.

"It certainly has. Anyway, we were about to write you when my husband was called to California on business. He'll be out there another week, and he's asked me to join him. I've taken the liberty of calling you, Mrs. Hewes, to see if it makes sense for me to stop over in Omaha. I know it's short notice, but I thought it would give us a chance to meet, and perhaps I might begin the application process."

"I would very much look forward to meeting you," Mrs. Hewes said. "Which day is most convenient for you?"

"Wednesday?"

"That would be fine. Shall we say ten-thirty?"

A few minutes later, when Andy hung up, she dug

a tissue from her purse and dabbed her forehead: lying was hard work.

Then she became conscious once more of the hard-faced men across the lobby. Her calls were finished, but not her errands. It would be a pleasure to make those rounds alone. Yet if she gave them the slip, might they call for reinforcements? Andy sighed. There was simply too much at stake; she would even go out of her way, if necessary, to help them maintain their surveillance.

Andy left the building by way of its Fiftieth Street entrance. Three blocks south, she turned right and from a number of electronics stores chose one with a window display of telephones and answering machines.

To her relief, the two men remained outside when she entered. Andy approached a salesman and inquired about pocket-sized calculators. She was examining the selection he'd placed on the counter when she asked if the store also happened to carry a gizmo that could determine if a telephone was being tapped. The salesman nodded. Andy told him she wanted one, and no, she didn't need to inspect it. Then she selected the least expensive calculator and paid for both items.

Leaving the electronics store, Andy walked west to the uptown BMT subway station at Seventh Avenue and Forty-ninth Street. Just as she finished climbing down the stairs, a train pulled in. There was a token in her pocket; it would be so easy to hustle through the turnstile and duck aboard, leaving those bastards high and dry. . . . Instead, she joined the queue in front of the token booth. By the time she'd bought four, the subway had pulled out, and her tails had joined her down in the station.

She took the next train to Fifty-ninth Street and Fifth Avenue. Emerging aboveground, she walked two blocks to the bank where she and Larry had maintained a savings account in trust for Patty.

Andy went inside and withdrew three thousand of her daughter's dollars. For the benefit of the eyes trained on her from the sidewalk, she bought five hundred dollars' worth of traveler's checks, making a production of signing each.

From the bank, Andy led the miniparade three blocks east to Bloomingdale's. She knew the next two hours would be the most difficult; it was almost impossible *not* to lose somebody inside that glitzy department store.

"Shit." Limpet One sank back as their taxi pursued the target's through Central Park toward the Upper West Side. "I can't stand to go shopping with Flo, and this broad makes Flo look like Speedy Gonzalez."

His partner grunted wearily. Then he said, "She sure bought enough stuff today—calculator, clothes, luggage. And the passport. Wonder where she's going."

"Beats me. But I got a hunch our client's already booked us seats to the same destination."

"You think he can access TWA's computer?"

Limpet One smiled.

His partner mulled it over for a few moments, then shrugged. "Anyway, good buddy, I thought we did a swell job keeping track of her in that zoo."

"It wasn't like she was trying real hard to lose us, was it?"

"Now that you mention it, she seemed pretty calm about the two of us all day. Yesterday afternoon, too. Strange."

"So's this whole gig, good buddy," Limpet One said.

As soon as Andy arrived back at the apartment, she dug out the gizmo she'd bought at the electronics store. Keeping the phone's plungers depressed, she picked up the handset and unscrewed the mouthpiece. Then she took the gizmo, an acrylic disc, and screwed it on.

When she released the plungers, the dial tone came on. So did a little red bulb imbedded in the acrylic disc: the line was tapped.

Andy found herself curiously unfazed by this grim confirmation; the day had gone too well, relief seemed too near. So that her listeners wouldn't grow suspicious over the continuing dial tone, she punched up a number and listened to the recorded weather forecast. Then she went back to her shopping bags.

These were almost unpacked when the phone rang.

"Hello?"

"Is this Mrs. Andrea Matteson?" a man asked.

"Yes it is," she replied, her attention swinging to the glowing red bulb in the acrylic disc.

"This is Western Union calling."

"Oh, uh—"

"We have a telegram from Merle Vaughan."

The dread invading her every cell drove out thoughts about the glowing red bulb. Andy gripped the handset tighter.

"The telegram reads: 'Have been trying to reach you, stop. Contacted Carol Fitzpatrick in Florida, stop. Report with sorrow that Philip died on Saturday, stop. You have my deepest condolences, comma, Merle Vaughan.' "

Once more the galaxy cartwheeled, this time not from passion but from anguish, and when the stars resettled, Andy understood that it was her special punishment to survive, perhaps forever, so that she would be forced to stand witness while all those dear to her shuffled—or were shoved—off this mortal coil. Though numb, her mind spewed out facts: of course she had known that Philip was going to die; guts busted apart, limbs smashed, brain most likely damaged, vital signs too weak to permit surgery—what recovery had been possible? Of course it was a blessing; how could this proud man have possibly accepted what had been perpetrated on his body? Andy's mind knew all this, just as it knew that Larry had died with neither pain nor knowledge; throughout the most tortured week of her life, her mind had employed such rational arguments to anesthetize her tormented soul.

But now the overload was just too great. Her mind didn't snap, but it retreated, leaving Andy aware of only the wail within her skull that would not cease.

"Hello? Hello?"

She was trembling badly, and her cheeks had turned into floodplains.

"Hello?" the Western Union man said again.

"Yes?"

"Do you want a written copy of the telegram, Mrs. Matteson?"

"No," she whispered, replacing the handset gently. Then, moving with the agonizingly deliberate speed of a severe arthritic, Andy lowered herself onto the sofa. Wasn't that considerate of Merle Vaughan to keep trying her? she thought. He must have had a hell of a time finding her here in New York; but then, he had obviously been as fond of Philip as she. Why wouldn't her eyes clear? It was as if each tear carried with it another precious unit of energy. . . .

When she awoke shortly before midnight, her forehead was too hot to touch. The fever stemmed from fury: though semidelirious, Andy now knew that she had two souls to avenge. And avenge them she would. She stumbled into the kitchen and quenched her ravenous thirst with a quart of orange juice. Then she groped her way down the back hallway and collapsed into bed. Even as her eyes drooped shut again, she was aware that the fire raging within would, by morning, have cleansed her of grief—and annealed her for the days ahead.

The Second Day

Five after six. When Andy's eyes flicked open, the bedroom still wore the gray shroud of predawn, and yet she could see its contents with preternatural clarity, as if in the light of a Barbizon noon. The ratchet of the digital alarm clock swinging to the new minute sounded like thunder. God, but she was hungry. She swung lightly out of bed and headed for the kitchen.

Seven-fourteen. The buzzer sounded in the apartment in which the two hard-faced men slept.

Limpet One jerked upright in his bed. When he finally realized it was the clock and not the alarm they'd rigged to the target's front door, he reached over and fumbled the off switch into submission.

The air in the room was stale, his mouth sour. He wanted very much to sleep for another day or three, but the cursed job was almost over; today was end game.

The previous night their client had telephoned. He could obviously access TWA's computer because he had informed them that the target held passage on today's late-morning flight from Kennedy to London's Heathrow.

"Do you wish us to book seats?" Limpet One had asked.

The electronically filtered voice: "Negative. Your directive is to establish continuous communication with me when the target leaves her building. Continue to report either until she reaches the airport or when it becomes apparent that she has changed plans. Questions?"

"The flight time?"

"Eleven-fifteen. Questions?"

There had been none.

Limpet One crawled out of bed, shook his partner awake, and headed for the shower. This was their fourteenth day on the job. If today was indeed end game, he and his partner stood to collect another four thousand dollars each to fulfill the one-month guarantee. The thought failed to cheer him.

Seven thirty-seven. Andy decided that the suitcase, packed with Larry's clothes, was full enough, so she zipped it shut and locked it.

She redirected her attention to the newly purchased overnighter. It was reversible. She flipped it so that its bright yellow side showed and then lined it with a plastic trash bag.

Into the mouth of the trash bag went a pair of high-heeled shoes; several changes of panty hose and underwear; two blouses and a skirt; a small toiletry kit, including travel alarm; and a stylish, new, navy-blue worsted suit. She zipped the overnighter closed.

Now Andy drew on a pair of panty hose, followed by jeans. She shrugged her way into an oatmeal-colored cable-knit sweater and then stepped into her boots.

She hefted the suitcase and the overnighter. Could she manage them in action? Yes, so she carried them to the vestibule.

From the front closet she fetched the new reversible raincoat and turned it so that its navy-blue side showed.

Back in the living room, Andy made a final check of her finances. She had slightly more than twenty-seven hundred dollars in cash. That should be enough, she thought, to avoid leaving a trail of receipts. There was also five hundred dollars in traveler's checks, which she would cash this morning, as well as American Express and MasterCard which, because they produced telltale slips, were good only on Phase One of her escape.

Andy felt her impatience mount, but it was only 7:53—and this was one day she couldn't afford to be early. So she went into the kitchen for a final cup of coffee and a final run-through of her notes.

Eight thirty-eight. Limpet One sat in the passenger seat of the Oldsmobile munching a bagel. When the black box on the dashboard beeped, he quickly slipped on the earphones.

"Dial," a woman said. "Going to?"

"Newark Airport," the target replied. "With a stop first at Rockefeller Center."

Limpet One turned to his partner. "Get the client on the line. The wheels are coming off—she's going to Newark Airport, not JFK."

"Where's the pickup, dear?" the dispatcher asked.

"Ninety-nine Riverside. That's the corner of Eighty-second."

"On voucher?"

"No, but I'll pay the corporate premium."

"Name?"

"Andrea Matteson."

"Okay. Hold on." There was a *click*, followed by Muzak's version of "Red Roses for a Blue Lady."

A minute later Limpet One's partner cupped the mouthpiece of the mobile telephone and reported, deadpan, "The cock-sucker's shaken."

Limpet One's mouth twisted in wry amusement.

The Muzak had segued into "Send in the Clowns" when the dispatcher finally came back on. "Matteson? Car three-two-two in twelve minutes. The billing will be the meter to Rockefeller Center, then the airport book rate of thirty-five dollars, plus a four-dollar premium and all tolls."

"Right," the target said. "Car three-two-two in twelve minutes."

When she broke the connection, Limpet One filled in his partner, who relayed the news to the client. His partner listened for a minute more, then hung up. "We got us a new directive—stay on her tail *real* tight and stay off the line to him unless it's a four-alarmer. Sounds like he's going to try to access the computers of every airline flying out of Newark this morning."

Limpet One pursed his lips. "His bowels're really in an uproar, huh?"

"Good buddy, not even that fucking filter could hide the quaver."

Slowly Limpet One's smile turned into a grin that matched his partner's.

Eight fifty-one. Andy finished brushing her hair and regarded herself in the mirror. What would she do if it didn't work? More important, what would they do?

She circled the apartment one last time, checking that lights were out and windows closed, all the while trying to impress images and memories deeper into her consciousness. In the vestibule she shrugged into her raincoat. Then, picking up suitcase and overnighter, she swung out the door, locked up, and rang for the elevator.

Eight fifty-four. A radio-dispatched cab drew up to the entrance of the building.

"Car three-two-two, good buddy," Limpet One said.

His partner turned the ignition key. The Olds kicked into life.

Eight fifty-six. Andy stepped from the building trailed by the doorman, who was carrying her bags. He started to place them in the driver's compartment.

"No, I'll keep them in the back with me," she said, opening the rear door. As he slid the luggage across the seat, she glanced at the Olds idling ten yards away. The plan *has* to work, she thought.

Andy climbed in, and the driver flipped the cab into gear. "First stop Rockefeller Center?"

"Right. The International Building, Fifty-first and Fifth. I'm picking up a passport."

The cab pulled away. In its wake, the metallic green Olds also angled out from the curb.

Nine-eleven. Cab 322 slid to a stop in front of the Fifth Avenue entrance of the International Building, and the target hopped out.

Limpet One's feet hit the sidewalk before hers.

Inside the building she took the escalator to the mezzanine, in her impatience walking up the moving steps. Real tight surveillance, the client had said; Limpet One matched her stride for stride.

On the mezzanine she turned left and then right and hurried down the corridor to the passport bureau. Limpet One followed her to the glass doors, through which he watched her pick up her passport.

When the target emerged, she refused to look his way though she passed within five feet of him. Instead, she hurried back down the corridor onto the descending escalator.

In the lobby he trailed her into a bank. She made straight for the special services window, where she cashed several travelers' checks. Then it was back through the lobby and out the Fifth Avenue entrance.

As Limpet One climbed into the Olds he said, "Nothing out of the ordinary. Any word from the cock-sucker?"

His partner shook his head and started after the cab.

Nine twenty-three. Andy pretended to check her makeup again. In the mirror of her compact, she could see the Olds one car back.

The cab was rolling down Fifth on the right-hand side of the avenue; the driver was obviously going to turn west on Thirty-fourth to take the tunnel to New Jersey.

Up ahead, the light changed.

Andy consulted her watch. "Driver?"

He half-turned.

She leaned forward and handed him three crisp, new twenty-dollar bills. "This should cover the call you answered. But I've changed my mind about going to Newark Airport."

Nine twenty-seven. As the target's cab glided south past Twenty-eighth Street and started to edge left, toward the center of Fifth Avenue, Limpet One muttered "Uh-oh" and reached for the mobile telephone.

By the time he raised the client, the cab had swung left onto Twenty-third Street, along which it proceeded east—away from New Jersey.

Limpet One was unprepared for the response to his report. An uncharacteristic chuckle floated eerily through the receiver, and then the electronically filtered voice said, "Splendid, splendid! I shouldn't doubt but that she's on her way to Kennedy to catch the London flight." Just as quickly, the self-congratulatory ebullience gave way to the familiar remoteness. "Your directive is to stay on the line and report any further evasive maneuvers. Questions?"

"Negative."

Nine thirty-four. Across Twenty-third Street and then the cab turned left onto First Avenue and headed back uptown.

Andy moved her suitcase and overnighter into position. She reached into a pocket of her raincoat; the American Express card was at the ready. Then she checked the mirror of her compact for the last time; the Olds was still one car back.

Up First Avenue and then the cab turned right onto Thirty-fourth Street—and ran smack into a line of cars waiting to get onto the ramp that led to the elevated highway. Beyond the highway Andy spied the East River.

An unholy racket could be heard even over the din

of traffic as a red-and-white helicopter lifted from a pad at river's edge.

Up ahead the light changed to green. The line of cars began to move.

Without turning, the cabbie said, "Get ready."

Nine forty-two. Instinctively Limpet One adjusted the earplug of his walkie-talkie; something was wrong.

The target's cab, separated from their Olds by a panel truck, had reached the intersection. The light was still green. So why wasn't the cab moving?

Horns started to blare.

His partner gripped the steering wheel tighter, preparing to swing out into the oncoming lane should the cab make a last-second dash through the light and onto the elevated highway.

The traffic light blinked to yellow.

"Fuck!"

The right rear door of the cab flew open, and the target was scrambling out and reaching back for her luggage, and then she was racing for the street that ran below the highway.

Limpet One bailed out of the Olds and sprinted after her.

Thanks to her head start, she was halfway across the street when the light turned completely against her and now vehicles were bearing down at speed from her right—a cacophony of screeching brakes and bleating horns—but even lugging her unwieldy bags, she never broke stride.

By the time Limpet One arrived at the intersection, the cross street was coursing with traffic. He had to stop and watch helplessly as the target continued through a gate, across a parking area, and up the stairs into the tan trailer marked New York Helicopter.

Nine forty-four. "Andrea Matteson," she gasped to the startled attendant behind the counter of the makeshift departure lounge. "Is my charter ready?"

"Uh, uh, yes, ma'am," he said. Recovering quickly, the young man picked up a microphone—"Customer's here, Waldo"—and then shifted his attention to the files in front of him. "Any other passengers, ma'am?"

"No." Andy slapped her American Express card on the counter and looked out onto the pad. The rotors of a small red-and-white helicopter were churning with increasing speed. She wheeled and looked back onto the street. The hard-faced man with the mismatched eyes stood impatiently on the far corner, waiting for the light to change.

Ker-chunk, and the attendant was handing over the charge slip and she was signing it and ripping off her receipt and he was passing her card back. Then the young man was fetching her bags and leading the way through the back door onto the apron.

Just before following him out, she snuck one last look.

Her pursuer had made it across three of the four lanes and was racing full-tilt toward the heliport gate.

Nine forty-seven. Limpet One slammed through the makeshift departure lounge in five giant steps and barreled out onto the apron.

Twenty-five yards away, the attendant was securing the helicopter door.

Through its porthole Limpet One could see the target's pale and anxious face. He bellowed "Hold it! Hold it!" but his words were drowned out by the craft's quickening chop; he started running again.

The attendant, stooped like a hunchback, turned and began to scuttle clear. Then he spotted Limpet One, who was both screaming and gesticulating frantically. The attendant hollered back, but his voice was also lost in the gathering din, so he shifted to intercept this onrushing lunatic.

Limpet One swerved right.

The young man refused to take the feint.

Limpet One swerved left—and then pulled up

short when he saw the wide-eyed face in the porthole
levitating as the helicopter's landing skids lifted from
the concrete.

"Goddamn it, man, you crazy?" the attendant
raged. "This is a restricted area! Can't you read?"

"Just trying to get aboard to catch a plane," Limpet
One wheezed, his eyes still tracking the rapidly climbing craft.

"You got to make reservations, man, you can't just
come running out here. . . ." The young man's voice
trailed off as his adrenaline count started to stabilize.
"Anyway, that was a charter. You couldn't've gotten on
no matter what."

"Hell," Limpet One said, his breath still ragged. "It
was my only chance of making my flight. JFK, right?"

The attendent grunted.

"When's your next flight?"

"About half an hour."

"How long to rustle me up a charter?"

"About forty-five minutes. Man, like you got to plan
these things ahead of time, you know?"

Limpet One nodded wearily. The helicopter was
by now just a dot in the sky.

Inside the Oldsmobile his partner, who had been
listening to the conversation on the apron through Limpet One's open walkie-talkie mike, spoke into the mobile telephone. "The target is en route to JFK via helicopter. Time and place of arrival unknown."

The electronically filtered voice: "Point of departure the heliport at Thirty-fourth Street and the East
River?"

"Affirmative."

"Repeat the target's attire."

"Raincoat, navy blue. Turtleneck sweater,
off-white Denim jeans, blue. Boots. Suitcase, black with
tan, red and green stripes. Also an overnight bag, yellow."

"Description copied. Your directive is to return to
base and await further directives. Questions?"

"Negative."

A click and the dial tone; Limpet Two gently replaced the handset in its cradle.

One minute after ten. Damn it, her schedule was decaying, Andy thought as she hurried across the tarmac from the chopper toward the TWA complex at Kennedy.

Once inside, her heart sank even more. She hadn't realized just how far the TWA terminal itself was from the helipad. Gritting her teeth, she hoisted her luggage and started down the long corridor.

Andy was bathed in sweat by the time she reached the check-in counter. As an attendant tagged her suitcase, she glanced at a clock: 10:16. Jesus—what if she showed up late and got bumped?

"Your flight will be boarding at gate—"

"Yes, I know," Andy blurted, wheeling away from the counter.

Ten-eighteen. Andy hurried past the other three women in the ladies' room and into an empty stall.

She took off the raincoat, reversed it from navy blue to powder blue, and then hung it on the door peg. She zipped open the overnighter, pulled out the plastic trash bag, and then reversed the overnighter from bright yellow to navy blue. She shucked boots, turtleneck, and jeans, threw then into the overnighter, and then plucked the top blouse from the plastic trash bag.

Come on, damn it, come on, all these lousy buttons, why hadn't she worn it under the fucking turtleneck? Finally she slipped on the navy-blue worsted skirt and suit jacket and then stood into the high-heeled shoes.

Was there time to apply makeup, as planned? No, so she crammed the plastic trash bag back into the overnighter, drew the zipper shut, and then grabbed her raincoat and left the stall.

It was late, dangerously late, but there was one more thing she absolutely had to do. Hurrying to the vanity counter, Andy dug from one pocket of her jacket a brush and barrettes and began to pin up her long, below-the-shoulder hair. Though the job was sloppy, it changed her profile dramatically; but had the two minutes it took come at the cost of her clockwork escape?

Ten twenty-nine. The taxi queue in front of TWA arrivals was to Andy's left.

She started for it. A grizzled man in a plaid lumberjack's coat offered to hail her a cab, but she was already past him, running on rubbery legs toward the vehicle at the head of the line. She wrenched open the back door and piled in.

"Where to, lady?" the driver asked as he flipped the meter.

"The United terminal."

"Aw, Christ, lady, there's a bus for—"

"Keep the change," Andy interrupted, thrusting forward a ten-dollar bill. "Just shut up and drive."

"Yes *ma'am*," he said, throwing the vehicle into gear before this whacko could change her mind about shelling out ten bucks for a ride of less than a mile.

Ten thirty-four. Andy gave the clerk at the United check-in counter her flight number and name.

"Here we are," the young lady said as she peered at her computer terminal. "How will you pay for the ticket, Mrs. Smith?"

"Cash."

Ten fifty-six. A public phone at the boarding gate to TWA's flight to London began to ring. The maintenance worker who happened to be leaning casually against the booth ducked inside and answered it.

An electronically filtered male voice: "Any sign of the target?"

"Nope."

"Repeat the description."

The maintenance worker suppressed a sigh.

"Height, five-nine. Hair, dirty blond, straight, below-the-shoulders. Eyes, gray. Wearing raincoat, dark blue. Jeans, blue. Boots. Look, is this snapshot we have recent?"

"Affirmative."

"Then we'll have no trouble spotting her. Relax. The flight isn't even boarding yet."

"The target checked her suitcase more than forty minutes ago," the electronically filtered voice said acerbically. "She should have entered your surveillance zone by now. Your directive is to requery your associates."

"Roger. Hang on." The maintenance worker activated his lapel mike.

In front of TWA arrivals, the grizzled man in the plaid jacket who pretended to be a taxi dispatcher, cupped one ear.

"Any sign of the target, Eagle Two?"

"Negative," the grizzled man said.

The maintenance worker spoke into his lapel mike again.

Outside TWA departures on the upper concourse, a man in a policeman's uniform turned his back to traffic.

"Eagle Three, any sign of her?"

"Yes, and I personally escorted her to a waiting limo," the fake cope said into his own mike.

The maintenance worker muttered "Smart-ass" as he picked up the phone and said, "All stations reporting negative."

"Then your directive is to make another sweep. Questions?"

"Nope." The maintenance worker hung up, left the booth, and started to drift through the thickening crowd yet once more.

Three after eleven. The flat, dull landscape bordering the runway blurred as the aircraft gained speed. Andy's eyes, which she usually squinched at takeoff, remained open; when what she saw began to tilt, she knew the Chicago-bound 727 was aloft, so she allowed herself a satisfied smile.

Three twenty-seven (Central Time). "*Mar*-velous! You look *smash*-ing!"

Andy hoped her grunt would be taken as assent; she couldn't stop staring at the mirror, in which the reflection of Mr. Bruno was blow-drying what remained of her hair.

The day before, by calling Chicago's O'Hare, she'd learned that, incomprehensibly, the country's busiest airport had not a single beauty salon on its premises; so here she was in the Woodfield Mall in nearby Schaumberg, trapped in Mr. Bruno's chair in an emporium with the unlikely name of Golbitz's Beauty City.

When she'd instructed him to severely trim her long locks, his eyes had flared like Fourth of July sparklers. Now Mr. Bruno laid down the tools of his trade and clasped his hands, clearly awestruck by what he had wrought. "So much trendier, don't you agree? I hope you don't mind my saying this, dear, but the moment you walked in, the moment I laid eyes on you. I thought to myself, Mr. Bruno, that long, straight look is very *passé*. But if she lets Mr. Bruno work his magic, well, then she would be a very *au courant* lady."

Andy nodded dumbly.

He began untying the smock around her. "I want you to live with this look for a while, dear. But I also want you to think very carefully about something else, okay? I want you to think about letting Mr. Bruno give you a set of really, really tight curls the next time you come in."

Sure, and if you dye my hair red and poke out my eyes, then I can go to costume parties as Little Orphan Andy, she thought, choking back a fit of laughter that arose less from amusement than from hysteria.

* * *

Five forty-two (Central Time). For the second time that day the landscape blurred and tilted. Andy stared out the window of the Omaha-bound American Airlines L-1011, watching vehicles and buildings shrink into toys. All the while she continued to tug at her hair, as if trying to lengthen it.

The Third Day

The raised brass letters on the mahogany door read The Hewes Service.

Andy suddenly felt like a teenager about to go to her first prom: hopelessly transparent. A visit to her hotel's beauty parlor had repaired some of Mr. Bruno's damage, and the valet service had pressed her travel-crumpled suit. Still she remained ill at ease, an imposter in the trappings of a suburban matron. Unconsciously, she fingered the new gold band, purchased also at Bloomingdale's, that encircled her ring finger. Then she raised one freshly manicured hand and turned the knob of the mahogany door.

The reception area was airy and sunny, exuding taste, culture—and money.

As Andy stepped inside, the receptionist said, with an expectant smile, "Mrs. Robert Lyall?"

Andy nodded.

"I'll tell Mrs. Hewes you're here." She picked up the telephone resting on a Chippendale secretary, pressed a button, and murmured into the instrument. On replacing it, she looked up. "Mrs. Hewes will be with you shortly. Would you care to have a seat?"

Andy walked across a rug she guessed to be an eighteenth-century Isfahan and sat in one of the wing chairs she knew to be a Sheraton. To her left, on pedestals in front of the picture windows, flourished several magnificent orchids. The walls were painted a subtly vibrant shade of peach. On a knickknack shelf across the room rested several exquisite pieces of chinoiserie. The music filtering through the hidden speakers was an early Bach concerto.

Even more impressive than the accoutrements, Andy realized, was the sheer size of the reception area. Space was surely at a premium at this, one of downtown Omaha's most prestigious business addresses, and yet the Hewes Service suite squandered it conspicuously.

In front of her stood a lacquer-and-gilt Coromandel trunk that served as a coffee table. On it were a selection of glossy periodicals: *Vanity Fair, Scientific American, Life, Town & Country, Fortune, House and Garden.*

Andy was thumbing through the *Vanity Fair* when her attention was caught by a stunning abstract photograph that proved to be of a computer's innards. When an upper-crust monthly such as this began sending back dispatches from the brave new electronic frontier, she thought, that frontier must be closing: the "future" was now. Her eyes slid to the text—and caught again. The essay was about the arcane games that geniuses played on computers. One sounded awfully familiar.

And then her mind flashed back to Ann Arbor and to that afternoon in Philip's office. Hadn't he mentioned Ergo Est? Yes, that was the legendary "ultimate game," if in fact it existed at all.

Andy lost interest in the article, her mind retreating to that last afternoon of love both superheated and tender. She withdrew so far into her memories that she almost didn't hear the door opening.

The handsome, silver-haired woman who approached looked like a Newport socialite. Her understated gray suit was set off by a mauve silk blouse with ruffled front and, on the lapel of her jacket, an ivory cameo set in white gold. In her mid-fifties, the woman radiated the pampered air of one whose daily morning exercise class almost—but not quite—counteracted the rich meal of the night before.

She smiled and extended a hand. "Mrs. Lyall? Larissa Hewes."

As Mrs. Hewes led Andy toward her office, she said to her receptionist, "Irene, please hold all calls."

Her corner office, furnished in Early American antiques, faced south and west; through its large windows Andy felt as though she could survey most of Nebraska.

"Quite a view, isn't it?" remarked Mrs. Hewes as she led Andy to a chair. Then, seating herself behind the refractory table that was her desk, she said, "One question that most of our prospective parents ask is, 'Why are you located in Omaha?' I like to point out that this is, after all, the home of Father Flanagan's Boys Town." Mrs. Hewes paused to smile at her own jest.

Then she launched into a well-rehearsed speech about The Hewes Service. A native Nebraskan who'd found herself widowed and her children grown, she had coped with her grief through volunteer work. The United Way agency that she discovered most gratifying specialized in adoptions. And yet, after several years of serving on its board, she couldn't help but notice that there seemed to be an unfilled need in the area of placing older children.

As Andy listened she intuited that so far, Mrs. Hewes was telling the truth; that a close check of her background would verify her boring recitation.

But then the warning bells began to sound.

"About three years ago," Mrs. Hewes said, "I decided to meet that need. Fortunately, my late husband had left me well provided for. I devoted the bulk of his estate to establishing The Hewes Service."

A bald lie unless the late Mr. Hewes maintained a second residence in Paraguay, Andy thought.

"It's been an experience filled with challenges," Mrs. Hewes continued blandly. "The youngsters whom we place must all be of exemplary character. And, of course, we do a tremendous amount of screening to insure that the parents they join will be able to provide the right kind of homes."

"Of course," Andy murmured.

"Now, Mrs. Lyall, unless you have questions about us, perhaps you would be so good as to tell me about your husband and yourself."

"Certainly," Andy said, suddenly wishing she had a cigarette. "We live in Old Lyme, Connecticut. Robert—"

"Old Lyme," Mrs. Hewes interjected. "Would that be near Fairfield?"

"An hour's drive," Andy replied, puzzled.

Mrs. Hewes turned and opened a drawer in the console behind her. From it she withdrew a folder. As she turned back, she riffled through the sheets in it. "My memory serves me correctly," she announced. "We had the good fortune to place a lovely young man with a family from Fairfield this past February. But, oh dear, I've interrupted you. You were saying?"

"Well, Robert, my husband, is a vice-president of Mutual Liberty Insurance in Hartford. I used to be a theatrical designer, but when we moved to Old Lyme, I began to pursue painting."

"How delightful, Mrs. Lyall. What medium do you prefer?"

"Uh, mostly oils. Still lifes."

Mrs. Hewes nodded approvingly.

As Andy continued her tale of how she and "Robert" had tried in vain to have a child, she sensed that her lies were ridiculously awkward. Yet, the silver-haired woman across from her seemed to hang on every word.

Ten painful minutes later, just as Andy was about to conclude her fictions, the phone on the refractory table chimed.

Mrs. Hewes frowned as she answered it. "Please, Irene, no calls. Oh. I see. . . . No, that's all right. Yes." She replaced the handset and looked at Andy. "I'm sorry, but something's come up. Would you mind waiting about ten minutes?"

"No, of course not."

"Thank you." Mrs. Hewes turned again and took from the console at her back a magazine-sized packet, which she offered Andy. "Additional information about The Hewes Service, along with our parents' application form. Perhaps you might like to look through these." Then she rose and left the room.

Andy opened the packet and withdrew a brochure slickly executed in four colors. As she placed the empty packet on the desk, she noticed the folder Mrs. Hewes had pulled out earlier.

Suddenly the office felt like the inside of an evacuated bell jar.

Though the folder was upside-down, Andy had no trouble reading its label: "Recent Placements." Along with her breath, time froze. Did she dare? What if she was caught? Could she brazen her way clear with yet another lie? Come on, come on, she thought, make a goddamn decision—

A knock on the door, and Andy snatched back her trembling hand.

"Mrs. Lyall," the receptionist said, peeking in, "would you care for some coffee or tea?"

"Uh, no thanks."

As soon as the door clicked shut, Andy grabbed the folder and opened it. Inside were over a dozen two-page reports.

The first page of the top report was dominated by the four-by-five color portrait stapled to it. The subject was a boy. Hair: sandy. Eyes: brown. Andy began to read the accompanying data. *Name:* Peter. *Age:* eight. *Date of placement:* early January. *IQ:* 137. *Health:* excellent. She skimmed down the biographical facts and figures. The only glaring omission: where The Hewes Service had located Peter.

She turned to the second page. *Name of adoptive father:* Thurston. *Age:* forty-two. *Occupation:* dentist.

Name of adoptive mother: Elizabeth. *Age:* forty-two. *Occupation:* housewife. *Number of previous children:* none. *Primary family residence:* Evanston, Illinois. *Family income:* $92,500. Andy breezed through some additional minutiae—bank references, clubs belonged to—and turned to the next report.

Subject Two was a boy. Hair: blond. Eyes: blue. *Name:* Henry. *Age:* ten. *Date of placement:* mid-January. *IQ:* 141. *Name of adoptive father:* Richard. *Age:* forty-six. *Occupation:* tobacco industry lobbyist. *Name of adoptive mother:* Su Anne. *Age:* thirty-nine. *Occupation:* charity work. *Number of previous children:* one, by husband's first marriage; male, age nineteen. *Primary family residence:* Falls Church, Virginia. *Family income:* $132,700.

Subject Three was a girl. Hair: blond. Eyes: green. *Name:* Tricia. *Age:* ten. *Date of placement:* mid-January. *IQ:* 139. *Name of adoptive father:* Alfred. *Age:* thirty-nine. *Occupation:* accountant. *Name of adoptive mother:* Bettina. *Age:* forty-one. *Occupation:* none. *Number of previous children:* none. *Primary family residence:* La Jolla, California. *Family income:* $88,900.

Subject Four was a boy. Hair: black. Eyes: blue. *Name:* Gerald. *Age:* nine. *Date of placement:* late January. *IQ:* 158. *Name of adoptive father:* Nelson. *Age:* sixty-three. *Occupation:* presiding partner of an investment bank. *Name of adoptive mother:* Megan. *Age:* thirty. *Occupation:* free-lance photographer. *Number of previous children:* three, by husband's previous marriages; male, age thirty-nine; female, age thirty-six; female, age nineteen. *Primary family residence:* Cornwall-on-the-Hudson, New York. *Family income:* $1,717,600.

After perusing ten of the reports, Andy reluctantly returned the folder to Mrs. Hewes's desk.

Just in time; in less than a minute the door was opening and the woman was at the threshold saying, "Let me know when that's ready for my signature."

As Mrs. Hewes stepped into her office, Andy looked up innocently from the agency's brochure.

"I apologize profoundly for having taken so long," Mrs. Hewes said.

"Oh, not at all. It gave me time to read your literature and study the application. Which brings me to a question—assuming that our application is approved, how long might it take?"

"That's difficult to predict, Mrs. Lyall. All I can say is, our screening process is so rigorous that we don't normally carry a long waiting list. In addition, it allows us to make a higher than usual number of first-try matches."

"I did notice how detailed the questions are," Andy said as she stood. "I hope the fact that Robert smokes an occasional pipe won't disqualify us."

Mrs. Hewes smiled encouragingly. "I shouldn't worry about that, my dear."

The two women walked to the door of the reception area. There Mrs. Hewes extended her hand again: "Please feel free to contact me if there are any more questions concerning your application. And do have a good trip West."

Andy's hotel, the Red Lion, was just three blocks away, so she started walking—and mulling over her forty-five minutes at The Hewes Service.

It had gone better than she'd dare hope. Having parachuted into Omaha in pursuit of her only real lead, Andy had obtained enough information to at least ring the agency's bell; how was Mrs. Hewes going to explain away the OvS connection? Plus, there had been the providential peek at the "Recent Placements" file.

Andy mentally reviewed the data culled from the ten reports.

Fact: The Hewes Service seemed to be placing about five children per month.

Fact: each was between the ages of eight and twelve.

Fact: though hair and eye coloring varied, each would certainly have been embraced by Hitler himself as embodiments of the Aryan myth.

Fact: each child appeared to be in excellent physical health, with an IQ rating in the "near genius" range or above.

Fact: each of the adoptive families was high-income and lived in an affluent community.

Fact: each husband was excelling in a profession or industry known for encouraging conservatism in matters both business and personal—including politics.

Fact: none of the families had other children living with them.

Fact: none of the families had Jewish surnames.

The one vital fact that Andy had not been able to uncover was the source of The Hewes Service's superkids. But she did have names and addresses. Suppose she could link the recent placements with the Realm culture that surely existed in their new communities. Would that, coupled with The Hewes Service's shady financial background, be enough to interest some organization—such as Larry's newsmagazine—in investigating this invidious and deadly game?

Still preoccupied as she entered the lobby of the Red Lion, Andy almost bowled over a departing postman. She apologized and continued to the front desk.

The clerk handed over her room key and then added, "Oh, Mrs. Lyall, some mail just arrived for you."

She looked at him blankly. Outside of Mrs. Hewes, who had recommended the hotel, nobody knew she was there, much less under what name.

"I didn't even get a chance to put it in your box," the clerk said, sliding forward a manila envelope bearing the distinctive blue-and-orange Express Mail label of the post office's overnight delivery service.

Her viscera began to churn as she read the label:

FROM: Wm. Smith
GPO

New York, NY

TO: Mrs. Robert Lyall
        Red Lion Hotel
        16th & Dodge
        Omaha, NEB 68102

And then her eyes swung to the handwritten notation below the label:

Please Forward To Andrea Matteson.

"Is everything all right, Mrs. Lyall?" the clerk
asked nervously.

Andy didn't answer. Instead, she clutched the
counter until she had regained sufficient strength to
make it to the elevator.

Up in her room, she tossed the unopened packet
onto the bed and plopped down beside it. Was "William
Smith" one of the hard-faced men she'd left at the East
River heliport some twenty-six hours earlier? If so, how
had he—or, more likely, the brains behind Realm—
traced her to Omaha? Andy looked at the time of post-
ing on the label. It had been mailed from New York at
3:27 P.M. yesterday.

There could be only one explanation: Mrs. Hewes.
Andy felt sick.

She thought her escape route so clever, but it had
been the work of an amateur. Of course they hadn't
bothered to pursue her; they had simply waited patiently for her to obligingly reappear between the cross
hairs.

Only once in her life had Andy ever given up on
anything—her marriage to Larry. It was time to make
it two failures. There was no way she could continue her
quest for the malignant perpetrator of Realm, not with
the hounds of hell again on her heels.

Three nights ago she had thought she would be
permitted no unilateral surrender. Perhaps she had
been wrong. Someone once observed that no action is

itself an action. Surely if she returned meekly to Ann Arbor and resumed her shattered life, sooner or later her tormentors would spot the white flag. Could she stomach the fact that she might well be forfeiting her privacy, that she must never again permit the word "Realm" to cross her lips?

Yes, Andy decided; anything would be better than the awful agony of waiting for yet another shoe to drop, be it the terror of an unexpected packet or the total trauma of a loved one's death.

Today was Wednesday. By Friday morning she could be on a beach in Bermuda, there to rejoin her daughter and her parents—not to mention the ranks of the sane.

Quickly, as if to ratify her resolve, Andy picked up the phone and asked for the long-distance operator. Her parents and Patty were away from the hotel, so she left a message that she would call back.

A shower would refresh. Andy was on the way to the bathroom when she remembered that the Red Lion boasted an indoor swimming pool. She called the front desk; yes, a bathing suit could be arranged.

Twenty minutes later Andy had changed into the borrowed black tank suit and was leaving her room. She noticed the Express Mail packet still lying unopened on the bed. After a moment's hesitation, she grabbed it.

Up and back, up and back, up and back, up and back; with each lap Andy could feel another layer of tension dissolve.

Finally, puffing like a spent marathoner and her muscles wrung to exhaustion, she stroked to the side of the pool and hoisted herself out. As she headed for her chaise, she became conscious of the attention paid her by two macho businessmen across the way. Probably my haircut, she thought and smiled to herself. Andy ran a towel over herself and then sank gratefully onto the chaise.

The orange juice she had ordered was on the

nearby table, next to the Express Mail packet. She took a long swallow, set the glass down, and then picked up the packet.

Andy opened it—and frowned at the smaller manila envelope inside.

But as soon as she read the mailing label, she relaxed; it had been mailed by her Ann Arbor landlord, the Boleys, to Larry's apartment in New York. The fact that her pursuers obviously had access to U.S. mailboxes left her curiously unmoved.

Andy examined the Boleys' envelope, which was still firmly sealed. Five seconds later, it wasn't.

Its contents consisted of a sheet of stationery folded around several unopened letters. Andy removed the rubber bands holding the packet together and smoothed out the note from Ginny Boley.

> Dear Andy,
>   Peter and I wanted to tell you again how sorry we are about the tragedies that have visited you. You deserve much, much better. Chin up, life will get better. You know that we are rooting for you. I am also writing to send along some letters that have come since you left. We are holding on to the bills and junk mail. If there is anything we can possibly do to be of help at this dark hour, you know the number. Andy, you are in our prayers.

Andy's eyes moistened. Why had she been so blind to the Boleys' friendship—because they didn't hold college degrees? Clearing her throat, she reached for the orange juice again as she began to flip through the enclosed envelopes. Judging from the return addresses, they were condolence letters.

Glass shattered against tile.

All eyes at poolside swiveled toward the explosion—except for Andy's, which were riveted to the name at the top left of the last envelope: *Hunt.*

A mop-toting busboy approached and asked if she was okay, but still she remained frozen.

This must be a cruel hoax, Andy thought. Philip had been in a coma until his death; how could he have known about Larry's accident, much less written a condolence note?

And then her eyes found the postmark: Philip had mailed it from Big Sur before his crash. . . .

Only upon realizing that this was not a message from the grave did she begin to breathe again. And then Andy became aware of somebody speaking to her.

"What?" she said, turning to the busboy.

"Uh, would you like another juice, lady?"

"Oh. No, no thanks."

Big Sur. The town was near Carmel on the California coast, and Carmel was fifty miles north of Lucia, and Lucia was where Philip had made his last phone call to her: *"My plane's landing, got to run. And, Andy—I love you."*

She slit open the envelope.

The single sheet inside, imprinted with the crest of the Lucia Lodge, bore a handwritten message:

Andy,
   What I've discovered out here is monstrous, but I've managed to get proof, and I'm flying that proof East tonight. This note's in case I don't get home in one piece. (Yes, it's that dicey.) If anything happens to me, check out a hush-hush private sanatorium that's between here and Big Sur. It's called Elysium. And check out a patient named Otto von Schwenk. Uh-oh, it's getting late and I've got a lot of miles to cover. Sure as hell hope this note proves redundant.
                                          Love, Philip

Otto von Schwenk—*OvS!*

Once again, tears welled. Two weeks ago, without realizing it, Philip had made the most momentous connection in the bizarre web that linked·

Rolf Schmidt and all the other young Realm Maestros;

The Hewes Service in Omaha;

OvS Enterprises/N.A., Inc. in Freeport, the Bahamas (courtesy of a Paraguayan lawyer who trucked with the remnants of the Third Reich);

And Otto von Schwenk, hiding in a Northern California sanatorium called Elysium.

If only Philip could have made it the last eight miles to her house unharmed; then he and the only other man she had ever loved would still be alive.

Andy dried her cheeks with the towel.

Surely this new revelation, coupled with the facts already established, would prompt an investigation. And then she remembered a project that Larry's magazine had attempted to mount about nine years earlier.

A correspondent had been tipped that a fugitive financier was using as his sanctuary a posh sanatorium in western Connecticut. Stonewalled by the head doctor and unable to penetrate the grounds surreptitiously, the magazine had finally turned the information over to the FBI. But the doctor—claiming that his relationships with patients were privileged—had managed to thwart even the FBI long enough to allow the financier to escape the sanatorium in the back of a bread truck. After a short ride to Westchester Airport, the fugitive had hopped his corporate jet to the extradition-proof Bahamas.

Andy stared moodily at the dappled waters of the pool. She no longer harbored any reasonable doubt about the Realm conspiracy, but she knew a disinterested observer might fairly judge it to be just a provocative confluence of circumstantial evidence.

No, the ultimate sacrifices made by Philip and Larry would go for naught unless she herself stalked Otto von Schwenk. And unless she herself could duplicate the hard documentation that Philip had acquired.

But if they had tracked her to Omaha, wouldn't they also track her to California?

Andy brightened. Not necessarily; Omaha had been a velvet trap baited with Mrs. Hewes. They had known that sooner or later, she would walk into it. But by arrogantly forwarding the Boleys' package unopened, they remained unaware of the contents of Philip's last note—and, therefore, the unearthing of Otto von Schwenk.

The key was to hit Elysium fast, before they suspected and could set up a defense. If she headed East out of Omaha and then circled back. . . .

Suddenly Andy realized she was breaking the vow made so recently up in her room, that she was again scheming like a huntress ready to place her life at risk. Madness? Yes—but it was a madness she could accept.

She began to gather her things. There were so many moves yet to plot, as well as another call to place to Bermuda—although now the message for Patty and her folks would be vastly different.

The Fourth Day

To her right, the drowning sun threw up one last dull orange flare to protest its swallowing by the Pacific Ocean.

It was cold in the gathering indigo gloom. Andy started to fiddle with the heater of the rented Capri. Then she noticed that the driver's side window was down. Now why in hell was the window down? Oh, yes, fresh air. Without fresh air she would surely fall asleep at the wheel. And if she fell asleep at the wheel, who knew but that she might not see Philip shortly?

The Capri started to drift to the right.

Cars are killers, she thought. If we can have gun control, why can't we have car control? It wasn't a gun that killed Philip, and it wasn't a gun that killed Larry.

Where did it say in the Constitution that we have the right to bear automobiles? Now, wouldn't that be a bitch for a woman to bear an automobile? And what would the gestation period be? She began to giggle.

Suddenly a shotgunlike blast peppered the right front fender.

Andy wrenched the wheel hard left. She heard a panicky *hooot* from the air horn of the big semi immediately in her wake and the howl of air brakes frantically applied, but she ignored these as she fought to dampen the Capri's violent fishtailing even as her eyes locked on the rearview. The mirror was filled by the dazzling headlights of the semi, which continued to draw inexorably nearer. She couldn't see them, but she knew those bastards were back there somewhere, safe in their metallic dark green armored car, waiting to try again. She'd fix them.

As the pedal hit the metal, the Capri skittered forward and barely out of the way of the sluing semi. She was wide awake now, so it was up on the accelerator and tromp down again to engage the passing gear; the engine whined wildly, and then the power was being transmitted through the drive shaft to the rear wheels, and the car was surging forward again. As the speedometer needle danced clockwise past eighty, Andy let out a whoop; this little buggy of hers could outrun an armored car any day of the week.

Eighty-five and climbing.

Wait a minute, she thought, the shots had hit her right front fender. That means they couldn't have been fired from behind.

Ninety and climbing.

Could they have snuck ahead and set up an ambush?

Ninety-two and holding.

But that made no sense. The side of the road had been empty, and besides, this section of superhighway was elevated; where could they have fired from? She glanced at the stream of oncoming cars on the other side of the divider. Why did all the drivers have their high beams on? Andy hunched forward over the steering wheel and blinked. They didn't; she was seeing double.

Eighty-five and dropping.

She blinked again, and her eyes ignited, the air stinging pupils left naked by tear ducts that fatigue had shut down.

Eighty and dropping rapidly.

Andy started to shiver violently. Getting a grip on herself, she braked, flipped on her turn signal, and began angling the Capri for the shoulder.

On leaving the pavement, the right front tire threw up a shower of gravel that peppered the underside of the the fender like—like buckshot.

Behind her, angry hoots of the air horn as the driver of the semi vented his rage at this dumb broad high on booze or drugs. The Capri shuddered in the airstream of the passing truck, and then the hoots dopplered into the distance.

Andy killed the ignition and rested her forehead on the steering wheel. Though she closed her burning eyes, the past thirty-six hours had exhausted her beyond sleep.

After finally reaching Patty in mid-afternoon of the previous day, she had feinted East from Omaha by booking tickets under the name Andrea Matteson for New York by way of Chicago.

Landing O'Hare, Andy had swung into a phone booth. The departure board served as her guide as she played dial-a-seat, calling the various airlines for the first available flight out, no matter what the destination.

Which was why, shortly after ten that night, she had found herself in Miami. Andy could have hopped a night flight to South America but decided against it. First, she would have to show her passport—and thus mark her trail. Second, who knew the schedule *out* of South America? So it was that she'd passed the night at an airport motel as "Jane Cooper."

Today had been even more frenetic. An early morning visit to another beauty parlor had produced another change of profile; gazing bitterly into the salon's mirror, she knew that this brunette would not have more fun.

From Miami to Dallas, where she had crisscrossed the terminal so many times, trying to determine if she was under surveillance, that an airport cop had taken her for a cruising hooker.

From Dallas to Denver, where after another half hour of hide-and-seek in the lobby, she'd purchased the last ticket—and was the last passenger to board—the flight to Los Angeles.

From Los Angeles to Oakland, where upon landing in early evening, she'd rented the Capri and started on the final leg of her transcontinental odyssey to Realm's poisonous fountainhead.

When at last Andy lifted her head from the steering wheel, the indigo of dusk had given way to the black of night. She started the car and pulled back onto the highway.

Three miles ahead a sign announced the town of Carmel. Elysium—and Otto von Schwenk—were oh, so close, less than fifty miles to the south. In between, though, lay beautiful but treacherous Highway One. Andy knew that to tackle this winding coastal two-lane at this hour, and in her condition, was tantamount to vehicular Russian roulette.

Despite her impatience, she pulled onto the Carmel off-ramp and began to search for a motel.

The Fifth Day

"You have reached area code four-oh-eight, six-zero-one, seven thousand," the prerecorded female voice intoned. "This is Elysium. At the sound of the chime, state your business and a number at which the Elysium staff can call you."

Pinnnnggg.

Caught off guard, Andy tried to remember what name she had checked in under. Jones? Cooper? No, that had been Dallas or Miami. Smith? Yes, Smith; Mrs. Robert Smith. Quickly she said, "This is Betty Smith. I'm calling to inquire about visiting hours." Then she gave the telephone number of the motel, as well her room's extension.

Ninety seconds later the phone rang.

"Mrs. Robert Smith?" a man asked.

"Yes?"

"This is Elysium. What is the guest's V.I.?"

"I beg your pardon?"

"The guest's V.I.," the man repeated.

"I'm sorry, I'm not following you."

"Every guest at Elysium has a Visitation Index," he said with some exasperation. "We cannot inform you of the hours you may visit until we know the guest's V.I."

"Oh. I'm afraid I don't know it."

There was a silence, and then the man said archly, "Very well. The guest's name, please?"

"Otto von Schwenk."

"Thank you. One moment." When he came back on, his voice, if possible, had grown even more curt. "Guest von Schwenk is permitted no visitors."

"But—"

The man hung up.

*   *   *

Eighteen miles south of the town of Big Sur, Andy rounded a long, sweeping bend and caught her first glimpse of Elysium.

It seemed a mirage.

This stretch of coastal Highway One had been chiseled high up the flanks of the palisades that form continent's edge. To her right, the land tumbled precipitously for a couple of hundred feet to the inaccessible, boulder-strewn beaches against which the Pacific crashed to a halt.

But the half-moon cove up ahead was like a tranquil emerald floating above the spuming surf. At great expense, part of the cove had been filled, raised, and graded until it was a terrace the size of several football fields. This plateau, which looked to be about forty feet above sea level, was carpeted with an immaculate lawn broken only by a few buildings and cottages and by a pair of macadam parking areas.

As Highway One continued to curve around the cove, Andy searched its shoulder for an overlook on which she could stop. There was none.

Intersecting the highway at the southern end of the cove was a driveway that swept down to the sanatorium. Andy slowed the Capri. The driveway was thwarted by a high metal gate that looked too heavy for even its three muscular—and pistol-packing—guards to budge. Nervously she stepped on the gas.

The road began to swing left; one minute and a half mile later, just around the next hairpin, the coastline reverted to its pristine and angry state.

She continued along it. The nearest overlook, which lay four miles further south, proved too distant and at the wrong angle for looking back on the half-moon cove. Andy stopped the car anyway; she needed to stretch her legs and to think.

The overriding impression given by Elysium was that of expensively cultivated impenetrability. But if people could get off Devil's Island, surely she could breach this littoral stronghold. All it required was time. Yet, that was the one commodity in short supply, for by now von Schwenk and his goons must know that she had gone to ground again.

Her mind latched on a ploy that had worked for a hundred movie heroes and one real-life fugitive financier: bribing some tradesman—the baker, the butcher, the launderer—to sneak her through the gate, hidden in the back of the delivery van. Which local merchants serviced the sanatorium? Once inside the compound, would she be able to conceal herself? Where and how could such information be obtained—or bought? Damn, if only there was some way of studying Elysium with her own eyes. . . .

Andy had been looking down at the roiling ocean. Now she swung her gaze one hundred and eighty degrees to the slopes that climbed above her. The summit should provide the proper vantage point; all she needed to do was find an access road to the top. She climbed into the driver's seat and started back north.

Even crawling along at twenty miles per hour, she almost missed it. Andy had virtually retraced her route to the half-moon cove—and was fretting about whether the guards would recognize her Capri—when she spotted a rusty chain strung between two trees. She swung the wheel hard right and nosed the car up to the chain.

Andy studied the crude path that pointed uphill. It consisted of two deep ruts on either side of a high hump that was in turn sprinkled with fist-sized rocks. Would there be sufficient clearance for the car? Did she care?

She got out and unhooked one end of the chain. Returning to the Capri, Andy flipped the automatic transmission into low and eased forward.

The trail proved even dicier than it looked. Not only did the car begin bottoming out so frequently that she began to worry about cracking the oil pan, but the ruts had been dug by a vehicle wider than a passenger car; consequently, she had to drive at a severe sideways tilt.

Fighting the disorienting driving position and the steepness of the grade, her vision obscured by the overgrown branches that slapped against the windshield, Andy slowly inched the car forward; it took almost three minutes to make it up seventy yards and around the first bend. There, she threw the car into Park, scrambled downhill to reattach the rusty chain, then got back into the car.

The ascending trail petered out more than one hundred yards short of the top. Here the incline was so sharp that she felt the need to chock all four of the car's wheels with rocks before resuming the climb on foot.

What remained of Andy's breath was swept away by the view from the summit.

To the east, ridges and valleys, all seemingly uncontaminated by man, marched to the horizon. North and south, the rugged coastline serpentined as far as the eye could see. To the west, the azure Pacific stretched toward China.

And almost directly below lay Elysium.

She needed binoculars. Then her stomach growled; she needed food, too.

Having driven down from the north, Andy knew that the first gas station-general store in that direction lay on the outskirts of Big Sur, some twenty miles distant. She pulled out her map and took a rough fix of her position. There was a town slightly to the south. She refolded the map and started back down to the car.

As Andy watched the rough-hewn man behind the counter bag her groceries, she asked, "By the way, what's that beautiful resort about five miles up the coast?"

He snorted. "Elysium, but it ain't no resort."

"Oh?"

"Nope. It's a cracker factory."

"You mean an insane asylum?"

He gave it some thought before replying. "Nah, that wouldn't be fair to real whackos. This Doctor Boll, the character who runs the joint, he mostly sucks up to rich folk. You know, the kind with skeletons in the closet that are still alive? Winos, druggies, fags, whatever you call them guys that like to flounce around in dresses—they got 'em all up there in that 'resort.'"

Andy was taken aback by the man's transparent hostility. "Well, at least having that place nearby must be good for business."

His mouth tightened. "Fat chance. This Doctor Boll character, he throws nickels around like barbells. You know who ships in the food? Some dago store up in Frisco. You think they hire us locals to do the cleaning and the laundry and the carpentry? Like hell they do—they got their own people."

The man laughed mirthlessly. "Near as we can figure, only two of us be making money off them. Johnny, who runs the Texaco station, because it's a damn far toot from here to anywhere. And me—it took me awhile, but I finally come up with a way. Look up there."

Andy followed his outstretched hand to a sign.

Picnic Baskets

Gourmet picnic baskets of roast beef/cold roast chicken/Dungeness crab/quiche & salad, plus fresh fruit, ½ bottle fine California wine (white & red). $17.95 per person, advance notice required. Hamper deposit $5.00.

"Never made a penny just selling sandwiches and beer," he gloated. "Didn't do too well with picnics, neither, until I jacked the prices and made 'em book ahead of time. Now, I get rid of maybe three dozen baskets a weekend. Regular customers, too—know how I know 'em? By their cars. There's the silver Porsche Turbo, the chocolate Mercedes roadster, the black Rolls, the white Rolls . . ."

Andy finally cut short his bitter monologue by handing over a twenty-dollar bill. Upon receiving her change, she picked up her groceries and the new pair of binoculars purchased at the local camera shop and beat a grateful retreat.

From her vantage point Elysium looked as pretty—and as animated—as a postcard. In the early afternoon sun the lush grounds were deserted, the buildings silent; even the guards at the highway gate were hiding in the shade. The ominous stillness was broken only by the sigh of gentle breezes and the wash of distant surf.

As Andy finished her sandwich, she kept thinking back to the grocer's angry assertion that the sanatorium contributed nothing to the local economy. That ruled out her fantasy of sneaking through the gate disguised as a tradesman. She drained the bottle of juice and picked up the binoculars again.

The half-moon cove faced almost due west. Two-fifths of it had been built up into a terrace. From this landfill's far edge, which ran along the sea, protruded a promontory.

Though the terrace was a safe forty feet above sea level, it was also in Andy's estimation more than one hundred and thirty feet below Highway One. The drop was so sharp that the only way down was through the guarded gate, by way of the double-switchbacked driveway cut out of the sheer hillside.

Once more she swept the sanatorium with her binoculars, searching desperately for inspiration.

At the southernmost edge of the grounds, which was to her left, a macadam parking lot lay empty save for a small fleet of minibuses and Audis, all painted an identical silver. Near it stood the compound's largest structure, a sprawling, two-story stucco building. From this ran a gravel path that bisected the velvet lawn. Midway across the lawn, the path forked. One branch pointed west toward the promontory and a row of twelve cypress-sided oceanfront bungalows. The other branch continued north to a pair of long, low stucco buildings reminiscent of a luxury motel; between them lay an Olympic-sized swimming pool. Finally, on the northern rim of the grounds, there stood another building. It was also two stories tall and also of stucco, but chunky and somehow lacking in grace. Because the small parking lot alongside held an assortment of older cars, Andy guessed that this was where the staff was quartered.

Now, activity at the gate. A guard was strolling onto the highway and peering north. A burgundy BMW approached. The guard spoke into his walkie-talkie, and the high metal gate began to glide open. The BMW darted through. It continued down the winding driveway and into the large parking lot, where it pulled into the space nearest the main building.

A distinguished-looking, white-haired man dressed in a natty black suit stepped from the car and strode into the building. Could this be Doctor Boll? Andy looked at her watch: 1:17.

Half an hour later, the somnolence was broken again. Men and women dressed in medical whites began to filter from the main building. Some turned toward the bungalows near the promontory while others headed for the two low stucco structures on the northern rim. Though traffic on Highway One was still light, the guards at the gate were also rousing themselves.

For good reason. Suddenly, like a desert arroyo after a flash storm, the two-lane highway was awash in cars; Elysium's visiting hours were about to start.

By five to two, the road was clogged in both directions as far as Andy could see. Yet, the gate remained shut. She used the time to survey the idling cars. Luxury models every one; even at $17.95 per hamper, that grocer to the south was probably charging too little.

At two o'clock sharp siesta time officially ended at Elysium. As if in response to an alarm, the sanatorium's patients—some in street clothes, most in bathrobes, but all escorted by a staff member—emerged from the bungalows and from the two low buildings. Back at the gate the guards began to let in cars, though they moved at the petty creep of French passport officials, checking each license plate against the list on their clipboards before allowing the vehicle through.

By two-fifteen, Elysium's velvet lawn teemed with small clusters of reunited families and friends.

But where, Andy wondered, was the guest permitted no visitors? Where was Otto von Schwenk?

She continued to stare through her binoculars until the last visitor had departed and the last patient led back to his room. Soon thereafter the staff started wheeling around large metal carts, from which they distributed dinner trays.

By the time Andy formulated a plan with even a twenty-five percent chance of success, the westering sun was only two fingers above the horizon. By the time she refined the plan so that it stood a fifty-percent chance, the skies were atwinkle with the first stars of evening. Damn it, why hadn't she thought to purchase a flashlight, she wondered as she groped her way from the summit down toward the Capri.

The Sixth Day

The sign to the right of the highway read:

> Santa Barbara   6
> Los Angeles   100

Up ahead, the flame-red Rolls convertible, its top down, remained in the fast lane, cruising south at seventy miles per hour.

Andy stared helplessly at first the sign and then the car. Three hours ago, anxiety had turned into frustration; two hours ago, frustration had turned into rage. Now, with Saturday afternoon virtually blown, there was only the emptiness that comes with knowing that she had guessed wrong.

The day had begun more auspiciously than she dared hope.

On weekends, it turned out, Elysium also had morning visiting hours. By nine-thirty, Highway One in front of the sanatorium was already gridlocked, and Andy was well into her list of arriving cars.

When she first spotted the flame-red Rolls descending from the north, she had added it to her page of highly visible—and thus easy-to-tail—candidates. As the car idled below her, she studied its two passengers. A handsome man in his forties drove; next to him sat a slim woman whom money was keeping youthful. On reaching Elysium's checkpoint, though, the Rolls had continued south on the highway, and Andy had scratched it off.

But twenty minutes later it returned. In the backseat: three distinctive picnic hampers. She smiled and added it back on her list.

The car cleared the gate, descended the driveway, and parked in the rapidly filling big lot to her left. The couple paused in the main building, then headed for one of the oceanfront bungalows. Ten yards short of the cottage they were met by an emaciated teenage boy accompanied by a male nurse. The man, the woman, and the boy greeted each other warily before retreating to the bungalow.

At ten forty-five the guards at the highway entrance shut the gate. Andy turned to her notes. Nearly two-thirds of the vehicles had arrived from the south. Of course the affluent could live anywhere, but it was a good one hundred and seventy-five miles to Santa Barbara, the nearest concentration of wealth, and almost another one hundred miles past that to Los Angeles.

On the other hand, San Francisco and the Bay Area lay but one hundred and sixty miles to the north. Andy thought this the better gamble, so she again scrutinized the dozen cars on her list that had arrived from the north. The most easily tracked: a lime Jaguar, a white 1957 Thunderbird, and the flame-red Rolls.

The first to leave, she decided, would be the one she followed.

Shortly after eleven, patients and visitors began strolling the grounds. Quickly Andy sighted her three targets.

The woman in the lime Jaguar was with an elderly gent.

The young man in the white T-Bird was with a person of indeterminate gender but who wore a dress.

The couple in the flame-red Rolls was with the teenage boy.

Several minutes before noon, the sanatorium staff started to wheel out the metal carts that carried luncheon trays. Here and there across the great lawn, visitors rose and hiked back to their cars to fetch picnic hampers.

Among them: the handsome driver of the Rolls. The food inside the baskets he brought back looked fine, but the boy ignored his, and the two adults only picked at theirs.

At 12:43 the driver of the Rolls stood. The woman started packing plates and utensils back in the hampers. When she finished, the boy finally stood and submitted to awkward hugs all around.

Andy swung her binoculars left. The woman in the lime Jaguar, talking animatedly to the elderly gent, was only halfway through her meal.

Andy retrained her binoculars on the promontory. The young man in the white T-Bird and his companion sat on the seawall holding hands, their luncheon trays still untouched.

Decision time. The flame-red Rolls?

Because minutes mattered, yes; Andy began scrambling down from the summit.

It took several minutes to reach the Capri, which was parked at the base of the rutted trail, around the first bend and just out of sight of the highway. She hurried past and down the final leg to the rusty chain.

Just as Andy was unlatching it, she heard a vehicle approaching from her right. It was the flame-red Rolls—heading *south*! And then her mouth snapped shut as she realized they were simply returning the hamper to the gourmet grocery.

By the time she wrestled the Capri the rest of the way down the rutted path, traffic had picked up noticeably on Highway One; visiting hours must be concluding, she thought. At the first break in the flow, she gunned her car onto the highway and swung south, toward town.

It was impossible to miss the ostentatious Rolls, which was parked several doors down from the grocery. Andy drove past, made a U-turn, and slid into a space across the street. It was 1:03.

Five minutes later, her concern mounting, she left the Capri, crossed the street, and peered into the grocery.

The couple wasn't inside.

She wheeled frantically—and almost collided with the woman, who was emerging from the card shop next door. Andy muttered fast apologies and continued walking. She stopped half a block away and looked in a store window: the reflected images of the man and the woman were vanishing into a coffee shop.

Andy headed back to the Capri, anxiety beginning to turn into frustration. For the longer they lingered, the less time she would have to purchase all the things she needed.

One thirty-two. The couple had taken a table near the front window of the coffee shop. Now the man was finally breaking off his earnest monologue and standing.

He dug out some change, plunked it on the table, and stalked out the door. A minute later the ashen-faced woman got up and followed him out.

Andy sighed with relief. Hand on the ignition key, she watched the sideview mirror and waited for the man to make the U-turn that would point his car north.

Instead, the driver pulled from the curb and continued south.

Could he be headed for the large Texaco sign down the road?

No; the Rolls sailed past the gas station and in less than forty seconds disappeared from her rearview.

Andy tried to control her rising panic. Was there time to hightail it back to Elysium and pick up either the lime Jaguar or the white T-Bird? She checked her watch: 1:40. Come on, come on, make a decision. . . .

Supposition: if visiting hours were still in progress, she stood a chance.

Supposition: if, however, they had ended around one—when the highway had grown heavy with cars pulling out of Elysium—then the Jag and the T-Bird would have at least a forty-five-minute head start. Which meant that even now they would be reaching the end of Highway One outside Carmel—and passing onto the trackless superhighway leading north.

Andy gunned the Capri to life, squealed through a quick U-turn, and roared off to the south.

The man at the wheel of the Rolls was no slouch; it had taken thirty minutes of hard driving along the twisting two-lane to bring the flame-red car into her sights. Then Andy had eased off and planted the Capri a good half-mile back, settling in for a long afternoon. That it had been: the two-car convoy had swept south out of the rugged Santa Lucia Range and down the flattening coast past San Simeon, past San Luis Obispo, where frustration had turned into rage, and now, past Santa Barbara.

Ninety-four miles remained to Los Angeles. Andy checked her watch yet again: 4:30. With each tick, the gamble she had so optimistically handicapped at fifty-fifty was growing more odds-against. At this late hour, was there even one chance in twenty that she could salvage her plan before Otto von Schwenk and his janissaries picked up her scent?

Six-fourteen. They were inside the Los Angeles city limits, eastbound on the Ventura Freeway. Up ahead, the Rolls eased over into the right-hand lane. So did Andy.

The sign "Laurel Cyn—1" came into view. The driver of the Rolls flicked on his turn signal. Maybe, just maybe, Andy thought, reaching for her signal.

The Rolls glided down the exit ramp and turned right onto Laurel Canyon Boulevard. When Andy again followed suit, her adrenaline was flowing.

Six twenty-six. They had surmounted the crest of Laurel Canyon Boulevard, and were snaking downhill toward Beverly Hills, when the Rolls slowed and then swung left into a driveway that climbed to a spectacular ridge-top house. Andy ignored the long line of cars behind her and braked almost to a stop. The mailbox at the foot of the driveway bore no name. But even in the gathering gloom she could read—and memorize—the number on it.

Six thirty-five. Speeding southwest on Santa Monica Boulevard toward the Beverly Hills office of Larry's magazine, Andy flashed past Rodeo Drive. Were any of its folded shops still open? she wondered. She'd need a pricey outfit to carry out her plan.

Two fast lefts and then a right, and she was cruising down Rodeo.

Near the Wilshire end, a door to a store opened, and several chattering salesclerks emerged.

Andy swerved the Capri to the curb, hopped out, and hurried over.

"Sorry, we're closed," the woman manager said through a gap in the door.

"Please, can I have just five minutes?" Andy pitched her voice at its most plaintive and babbled on. "The freeway was murder, and there's a party up in Bel Air, and I won't take long, really I won't—"

The manager opened her mouth to interrupt.

Andy's eyes darted to a prominent display of cashmere sweaters. Gesturing to it, she said, "I drove all the way in from Trancas just to buy one of those. And a matching skirt, of course."

The manager turned and looked. The sweaters to which Andy pointed were six hundred dollars a copy. There was no clerk remaining in the store to claim the commission. She turned back and with an unctuous smile opened the door.

Six minutes later—and eight hundred dollars poorer—Andy was running to the car with a bag that contained a gun-metal gray cashmere sweater and a pair of cream-colored linen culottes.

Andy was about to get into the Capri when she noticed the window display of another store farther up Rodeo. She hesitated, then locked her new clothes inside the car and headed for the store, which was an electronics boutique.

If nothing else, the sullen drive south that day had given her the time to formulate a tentative solution to one problem that had plagued her since she began her quest in New York. As it stood, her family and friends had no idea of where she was; nor could they, given the scarifying surveillance capabilities of von Schwenk's goons. But suppose harm befell her within Elysium's walls. Andy needed some kind of insurance policy so her parents would at least have something tangible to take to the authorities.

The boutique was crammed with the high-ticket spawns of microchip technology: personal computers, satellite dishes, component televisions, video recorders, and space-age stereos.

A young salesman came forward.

When Andy described her rather mundane needs—a miniaturized microphone, an easily concealed short-wave transmitter, a tape recorder—he matter-of-factly led her to a display case. Bugging must be common in Los Angeles, she thought; or at least among those Angelinos who could afford to shop at places like this.

"How far's the recorder going to be from the transmitter, ma'am?" the salesman asked.

Andy calculated the distance between the sanatorium and the nearest motel to it. "About seven miles."

The salesman shook his head. "No can do. Nobody needs a transmitter that powerful."

"What do you mean?"

"Most times, surveillance is done by teams. A low-powered transmitter and a parabolic dish is much better. Catch my drift?"

Andy shook her head.

The salesman reached into the case and removed two transmitters, one the size of a safety match and the other the size of a cake of soap. "This little bugger'll transmit more than a mile," he explained. "The big one is much clumsier, but it'll only throw a signal maybe five miles, line of sight—that means no buildings in the way. You see, ma'am, the size-distance trade-off isn't very good, so just about everybody takes the little bugger and puts a dish on it."

Andy's spirits sagged. "I don't have a 'team.' I'm doing it myself."

The young salesman's optimistic response surprised her. "Give me a couple of minutes and let me see what I can come up with." He put the larger transmitter back in the case, picked up the smaller one, and began to whistle tunelessly. Then his face brightened. "Not to be prying, ma'am, but would you be doing your thing around lots of people? That is, you know, in a house or something that'd be near a mailbox?"

"Why?"

The salesman grinned. He hurried to another case and returned with three microcassette recorders—a Sony and two Aiwas—the size of a pack of one-hundred-millimeter cigarettes. "Give me fifteen minutes, and I can wire one of these suckers to remote-receive off this here transmitter. If you're going to be near a mailbox, you just wrap up the recorder and drop it in beforehand. It'll record whatever you say, and you get the whole shebang delivered right to your door a couple of days later!"

Andy thought it through and began to smile.

Eight-twenty. The weekend night man at the magazine office hadn't wanted to let her in. Finally she'd gotten him to track down Andersen, an old acquaintance who was current chief of bureau, at a small dinner party at Goldie Hawn's. As soon as Andersen heard what she needed, he'd cleared Andy to use the bureau's facilities.

Now she was flipping through the reverse telephone directory, which listed subscribers and their numbers by address rather than alphabetically. Lauderdale Avenue, Laughlin Street, and finally Laurel Canyon Boulevard; Andy ran her finger down the column, stopping alongside the street number engraved in her memory. Two phones were listed: Joyner, Matthew and Joyner, Renee.

She picked up the phone and started to dial Elysium.

Wait; the call would be answered by a machine asking for her name and number. The previous morning, at the motel in Carmel, Andy had given the name "Betty Smith"—yet when the man from the sanatorium had called back, he'd addressed her as "Mrs. Robert Smith." Obviously he had checked with the motel's front desk. Would they also check phone numbers? If so, she couldn't afford to give the newsmagazine's.

Andy replaced the handset and picked up the Yellow Pages.

It took three calls to locate a store that both sold what she still needed and would also be open until midnight.

Two more calls, and she located the type of car that would complete her charade.

Time was still critical, but Andy allowed herself a few seconds to savor her accomplishments of the past two hours. The odds no longer mattered, for the last trick was about to be played—and she felt she held the trump.

On leaving the magazine office, she drove out Olympic. The car rental agency had three expensive imports available. Andy dipped into her dwindling supply of cash to pay the deposit and left the lot behind the wheel of an orange Porsche 911SC Targa.

The next stop was Sunset and Fairfax. Twenty minutes later she was tossing two more shopping bags into the Porsche. One held a white polyester nurse's uniform, opaque white panty hose, white, crepe-soled, lace-up shoes, and the least garish wig she could find. The other held a cardboard box, a roll of gift wrap, a bright red bow, sundry stationery supplies, and stamps.

Andy continued along Sunset until she saw a crowded tavern. She grabbed her overnighter, went inside, ordered a drink at the bar, and paid for it. Then, bag still in hand, she ducked into the ladies' room. After bolting the door, she stripped off jeans and sweater and climbed into her navy-blue suit. Finally she washed her face and applied makeup.

The transformation was substantial; the bartender who'd served her gave her an appreciative once-over, obviously not connecting her with the bedraggled customer who'd ordered the untouched drink.

Andy hopped back into the Porsche and made for Ma Maison, one of Los Angeles's toniest restaurants.

It was almost ten-thirty, but the small, pink-walled lobby was thick with waiting diners. She was searching for a pay phone when the maître d' glided up. "May we help you, madame?"

"Yes, I'm with the Coppola party."

The hint of a frown creased the man's tanned face. "One moment, please." He went back to consult the thick ledger, then returned. "I'm sorry, madame, we have no reservations tonight for Mr. Coppola."

"That's odd. I'm sure Francis said Ma Maison at ten. A table for eight—it's supposed to be a surprise party. May I use your phone?"

He pointed Andy to the back.

She found the booth, ducked inside, and placed her call.

"You have reached area code four-oh-eight, six-zero-one, seven thousand," the same prerecorded female voice intoned.

At the *pinnnggg* Andy said, "Hi, Renee Joyner here. I'm in a booth at Ma Maison, in Los Angeles." She read off the number on the dial and hung up.

Ninety seconds passed, and then another ninety. She had been right to be cautious; they must be checking out the number.

Almost four minutes after she'd rung off, the phone finally trilled.

"Mrs. Matthew Joyner?" a man asked.

"That's right. I'm sorry to trouble you so late, but something's just come up."

"Yes, Mrs. Joyner?"

"It's Matty's sister. When we got home, we discovered that she had flown in unannounced from the Far East. The problem is, she has to leave for New York first thing Monday." Andy was about to embroider the story, but some instinct told her to stop.

After a short silence the man said, "And she would like to visit Barry tomorrow?"

"That's right."

"Well, Mrs. Joyner, I must point out that rules are rules. Visits really must be arranged in advance—we must remember the welfare of our guests."

"Believe me, nobody appreciates your concern more than Matty and I. But Barry hasn't seen his aunt in two years."

"Mrs. Joyner, let me see what I can arrange. Please hold."

Seconds stretched like minutes, minutes like hours: Andy's whole quest hinged on this final trick. Could she finesse it?

"Mrs. Joyner, I have good news for you," the man finally said. "Doctor Boll is permitting the visit."

"Thank you ever so much," Andy said with unfeigned joy. "Truly."

"What is the visitor's name, please, and her time of arrival?"

"Lois Dickson. She should be there between two and two-thirty. And, oh, could you please not tell Barry? We'd like it to be a surprise."

"Of course. Will she be driving either of the cars we have on record, Mrs. Joyner?"

"No. Could you hold on a second, please? Oh, Lois"—Andy cupped the mouthpiece, dug out her keys, and read him the Porsche's license number.

As she made her way from the restaurant, the maître d' caught her eye and arched an inquisitive eyebrow.

"My error," Andy said with a grin she hoped looked sheepish. "I feel like such a fool—he didn't say 'Ma Maison,' he said *'chez moi.'* "

Andy was too wound up to sleep just yet, so she aimed the Porsche north. By eleven she had made the freeway. By midnight she had made the outskirts of Ventura. Her reflexes were decaying, and her body was turning into lead, but she gritted her teeth and roared past the exits; the further she could push that night, the less she would have to drive the next morning.

Twenty minutes later, Andy's stinging eyes began to see double.

The next major town was Santa Barbara. She stopped at a 7-11 near the off-ramp and picked up juice and a roll for morning.

The motels were clustered along Cabrillo Boulevard. Most had Vacancy signs blazing. She chose the Travelodge.

Up in her room, Andy discovered that her mental circuits were still overloaded. To unwind, she fetched ice to chill the juice, filled the one-cup coffee maker, and set her travel alarm. Damn it, in her fatigue she was forgetting something: Patty. What time was it in Bermuda? She called the Princess Hotel. It was 5:00 A.M. on the other side of the continent; Andy left a message that she would call again in eight hours.

She undressed and switched off the light.

It took two more hours before she could switch off her mind, too.

The Final Day

Terror being the enemy of sleep, the travel alarm rings unanswered in room 217 of the Santa Barbara Travelodge.

Andy has been standing in the shower so long that her fingertips are puckered and almost translucent. Yet she remains under the pounding water, willing it to at least thaw muscles knotted by too much driving and too little rest.

To no avail.

Similarly, she cannot stop the dream-corroding free associations that even in wakefulness richochet out of sequence and beyond control: the watery-eyed Rolf and his snakelike father; flowers thumping onto Larry's coffin and Philip ensnared by the intensive-care tubes and wires; metallic green surveillance vehicles and the hard-faced man with the mismatched eyes.

But now there are no more pursuers to flee and only one phantom left to stalk—the diabolical cipher that is Realm's creator, Otto von Schwenk. *And the chase must end today!* On that thought, she steps from the tub and wipes condensation off the mirror over the sink.

The image staring back is that of a stranger's, for the desperate flight from one rim of the continent to the other has exacted a heavy toll. Her hair is far too curly, far too short, and far too dark. When and where did she have it chopped, when and where did she have it dyed? She no longer remembers. Her cheeks, normally lean, seem on the verge of collapsing inward, but the flesh below the eyes is dark and puffy. Andy leans forward. Her pupils are dilated, the whites laced with reddened capillaries.

The mirror starts to mist over again, so she cracks open the bathroom door.

Outside, a foghorn bays.

When Andy emerges from the bathroom, she crosses to the shopping bags at the foot of the bed. From the one emblazoned with the name of the Rodeo Drive boutique come the cream-colored culottes and the gun-metal gray cashmere V-neck. She dresses quickly, then puts the nurse's gear and wig into the cardboard box. Next she takes out the microcassette recorder. The salesman had set it up to tape for ninety minutes without having to change sides. She examines the machine. Even swathed in shock-absorbing bubble wrap, it's close enough in size to a pack of cigarettes that she's decided to package it like a free tobacco manufacturer's sample. Andy slides it into a small white cardboard mailer and licks on several dollars' worth of postage. This, too, goes into the large box, which she then wraps with gift paper and decorates with the bright red ribbon bow.

Andy's pathetic breakfast of canned juice, sweet roll, and instant Maxwell House coffee tastes even worse than it looks, but she gags it down; her schedule's far too tight for food stops.

At precisely 9:00 A.M. she picks up the phone and places a long-distance call.

"Bermuda Princess Hotel, good afternoon."

"Room six-thirty-nine, please."

No answer—but there is a message awaiting her at the front desk: due to a previously booked excursion, her parents and Patty will have to call her in New York around six, their time.

Andy wants to cry out in frustration. Why at critical passes do the wheels always seem to fall off right at the start? Stop the self-pity and *think*, she tells herself. Six, Bermuda time, would be two in the afternoon in California, at which hour she should be breaching the radio-controlled gates of Elysium and searching the immaculately groomed compound for one particular inmate. . . .

The desk clerk clears his throat discreetly. "Will there be a message, ma'am?"

"Yes," she says. "Please leave a note that Andy's in Connecticut and can't be reached. I'll call again about six-fifteen, your time."

Even as she replaces the handset, her mind races to rejuggle her timetable.

Come on, come on, the clock's running. A fast check of the room; then, carrying purse, overnighter, and gift-wrapped "present," she heads for the door.

And stops short. For the past seventy-two hours, since Omaha, she's been below their radar. Still, she backs up to the window and inches open the curtain.

Fog shrouds her entire field of vision. The murk is so thick that the Pacific Ocean, just across Cabrillo Boulevard, is invisible and the cars crawling along Cabrillo mere wraiths. She scans the parking lot; none of the vehicles in it is painted that distinctive metallic green.

Yet, the reassurance proves ephemeral. When Andy finally steps out the door, the foghorn's moans sound deeper and more piercing. Tires sizzle spookily on wet macadam. In the distance surf crumps dully onto packed sand. Her adrenaline spurts and raises goose bumps on her arms.

At the motel office, Andy settles her bill and then asks to use the typewriter. She rolls in an unobtrusive plain white mailing label and addresses it to herself, care of her parents' home in Connecticut.

Now she hurries to the rented Porsche. Moisture has beaded into tiny drops on its slick orange skin. She throws her gear in the rear well and starts to swing into the driver's seat. Too claustrophobic; despite the weather, Andy removes the roof panel and stores it in the trunk.

The Porsche kicks to life with a throaty rumble.

Wipers on. Fuel, two-thirds. The time, 9:09—no, 9:10.

The fastest way to the freeway is to the right, but because even paranoids have real enemies, Andy swings the wheel left.

Visibility: under thirty-five yards. The fog plays acoustical tricks, muting the sounds of other cars even as it amplifies the throbs of her own.

One block south, then two. Suddenly in the rearview she sees headlights pulling away from the curb, and then, some fifty yards back, that vehicle begins to edge into her lane. . . .

Andy accelerates slightly.

So does the vehicle behind.

She surveys the oncoming traffic. A Greyhound bus has just about finished passing a long line of cars.

Patience, patience, Andy tells herself as she downshifts into second and tightens her grip on the steering wheel.

The oncoming Greyhound begins to slide past on her left—

And *now:* hard left on the wheel and punch the gas; tires spin vainly on the slickened road, then more gas and finally the Porsche skitters through the gap between the rear of the Greyhound and the looming front of the next car, and then it's surging down the side street.

In the rearview, the black pickup truck that was behind her continues serenely down Cabrillo.

Slowing the Porsche is easy. Slowing her heart isn't.

Nearby, church bells begin to toll. Andy overrides the chimes, and their haunting reminder of Larry's recent funeral, by switching on the radio: "*—rent temperature in Los Angeles, seventy-eight, and we're projecting a high of eighty-eight. Along the coast to the north, a heavy fog, possibly burning off by early afternoon . . .*"

Shit, she thinks, it'll be white-knuckle all the way. She punches to the FM band and fiddles with the dial until she finds a classical station.

Under the overpass, left onto the ramp, and then onto Highway 101 North; Andy snicks the Porsche effortlessly up through the gears and into fifth. At speed, the wind a tangible companion and Bach issuing from the radio, she feels cleansed and free and curiously invulnerable in her hurtling steel cocoon.

Then her eyes drop to the speedometer: eighty-five.

Startled, she backs off. But the dashboard clock already reads 9:18, so when the needle dips below sixty-five, she plays with the accelerator, searching for the groove that will land her at Elysium—where Otto von Schwenk remains ensconced—in four hours and forty minutes.

"Room six-thirty-nine, please."
The phone rings twice. "Hello?"
"Hi, Patty."

"Mom!"

"How was the cruise?"

"Fine," the girl answers without much enthusiasm. "Grandma and Grandpa had a good time. But guess what? We're going to a movie tonight, and tomorrow Grandpa promised I could go wind surfing again. You ought to see me on one of those boards, Mom. I'm a wizard—truly. Can we buy one, huh? I'm sure I can use it on Wall Lake . . ."

As Andy listens to her daughter's comforting chatter, she watches a man enter the gourmet grocery and pick up four picnic hampers. Still time to abort, she thinks. Rather than drive the last four miles up Highway One, she can be back in Los Angeles in time for the red-eye East and be hitting the beach in Bermuda by noon tomorrow.

". . . hold on a sec, okay?" And then another voice comes on the line. "Andy?"

"Hi, Dad."

"I hope you're calling to tell us you're coming out."

"I'd sure like to."

"We tried you yesterday."

"I was, uh, I was up in Connecticut."

Silence in which Andy can almost hear his frown; her father has always been attuned to her lies and evasions. Finally he says, "Listen, honey, your mother and I think you've been pushing yourself too hard."

"You're probably right, but I've just about got everything wrapped up."

"Then fly out tomorrow or Tuesday. Those loose ends won't run away."

"Dad! I—" Andy closes her eyes. Lighten up, she tells herself; this is one phone call that she must not let deteriorate into anger. "I'm sorry. You're right, Dad. It's just that I've got two appointments left, the last on Tuesday afternoon. Maybe after that."

"Sounds good. We all miss you, Andy."

"And I miss all of you. Let me say hello to Mom,

okay? And, Dad—thanks again for everything. You've
been—you've been just great."

After speaking briefly with her mother, Andy asks
for Patty again.

"Hi, sweetie. This is just to say I love you."

"I love you, too."

Last chance, Andy thinks. Her palms feel suddenly
clammy. Finally she clears her throat. "Take care of
yourself, Patty. I'll—I'll see you real soon."

"Promise?"

"Promise," Andy whispers. She hangs up, dries her
eyes, and walks out of the store to the car. As she turns
the ignition key, she checks the dashboard clock: 2:19.

The guard's mirrored sunglasses glow orange as he
leans over to check the Porsche's license plate. He consults his clipboard, sashays back, and sticks his face in
the open top. "Name?"

"Lois Dickson," Andy replies, her neck craned uncomfortably upward.

"This be your first time here, ma'am?"

"That's right."

"Okay. When you come off the driveway, you'll
want to hang a left and park it in the lot directly in front
of you. Then you'll want to sign in at the main building."

"Got it." She slides the stick into first—and shivers
involuntarily as the snout of the Porsche pushes
through the gate and into Elysium.

The grounds teem with patients and visitors. That
cheers her; the more bodies, the less hers will be noticed, right?

In the parking lot Andy shuts off the engine. Why
doesn't she want to get out? Finally she steps out onto
the blacktop. Why are her legs so unsteady and her lips
so dry?

Fifteen yards from the main building, she stops and
retreats; in her anxiety, she's left the all-important
"present" in the car.

The cavernous lobby of the main building feels like

a tycoon's hunting lodge. From the high, vaulted ceiling hangs an ornate chandelier. The right-hand wall is dominated by an oversize fireplace, above which are mounted the heads of bagged trophies: grizzly, mountain ram, puma, elk. The left-hand wall is taken up by paintings, mostly tacky Alpinescapes. The massive furniture is of hardwood and leather. Does Doctor Boll gather the staff here after hours to quaff steins of beer and sing the *Horst Wessel* song?

Across the lobby, at the desk, two blond surfer types are logging in some half-dozen visitors. Andy's lips compress in disappointment: to the left of the desk stands a mailbox. Back at the motel, she had without thinking thrown the microcassette recorder into the gift-wrapped box. That means changing into the nurse's uniform and then coming back to the lobby, thereby increasing the chances of exposure.

She starts across the room. Halfway there, she notes two corridors extending from the lobby. To her left are offices. To her right seems to be the nurses' station, for a forbidding, white-uniformed woman has emerged from a blind alcove and, sheaf of papers in hand, hurries toward the lobby.

Andy moves to intercept.

Suddenly her blood runs cold—the uniform she bought in Los Angeles doesn't look at all like the one the approaching nurse wears! Andy recovers just in time to ask for the ladies' room.

Without breaking stride, the nurse gestures down the right-hand corridor.

Andy turns and walks, nonchalantly she hopes, toward the door marked Women.

The room is empty. It also lacks a lock; but of course there wouldn't be one, not in an institution like this. She ducks into a stall and begins ripping at the gift-wrap covering the "present." Her sweater and culottes are off when she makes a vow informed by gallows humor: if I get out of this one, I'll never make another quick-change in a public facility, ever. Now into the dress, then pull on the opaque white panty hose, step into the shoes and lace them—come on, come on.

Andy carefully removes the matchstick transmitter. With the pin that the young salesman at the electronics boutique had soldered on, she attaches it inside the collar of the nurse's uniform so the tiny microphone head just protrudes from the top buttonhole. Next Andy opens the mailer containing the microcasette recorder. She pushes aside the wrapping and depresses the Record button; for the next ninety minutes, everything she hears or says will be preserved on tape. She seals the package, then fishes from a culotte pocket the mailing label typed back at the motel, and presses it into place.

Andy slips the all-important package into the right hip pocket of the uniform. Finally, she pulls on the wig, adjusting it as best she can.

At the sound of footsteps in the corridor, she freezes. Only when they click past does her breathing return almost to normal.

Andy steps cautiously from the stall. The trash receptacle is recessed into the wall to the right of the sinks. Ten seconds later, box and gift wrap are squashed down into it. She scans the room for a place to hide her new cashmere sweater and culottes. There is none so, with an irrationally heavy sense of regret, she stuffs them into the trash receptacle, too.

Forty-five seconds at the mirror, and the wig fits as well as it ever will.

Now, ear to door; nothing.

Andy swings it open. Relax, act natural, don't hurry. . . .

She looks up the corridor toward the lobby and begins cursing to herself. The formidable nurse who had directed her to the ladies' room seems rooted in the middle of the room, deep in conference with several men wearing white doctors' smocks. Andy considers her options—risk recognition if she goes back to mail her package or hope there's another mailbox in the other direction—and turns left, away from the lobby.

Two nurses approach. Surely they'll laugh at my wig, she thinks, surely they'll spot the glaringly bogus uniform . . .

They don't.

Fifteen yards down the corridor, behind a chest-high counter, lies the alcove from which the formidable nurse had emerged. The desk in it is unoccupied. Next to an ashtray in which a cigarette still burns stands a metal carousel—the patient charts?

Beyond the alcove and overlooking it is a glass-windowed office. A middle-aged woman in civilian clothes sits inside, speaking on the telephone. The glance she gives Andy proves cursory.

Move, damn it, move before whoever left the cigarette burning returns.

Another heartbeat of hesitation and then, summoning courage from some unsuspected reservoir, Andy rounds the counter and begins flipping the arms of the carousel.

There it is: von Schwenk, Otto. Bungalow Two.

Andy looks about for a mailbox or, failing that, an "Out" box. Shit—nothing. And the formidable nurse remains in conference in the lobby.

Andy grits her teeth and leaves the alcove.

The harsh mid-afternoon sun sears eyes grown accustomed to the gloom of the main building. There are people all about, yet Andy is no longer self-conscious about her clumsy disguise; it's as if, having penetrated so near, a magnet is impelling her down the path to the fork and from the fork left toward the promontory and the bungalows along it.

Out here, the winds seem to be freshening. For an instant Andy fears her wig might blow away, but she fights back the temptation to clamp a hand on it. Forty feet below, the waves crash with enough force to drown out the drone of traffic from Highway One, drown out the conversations on the lawn behind her. The prime-val beauty arouses all Andy's senses to the fullest; what a pity, she thinks, that she can't linger to enjoy it.

Bungalow Two sits at the very tip of the promontory, its door shut.

Andy knocks.

She counts to ten, raps again, and then turns the knob.

Inside, music plays at considerable volume. Perhaps her knocks went unheard? Andy steps into the vestibule and from rust-heavy vocal cords manages to produce a loud and cheery "Hello!"

No answer.

Damn, the music's familiar.

Pulse racing, Andy steps from the vestibule. The bungalow proves bigger than it looked from the outside. To her immediate left, a dining alcove that can seat eight; to her right, one open door leads to a bathroom, the second to a spacious bedroom; and straight ahead, behind a large chrome-and-glass étagère that serves as a room divider, lies the sun-dappled living room.

"Hello," Andy calls out again. "I've brought you a snack!"

The only response is another thunderous blast of orchestral music. Then she recognizes the composer, and her spine ices: Wagner—Otto von Schwenk is listening to the musical laureate of the Third Reich, Richard Wagner.

Five cautious steps forward, and she can see that both bathroom and bedroom are empty.

Andy continues to the étagère.

Through it she sees a huge picture window that looks west over the Pacific. In front of the window, less than twenty feet from her, a high-backed wheelchair faces the ocean. The wheelchair is jiggling; could von Schwenk be keeping time with the steadily loudening music?

Suddenly the room plunges into total silence.

Andy stops in mid-step, trying to still her pounding temples and rasping breath. The record; it's only the phonograph needle hitting the blank grooves between cuts. She wipes her mouth with the back of a hand and continues forward.

Now the opening strains of Wagner's most familiar passage, "The Ride of the Valkyries."

"Mr. von Schwenk?" she calls out over the rising woodwinds.

Again, no response.

Andy has edged halfway to the wheelchair when something in the picture window catches her eye. Not the ceaselessly moving blue-green Pacific but, rather, a black speck on the horizon that's paradoxically both stationary and growing in size.

She blinks away the apparition. As she resumes her stalk, the swirling, skirling music continues to build; the daughters of Wotan are gathering for their ascent to Valhalla.

Now the wheelchair is just six feet away.

Something draws Andy's attention back to the picture window. The speck is no longer on the horizon and no longer small. It's achieved the size of a Tinkertoy. A helicopter. A helicopter hurtling in at wave-top height. She frowns. Why does it look so disconcertingly familiar?

Andy tears her eyes from the picture window and refocuses on the problem almost at hand. A penultimate step, and she's so close she can clearly hear Otto von Schwenk's labored wheezes over the crescendoing Wagner.

Green . . .

The goddamned helicopter's painted green, that distinctive metallic dark green, and the pilot's blown it because he can't possibly climb fast enough to clear the promontory. Christ the thing's coming right through the fucking window.

Shaking with fear and dread, knowing that somehow her mission has been irretrievably blown, Andy lunges the last step and confronts the figure in the wheelchair.

And finds her panicky stare returned by the laughing eyes—one brown, the other black—of Otto von Schwenk.

The gasp that explodes from her lips goes unheard because now the fat ladies are shrieking, the entire bungalow reverberating from the shrill "Hojotoho! Hojotoho!" of Wotan's furies and the marrow-curdling throbs of the helicopter as it slams past a mere few feet overhead; in this bedlam Andy recoils backward, her mind trying to grasp the fact that in the wheelchair sits the thug with the mismatched eyes who had hounded her across Ann Arbor and New York, his hard face unsoftened by the pale smile on it, and his hard body sheathed in a suit cut from metallic dark green cloth.

Andy retreats another step—right into a steely embrace.

Her head whips around. The hands clutching her biceps belong to the other thug; he, too, wears a metallic dark green suit.

The man with the mismatched eyes begins to rise from the wheelchair.

"I—I—mistake . . ." Andy's protests are lost in another chorus of "Hojotoho! Hojotoho!"

The two thugs start to drag her toward the front door.

And then Andy's brain unthaws; they can't take me away in broad daylight, she thinks, not in front of all those witnesses outside.

The thugs quick-march her through the door.

Twenty yards away, the metallic green helicopter squats on the lawn. Its rotors are still churning, shattering the stillness, bending the grass. They are also, she realizes suddenly, driving visitors, patients, and staff back in a rough semicircle—and thereby isolating her from potential rescuers.

Andy starts to struggle.

Pressure applied cruelly to her biceps brings an end to the struggles, as well as tears to her eyes.

"Help! Help!" But Andy's cries evaporate like sighs in a hurricane, so she digs her heels into the turf.

The thugs snap her forward with ankle-numbing force and continue inexorably toward the waiting craft. Now the rotor wash plucks at her wig. Andy feels it lifting, and then the pins that hold it pulling out, and then her head seems suddenly vulnerable. Reflexively, she turns: the Dyncl mop is cartwheeling back toward Bungalow Two.

The door of the helicopter flies open. Andy is shoved up and in, and then the two thugs are scrambling aboard after her.

She feels the greenhouselike heat in the cockpit, smells the stench of gas and hot machine oil. Through the Persplex canopy, the people on the lawn appear unmoved by what they are seeing; could the dragging off of a deranged nurse be an everyday occurrence? Now rough hands cinch a harness-style belt tightly around her. The pilot snuggles back in his seat and inches open the throttle. As the whine of the overhead engine drops two octaves, the craft surges clear.

Fifty feet above the lawn it hesitates before circling over this cuckoo's nest and tilting oceanward.

At that instant Andy's vision is cut off by the blindfold being wrapped over her eyes.

Eyes open or closed, it's the same: nothing. Better closed, more like sleep—but who can sleep in din like this? Do helicopter pilots go deaf, like rock musicians? Let's see, I'd counted up to sixty how many times, eight? Add another thirty seconds for this digression, so pick it up at thirty-two, thirty-three, thirty-four. . . . Good thing I didn't eat or drink much today, or I might have embarrassed myself in front of all those people back on the lawn; about the only thing I got right all day. . . . Pick it up at forty-two, forty-three. . . . Why has it gotten so cold in the cabin? Are we flying that high?

Maybe we're headed away from the sun, which would make it east. . . . Let's call it nine minutes airborne, okay? Wonder how fast this thing goes . . .

But now the willpower to continue her mental gymnastics begins to wilt, and Andy's mind returns to picking on its too-fresh scab.

The cleverness with which she'd tracked down "Otto von Schwenk" was nothing compared to the cleverness with which she'd deluded herself. No wonder the two thugs had disappeared from her trail; they'd merely leapfrogged ahead to Elysium and waited as patiently as a spider in a swamp in August. The wave of nausea that sweeps over her has nothing to do with the turbulence of the helicopter ride. Come on, come on, she pleads with herself, you're still breathing, so fight against the terror and the paralysis. There, that's better. Why don't we pick it up from nine minutes and fifteen seconds, sixteen, seventeen . . .

She feels the helicopter both slowing and descending. Elapsed time: more than thirty-five but fewer than forty-five minutes. A hand yanks her blindfold yet tighter. Andy's puzzled until she realizes that it's being unknotted. Now fabric slides across her cheeks. Her eyes pop open, but the sunlight blasting through the Persplex canopy renders her dilated pupils momentarily sightless.

When her vision returns, she finds herself staring down at another brilliant greensward whose curving western boundary is the Pacific. As Elysium was unmistakably Northern Californian coastal—a precious foothold carved from unforgiving rocks—so the compound beneath her is expansively Southern Californian. Andy surveys its eastern edge and sees not craggy palisades but rolling scrubland, the dun coloration broken only by clumps of high chapparal. On the vast estate itself, low-slung buildings of glass and concrete are fanned in a semicircle near the ocean. From these, palm-lined walkways run fifty yards inland to a sprawling one-story structure. This main building, which has three wings, is windowless. Adjacent lies a concrete landing pad. The helicopter dips toward it.

On touchdown, the two thugs hop off. One turns to offer Andy a hand. She ignores him.

During the short walk to the main building, she scans its facade for a sign, for a symbol, for anything that will tell her where she is. Nothing.

Andy and the two thugs bracketing her have almost reached the entrance when the glass doors slide open.

Suddenly she feels transported back two decades, to her own undergraduate days. For the quintet of young men and women stepping out is if nothing collegiate: clean-cut, dressed casually in polo shirts and jeans or shorts, sockless on this warm spring day, and all toting ring-binder notebooks.

Surely they'll help her. . . .

Just as quickly, hope vanishes. Their notebook jackets are of that metallic dark green, as are the small rectangular pins that each wears over the left breast. One of the young men glances at Andy, taking in her disheveled hair and her rumpled nurse's uniform; his eyes are unquestioning, as if she were part of some Medivac team.

Andy is ushered past the group into the "lobby," a chocolate-walled space measuring but eight feet wide by six feet deep. Opposite stands a metal door. Embedded in the wall to the right of it are a television camera, a video screen complete with built-in keyboard, and a metal half-cylinder. Jesus, she thinks, this is like one of those twenty-four-hour, automatic-teller banks.

The thug with the mismatched eyes continues to the keyboard. He pulls a slip of paper from his pocket, consults it, and punches in an entry. Then he turns and gestures for Andy to step before the television camera.

She obeys.

The half-cylinder opens. The thug reaches in for a

piece of celluloid the size of a credit card and hands it to Andy.

It reads ENTRYWAY: B. ROOM: 5.

The metal door to her left hums open, and the thug jerks his head toward it.

Andy steps through, and the door hums shut.

She is alone in a bright blue room only slightly larger than the "lobby." Near the ceiling, another television camera. Ahead are four more metal doors, each flanked by a slot to receive celluloid cards like the one she holds.

Andy ignores the overhead camera and tries the card in three doors.

Nothing.

She sticks it into the last slot; door B slides open.

Andy steps into a stainless-steel cubicle. Now why the hell would a one-story building have an elevator? Instead of a panel of buttons, another slot; she inserts the card, and the door closes. Her stomach floats upward as the car begins to descend.

The corridor Andy steps out into is painted and carpeted in white. There are eight doors. Three minutes later, she has tried the card without result on seven of them. She sighs and sticks the celluloid into the remaining slot; this time, it works.

As the door opens, a low, dark shape lunges at her.

Startled, Andy jumps back into the corridor. She blinks, and then her heartbeat starts to fade back to merely normal. The shape isn't an attack dog but rather a wheeled machine about three feet high, two feet wide and four feet long with a single glowing eye—a robot mailcart, the kind that follows an imbedded electronic track. It has rolled forward into the doorway, where it sits, its eye winking on and off.

Andy waits for it to move aside.

It doesn't.

Then she realizes that the machine's "eye" is a photoelectric cell, and that as long as it senses her standing in its path, it will remain motionless. A hell of a high-tech standoff, she thinks wryly, slipping the celluloid card into the right hip pocket of her uniform.

Her hand encounters something hard—the microcassette recorder she had failed to mail at Elysium . . .

Andy moves aside.

The machine lurches forward.

Dare she? But what other choice is there? As the robot mailcart purrs past, she takes out the package in her pocket and slips it into one of the compartments on the side marked Outgoing.

The machine turns left and continues down the corridor. Andy, meanwhile, turns her attention to the room, an expanse as spacious—and as deserted—as a corporate conference room on Sunday.

She edges inside the door. It shuts behind her with a pneumatic *thunk*, but she ignores the menacing sound, for her attention is already transfixed by the large drapes that stretch across the far wall. On it is a design of four letters boxed in a rectangle; the logo has been woven into the cream-colored fabric with thread of that distinctive metallic dark green.

Suddenly time goes out of joint. Vast chunks of memory boil up from the deep subconscious. . . . With her mind spinning like a dog after its own tail, Andy sees but does not quite register the rest of the room:

To her left, an ultramodern seating cluster; directly ahead, a polished rosewood desk flanked by a computer terminal; in front of the desk, two modernistic chairs; and behind the desk, a high-backed executive chair that's swiveled carelessly in the opposite direction.

Slowly, Andy's dizziness subsides.

Why is she alone in this room?

And then her eye catches on the rosewood desk and the telephone on it. Of course the line will be monitored, and of course her call will be cut off, but anything's better than just waiting passively for the tumbrels to roll.

Andy hurries toward the desk.

Five feet from it, she lets out an involuntary cry as the high-backed executive chair snaps sharply about.

A self-satisfied smile creasing his face, Merle Vaughan says, "Hello, Mrs. Matteson."

And then Andy knows for certain that she's been catapulted into a universe where one plus one equals five.

Vaughan gestures toward one of the steel-and-leather chairs in front of the desk.

Andy wavers and then sits.

"You have come in search of answers, dear lady, and answers are due you," Vaughan says. "But first, may I offer you a refreshment?"

Andy shakes her head. The numbness will not go away. Then, despite herself, her eyes swing from Vaughan to the metallic dark green SOTA logo on the drapes behind him.

He follows her gaze. "Do you approve of the color?" he asks. "Would you care to know its origin? It is the hue one obtains if, during the process by which titanium is alloyed, one adds a generous dash of green. Not any green, mind you, but the precise green that the United States Treasury uses to print its currency. In that it is our mission to marry technology and commerce, we at SOTA think the color terribly apt.

"By the way, my dear, did Philip ever explain our acronym? No? The letters stand for 'State-of-the-Art.' A trifle cute, to be sure, and yet . . ."

As Andy listens to the patronizing prattle, she realizes that the more this psychopath reveals, the less likely that she'll ever escape her high-tech dungeon alive. Not that Vaughan looks capable of using force to detain her.

She stands abruptly. "I wish to leave."

Vaughan leans back in his chair. "I'm afraid your chances are not good."

"How're you going to stop me?"

"By lifting neither hand nor the phone, Mrs. Matteson. There are only three ways off the grounds. Via the front gate—but you lack an exit pass, a fact the guards would not look upon kindly. Or you could overpower the pilot of the helicopter that brought you here and fly the beastly craft away yourself. Or you could swim. It's only six miles to the nearest public beach.''

Looking at Vaughan's complacent smile, Andy suddenly understands the term "the banality of evil" and sits again.

"As I was saying," Vaughan continues affably, "during the seventies, Wall Street was much enamored with the so-called 'genetic research boutiques.' They couldn't print our stock certificates fast enough. Basically, each of the Big Four—Cetus, Genetech, Biogen, and SOTA—has devoted most of its efforts to traditional, cutting-edge research. You know, recombinant DNA, synthetic enzymes and hormones, anticarcinogenic viruses."

Vaughan leans forward and steeples his fingertips. "Unlike the others, though, we at SOTA feel a publicly held corporation ought consider not only short-range goals but also its long-range obligations.

"The two are not always synonymous. Short-range, genetic research has been succeeding exponentially—breakthrough piled on breakthrough. Sooner rather than later, though, we shall have achieved most of the major breakthroughs. These shall be patented, perfected, and licensed. What then? Do we merely sit back and grow fat on royalties?

"We found that scenario unacceptable. Therefore, SOTA established a secret department, of which I am the director. My charter: wield an interdisciplinary scalpel to probe other, nongenetic frontiers of the biosciences. To date, the most visible fruit of my little team's labors has been the creation of the game called Realm.''

Andy regains her tongue and blurts, "You call that perversion 'scientific research'?''

Vaughan chuckles indulgently. "I believe you are familiar with the rules of Realm? Yes, well, can you not appreciate how it is a perfectly conceived experiment in behavioral modification? How it brings into play such theories of social engineering as reward-and-punishment, submission to authority, peer pressure?"

"You dirty shit," she says softly.

"Now now, Mrs. Matteson. Please. My little group merely examines whether behavior can be modified through the application of certain keys. No harm comes to Realm's participants."

"What do you mean 'no harm'? You're screwing around with half-formed minds!"

Vaughan shakes his head benignly. "We take the most stringent precautions against just such possibilities. I assure you, dear lady, that our aims are purely scientific, our search only for knowledge and methodology."

"What if there are no 'keys'?" Andy challenges. "What if the only way to modify behavior is brainwashing?"

Vaughan shrugs. "We terminate Realm and refocus on other promising areas of research."

"Just like that?"

"Just like that. Our financial exposure to date is no more than nine-point-six million. You must understand that SOTA could well use an R-and-D write-off of that magnitude."

"Who writes off all the kids you leave bent?"

"Has your daughter Patricia been 'bent' by Realm?" Before Andy can open her mouth, Vaughan adds, almost to himself, "We scientists really must find a way to end this traditional hostility toward innovative research."

Andy laughs derisively. "I didn't know scientists spent so much time worrying about their shareholders."

Vaughan sighs. "Ours don't. As team leader, that role is mine. In fact, my main responsibility has become to anticipate the commercial applications of SOTA's non-genetic research. If the Realm project proves successful, for instance, Madison Avenue should be most interested, wouldn't you think?"

Suddenly, random factoids that had been shunting blindly through Andy's mind veer toward each other; and the heat of their fusion burns away the final curtain of uncertainty. The naked truth is horrifying in its evil. "No," she says. "No, selling a way to modify behavior to advertisers would be like kissing your sister. The clientele you're after is much, much bigger. Moscow? Or is the KGB already running a parallel project? Then how about one of our neighbors to the south, some banana republic with a restless populace?"

Vaughan studies his manicured nails in silence.

"Come to think of it," Andy continues, "how many of SOTA's stocks are registered in Latin America? And bought with Third Reich booty that's been laundered into pesos, cruzeiros and what-have-you's?"

Vaughan looks up with genuine amusement. "Were we that successful in creating the illusion of *Der Realm*? My dear Mrs. Matteson, we are most definitely *not* propagating the boys and girls from Brazil!"

"But Otto von Schwenk?" she protests. "That lawyer Stroessels? Rolf Schmidt and all those other Aryan kids I saw up at Hewes?"

"Red herrings—or, to be more precise, brownshirted herrings," Vaughan replies with a grin. "Yes, we set up The Hewes Service as a way of controlling the experiment. But there's nothing mysterious about the fact that our children tend to have blond hair and blue eyes. Simply put, those attributes are in greatest demand."

"Then where do *you* get them?"

"What would you have me tell you, that they come from some breeding farm? No, we scout foster homes much as professional ball teams scout colleges. We look for two criteria: a youngster with the requisite traits and an uncaring family. When we find such a situation, the family is offered a generous stipend."

"Buying children is illegal, mister," Andy retorts.

"Our transactions are not. Were I a lawyer, dear lady, I should be able to explain exactly why. In any event, our children are detraumatized through psychiatric counseling before placement by The Hewes Service. So you see, there is nothing sinister about their comely appearances."

"Oh? Then why is Realm limited to only beautiful children?"

"Beautiful—and extraordinarily intelligent," Vaughan says professorially. "For a very good reason. By early adolescence, certain key personality traits are already well-formed. We at SOTA lack the resources to test our theories at every socioeconomic stratum. Consequently, we concentrate on the best and the brightest. The children allowed to participate in Realm are, in the main, destined for fruitful, productive lives. For instance, have you any doubt that your own Patricia won't leave her mark on society?"

"Jewish kids leave their marks on society, too," Andy says sharply.

"Dear lady, your fixation on the master race is becoming boring. Many Jews play Realm. That Ann Arbor had none is an idiosyncrasy, the reason for which shall soon become apparent."

Vaughan glances at his watch and frowns; when he resumes, his speech takes on a subtle urgency. "I'm sure you will accept that genetic engineers are not above industrial espionage. Because SOTA's stake in my little team's experiment is considerable, we periodically test its security. How? By creating circumstances that will prompt a concerned individual to investigate the game."

"A parent!" Andy gasps.

"Exactly. A parent motivated by fear for her child. But not just any parent—our ideal candidate must also be intelligent and resourceful.

"Of course, the way we induce curiosity varies from locale to locale. Ann Arbor happens to be a liberal town. Our analysts calculated—correctly, it turns out—that any extracurricular activity excluding Jews would come under attention. Therefore, when your town was targeted for a security evaluation last summer, Jewish children were banned from the next round of gaming."

"But it wasn't my town then," Andy counters. "I wasn't even in Ann Arbor last summer."

"Nor were you our first choice, dear lady. When that person proved inadequate to the challenge, our analysts came across your profile. We ran a check—"

"You came to the sherry party to size me up," Andy interrupts, more of her mental fog clearing. Now she remembers what was nagging at her that afternoon at Philip's apartment and then again in New York when she received the "Philip-is-dead" telegram from Vaughan. "You already knew who I was, and that's why you've always addressed me as '*Mrs.* Matteson.'"

Vaughan bows his head in acknowledgment. "Needless to say, you more than passed muster, and hence your inclusion into Realm Eight."

"Eight? But there are only seven Levels."

"Quite so, quite so—in the children's version." Vaughan's smile is like dry ice. "Level Eight is an experience reserved for adults."

The fragile bridge that Andy's been building toward reality snaps. Even as she hears herself screaming, *"This is not a game, you crazy bastard,"* she knows that it is. And that the ante is life itself—hers.

By way of response, Vaughan presses a button recessed in his rosewood desk.

Behind him the heavy drapes bearing the SOTA logo part to reveal an oversize video screen.

Vaughan swivels to the computer terminal next to his desk. He taps on its keyboard, and words materialize in the center of the giant screen:

```
REALMLOG/Level Eight
SUBJECT: Andrea L. Matteson (USA)
MAXIMUM MOVES PERMITTED: 12
```

Vaughan touches another key; more lines begin to scroll up, like the credits at the end of a movie:

MOVE	ACTION	REACTION	ALM	RS	RESOLUTION
1	Assess subject ALM	None	22	40	Cont M-2
2	Introduce porno prior drug lecture	ALM to police	09	41	Cont M-3

Vaughan lifts his finger from the Scroll key. "The column headed RS represents Realm Security," he says helpfully. "The numbers in that column, as well as yours, are the equivalents of die tosses—using, of course, Realm's forty-nine-sided die. In your absence, the computer randomly generated both your throws and Realm Security's. The interplay of these two values determines the next move."

He presses the key again, and the remainder of the Realmlog scrolls up:

3	Reveal Realm booklet	ALP to P. Hunt (Player #5)	13	18	Cont M-4
4	Pressure: wiretap & Breathalyzer	(DEM)	39	33	Cont M-5
5	Accident: Player 5	ALM to L. Matteson (Player #8)	48	16	Cont M-6
6	Pressure: overt surveillance	(DEM)	19	21	Cont M-7
7	Accident: Player 8	ALM to police	42	36	Cont M-8
8	Pressure: overt surveillance	ALM escapes surveillance	25	09	Cont M-9

9	Allow Hewes penetration & pressure: Express Mail packet	ALM disappears	32	49 Cont M-10
10	Allow Elysium penetration	ALM detained	02	11 Cont M-11
11	Reveal SOTA secrets	**END GAME**	??	?? ?????????

After giving Andy several seconds to absorb the Realmlog, Vaughan says, "I believe that the Actions and Reactions are self-explanatory except for the notation DEM, which stands for 'deus ex machina.' This is an occurrence that effects not only you but also bystanders. You see, once you involve bystanders—as you did twice—they, too, become participants.

"When Player Five, dear Philip, entered the game, he had the good fortune to link Realm to Otto von Schwenk Similarly Player Eight, Mr. Matteson, linked Realm to the Hewes Service. Alas, both expended too many Arsenal Points on their quests and thus left themselves, uh, fatally vulnerable."

"Murderer," Andy whispers savagely.

"Hardly, my dear. It was not *I* who brought them harm." Now Vaughan's smile returns, and his voice grows unctuous. "May I observe that you have provided Realm Security a challenge that has had no equal? It goes without saying that the die rolled very much in your favor. Still, it is your ingenuity—and, yes, your sheer pluck—that has made you the only participant to gain entry into this chamber. In fact, Mrs. Matteson, you are the only Realm Eight participant to even survive Move Seven!"

As the deadly implications of Vaughan's congratulatory remarks sink in, Andy feels the air growing so viscous that all motion is slowed.

Thus, Vaughan's hand appears to be laboring through water as it dips into a drawer of his rosewood desk. And when it emerges to release a forty-nine-sided die, the prickly chunk of ivory consumes one eternity dropping onto the polished tabletop and a second, third, and fourth bouncing to rest. His words, too, seem to rise from some fathomless sea: "And . . . now . . . my dear . . . it's . . . end . . . game . . ."

Andy blinks.

"Come come, Mrs. Matteson. The final Action has been taken by way of my revealing to you the scope of Project Realm. All that remain are the last two tosses of the die."

Andy continues to stare at the ivory pellet.

"I assure you that your chances of achieving your liberty are statistically fifty-fifty," Vaughan says coaxingly.

Andy remains motionless.

"Perhaps you prefer that Realm Security roll first?" Obtaining no response, Vaughan sighs and taps the keyboard. The last line of the overhead screen changes:

```
11   Reveal SOTA   **END GAME**  ??   46 ?????????
     secrets
```

Vaughan swivels back to face Andy and nudges the glistening bone-white die nearer to her.

"No," she says.

"I beg your pardon?"

Andy blinks again. "Do what you have to do, but I'm not giving you the satisfaction of playing. It's meaningless—you can't afford to let me leave."

Vaughan looks hurt. "You doubt our word?"

"What do you think, mister?"

"You labor under a misapprehension, dear lady—namely, that should you regain your liberty, you would represent a loose cannon that could somehow harm SOTA. I beg to differ. If you would be so kind as to examine these."

Despite herself, Andy picks up the folder that Vaughan has slid across the table.

Inside, on forms imprinted Elysium, are sheafs of doctors' reports and nursing charts on a patient named Andrea Lyall Matteson. There are also photographs: of Andy reading in her room, swimming in the Olympic-sized pool, picnicking on the great lawn.

"It would seem that the successive deaths of two loved ones placed you under severe stress," Vaughan says sympathetically. "Fortunately, you recognized this. You sent your daughter, Patricia, to Bermuda with your parents while you yourself flew West to check into Elysium for observation and some much-deserved rest."

Andy picks up one of the doctors' reports. The names of the various medications prescribed for her contain six syllables each. She studies several of the photographs. The retouching is flawless.

"We have no doubt but that we can discredit any story you choose to convey to the outside world," Vaughan says. "Bearing that in mind, Mrs. Matteson, do you not feel it fitting to determine your own fate at end game, rather than allow the computer that honor?"

The photographs slip from Andy's hand onto the floor. Surely it's all a nightmare. But can a nightmare last two weeks? Surely the drained husk sitting in this chair can't be *her* body. Surely the mushy gray matter attempting to process this surreal data can't be *her* brain. God, a cigarette would be nice. And maybe—mercifully—it would cause instant lung cancer . . . Gallows humor gives way to the despair that's crushing her like a boa constrictor. She reaches for the die.

"That's the spirit!" Vaughan says excitedly.

A flick of the wrist and the prickly ivory pellet clatters across the polished rosewood. It strikes the telephone, rebounds, and spins to a stop.

Vaughan cranes forward, his glowing eyes in search of the glowing facet.

His eyebrows arch—in triumph or disappointment?

Wordlessly he turns back to the computer terminal.

Suddenly the pregnant silence is rent by the sibilant hiss of the door. Even before Andy can react, Vaughan is turning toward the sound; now his eyeballs are bulging with fright, and he begins to stand. "No, no, *no . . .*"

Then Andy, too, rises and turns. Why can't she focus her vision?

Vision focused. In the doorway looms a tall, lean man. His clothes are shiny, as if wet, and he looks awfully familiar. . . .

"No, my boy," Vaughan begs, "I implore you, in the name of God, *No!*"

It is Philip.

Philip Hunt. Philip didn't die after all! And somehow Philip's outsmarted Merle Vaughan, somehow Philip got into the SOTA stronghold—obviously Philip swam in, which explains the wet clothes, and all to rescue me. . . .

Andy, tears of joy staining her cheeks, lurches from her chair toward him.

But Philip doesn't seem to notice her; instead, he slowly hoists the skin-diver's spear gun in his hand and sights down its slender steel shaft.

Behind her, Vaughan's feverish pleas have degenerated into gibberish.

Andy stops in mid-stride, her eyes riveted on Philip's trigger finger. It is easing backward.

The front end of the spear gun blurs, producing a note like the casual pick of a guitar chord, and as the sound fills the room, something flits past her head, coming so near that she feels the *thrruuummmm* of its passage.

A liquid gasp in back of her . . .

Andy wheels.

Blood spews from Vaughan's mouth, but he makes no effort to staunch the flow because both his hands are working at the arrow piercing his throat. Pink bubbles foam at the corners of his mouth, which flaps soundlessly. And then he crumples onto the rosewood table, and his weight tugs him over the edge. As he slides floorward, he sweeps in his wake papers and folders and telephone and pens.

The limp *thud* seems to shake the very room.

Andy sways. She grips the edge of the table, hard. When her eyes unglaze, all she can see of Vaughan is his legs. They are enough; shivering, she turns from the man she knows to be dead toward the man she knew to be dead.

Philip approaches briskly.

For the third time in fifteen seconds, Andy's heart stops. Why is Philip's face contorted in savage exultation? And his clothes—it's not a wet suit, it's a perfectly dry jogging outfit. Why is Philip wearing a jogging outfit cut from metallic dark green cloth?

He strides past without acknowledging her presence. Then, as he kneels over Vaughan, the corners of his mouth curve upward in a tight smile.

"Did you? . . . Is he? . . . Why?" Andy tries to override her almost terminal confusion, but without much success. "What—"

"The bastard tried to subvert our project," Philip replies, still staring at the corpse.

"*Our* project?"

Philip begins to scan the floor around the body.

"*Our* project? You were in on it from the beginning? Oh, my god. You singled me out last December? And became my friend, and my— Jesus." Yet again the galaxy cartwheels, but this time the stars refuse to resettle. In Andy's brain memories stack up—memories of dates and hospital vigils, of panic and passion, of laughter and pain—one on the next in a collage that defies comprehension.

Finally one image bursts to the fore, an image of a moment not shared with Philip, and that image recy-

cles through her mind's eye: once more the can of
Campbell's soup drops onto the balsa platform; once
more the X members compress; only this time the
weight proves too great because the thin slivers of wood
are snapping right and left, the can tumbling . . .

Slowly the image fades. Slowly the bitter roar re-
cedes from Andy's skull. Only then does she begin to
grasp the depth and finality of her betrayal.

Philip stands. "What number did you roll?"

"What?"

"The die. Vaughan didn't have time to enter your
roll."

"Philip!"

He opens his hand. In it is the die Vaughan had
swept to the floor. He places the ivory pellet gently on
the rosewood table. "The game isn't over, Andy."

"Are you out of your mind? There's a man lying
de—"

"Vaughan brought it on himself," Philip interrupts.
"He went bananas when he saw how far you were penetrating. Realm Security was his baby, so he tried to
fudge the data. Do you realize what that means to a sci-
entist, fudging data? This project has cost far too much
to just let it go down the tubes."

"Tell me about the cost, you bastard," Andy says,
anger starting to melt shock. "Tell me about Larry."

Philip shrugs. "I could blame it on Vaughan—he
was the one who contaminated the program—but that
would be wrong. No, what happened to Larry happened because—because his number came up wrong
in the computer."

"Bullshit. Computers don't hire hit men."

Philip returns her accusatory stare for a few heart-
beats before saying, "It's end game. Please roll."

"Fuck you. You've used me enough."

"You've gone through too much to let the computer determine the outcome."

"Why can't I let it? Because that would only be
murder, and you want to witness a suicide?"

"Andy, believe me. Your fate's not predetermined."

She laughs scornfully and gestures to the weapon he still holds. "How will it be this time, Philip? With that? Another car crash? A bottle of sleeping pills forced down my throat? Or don't you remember that five minutes ago I saw you commit murder?"

"Nothing of the sort," he replies blandly. "As far as the world knows, you're still in the booby hatch you checked into seven days ago."

Reflexively, Andy glances down at the Elysium forgeries. They lie soaking in a pool of Vaughan's blood.

As if reading her mind, Philip says, "The originals are in a safe. Come on, roll—the deck isn't stacked. Really."

Andy shakes her head.

"If the right number comes up," Philip coos seductively, "it's no more phone taps, no more guys in green suits, no more terror—we're out of your life forever. Do it for yourself, Andy. And do it for her. . . ."

He takes from one pocket of his jogging outfit a folded piece of paper and throws it on the table.

Andy regards it with mounting dread. Finally she picks up and unfolds the sheet, which is a grainy photograph, the kind the wire services transmit.

The shot of her parents and Patty boarding a cruise ship in Bermuda was obviously taken that same morning.

"Get us out of your lives," Philip says softly. "Roll for yourself and for Patty."

Andy is mesmerized by the photo. Gee, Patty looks swell. The girl's going to be one beautiful broad when she grows up. Smart, too. And tough. Andy feels a stinging sensation at the tip of her nose. Not now, she thinks, not in front of this sadistic son of a bitch, so she wipes her nose and fights back the tears of longing and regret.

Slowly her hand reaches for and enfolds the die.

"Andy."

She looks up.

"I want you know it wasn't all a lie. Really."

Why didn't she see through this guy's painfully transparent act? Patty sure did. Andy draws back her hand. Patty. Patty eating chocolate rum cake down in the Village. Patty eating chocolate rum cake and nattering on about some arcane Realm rule, what *was* that rule?

The forty-nine-sided die hits the polished rosewood table, bounces once, bounces twice—and then Andy smothers it and scoops it from the tabletop.

Philip jerks upright, as if on a string.

"I want an Arsenal Point Summary," Andy says coolly, remembering at last.

Philip's face unclenches into a wry smile that owes as much to respect as amusement. He pivots to the computer keyboard, which is flecked with Merle Vaughan's blood, and begins to tap.

Up above, on the oversized screen, the Realmlog gives way to a list of the Level Eight participants:

1) Realm Security
2) Merle Vaughan
3) Patricia Matteson
4) Andrea Matteson
5) Philip Hunt
6) Eric Schmidt
7) Surveillance Team
8) Lawrence Matteson
9) Larissa Hewes

Andy ignores the various numbers alongside each name and studies the players. Finally she demands, "Who's attacking my Configuration? You or Realm Security?"

"Realm Security," Philip replies neutrally.

"Shift all my Arsenal Points to that border."

Philip taps the keys again before calling the Realmlog back onto the screen.

Once more Andy picks up the die and raises her

hand. Then she pauses. "If this comes up a loser, I hope
you have the balls to do the job yourself." An instant
later her hand descends and opens.

As her life fractures into forty-nine facets, she
crosses her arms over her chest; it has grown cold, so
cold, down here in Hell's antechamber. . . .

The die bucks and clatters and teeters to rest.

Philip peers at it, enters the number that appears
on the glowing facet into the computer, and pushes a
tab.

The screen changes:

```
11    Reveal SOTA    **END GAME**   04    46  ???????
      secrets
```

He takes a deep breath and pushes another tab, his
eyes dart back to the screen, which is changing for the
last time:

```
11    Reveal SOTA    **END GAME**   04    46  ALM at
      secrets                                 liberty
```

Philip sighs—is it relief or chagrin? Then he stands,
steps over Vaughan's corpse, and rounds the rosewood
table. "Come on."

"I'm really free? Free to go?"

"Yes."

"Oh."

"Your card," he says.

"Huh?"

"The piece of plastic you got from the machine upstairs."

Andy pats her pockets absentmindedly. "I—I must
have lost it."

"Forget it," he says wearily. "Come on."

At the door Philip pulls out his own card and inserts
it into the slot. Andy follows him out without a backward glance. Into the elevator now, the two of them still
avoiding each other's eyes as it ascends, and then

through the bright blue chamber and into the tiny chocolate-walled "lobby." Two more strides, and the glass doors slide open.

Andy steps into the waning afternoon and begins to suck in deep drafts of fresh air.

The metallic dark green helicopter sits on the concrete pad twenty-five yards away. They head for it.

"Oh!"

Philip feels something striking his legs. He turns.

Andy, having tripped, sits on the ground, massaging her left ankle.

"Here, let me give you a hand," he says, bending over to take her arm.

Wordlessly Andy pulls it away.

Philip flushes.

Andy stands and continues toward the chopper, never looking back as she stoops under the churning rotors and climbs through the open door.

The only person aboard is the pilot, for both hard-faced thugs have disappeared. Andy chooses a seat on the far side of the craft and begins to buckle herself up.

The pilot inches the throttle forward, and the helicopter lifts.

Forty-five seconds later, Andy shields her eyes from the westering sun that pours through the Persplex canopy and looks earthward: the lone figure near the main building has shrunk to the size of an ant.

The speck on the horizon has long since vanished, yet Philip remains on the lawn in front of the building, gazing north into the encroaching twilight.

"Splendid performance, sir."

Philip turns.

Merle Vaughan stands dabbing with a damp towel at the fake blood on his throat.

Philip nods distractedly. "When we blocked out the scenario on the phone, I didn't think it would work so smoothly."

As Vaughan continues to clean himself up, he winces; an angry, real-life welt has surfaced just below his Adam's apple.

"How did that happen?"

Vaughan holds up a prop arrow consisting of front and back ends separated by a semicollar of fresh-colored plastic. "Weren't you supposed to distract the young lady by yelling 'Duck' or some such phrase? Yes. Well, when you didn't I panicked and just jammed the damn thing on."

"Just one more fuck-up in a fucked-up game."

Vaughan sighs in agreement. "A rather unpredictable sort, wasn't she? I'm afraid Mrs. Matteson has done neither of our scores much good. I was unable to prevent her from penetrating my office before the deadline, yet you were assessed those penalty points for her former husband's de—"

"Come on, let's go check the damage," Philip says impatiently.

Vaughan regards his opponent with newfound interest before turning back toward the main building.

Philip starts to follow, but his eyes pivot once more to the northern skies. Catching himself, he quickens his pace to catch up.

The two men are waiting for the elevator when Vaughan says, "What do you think of our headquarters here at SOTA, sir?"

"Sinister. You're ass deep in security toys."

As the elevator doors open, Vaughan says chidingly, "Come come, Mr. Hunt. Your offices in North Carolina must be heavily guarded, too."

Philip shakes his head.

"But surely you have many research secrets to protect," Vaughan persists.

"Maybe we trust our people more."

Rather than retort, Vaughan endures the rest of the short ride in silence.

When they enter his office, Vaughan heads for his rosewood desk and begins to tidy it up.

Philip continues past him to the heavy drapes that bear the SOTA logo.

"Will you join me in some brandy, Mr. Hunt?" Vaughan asks.

"Fine," Philip replies, searching through the folds of the drapes for the spear-gun arrow he fired wide. He finds it, works it free, and carries it back to the rosewood desk. There, he pitches it into a wastebasket, where it lands next to the prop arrow and Vaughan's red-stained towel.

Vaughan glances up from the computer keyboard. "I'm almost finished with the report. Would you do the honors and pour?" he asks, nodding to the decanter and snifters that sit on his rosewood desk.

Philip unstoppers the decanter and fills the snifters. He knows he's been acting surly and that Vaughan has been testing that touchiness; in a game without end, a good player always tries to accumulate ammunition for the future. Time to lighten up, Philip thinks, so he says, "Does SOTA really have a Realm Security drill, or did you create it just for our match?"

"Oh, good heavens, Mr. Hunt, it's as real as Realm. And I'm happy to say that so far, our security seems faultless. I was not lying when I told Mrs. Matteson that she is the only participant who has learned of Mrs. Hewes's existence, much less encountered the good lady." Vaughan stands and picks up the second brandy snifter. "I have logged on. If you would be so good as to approve my report and then log yourself on?"

Philip sits himself in front of the keyboard. Vaughan's summary of Realm Eight's final move appears up on the giant screen. He scrolls through it, making several minor changes. "Fine by me," Philip says. "Now what?"

"Go to the command field and log on."

Philip manipulates the cursor to the top of the screen. Then he punches in his eight-digit entry code, followed by his seven-letter password.

"Good," Vaughan says. "It's all set up for an interface. Just enter the Realm Eight reference number and hit triple-shift Fetch."

As Philip does so, a link is forged between SOTA's computer in Point Conception, California, and the National Security Agency's Loadstone computer in Fort Meade, Maryland.

New words flash onto the giant screen:

```
ERGO EST WELCOMES MERLE VAUGHAN
AND PHILIP HUNT
GAME IN PROGRESS: ANDREA L. MATTESON
(USA)
PLEASE ENTER PROJECT STATUS
```

Vaughan sees Philip shaking his head and says, "What is it, Mr. Hunt?"

"Nothing, really. It's just that every time I sign in on Ergo Est, I feel a real letdown."

"Oh?"

"It looks exactly like every other computer program. If one of your colleagues came in right now, he'd think we were engrossed in some SOTA exercise like Realm. But—but this is Ergo Est."

"And you'd prefer more ceremony?" Vaughan says wryly. "Perhaps a few bars of the theme from *Rocky*? At the risk of sounding like a stuffed shirt, sir, I daresay that the older you become, the more you'll appreciate understatement."

"*Touché*," Philip says. "What do I do next?"

"Define the report and hit Send."

As Philip does so, the Realm Eight data flashes east across the continent to Loadstone, on which Ergo Est lives; an eyeblink later, data absorbed and evaluated, new words appear on the giant screen:

```
PROBABILITY SUBJECT BEING BELIEVED: 0.014
END GAME POINTS AWARDED:
MERLE VAUGHAN:  38
PHILIP HUNT:  37
```

Vaughan grunts in disappointment. "My congratulations, Mr. Hunt. You made a remarkable showing in the face of a twenty-five-point penalty. And still—and still, if my men had not lost her coming out of Omaha and if I could have delayed her another thirty-six hours—"

"And if your aunt had a penis, she'd've been your uncle," Philip snaps. Then he softens. "Sorry. No, you would have scored in the mid-sixties. But like I told you, she's one resourceful lady."

Vaughan takes another sip of brandy. "No use putting off the bad news, sir. Would you please be so good as to punch up the cumulatives?"

Philip taps in a new instruction.

The giant screen flickers and then displays a list of Ergo Est's two dozen international participants. The two men study the rankings with dismay; their disastrous scores have dropped Philip from sixth to ninth and Vaughan from eleventh to twelfth.

"Chebrikov looks uncatchable," Philip mutters.

"Not true, Mr. Hunt. One sound trouncing, and we're all alive again." Vaughan watches Philip bolt down the last of his brandy, pour himself another, and then attack the refill. "I realize I'm prying, sir," he says, "and you certainly have the right to tell me to butt out. But your continuing agitation—might Mrs. Matteson be its source?"

Philip's face tightens, and his eyes flash, but he does not answer.

"Mr. Hunt?"

Finally the electric silence is broken: "Vaughan, what do you want me to tell you, that you're a fucking genius?"

"Sir, you have my apologies. But you knew about the warnings against fraternizing with subjects, and you knew—"

"That's not it," Philip interrupts, spacing each harsh word like a sentence. "Don't you realize that she's still dangerous?"

"Oh, come come. Ergo Est rates the probability of her being believed at one-point-four percent."

Suddenly Philip sinks back into his chair; his tension seems to evaporate, to be replaced by resignation.

"Mr. Hunt, surely she realizes she can never expose us."

"She knows."

"Then surely we have no cause for concern."

Philip continues to stare broodingly at his snifter. Once again the silence grows. Finally, sensing that the question is about to be repeated, he answers it—with a melancholy shrug.

Epilogue

The sun streams through the living room windows. On the tape deck, Galway plays Vivaldi, the clean notes of the flute chasing away the silence.

It is late Saturday morning in Ann Arbor. Patty had dashed out right after breakfast to pitch in on a charity car wash in the junior high parking lot, so for the moment Andy has the apartment to herself.

She sits at the drafting table staring into the contract-law manual for her course, Professional Practice II. The finals loom, and there is much to catch up on; yet, a yawn escapes. She looks up. The Sears Roebuck furniture no longer offends, for along one wall of the room rests a stack of knocked-down, corrugated cardboard packing boxes. And in three weeks—twenty-three days, to be exact—they will be full, sealed and aboard an eastward-bound van.

The decision to move had come from the gut, made while lying beside Patty on a beach in Bermuda. But now that her nerves were no longer aquiver, her body no longer terminally bruised, Andy remains unsure of her motives. Is it her unrequited longing for Manhattan's soothing chaos? Or is it her need to escape from Ann Arbor and all its Realm associations? Last Wednesday, while parking downtown, she had spotted Keresey, the cop who had trumped up the Breathalyzer test. If her reaction was so strong, how would she feel the first time she ran into Chief Eric Schmidt?

Not that moving would lessen the chances of being sucked back into the SOTA madness. Since choppering out of Point Concepcion, Andy's privacy has remained unbreached and her field of vision free of that distinctive metallic green; but that reprieve, she knows all too well, can be canceled anytime, anywhere.

Andy sighs. More coffee? Why not?

She is refilling her mug when she hears the door downstairs slam and then two sets of footsteps on the stairs. Who is her daughter bringing home?

"Hi, Mom," Patty says, letting herself in. "Ginger's here."

"Hi. How did you guys do?"

"Made out like bandits," Patty replies, her voice drawing nearer. "Truly. More'n two hundred dollars."

Ginger enters the kitchen first. "Hi, Mrs. Matteson. Hope you don't mind."

"Of course not, Ginger." Andy looks past the girl at her daughter and suppresses a smile. Patty's hair is even blonder, and her Bermuda-acquired tan even deeper, thanks to the strong, late-spring sun. Combine that with the yellow tube top and white cutoff jeans covering—after a fashion—her willowy frame, and the girl seems, at least in her mother's eyes, as vibrantly alive as a wild sunflower.

Patty walks over and wraps an arm around Andy's waist. "We're going to bike up to the Arb this afternoon. What's for lunch?"

"Grilled cheese sandwiches?"

The girl wrinkles her nose.

"Tuna fish? Eggs?"

"Eggs."

"Good. You know where they are. And while you and Ginger are at it, I'll have two, easy over."

"Oh, Mother." Patty groans and shuffles toward the refrigerator.

As Andy leaves the kitchen she asks, "By the way, has the mail come yet?"

"On the little table," Patty replies.

Andy takes a sip of her coffee, looks toward the table in the vestibule—and freezes.

There, among the bills and advertising circulars, sits a little white cardboard box much like the kind in which tobacco manufacturers mail free samples. After all this time, she thinks; but obviously the package made it through SOTA's mailroom to her parents' home in Connecticut, whence it had been forwarded.

Andy glances furtively into the kitchen. Patty and Ginger are giggling, their heads in the refrigerator. Good, she has time.

She darts to the table, picks up the package, and hurries to her bedroom. Her finger trembles as she uses the nail to slit the sealing tape, her hand shakes as it pushes aside the bubble wrap and slides out the recorder.

The microcassette has played all the way to the end, as it should have.

Andy presses Reverse. When about a quarter of the tape has rewound, she presses Stop, takes a deep breath, and punches Play:

"... *that successful in creating the illusion of* Der Realm?" Merle Vaughan is saying.

She hits Fast Forward:

"... *bastard tried to subvert our project,*" Philip Hunt is saying.

Again, Fast Forward:

The *whack-whack* of helicopter blades gaining speed ...

Andy closes her eyes. It was on the way to the chopper that she'd pretended to trip; and while Philip had been trying to help her up, she'd pinned the matchstick-sized transmitter to the bottom of his jogging pants. Had the device continued to work? And then she has her answer—yes!—for the helicopter's sounds begin to recede.

But the next voice on the tape provokes a gasp. "*Splendid performance,*" Merle Vaughan is saying. Merle Vaughan? With an arrow through his neck? As if proximity would enhance clarity, Andy draws the recorder closer to her ear.

*   *   *

Ten minutes later, Patty yells from the kitchen that lunch is ready.

"Be right out, dear," Andy replies, an enigmatic smile creasing her face. She returns her attention to the recorder, on which Philip Hunt and Merle Vaughan are plotting their next games of Ego Est. It'll keep, she thinks as she turns off the machine and ejects the cassette.

She moves now to her desk. From the back of the top right drawer she pulls out an envelope. The piece of celluloid marked ENTRYWAY B. ROOM 5.—until this moment her only hope of substantiating her story, not to mention her only link with sanity—lies inside.

As she drops the telltale microcassette next to it, Andy Matteson's smile hardens.

ABOUT THE AUTHOR

TONY CHIU, who was born in Shanghai, has been a Senior Editor of *TV-Cable Week,* a writer and editor for, among other publications, *The New York Times* and *People.* He is currently at work on *Visible Mark,* his third novel.

THE BLISTERING NEW THRILLER BY
THE BESTSELLING AUTHOR OF
AN EXCHANGE OF EAGLES

THE KREMLIN CONTROL

OWEN SELA

With a single, cryptic clue to guide him, KGB officer Yuri Raikin pierces the heart of a monstrous secret hidden for three decades . . . A secret that explains a general's death and an agent who should have died . . . A secret of conspiracy that reaches from Moscow to Zurich to Washington . . . A secret so explosive that it could topple the walls of the Kremlin—and shatter world peace forever.

Read **The Kremlin Control,** a stunning novel of Russian intrigue and treachery, on sale August 15, 1984, wherever Bantam paperbacks are sold, or use the handy coupon below for ordering:

*A masterwork of mounting suspense, in the grand tradition of
Alfred Hitchcock and Mary Higgins Clark*

WOMAN
IN THE
WINDOW

Dana Clarins

It began on the happiest day of her life. Natalie Rader
was on top of the world. Freed from her empty marriage,
newly single and loving it, she was celebrating her first
million-dollar deal. Now, as night descended on the city,
she stood gazing through her third-story office window.

Suddenly, on the street below, a man was running toward a
construction site. Natalie saw him clearly, and she saw what
he threw over the fence: a gun. As she watched in horror, the
man looked up. His eyes locked with hers . . . and Natalie
Rader's well-ordered life was about to come apart. . . .

Don't miss WOMAN IN THE WINDOW, on sale July 14,
1984, wherever Bantam Books are sold, or use the handy
coupon below for ordering:

SPECIAL
MONEY SAVING
OFFER

Now you can have an up-to-date listing of Bantam's hundreds of titles plus take advantage of our unique and exciting bonus book offer. A special offer which gives you the opportunity to purchase a Bantam book for only 50¢. Here's how!

By ordering any five books at the regular price per order, you can also choose any other single book listed (up to a $4.95 value) for just 50¢. Some restrictions do apply, but for further details why not send for Bantam's listing of titles today!

Just send us your name and address plus 50¢ to defray the postage and handling costs.